What
we did
for
Love

Teresa McClain-Watson

What we did for Love

sepia

BET BOOKS™

BET Publications, LLC
http://www.bet.com

SEPIA BOOKS are published by

BET Publications, LLC
c/o BET BOOKS
One BET Plaza
1900 W Place NE
Washington, DC 20018-1211

All Kensington Titles, Imprints, and Distributed Lines are available at
special quantity discounts for bulk purchases for sales promotions,
premiums, fund-raising, and educational or institutional use. Special
book excerpts or customized printings can also be created to fit specific
needs. For details, write or phone the office of the Kensington special
sales manager: Kensington Publishing Corp., 850 Third Avenue, New
York, NY 10022, attn: Special Sales Department, Phone: 1-800-221-
2647.

BET Books is a trademark of Black Entertainment Television, Inc.
SEPIA and the SEPIA logo are trademarks of BET Books and the BET
BOOKS logo is a registered trademark.

ISBN 1-58314-461-7

First Printing: July 2004
10 9 8 7 6 5 4 3 2 1

Printed in the United States of America

ACKNOWLEDGMENTS

To my Lord and savior Jesus Christ for giving me the gift of writing and allowing me to enjoy that gift.

To Minnie McClain-Hogan, Marion McClain, Bartholous Woodley, III, Marilyn Enos-Upthegrove, Steven Murray, Annie Ruth Brookins, Annette White, Deborah Lee, Betty Gainous, and numerous other family, friends, and well wishers for their continued support.

To Glenda Howard, my editor, for her excellent suggestions and editorial expertise.

And to my husband John. My inspiration.

What
we did
for
Love

CHAPTER 1

It bordered on obsession. *And that's the problem,* Josie thought, as she downshifted her Mustang along the windy slopes of Rolling Ridge and cruised onto Saint Cloud's County Road 4. Each morning she woke up thinking about Ben. She went to bed thinking about Ben. She spent the entire balance of her days doing her work, getting it done, and thinking about Ben. It was so unlike her, so *not* her, that even she was concerned.

She'd thought she had it together before Ben came along. She'd thought she was the personification of the go-getter, upwardly-mobile sister who wasn't about to let some man have her tripping. When the brothers tried desperately to run their lines on her, with all kinds of creative rhymes in their talk, she knew better. They were nothing more than players with a rap, in her opinion, brothers who knew how to twirl a phrase, but also how to break a heart. And they were all the same to her.

Yet Ben, to her great dismay, was different. She drove into the parking lot of the *Saint Cloud Herald* newspaper building wondering why he was so damn different. He *was* gorgeous; even by her standards the man had sex appeal oozing from every pore over his fine, muscular frame. But he was so unlike her in every conceivable way that she still could not believe their union.

She was a twenty-nine-year-old, hazel-eyed beauty who favored African attire, braided hairstyles, and the truth at all costs. She was a staunchly liberal journalist who spoke her mind freely and fought to the end for the causes she believed in. Ben, on the other hand, was a forty-nine-year-old, conservative former judge who chose his battles carefully. He believed that truth was always layers deep and becoming a crusader for a cause was often a fool's game that required considerable thought and planning, not the knee-jerk emotionalism Josie often displayed. He was calm in the face of turmoil. Josie flew off the handle at the first inkling of trouble. He loved jazz; she loved hip-hop. He was well experienced at love; she had never been in love a day in her life, until a year ago—when she met him. *And that's the rub,* she thought, as she hurried out of her Mustang with her hobo bag and her briefcase and began running toward the building's entrance, already forty minutes late.

She had zero experience with that thing called love. When she was in her teens and early twenties she prided herself on steering clear of romance. She would throw shade on any brother who even thought about profiling her. Love was a game to people and she wasn't playing it. She'd seen her mother and sisters and every female she'd ever known play the game, falling madly in love every other week with some new Mister Right only to end up mad and sad and deep-down brokenhearted. *Forget that,* she thought. She was keeping her heart to herself. And she did, for years, until Ben came along. Until this calm, smooth brother she thought would be the last human being on earth she could ever fall for knocked her so off stride that, to this day, she was still stumbling and bumbling and acting, as her mother loved to say, like a *zip-dang* fool.

She entered the revolving doors of the *Herald* and hurried up the stairs. Her heels were high, a pair of Rowe stilettos, forcing her to take deliberate steps. Her outfit, an African-style, flared-legged pantsuit made of hand-loomed Yoruba fabric, hung loosely under her full-length wool coat. At the top of the stairwell was a large portrait of the newspaper's founder, his broad, red-cheeked face and grotesquely huge, blue pop-eyes almost frightening at first glance. In the glass of the frame Josie watched her reflection as she advanced up the stairs. Although she was almost universally considered attractive, with a nicely proportioned body made sexy by her large breasts and plump backside, she cringed when she saw herself. She couldn't see what all the fuss was about. She couldn't see what men saw, that her pear-shaped hazel eyes contrasted beautifully with her deep-brown skin tone and her sultry lips, that her braided hair cropped into a low-cut bob hung like a wrap against her long, thin neck, and that her African attire gave her that confident, sister-with-an-attitude ethnic flare. Her appearance was a turn-on.

When she looked at herself lately she didn't see the turn-on. What she saw was a pathetic female who projected, not attitude, but fear. *And it shows in spades,* she thought, as she entered the narrow corridor on the second floor and hurried for the newsroom at the end of the hall. She was nowhere near the together sister she used to be, nowhere near the kind of woman she thought she'd be by now, and she jokingly told herself that it was all Ben's fault.

Norm, one of her fellow reporters, a short, rail-thin man with short blond hair, was just leaving the newsroom as she approached its double doors.

"You're late," he said.

"Is that clock right?" she asked, looking up at the clock above the entrance doors.

Norm smiled. "It's right," he said. "It's always right. You're always late."

A frown appeared on Josie's face. The last thing she needed was his little flip remark.

"What*ever,* Norm," she said as she fluffed her braids, took one more deep breath, and then marched into a newsroom loaded with rows and rows of desks with computer screens, ringing telephones, and busy white folks.

Six months on the job and she still wasn't comfortable here. She still felt she had to prove herself day in and day out, when she had already made her mark on the world of journalism years before. But that was back in Florida. That was back in the day when she was the undisputed slash-and-burn queen. But here, in Minnesota, they weren't feeling her.

"One time, Josie," Ron Depp said as she moved briskly toward her desk. She thought she was out of view. She thought she had slipped in undetected. But Ron, the city editor and her immediate supervisor, wasn't in his office as she had thought, as she had hoped, but standing at the fax machine not five feet away.

She turned quickly at the sound of his voice. He stood like a huge pumpkin, his bright red cheeks sagging over his fat neck, his round shoulders and protruded chest reminding Josie of a sumo wrestler. She was busted. There was no way around it. So she did what she normally did and slung her purse, briefcase, and keys onto her desk, took off her coat, and tried like hell not to show any interest whatsoever in what he had to say.

"What's up?" she asked cavalierly, looking away from him as if her chronic tardiness was no big deal at all.

"One time," he said, again.

She looked at him again. She hated it when he spoke in code. "One time what, Ron? What are you talking about?"

"You don't know what I'm talking about?"

"No, I don't," she said.

"I think you do."

"But I don't."

"I think you do."

"Okay, whatever," Josie said, her temper trying to flare. She decided it best to just forget Ron and get busy. She began putting her purse away in her side-bottom drawer.

But Ron wasn't ready to forget her. He left the fax machine and walked over to her desk, his big bulk and six-six frame causing him to take slow, measured steps. Josie was, by far, his most difficult reporter, a woman whose tenacity alone would often get her that big story, but whose big mouth and hot head made him care less whether or not she did get the story. Like today. He was her boss, yet she was behaving as if he didn't have the right to even question her about her problem.

"One time," he said once again as he stood in front of her desk. Josie rolled her eyes. "It has been exactly one time that you've walked into this newsroom at the hour you're supposed to. One time, Josie. It was so remarkable, so unprecedented for you, that I actually considered issuing a press release."

"I'm late, Ron, it's obvious. So what do you want me to say? I'm sorry for being late? Is that what you want? Okay, I'm sorry. I'm sorry for being late. It won't happen again," she said.

Ron smiled, but it was a sinister smile. "That's a familiar tune," he said. "'It won't happen again,' she sings. The same song she sang last week."

"I was on time last week."

"And the week before that."

"Look, I said I was sorry."

"And the week before that!"

"What's up with you?" Josie asked. "It's not like I'm trying to be late on purpose, Ron, damn!"

Ron looked at Josie hard. "Who do you think you're talking to?" he asked her. "I'm the boss around here. Not you!"

Josie folded her arms and began her nervous leg-shaking. She knew she was treading on troubled waters and if she had any sense at all she'd keep that trap of hers mute. And to her own astonishment, she did. But Ron didn't.

"You listen to me, Josie Ross," he said, her name spewing from his lips as if it were a contaminant. "If it wasn't for your boyfriend and his friendship with my boss, you wouldn't have this job at all. Don't you forget that. I didn't want you here. I never believed for a second you deserved to be here. Just having you in this building does a disservice to the entire journalistic profession. That newspaper in Florida didn't fire you without cause, let's not kid ourselves. You were run out of town on a rail, lady, so don't try to act like you're such hot shit around me. I know what happened. I know the truth. All right? And, as to your cute little comment that you don't try to be late on purpose, that may be true. But what's equally true is that you certainly don't try to be on time!"

Josie exhaled as the sting of his words settled in. She used to think Ron was okay. He would get on her nerves with his code speak and lack of concern for the problems of the world around them, but she'd still thought he was cool. She'd had no idea he harbored such strong feelings against her.

"I said I was sorry," she said in a low voice, her emotions welling up like golf balls in her throat, "and I'm not apologizing again."

"Good," he said. "Keep your apologies. Just get to work on time!" He stared angrily at her, and then walked away.

She sat down, and then looked around the newsroom. Those eyes that moments before she just knew had been fixed on her and Ron suddenly shifted back to their own business. Now everybody knew, she thought. Everybody knew that the woman they couldn't stand anyway was a fraud, that the only reason she was there at all was because Ben had called in favors. Now the respect she already lacked from her peers was about to reach even lower lows. They knew there was something about her. They thought it was her big mouth or her everything's-a-crusade liberalism or that out-there African dress style of hers that they never could equate with professional attire. But now they knew better. They didn't like her for far more honorable reasons. She hadn't earned her place. She didn't deserve to be there, to be one of them. They had finally figured it out. Ron, Josie believed, had just given them the weapon to hammer her with.

But as she pulled out the files of the stories she had been working on, she decided that the word might be on the street, but she wasn't letting it worry her. She hadn't asked Ben to pull any strings to get her the job, but when he did she wasn't about to turn him down. And Ron was right. She hadn't gotten fired in Florida without cause. Just a year ago she had been one of the most heralded reporters in Jacksonville, a journalist known far and wide as the slash-and-burn queen for her hard-hitting, take-no-prisoners reporting style. Ben was at the top of his profession, too, a well-respected conservative judge with only the sky as the limit as to how far he could go.

But when the governor of Florida announced his intention to nominate Ben to a seat on the state supreme court, all hell had broken loose. Three different females accused him of sexual harassment and that had changed everything. The politics surrounding the scandal became so heated that the governor had had no choice but to rescind the nomination. The conservatives cried foul. The liberals rejoiced. And Josie was stuck in the middle. She hated Ben's politics, but she loved Ben. But their relationship had been young, only a couple of months old, when the allegations surfaced, and Josie had found herself devastated. She didn't know what to believe. And Ben hated her indecision.

Ron mentioned her getting fired as if it were a simple case of incompetence, when it had nothing to do with her ability to do the job. In the end she did a damn good job, because she had ultimately exposed the women liars and exonerated Ben. But the damage had already been done. Ben had lost his moral authority. Under intense pressure he resigned his post as a criminal court judge, ending an exemplary eighteen-year career in the judiciary.

And to make matters worst, Josie's exoneration of Ben had almost gone unheard. The newspaper she worked for at the time, the *Jacksonville Gazette,* was a hotbed of liberalism and was not about to print a story clearing the name of a conservative judge they didn't want anywhere near the highest court in the state anyway. So they wouldn't run the story. But Josie, being who she was, wouldn't give up. When she took her story to the competitor, to the very conservative *Daily*

News, who couldn't print it fast enough, she was fired. And she wasn't run out of town on a rail, as Ron insisted. She gladly left. She gladly left with Ben.

Josie thought about that Florida scene. She thought about it as she pulled up the computer file of her story on campaign-finance reform, and tried to make final revisions. Ben survived Florida. He had friends in high places all over the country, friends who knew he had been railroaded by liberal activists who had stopped at nothing to see him fall, and these friends looked out for him. Josie, however, wasn't as well established. In Florida she was respected and feared for her hard-hitting style. Now she was marked and derided and treated as if she were less than incompetent. And it wasn't about to get any better in Saint Cloud, thanks to good old Ron and his little sly remarks. And that was why, when he came back out of his office some two hours after he had put her business in the street, she rolled her eyes.

"Lose the attitude, Ross," he said as he walked up to her desk.

"I don't have an attitude."

"And I don't have a weight problem."

"Is there something you wanted? Or just badgering me is the goal?" she said.

He smiled and shook his head. "You're something else, Josie."

"I have work to do, Ron."

"Get over to city hall."

"City hall? Why do I need to go over there?"

"Maybe because I'm the boss and I told you to go over there."

"Why, Ron? What's going on?"

Ron exhaled. She was too much. "Mayor Keating's having a press conference," he said.

"A press conference? That wasn't on his manifest for today."

"It is now."

"Dang. That man loves the cameras. What's this one about?"

"Josie!"

"You want me to cover a press conference without bothering to tell me what it's about?"

"It's about his Better Saint Cloud Road Improvement Plan. All right? Is that enough information for you?"

Josie hesitated. "Yes," she said.

"Good. I'm glad I can please you every now and then. Just get over there and check it out."

Josie stood up quickly. He didn't have to ask twice. She was grateful to be leaving that building, not to mention his sight.

Although she left as soon as Ron gave her the assignment, she still managed to be late, walking into the city hall pressroom a full fifteen minutes after the mayor's news conference had begun. She flashed her press badge at the security guard and hurried to a seat near the back of the room. She sat down and immediately stood out like a sore thumb. Not only was she the only black and the only woman in the cramped press room, but she had the biggest mouth, too, for which she was well known, if not very well regarded.

But what they didn't know was that Josie constantly tried to hold her tongue. And she was trying to hold on through the press conference. But when the questions her fellow reporters were asking the mayor were ridiculously complimentary without even touching on the real issues, she couldn't hold back any longer.

"Where's the diversity?" she asked as she stood up. Everybody in the room, including Mayor Keating himself, turned and looked at Josie.

"Good afternoon, Miss Ross," the mayor said.

"Good afternoon, Mayor. You said your—"

"I missed you when this press conference first began," he interrupted.

Josie knew what he was doing. He was trying to get her so preoccupied with her tardiness that she would opt out of asking the tough questions. She wasn't going to fall for that.

"You said your Better Saint Cloud Road Improvement Plan would be a model of diversity. That's what you told the voters when the initiative was being debated. Yet, now, at its implementation, not one minority contractor won a bid. How can your plan be diverse, sir, if no minorities are represented?"

Mayor Keating stood behind the lectern and smiled. He couldn't stand Josie Ross. He couldn't stand her the day his good friend Ben Braddock introduced her to him. He found her overconfident attitude and big mouth too much to take, and he couldn't stand her even more the moment he learned that she was the new political reporter for the *Saint Cloud Herald*. Al Sharpton, Junior, was what he called her behind her back.

"It was just a matter of time," he said. "Wasn't it, Miss Ross?"

Josie at first looked around, as if she had missed something. Then she looked at Keating. He was a tall, blue-eyed, sandy-haired man who always had what Josie considered a constipated look.

"Excuse me?" she asked him.

"It was just a matter of time before your verbal onslaught would begin. But you're getting better at it, I must admit. You've been here, what, five minutes? And already you're on the warpath."

The other reporters laughed. Josie, however, failed to see the humor. This was a press conference, not a love-fest, and she was completely right to ask the tough questions. Keating knew what he was doing. He was playing the game. He was luring the press into his world, telling them a few jokes, making them laugh, calling it a day. But Josie wasn't about to play along.

"My question," she said, "is a simple one, Mayor. You promised the voters diversity when they voted to approve your initiative. Where's the diversity?"

"There's diversity, Josie," Keating said, still smiling, still trying not to show his irritation. "This was a fair process."

"Even you can't believe that, Mayor Keating."

There was an aghast hush over the pressroom when Josie spoke those tough words. Keating wanted to zing her back, but he knew he couldn't. Not directly anyway.

"She's calling me a liar, folks," he decided to say as he looked at the pool of reporters staring back at him, his smile slapped on even wider. "Isn't she sweet?"

The reporters laughed once again. Josie looked at her colleagues as they played along, and she was astonished at how easily they continued to fall for the mayor's obvious rope-a-dope. She could have fallen for it too; she could have smiled and told the mayor how he had a point there, and allowed him to move on to the next reporter. She would have been justified. Mayor Keating was, after all, another one of those close, personal friends of Ben's, and Ben wouldn't appreciate her piling on like this anyway. But she had a job to do.

"You didn't answer my question, Mayor," she said. "Isn't your Better Saint Cloud Plan nothing more than a taxpayer-funded giveaway for the rich?"

"No," the mayor said curtly. "Next question, please?"

"But how can you say *no* when even the NAACP, which has had a very good relationship with your administration, publicly voiced serious concerns?"

The mayor sighed. Out of respect for Ben he had, in the past, given Josie Ross a lot more latitude than he felt she deserved. But enough was enough.

"The citizens of Saint Cloud clearly support every aspect of my plan, Miss Ross. They understand fully that our wonderful city is well overdue a cosmetic make-over. You and the fringe elements of our community may not support it, but you never support anything, so please excuse me if I don't find your comments alarming."

"So you consider the NAACP a fringe element of our community?"

"Don't put words into my mouth, Miss Ross."

"You put those words into your own mouth, sir. You were the one who referred to those who didn't support your plan as fringe elements. Not me."

The mayor smiled and shook his head. "What is it, Miss Ross?" he asked. "What is it this time? Still trying to make a name for yourself? Trying to create racial tension where none exists? Is that what you're up to? Is that your game this time?"

"I'm not playing a game, sir. I'm sure there are many citizens who—"

"Who think like you?" the mayor interrupted. "Who want to see our community torn apart by people like you? No. You're what's wrong with this community, Miss Ross, not my initiative. The people of Saint Cloud support me, and you and your liberal buddies can't stand that fact. My plan is a good plan. My plan is a sound plan. And my plan is supported by all those who can see beyond your race-baiting rhetoric and appreciate what I'm trying to do."

"But, why, Mayor Keating," Josie began, determined not to be diverted, "was every single contract under your initiative given to non-minority contractors? Why did you allow your rich cronies to bid for the contracts expected to go to minorities by letting them suddenly make their wives the owners of the companies and therefore be entitled to minority status?"

Keating's smile, by now, was completely gone. "As usual, Miss Ross, your facts are as wrong as your argument, and it's quite obvious that the only thing you're interested in doing is manufacturing a racial incident in our beloved community. And I will not have it! Now next question, please!"

"Why can't you just answer my question, Mayor Keating?"

"Why can't you just shut the hell up, Miss Ross?"

The mayor's anger was unhinged, and Josie knew to back off. The other reporters in the room looked at her, glared at her, because they were also tired of her unending crusades. Something that seemed so simple, such as a plan to improve the city's roads and bridges, was turned upside down by her. Now a road improvement plan is a minority-rights issue? They just didn't see it.

Josie couldn't see how they didn't. She sat quietly for most of the remaining time, but the questions her colleagues were asking of the mayor, questions that were so flattering and condescending, nauseated her. How could they call themselves journalists, she wondered, and be so deferential? She left the building.

Outside of city hall it was a cold Minnesota morning. She buttoned her wool coat and hurried along busy Second Street to her car. She hated Minnesota, especially on days like this, where not only was the weather freezing her behind off but snow flurries had the nerve to be floating around in the air too, as if being cold was supposed to be cute. Folks dreamed of white Christmases, and Josie enjoyed the snow at Christmastime herself. But a white February? That was too much. She wasn't used to that. Februaries in Florida were heaven-sent compared to this, where a light jacket would do you, but here, in the heart of Saint Cloud, on a biting cold February morning, she felt like an ice cube even in a wool coat.

Her car, a four-year-old, flame-red Mustang, was parked within a few hundred yards of the splashing Mississippi River. She plopped down in it and quickly turned on the heater. She leaned back against the headrest and found herself staring in the rearview mirror. She wished to God she wasn't so passionate about every damn thing. She wished to God she could know the facts and ignore them, the way the mayor did, the way her own colleagues did. She tried when she first arrived in Minnesota. She tried her best to go along to get along, because she'd already been through too much turmoil back in Florida and wasn't trying to live her life that way again.

But she couldn't do it. The truth kept getting in the way. And whenever her colleagues acted as if truth didn't matter, that there were more expedient things to worry about, she corrected them. Early on they may have respected Josie Ross. They may have even admired her tenacity and passion, but she'd riled them too much with her almost inexplicable liberalism that, to them, bordered on naiveté. She was a truth-seeker to her core, without limits, a woman who would drive over a cliff if the facts led her that way. That was a little too much devotion for them.

Although that truth-seeking of hers may not have had its limits, it certainly had its price. It made for a lonely existence, for one thing, where people would rather not deal with her because truth required too much energy. The only person who even bothered with her was Ben, and he was now the senior vice president of one of the largest corporations in the state and had little time or energy for her, either. At least he respected her devotion. And he was all she had.

She pulled out her cell phone and called his office, but he wouldn't even come to the phone. It took Whitney, his secretary, nearly three minutes to get back on the line. "Mr. Braddock is tied up in a meeting right now," she said. Josie sighed. She'd heard that one before.

"Did you tell him it was me, Whit?"

"I told him, Josie."

"I need to talk with him."

"I know. I told him that too. But he's really very busy. He said he'll see you tonight."

It was his usual response to Josie's daily phone calls. She could rarely get through to him on her first try, and sometimes not at all, which didn't help anything. But that was Ben. You either take him or leave him, and she couldn't quite do either.

"Did you see the mayor's press conference?" she asked Whitney.

"Yeah, I did. I saw part of it anyway."

"My part?" Josie asked.

Whitney laughed. "Yep. That was the only part worth watching in my opinion. Me and some of the other secretaries were cheering you on too."

"Yeah?"

"Oh, hell yeah, Josie. Mayor Keating is always running these scams on the voters and somebody needed to say something. We knew exactly what you were talking about."

Josie was glad to hear that. She hadn't expected a cheering section. But then she hesitated. "Did Ben see the press conference?" she asked Whitney.

"You know how Mr. Braddock is, Josie."

"Did he see it?"

Whitney paused. "He saw it," she said.

"Was he cheering me on too?" Josie asked. Whitney didn't say anything. Josie closed her eyes. "Okay, Whit. Thanks." She said this and turned off her cell phone. She was going to get that much-needed attention from Ben now, she was certain of that. She was also certain that there wasn't going to be anything positive about it.

But within moments, as if Whitney were calling back, her cell phone rang. She answered quickly. But it wasn't her boyfriend's secretary. It was her boss's.

"Is this Miss Ross?"

"Yes, it is."

"Hello, Miss Ross. I'm Mr. Graham's assistant. He wishes to see you."

Josie's heart dropped. Herbert Graham, the managing editor of the *Saint Cloud Herald,* never requested to see a reporter unless that reporter had done something grand, like win a Pulitzer, or something horrific.

"Are you there, Miss Ross?"

"Yes, I'm here. I'm sorry. When did Mr. Graham need to see me?"

The secretary hesitated as if she could not believe Josie asked such a question. "At once," she replied, and then hung up the telephone.

CHAPTER 2

Benjamin Braddock leaned down from his six foot frame and grabbed his ringing desk telephone. It was Sam Darrow, the company's public relations director, asking if he could spare a few minutes. "I think I can squeeze you in, Sammy," Ben said lively, although he could barely stomach Sam and his nauseating ambitiousness. But the young man knew everything about anything that went on at Denlex, as if he were a human tabloid. Although he was only mid-level management, he was still the man every top manager in the company knew to keep close.

Ben hung up the phone and leaned back in his chair. It had been a long day. Denlex, a mass-market catalog giant headquartered in Saint Cloud, also had plants in eight other states. As senior vice president, Ben oversaw all plant operations and often would find himself putting out fires of controversy and incompetence that sometimes ran rampant in the corporation. And today was no exception. The Portland plant, after fifteen years in operation, still seemed unable to get its act together. Its workers threatened to strike, females threatened to sue, and a backlog unlike any the company had ever seen threatened to shut the whole plant down.

But if dealing with that wasn't bad enough, it was also a day of strangeness for Ben. First, Wayne Murdoch, the company's president and CEO, had called him to his office. He wanted answers, he'd said, about the chairman of the board.

"What about the chairman?" Ben asked as he stood in front of the old man's desk.

"What's he up to?"

Ben hesitated. Murdoch was sixty years old, with milky blue eyes and snow-white hair, a man brilliant in business but eccentric as hell. He purposely wore a black shoe and a brown shoe everyday, never rode the elevators, made his driver start the limousine before he got into it in case, he'd say, "a bomb blows," and was constantly suspicious that some grand conspiracy to dump him as CEO was always on the horizon. Ben was second in command behind Murdoch, and many senior executives often ran to Ben when Murdoch and his ways were just too crazy for them to abide. But Ben never went to the board. Murdoch was no prize, but he had given Denlex nearly forty years of his life. That should account for something, he felt.

"I don't understand what you're talking about, Wayne."

"The chairman, Benjamin. The chairman. You know. What's he up to?"

"I have no idea what he's up to."

Murdoch looked at Ben. Ben was a muscular, unusually handsome man, with smooth brown skin, a thick, black mustache, and large, bright brown eyes that looked almost as gold as grain. His hair was not like the wild styles of the day, but trimmed neatly to the skull. He was a forty-nine-year-old dynamo who looked younger than his years and, in Murdoch's eyes, a prototype CEO if ever there was one. Trusted. Respected. Conservative. And a black man too? Murdoch would shake his head. It would be the first time in the company's fifty-year history for an African American to take the reins, an historic event which, to Murdoch, made it more possible.

"You don't know, do you?" Murdoch asked him.

"Don't know what?"

"They're keeping you in the dark too, I see. Never a good sign. That's why you keep your enemies closer. Your friends close, but your enemies closer. But thanks for coming by anyway, Benjamin. Have a nice day."

And that was that. A one-minute meeting about nothing.

Then Herb Graham had called. Herb was the managing editor of the *Saint Cloud Herald* and the man Ben had turned to when Josie needed a job. He and Herb went way back, back in the day when they both served on the board of Alcoa, and Herb had been more than willing to help out the lady friend of a man he so greatly admired. But it apparently had gone too far today, because Herb had had enough.

"I had to let her go, Ben," he'd said over the telephone.

Ben leaned back and listened to his old friend, listened to him calmly say that he just fired the woman Ben loved, that he just made life that much more complicated by *letting her go*. She deserved what she got, Ben felt. He'd seen that press conference, but Josie was a different breed of woman. Although she was pushing thirty years old and should be beyond those unthinking ways of hers, she still had a lot of growing up to do. A firing for most people would be hurtful but, if he knew Josie, a setback like this would probably be crippling.

"Did you see the mayor's press conference today?" Herb had asked Ben.

"Some of it, yes."

"She got into a yelling match with the mayor. The *mayor*, Ben. I could not believe my eyes. That's just not done and she should know it." Then Herb exhaled. "Dammit, Benjamin. That woman is a loose cannon I'm telling you. She can't be tamed."

Since Ben had no intentions of taming her, he hadn't responded to Herb.

There was a slight hesitation, as neither man seemed willing to move the conversation along. Then Herb finally had said: "She can't represent my paper."

Ben had sighed and closed his eyes. "Understood. I thank you for giving her a chance."

"I was glad to do it, you know I was. I'm just sorry it didn't work out."

"Okay."

"No hard feelings?"

"Of course not."

"Good. Because I value your friendship, I really do. I knew you'd understand. I mean, goodness gracious, man. How do you put up with her? That woman would drive me to drink, or to kill myself. One of the two. She's too much lady for me." Herb had said this and laughed. Ben pulled out a cigarette. "But listen, while I have you on the phone. The weather's supposed to be unseasonably decent

Saturday. At least that's the forecast now. How about we meet over at the club and see if we can get in a few rounds of golf?"

Ben sighed. It was a brutal business. "It'll probably have to be indoors golf, Herb," he'd said.

Herb laughed. "I hear ya. I'll check back with you later in the week. All right?"

"Okay."

And that was how it had gone. I'm firing your lady today and let's play golf tomorrow. Ben had hung up the phone.

Josie had called before and again after her meeting with Herb Graham, called no doubt to try and tell her side of the story to Ben, but he was too upset to allow her calls through. As he'd watched that press conference and her refusal to leave that minority-contractors issue the hell alone, he'd wanted to yell through that TV screen and tell her to knock it off himself. He'd see her tonight, he told Whitney to tell her, hoping that by nightfall his anger would have subsided and he could better handle without adding fire to what was certain to be an already emotional scene.

Then Sam Darrow came into his office with more strangeness. Sam was a thirty-something white man with short, slick black hair, big, green eyes, and narrow, almost nonexistent lips. He was a well-connected staunch supporter of Ben, who saw all and heard all. He hoped that someday his hard work would pay off with the ascension of Ben Braddock into the CEO's chair, and he into Ben's.

He sat down in front of Ben's desk and smiled. "Hey, buddy," he said. "How's it going?"

"Good."

"How's your health?"

Ben hesitated. "My health?"

"Yes. How is it?" Sam asked, again.

"It's fine."

"You sure?"

"I'm positive."

"You don't have any ailments, do you?"

"Ailments?"

"Yes. Sicknesses. Diseases. STDs?" he asked.

Ben leaned back. The nerve of the young man astounded him. "What are you talking about, Sam?"

"You work out, don't you?"

Ben didn't respond. He stared at Sam instead.

"Yeah, I can tell," Sam said. "You're a muscular man. Really buff. You work out. But have you ever taken steroids or been on any psychotropic drugs? Any hallucinogenic drugs?"

Ben frowned. "Why?"

"Just say no."

"Don't tell me what to say. Why do you need to know any of that?"

"Do you have an as yet unexposed weakness I need to know about?" Sam asked. Ben thought about Josie when asked about his weakness. But he still didn't answer the question.

"What's with the questions, Sam?"

"Something's in the wind, bud. Something big. But before I can make an announcement I need to confirm some things with my sources. Lunch tomorrow?" Ben hesitated. Something was in the wind all right. Him twisting in it.

"Yes," he finally said.

"Perfect," Sam said and stood up, his eagerness almost sickening to Ben. "Oh, by the by, I saw Josie on the idiot box this afternoon. She's a fireball, ain't she?" Ben didn't respond. Sam laughed. "I wouldn't want her to be an enemy of mine, I'll tell you that much," he said. "Reel her in, is my advice," he added, and then slipped back out of Ben's office.

The telephone rang and Josie looked at the clock on her bedroom wall. Eleven forty-nine P.M. She grabbed the receiver, certain that Ben had gone home instead of coming by her place as he had promised.

"Where are you?" she blurted out before he could say hello.

But it wasn't Ben. It was Scotty Culpepper, her old friend from Florida. Josie lay her head back on her pillow and sighed.

"What is it now?" Scotty asked, knowing the saga of Josie and Ben like the back of his hand. Josie was, as Scotty often said, practically a virgin when she met Ben. She didn't know how to handle love then and in a lot of ways still didn't. She nearly drove Scotty insane.

"Ben was supposed to come over," she said.

"And let me guess, he hasn't made it yet and you're about ready to pitch a fit?"

"Right."

"He's probably still at work, Josie. You know he's always working late. Why don't you just call him?"

"I can't."

"You can't? And why the hell not?"

"Every time I call to see if he left the office he always finds out and gets upset. He doesn't like weak women, remember?"

"Do I ever. But you're hardly weak, Josie. You just don't know what you're doing."

"Very funny. But I know what I'm doing, thank you. I just don't know what *he's* doing."

"Why you got to know? After what y'all went through in Florida I thought you figured out by now that he's a righteous brother. You had to have figured out that much by now."

"I think I have, Scotty. But he just . . ."

"He just what?"

"Nothing. Just nothing. Let's talk about you. How are you?"

"No, now girl, we're talking about you."

"I know you didn't call just to hear me bitch and moan. And if you did, tough. Now what's up?"

There was a pause. Josie knew what that meant. "Not again, Scotty."

"I don't want to hear it, Josie."

"What did what's-his-name do this time?" she asked.

"What's-his-name's been gone, girl. I kicked him to the curb two weeks ago for your information. Bruce came back."

"Oh my goodness. Not the thug, Scotty. Tell me you didn't let that thieving thug come back into your life?"

, "Okay. I didn't let that thieving thug come back into my life."

"You let him back? After he stole your credit card, your car, Scotty? You let him back? How can you keep taking yourself through that crap, over and over again?"

"He's gone now, anyway, so that's over." Scotty said.

"What happened?" She could hear Scotty sigh. "What happened?" she asked again.

"He said I was stifling his creativity and he had to leave."

Josie laughed aloud. *"You* were stifling *him?"*

"Ain't he a trip?"

"That asshole!"

"I know. But it still hurts," he said. "And if he were to knock on my door right now I still would let him in, girl."

Josie thought about Ben. She knew the power of love now and how it could absolutely turn your life, not to mention your standards, upside down. She nodded her head.

"Yeah," she said. "Know what you mean."

"But enough about me. How are you?"

"I told you I'm okay."

"Still getting used to Saint Cloud?"

"It's too damn cold here."

"I couldn't believe y'all settled on Saint Cloud, Minnesota. I know you said y'all wanted to give the Midwest a try, but damn. Minnesota? Of all the places y'all could have picked y'all settled on Saint Cloud, Minnesota?

"Don't say y'all—Ben. You know he wasn't going anywhere without a job, a house, and everything else lined up. I thought we were going to be daredevils, you know? He resigned his judgeship and you know what happened to me. We were free. We could have just explored America together for the rest of our lives."

"That don't even sound like no Ben."

"I know. But I was still hoping. Until Ben casually mentioned that this friend of his, the chairman of the board at Denlex Corporation, needed a good, conservative gentleman such as himself to fill their VP vacancy. 'Denlex?' I asked. 'Where is it?' That's when he mentioned Minnesota."

"And you followed him like the good little whipped puppy you are."

"Damn straight. I wasn't letting him get away."

"I hear that. But I'm still surprised they hired him, and at the top like that. Denlex didn't care that women had accused him of sexual harassment?"

"They knew it was lies, that's why. Especially after my article appeared in the *Daily News*. They knew Ben had gotten a bum rap. You just don't know, Scotty. His friends really stick by him. I was the only one who ever doubted him." Josie shuddered at the thought of what could have been and decided to change the subject. "So," she said, as if it was a relief to be able to move on, "how's the Culpepper Art Gallery getting along these days?"

"Fine, child. You know I take good care of my business, thank you. Fran quit."

"Get out! Really? Now that's what I call good news. But why did she quit?"

"Don't know, don't care. I was truly tired of her bitching, anyway, you hear me? Got me a new, more talented assistant now. His name is Daniel."

"Oh, Lord. Here we go."

"It's strictly professional, Josie, damn. I don't play that with my business, you know me. I'm passionate about my work too."

Work, Josie thought. Another sore subject. "Anyway, Scotty, I'd better get off this phone."

"The sex still good?"

"No, you didn't ask me that."

"Well is it?"

"It's great. Okay? When I can get it," she said.

"When you can . . . what? When you can get it?"

Josie had said too much already. She closed her eyes.

"Come on, Josie. Fess up, girl, you'll feel better for it. Ben still refusing to give it up?"

"He gives it up. Just not on no regular basis."

"Why the hell not?"

"He thinks I still have a lot to learn emotionally. You know how he is," she said.

"Well, it's true."

"It's not true. I'm almost thirty years old, Scotty."

"You're beautiful, Josie. You're smart. Lord knows you're passionate about everything. But a sophisticated, mature lady you are not."

Josie rolled her eyes. *Why not?* "If you say so."

"I know so. Men always were the baddies in your life. You grew up with a mama always crying over some man. Your sisters were always depressed over some man. Your brothers ain't worth sweeping out the door. So you hated men."

"I did not hate men, Scotty."

"Okay, you disliked them. Then Ben Braddock comes along. The first man you truly loved. And he's no joke, let's get real, girl. He also happens to be the best-looking brother on the face of this planet."

Josie smiled. "Okay!"

"And his good-looking ass rocked your world. That's all there is to it. He rocked it. But he's light years ahead of you in the romance department, girl. You're a babe in the woods compared to him. I mean, he's been around, know what I'm saying? How many times has he been married?"

"Once."

"That's it?"

"Yep. Until his wife became ill and died."

"And he never remarried?"

"Never."

"I don't know, girl. Your hopes for wedding bliss don't look so good if the man been single this long," Scotty said.

"I didn't have any plans for wedding bliss."

"Sure buddy," she said. Then Scotty laughed. "So, just how often do you get the honor of a roll in the sack with Ben?"

Josie smiled. "None of your business, Scotty, okay?" Scotty continued laughing.

"What is so damn funny?" she said.

"Now you're twenty-nine years old and still practically a virgin!"

Josie wanted to laugh herself, but she didn't. "Bye, boy!" she said to the still laughing Scotty Culpepper, and then hung up the phone.

She got out of bed and walked downstairs. She lived in a two-bedroom townhouse on Cypress Road, a thoroughly modern home with 1,600 square feet of black and white checked floors, cathedral ceilings, bright white walls, and gorgeous black leather furnishings. Ben purchased the home for her when they first relocated to Minnesota, and furnished it as well, which was fine with her because she was unemployed at the time, in need of a serious helping hand, and she also didn't have a clue about interior design. But now, as she stood in her quiet kitchen and poured herself a tall glass of water, she wondered if it was such a great idea after all. She felt beholden to him now, when the last thing on earth she wanted was to be beholden to some man. *But that's love for ya,* she thought. She was thrilled when he did things for her. The same woman who wouldn't allow a man to open a car door for her had allowed one to buy her a house. Just because she fell in love. Just because that foolishness called love she had thought wouldn't kick her around had knocked her to the ground.

But there was another way, she thought, as she headed back upstairs to bed. She still hadn't fully resolved in her mind why Ben didn't just keep his cash and let her move in with him. He had a huge home in Walden Woods after all. A beautiful, palatial home. And he lived there all by himself, like some recluse, when Josie would have been more than willing to share those quarters with him. But he wasn't about to go for that. He was a conservative to his heart, which meant, as Josie saw it, that he had this great Christian philosophy that wouldn't allow him to go out there too far. Or, as he'd once said himself, he wasn't going to overdo it. Shacking up, in his view anyway, was definitely overdoing it.

But he covered himself, Josie thought, because he wouldn't marry her either. He claimed she wasn't ready yet, that her lack of experience rendered her virtually numb to the ways of romance, a truth, Josie felt, he never seemed comfortable admitting. He had fallen in love with a woman who didn't know squat, when his interest had always tended toward more sophisticated ladies, and it probably bothered him. Now Josie rarely saw him, being forced to take his rationed-out romance whenever she could get it. But if he had listened to her, she believed fervently, everything would have been different. She would have been able to see him more, at least every night, not once or twice a week. And their romance, which seemed stagnant to her, would have made more progress by now.

She was back in bed by the time Ben arrived at her townhouse. It was late, well after midnight, so he used the spare key she kept outside to let himself in. He was exhausted. Another long-behind day. He poured himself a drink at Josie's small bar, and then walked slowly up the stairs to her bedroom. He didn't have the energy for any confrontation with her and, to avoid one, he had thought about not coming over at all. But he'd promised to come by. And Josie had yet to allow him to break a promise to her.

Instead of her greeting him with a warm hello as he stepped into her bedroom, she immediately wanted to know where he'd been.

"At work," he said calmly, standing there.

"This time of night, Ben?"

"Yes."

"But it's after midnight."

He stood there staring at her, his body near collapse with exhaustion, and he wasn't about to argue with her. He walked over to the chair and sat down, his glass of scotch cold in his hands as he took a sip, his lit cigarette hanging limply between his fingers. Josie was lying on top of her covers, wearing a see-through, micro-short chemise he remembered buying for her, although he couldn't remember for what occasion he'd purchased it. Her large breasts could be seen visibly underneath the chiffon material, and that small section of her pubic hair, unshaved beyond her bikini line, glowed like sweet darkness as her gown clung against it. Ben leaned back and crossed his legs.

Josie turned her body sideways, to face him, and it was no accident that she was wearing her most provocative sleepwear. She wanted to relax him, because she needed his help again, but she just didn't quite know how to break the news. Besides, she was still reeling from the lateness of the hour. Getting off work at midnight? She wasn't buying that for a second.

"What were you working on?" she asked him. Some female? she wanted to add.

Ben, however, rarely went there with Josie. He had already told her what he was doing. That conversation, as far as he was concerned, was over.

"You called the office quite a few times today," he said, deciding to get to the point. "What's up?"

Josie swallowed hard. She wanted to get on with it too. "I know Herbert Graham is a friend of yours," she began, "but the man just ain't right, Ben. He wouldn't even listen to me. I know it got heated at the mayor's news conference today, I know it did. But I was just doing my job. The job Mr. Graham was paying me to do, by the way. At least that's what I thought. Until . . ."

Ben took a slow drag on his cigarette. He was most disappointed in Josie when she fell for her own bs. She'd gotten herself in a hell of a mess, but it was the boss's fault now, not hers. It took all he had to contain his anger. "Until what, Josephine?" he asked her.

Josie looked at Ben, her beautiful gray-green eyes wide and devastated. "He fired me today," she said.

Ben hesitated. Something about those big eyes of hers softened him. "I know."

Josie, however, was shocked. "You know? How did you know?"

"Herb called and told me."

"When?"

"After you met with him."

"After I met . . . And you didn't call me or come and see about me? You knew I had been fired and you wouldn't even take my calls?"

Ben stared at Josie, stared at this woman he still couldn't believe he loved. But he did. Deeply. "Yes," he said.

"But why? I needed you."

"You were out of line today, Josephine."

"Because I told the truth? How can you say that? Todd Keating knows what he's doing. Not one minority contractor received a bid on that road improvement initiative and that was no accident."

"I know that."

"Everybody knows that. But nobody says a damn thing. It was my job to point that out." Ben didn't respond. He just sat still and stared at Josie. "I didn't deserve to get fired because I told the truth. How can you say that?" Then she hesitated. "Mr. Graham was so nasty to me, Ben, you should have been there. He said I insulted the mayor and that wasn't even true. All I did was what any good journalist would have done and questioned why no blacks were getting any of those 'Better Saint Cloud' contracts. That's all I did. But Graham didn't even wanna hear that. He said I was an embarrassment to his paper. He said he couldn't believe a man of Ben Braddock's stature would have recommended a loose cannon like me for such a position of trust. I almost puked."

Josie glanced at Ben, to see if his gorgeous face showed the least bit of sympathy for her position. But there was none. She had been fired from a job he had had to call in favors to get. Fired because of her mouth again. Because of her loose lips. That was all she saw on Ben's face. She felt like a failure, like she had let him down, not to mention herself, once again. "I want my job, Ben," she said.

Ben shook his head. "I know better than that," he said.

"What?"

"You don't want that job. Because if you did you would have thought about that job before you decided to become the advocate for wealthy minority contractors."

"It wasn't like that."

"It was exactly like that! I saw that press conference, Josephine. When the mayor denied your claim of racism you don't stand there and badger him about it, you move the hell on! But not Josephine. Her mouth takes over. She calls the man a liar to his face."

"He is a liar! It's the truth. And I believe in telling the truth."

"And that's fine. I have no problem with you standing up for what you believe in. You'd better never stop doing so. But what drives me crazy is the way you do it. You never count up the costs first, Josephine. Never. Beliefs aren't free. They come with a price. And if you aren't willing to pay that price then dammit don't stand up! Now you've lost a good job, a job you told me you wanted. So don't come to me when the cost is too high, because you should have thought about that before!"

Ben leaned back. What he hated most was losing his temper. It did something to his entire body chemistry, usually making him sick to his stomach. And he was already exhausted too. That was why he doused his cigarette in his now empty glass and sat it down on the bedroom floor.

"I'm going home to bed," he said, rising to his feet.

Josie couldn't believe how insensitive he could be sometimes. She had just spilled her soul to him, telling him all the chilling details of how his so-called friend fired her, and he was going home? But she held her tongue. She had done enough damage for one day, she decided.

Ben walked over to where Josie was lying and sat on the edge of the bed, his hands resting on either side of her narrow shoulders.

"We'll talk tomorrow."

"I'm sorry, Ben."

"I know."

"We came all the way to Minnesota to get away from mess. Now it's starting back up again."

"Don't say that, Josie. You hear me? Nothing's starting back up. We're okay. We're going to be okay. And you're still my girl. All right?" He said this and smiled.

Josie rubbed his mustache with the tip of her finger and then massaged the lines on the side of his eyes. "You mean it?" she asked him.

He nodded. He meant it. Then he kissed her softly on the lips. He could feel her relax as he kissed her. And when he looked into her eyes, those gorgeous hazel eyes that had captured his heart in the first place, he could see her pain. And her need. It had been months since he had allowed them to go there, believing rightly that going slow was an absolute necessity for an emotionally inexperienced woman like Josie. But he also knew how lonely she was and how Minnesota had not been what she had hoped, and how he disappointed her most of all. He kissed her again.

She wrapped her arms around his big body and opened her mouth wider. His tongue explored her mouth as he raised her body up to him. The longer they kissed, the closer their bodies became. Until Josie removed her lips from his and smiled as she grabbed the hem of her chemise, wiggled her body up, and then slipped the gown over her head. Ben's eyes became transfixed on her naked body before him, all sweet and tender, as if it were a ball of desire begging him to touch it. He stared at it. He stared as if amazed by the beauty of what he was blessed to see. Then he touched it, and stroked it softly, tenderly, passionately, all over, and Josie moaned and groaned and begged for more. His touch was what she had to have, what she was beginning to feel she could not live without, and she looked into his eyes. He had to see it too. She had to get him to understand the depths of her love for him.

But he already understood. He understood better than she did. That was why he placed his hand on the side of her face and kissed her again. He thought that would calm her down, but it only riled him up. He was tired. And burdened. And unable to be reasonable anymore. Josie was ready, willing, and more than able to be unreasonable too.

He stood up. Stared at her one more time. And then removed his clothes.

Cypress Road was pin-drop quiet at midnight as all manner of activity that once dominated the landscape had packed up and gone indoors. A dark blue Corvette sat in the shadows of the quiet street, just across from Josie's townhouse. The car had dark tinted windows and headlights that pointed out like two watchful eyes of a lurking peeping tom. It was parked there by no accident, but because Ben's Mercedes was there, parked in the driveway of his girlfriend's home. And as soon as it could be seen from the street that the light in Josie's bedroom had gone out, that former criminal court judge and one-time supreme court nominee, Benjamin Braddock, would not be coming out of that house any time soon, the car, the dark blue, lurking Corvette, slowly drove away.

CHAPTER 3

Her job search turned up blanks. She went everywhere—from Saint Cloud to Hutchinson to Brainerd—to newspapers, weeklies, and monthlies in the Twin Cities, but nobody was interested. Her reputation preceded her. And that was the problem. She was liberal, it was no secret, when many Minnesota papers preferred to stay away from such blatant extremism, and she had been fired very publicly from two coveted newspaper jobs in less than a year.

But she didn't want to go home still unemployed, still at the mercy of others because she couldn't get her act together. That was why she decided, and it didn't take much effort, to try it her way. She had been thinking about it even before the *Herald* got rid of her, but she knew Ben wouldn't go for it. But it was her career, not his, she decided. She was the one who had to work the job, so she became determined to get a job she wanted, where her passion might actually be appreciated. The mainstream press was done with her and, perhaps, she was done with them. She fully understood now that she never really fitted into a world like theirs anyway.

So she stepped through the doors of the *Bullhorn Journal,* a proud-to-be-liberal, fringe weekly located on the east end of Saint Germain on the bottom floor of an otherwise deserted warehouse. She sat in a small chair against a wall that was badly in need of a paint job, patiently waiting for nearly an hour for the editor to call her name.

Deuce Jefferson, the editor, wasn't waiting for her, however. He sat in his office reading over the latest unemployment statistics, as if he had nothing better to do. It was Rain, the assistant city editor and his trusted friend, who came into his office asking why he hadn't bothered to see the applicant yet.

"What applicant?" he asked.

"Deuce, come on, just the young lady who has been sitting outside your office for about an hour now."

"Young? How young?"

"I don't know, look on her application. She looks to be about twenty-three or twenty-four."

"That's too young."

"Yeah, right. Then you've got to fire half your staff. Look, Deuce, I know you hate interviews, but just see the woman. Demi says she's well qualified."

"If she's not a moron then to Demi she's well qualified. Don't talk to me about Demi, anyway. Did you see these unemployment stats, yet?"

"Not yet. And it's probably because I have too much work to do while my boss has too much time on his hands."

Deuce looked up from his papers and smiled. Rain was his girl, a chunky, thirty-year-old woman with fat thighs and hips and a large, round, hog-shaped head, but with a beautiful smile, and the kind of wit he adored. She was also crazy as hell, which turned him on too. He considered long ago coupling up with her, because there was something about Rain, but she knocked that notion out of the way almost as quickly as he thought it up. "Not on your life," she told him. "You're my friend. We sleep together and just like all your prior romances our relationship will be toast. Then you'll wanna fire me. No way, partner. We stay friends. I'm not interested in taking that chance." And he agreed. And stayed away from such thoughts about Rain.

"Okay," Deuce said, folding his papers, "where's her ap'?"

He fumbled around on his messy desk searching for the application. Rain, however, found it on the floor near the waste basket. "Why am I not surprised?" she said as she picked it up.

He snatched it from her. "Just give it to me and leave," he said jocularly, and she did.

He skimmed through Josie's application quickly. A graduate of 'Bama's journalism school, a reporter and later the assistant city editor of the *Jacksonville Gazette*. And then a reporter with the *Herald*. The *Herald?* Deuce looked at the name again. Josephine Ross. Then he smiled. He remembered her. He remembered her from the mayor's press conference. She was the woman with the braids. The sister with the attitude.

He hurried out of his office to greet his applicant. Josie stood when he walked into the newsroom. He was of medium height, a late-twenties type with a kind face, and angular good looks. He wore that wild-but-neat, part-twist and part-Afro hairstyle that reminded Josie of that brother on *CSI*. He dressed casually in a pair of khaki pants, a brown-and-gold paisley shirt, and a pair of Timberlands. He sported the kind of muscular but slender body built more for a fashion runway than a newsroom. But his eyes were what kept Josie's attention. Big, beautiful, oval-shaped eyes, like Magic Johnson's, but not cheerful like Magic's, but sad, and black as coal.

"Come in, Miss Ross," he said and Josie walked eagerly toward him. "I'm Deuce Jefferson." He said this as he stood at his office door and extended his hand, and Josie gladly accepted it. A friendly face after a day like the one she'd had was a welcomed sight. "I'm the city editor and managing editor and any other kind of editor for the *Journal*. Please," he said as he moved aside and allowed Josie passage in.

As soon as she walked into his office she turned and faced him. He was even better looking up close, she thought. "Before we get started, Mr. Jefferson, I just wanted to tell you—"

"Oh, no you don't. We don't play that here. No 'Mister' nothing. Deuce, please."

Josie, who thought she had just made some terrible mistake, smiled. "I'm sorry. I'm just a little nervous."

"No need for that."

"Thank you," she said.

"So?"

"Sir? I mean, what?"

He smiled. "What did you want to tell me?" he asked.

"Oh! Right. I just wanted to tell you how much I appreciate the opportunity to be interviewed. That's all I wanted to say."

"That's what they tell you to say in those interview books, don't they? The dos and don'ts?"

Josie hesitated. "I think so."

"Then is it true, or is it recommended? Do you truly appreciate this opportunity?"

"Oh, yes. Very much so."

"Good. Nothing wrong with that. Appreciation is near-extinction nowadays, anyway. Have a seat."

Josie sat down in the small, metal chair in front of Deuce's desk, a desk covered completely with papers and books and stacks of files. Deuce, in fact, leaned against the front of his desk, because he probably would not have been able to see Josie's face if he sat behind it. She handed him her resume. He glanced at it quickly. Then he threw it on the desk to get swallowed up with the other words on paper he seldom read.

"So," he said, "you're Josephine Ross?"

"Josie. If you don't mind."

"Not at all. Josie. I remember you from the mayor's press conference."

Josie hesitated. Surely he wouldn't hold that scene against her too. "Let me just say this about that," she said, feeling defensive. "I know I gave the mayor a hard time, and I know you might think I was out of line, but I disagree. I was only telling the truth."

"I know you were. Damn straight you were. I like your style, Josie Ross."

Josie had to digest what Deuce had just said. "Are you sure about that?" she asked. "That style is what got me fired from the *Herald.*"

"They fired you because of that?"

"That's what they said."

"Because you questioned the mayor?" he asked.

Josie nodded. "Yep."

"Damn. But don't even sweat that. Your performance may have gotten you fired from the *Herald,* but here at the *Journal* you won rave reviews."

Josie smiled. Comradery at last. "Thank you," she said, heartfelt. Even Ben didn't seem to understand. "Thank you very much."

Deuce folded his arms and stared at Josie. She was dressed in a grainy gold and gray, African-style pantsuit that he thought illuminated her beautiful brown skin. Her heels were high and her earrings wooden, and whenever she smiled her cheeks lifted. *An African princess,* Deuce thought, as he stared at her big hazel eyes and sweet, innocent face. She was so gorgeous in every way that he wanted to know immediately if she was married. He didn't suspect that she was—there was no ring and a woman of conscience like her was probably too hot to handle for most brothers—but he decided to make it his business to find out.

"How long have you lived in Saint Cloud?"

"I've been here for eight months."

"Like it?"

"Nope."

He smiled. "Okay," he said.

"I mean, I'm sure it's a very nice place. I'm just still trying to get used to the weather."

"That's right. You're a Florida transplant, aren't you?"

"Yes."

"Why Saint Cloud? Especially since you don't even like it."

"A very long story," Josie said.

"Following your husband, something like that?"

"I don't have a husband, but something like that."

Deuce nodded. A boyfriend probably, but he took that to mean she was still fair game. "So you want to be one of our roving reporters?"

"Yes. Yes, I do."

"You were an assistant city editor at the *Jacksonville Gazette.* Weren't you?"

Josie hesitated. "For a brief period of time I was, yes."

"What happened?"

"My style, once again, clashed with theirs."

"That's what I don't get. Why would you, knowing the deal, knowing how those people are, go to work for a mainstream, some would say, conservative daily like the *Herald?* After what happened to you in Florida? You enjoy torturing yourself or something?"

Josie smiled. "I just might. I don't know. I just did it." She did it because Ben told her that was what she was going to do. If she was going to go back into journalism, she was going to work for the best newspaper in town, Ben had said.

"The *Journal* was your last choice, wasn't it?"

"Yes. I ain't even gonna lie. Now you're my only choice."

"Damn. Dead last?"

"Dead last," Josie said.

Deuce shook his head. "I don't know what they be thinking. You're obviously a talented reporter. I think you were the best one at that press conference. But they hate talent, don't they?"

"They hate something."

"Well, the good news is that we don't. We thrive on it, in fact."

Josie smiled. Deuce loved the way her lips poked out and then slid into a line of perfection when she smiled. "Does that mean I'm hired?" she asked him.

"Oh, hell yeah. With your credentials? And your style, I might add. I'd be a fool not to take you on. And my mama—"

"Didn't raise no fool. I know."

Deuce smiled and so did Josie. She was pleasantly surprised. She found herself easily relaxed around Deuce, who seemed so naturally affable. She couldn't have feelings for any man but Ben, but she also found herself easily attracted to him. She liked his kind face, and his perfect model's body, and the fact that he didn't judge her or criticize her style or try to put her in some box right away. It was an attraction that almost threw her for a loop. She didn't expect it, and she definitely didn't encourage it. But it was there.

By the time she left Deuce's office, he was attracted to her too, more than she would ever know. Because he was convinced, after only a few minutes with that hazel-eyed beauty that just graced his land, that he had just hired the undeniable, perhaps even unobtainable, woman of his dreams.

Benjamin Braddock decided to walk. It was an unusually mild day for Saint Cloud, 59° in the shade. He left his office on the top floor of the mammoth Denlex corporate headquarters much earlier than the time he agreed to meet Sam Darrow for lunch. He was comfortably yet elegantly dressed, a striking figure out on Seventh Avenue in a dark blue pinstriped suit, a pair of expensive Artioli shoes, and a dark blue fedora, all in perfectly coordinated detail. His suit coat flapped freely as he walked, his belly slightly protruding over his belt, which worked for him because he was big and muscular and seemed to need the extra

weight. The women he passed along the streets of Saint Cloud certainly didn't seem to mind, glancing at that muscular body of his with
obvious approval. They eyed him with double takes as they walked by
him, and that same reaction of females whenever he entered a room or
even walked down a city street always amused him.

He arrived at the restaurant called Rhonda's, and entered through
the heavy double-doors just as the smiling, familiar face of the maitre
d' greeted him. He sat down, ordered brandy, and fully expected Sam
to be late as usual. That was why he brought a newspaper along, the
Saint Cloud Herald, and he checked to see if there was any mention
of Josie's firing or of her supposed embarrassment of the mayor. She
was a great lady who never got any breaks, he felt, who still managed to remain true to her beliefs even when her brand of liberalism
was long out of style. He thought about Josie, and how she clung to
him last night, and how tender her body felt against his. He hadn't
made love to her in months, and it showed, as he couldn't get enough
of her. But even after they made love and after she finally fell asleep
in his arms, she was restless all night, tossing and turning, as if she
couldn't get over what the *Herald* had done to her. Her firing was a
monumental wrong in her eyes, a grave injustice, yet the folks at the
Herald apparently didn't think so. They didn't consider it worthy of
even a mention in their own paper.

As Ben continued reading the *Herald,* amazed by some of the
lame stories that did make the cut, Meredith Chambers walked into
Rhonda's. She explained to the maitre d' exactly where she wanted
to sit, and he escorted her to the table of her choice. She wore a tight-
fitting, yellow business suit, bright enough and with a skirt short
enough to catch the eye, but just understated enough to catch the attention of a particular eye.

And it worked. Ben Braddock merely glanced at her as she moved
past his table, but when he realized what he'd just seen, he did as females often did to him and took another look. She was a stunner, he
thought, as she sat down at the table three rows away from his,
crossing her remarkably shapely legs and slinging back her long,
straight hair with a sexy, coquettish flip of the hand. Her face reminded him of Lola Falana in her heyday, with those large, stunning
eyes, full, luscious lips, and high cheek bones that gave her grace
with her beauty. He would put her age around the late thirties,

maybe older, and everything about her was a turn-on. Before he met Josie she was exactly his type, the only kind of woman he bothered with: mature, confident, and seductive.

The peripheral sight of Sam Darrow coming toward his table broke his stare. Sam, ever smiling, ever anxious to tell the news, plopped down in the chair in front of him and ordered a pipeline.

"A what?" Ben asked when the waiter left their side.

"A pipeline. It's . . . you know it's . . . oh, you don't wanna know."

Ben smiled and folded his newspaper. "So," he asked, not at all anxious to spend a lot of time with Sam, "what's the big news?"

"You came to Denlex, what? A year ago, right?"

"Eight months, but go on."

"When the chairman brought you on board, there were rumors."

"There always are."

"But these particular rumors wouldn't go away. It was just assumed that Wayne Murdoch, wonderful man that he may be, was on the way out."

"And?"

"And you were on the way in. That's why you were brought here. To replace Murdoch. Those were the rumors anyway. And according to my sources, those rumors are true."

Ben leaned back. Wayne Murdoch, the president and chief executive officer of Denlex, hinted as much today, saying over and over in his private meeting with Ben that he was tired of office politics, of how he had given forty years to Denlex and what does he get in return? More politics. He wasn't specific with Ben, and Ben didn't ask for specifics because the writing was on the wall.

"I've been hearing about Murdoch's fate since I got here. It's just good, old-fashioned, company gossip, Sam."

"Not anymore," Sam said. "They're prepared now to ask for Murdoch's resignation. No more talk about it. They've got a timeline."

Now Ben was genuinely shocked. But Sam wouldn't know it to look at him. "Do they?" Ben asked.

"They do. And they want him out soon. Very soon. And Murdoch will agree to go."

Ben started thinking about Murdoch and he couldn't help but empathize with the man. Murdoch had given Denlex forty years of his life, forty long years, and how does it end? With rumors and gossip and everybody knowing more about his impending doom than he would probably ever know. But that was the name of the corporate game. Do it to them before they do it to you. It was a game Ben hated. Because it was a boomerang. Because just as surely as it was Murdoch's day, his day would come too. Ben was forty-nine years old, and his birthday wasn't that many months away. The big five-oh was just around the corner for him. Murdoch was sixty. Just ten years older. And already being led out to pasture.

"The hunt is on for a successor," Sam continued, so excited by the misfortunes of his fellow man that it sickened Ben, "and from what I hear it's already over."

Ben didn't say anything. He did as he normally did when news came too quickly. He listened.

"My sources tell me that you, not anybody else, but you are the heir apparent." Ben still did not respond. "Say something, man, come on. I'm telling you what I know."

"I don't think so, Sammy."

"Why the hell not?"

"I may be on their short list but I doubt seriously if I'll make the final cut," Ben said.

Sam nearly jumped out of his seat. "Are you kidding me? I'm telling you CEO is yours to lose. And it'll be historic too! You'll be the first African American ever to occupy such a position of esteem in the fifty-year history of Denlex, Ben. They'll be begging you to take it. Just to make history alone. The time is ripe for this thing to happen. They'll be merely going through the motions with other names, it'll just be for show. Trust me on that."

Sam had a way about him, an almost inexplicable way of drawing others into his web of excitement. Ben could feel it coming on too. He could feel that surge of energy that that excitement required, where the impossible was suddenly possible, but there were still too many unanswered questions.

"How many others are in the running?" he asked Sam.

"Just window dressing."

"How many?"

"I'm telling you they don't stand a snowball's chance in hell—"

"Sam, did I ask you a question?"

Sam looked at Ben and wondered why he even bothered. Ben

never treated him as an equal, not even when he was bending over backwards to keep Ben's name in the public eye and in the board's good graces. You would think the man would show him some kindness. But never. Always straight-shooting Ben. Never emotional. Never unhinged. Never once showing an ounce of ambition.

"Two other men are in the running," Sam finally said. "Both are outsiders, long resumes, little personality, window dressing like I said. You're the only inside man up."

Ben nodded. It was promising news to be sure. He figured he would be on a short list of maybe eight, ten names. But one of three? It was some damn good news if it were true. But he couldn't stop thinking about Florida. That had been promising news too, the day he got word that the governor of Florida planned to enter his name for the vacancy on the state supreme court. It had been, in fact, a dream come true. But his dream became a nightmare when woman after woman began to surface, claiming that he had sexually harassed them at some point or other in his judicial career. He had been a well-respected, conservative, criminal court judge then, and the allegations had devastated him. The governor had rescinded the nomination, the press had a field day scandalizing his name, and for a while even Josie believed the women. By the time the truth came out, when Josie decided to stop going for the obvious and look beneath the web of lies those women told, Ben had already resigned his position in the circuit court.

But the liberal newspaper Josie had worked for and loved so profusely, her beloved *Jacksonville Gazette,* had refused to print her story. Ben Braddock was a conservative asshole and they weren't about to try and resuscitate him with something as simple as the truth. So she had taken her story to a rival, conservative newspaper. They gladly printed the story and Josie, subsequently, was fired. The damage to Ben's career, however, was already done. Many believed he recovered. He was, after all, the senior vice president of one of the largest corporations in the Midwest, but Ben knew better. He was scarred for life by the hell he had gone through in Florida and the responsibility he felt for what happened to Josie's career. That was why good news no longer carried the weight it once had. That was why his emotions, which he kept hidden beneath the surface, remained dormant even on his best day. Sam could assure him until he was blue in the face, could tell him a zillion times that the victory was in the bag, that the position was his to lose, but Ben wasn't about to dance a jig just yet.

The same dark blue Corvette that had sat outside Josie's townhouse the night before sat outside Rhonda's restaurant today. Meredith Chambers, her yellow business suit sparkling against the gray Minnesota sky, stood outside the restaurant as the Corvette cranked up, completed a U-turn on Second Street, and then drove up to the curb where she stood. She opened the front passenger door and quickly stepped inside. The driver, Hines Lowe, an olive-skinned man with bushy red hair, removed the dark glasses that covered his small, slanted eyes and looked at her.

"Did Braddock notice you?" he asked anxiously.

"That is a nice restaurant, Hines. We simply must come back and sample their cuisine."

"Did he notice you?"

Meredith slung back her long hair and smiled, so confident in her seductiveness that she was practically giddy. "Oh, yes," she said. "He noticed."

Ben lived in Walden Woods in a big, sprawling, brick home, fourth from the corner on Old Spanish Trail. Josie drove into the circular driveway and parked her Mustang just behind his Mercedes. Inside his garage were two other vehicles, both of which he almost never drove, a Cadillac Seville STS and a brand-new Nissan Frontier pick-up truck. It seemed like such a waste to Josie, to have all of those cars, but that was Ben's business and he never discussed his business with her.

Ben was inside his home cooking when the doorbell rang. He removed the boiling pasta from the burner and hurried to answer the door. When he saw it was Josie he smiled. Then he kissed her quickly on her forehead and rushed back to his kitchen. She was still walking on air after securing employment, but still trying to find the right words to tell Ben exactly who her new employer was. The *Bullhorn Journal* was known primarily for one thing: criticizing the big corporations as often and as recklessly as they could. Ben's Denlex, particularly its overseas plants, but a few of its stateside plants as well, scored an environmental grade of F as far as the *Journal* was concerned and was therefore a constant target. Now she had to tell Ben that the one newspaper he rightly despised was her new employer.

"Something smells good up in here!" she said cheerfully as she walked into the home that looked almost antiseptically clean, like a show house, like a place so together that very little living appeared to be going on. His furnishings were all antique Victorian and seemed untouched by human butts, and the artwork that hung on the walls, from Renoir to little-known Otto Gellen, only enhanced the sterile feel. What this house needed was a woman, Josie once told Ben. He, of course, didn't say a word.

"You heard me?" she asked him as she walked into his kitchen. "What's for dinner?"

"Pasta," he said. "How was your day?"

She sat down at the kitchen table. *Give little information,* she thought. "Good," she replied.

"How did your job search go?"

"It was tough. I ain't even gonna front. Nobody would hire me, I mean they wouldn't even consider it, Ben. I've been fired from two jobs in less than a year, and the word had traveled fast. They were looking like something was wrong with me."

Ben sighed exhaustively and looked at Josie. In a lot of ways she was refreshing, fighting to the end for what she believed in, no matter what the cost, but in other ways she was just too gung ho. She was also the sweetest, kindest human being he'd ever met, somebody he could never leave out in the cold.

"Want me to see what I can do?" he asked her.

Josie quickly shook her head. She should never have allowed him to get her that position with the *Herald* in the first place. She was ill-suited to work at a newspaper like that and Ben should have known it. Or, at least, she should have.

"No," she said. "But thanks, anyway. Thank you. Actually, and incredibly, I have a job."

Ben frowned. "I thought you said nobody would hire you."

"They wouldn't. Not in the mainstream press, anyway." She said this and looked at Ben, her big hazel eyes filled with anticipation. He knew something was up, something he wasn't going to like, so he continued cooking.

"I tried with the big boys, Ben. I tried my best. But I don't think I'm really suited for that," she said. Ben's heart dropped. And he hesitated.

"I see," he said as he poured scallops and vegetables into a wok and began to stir-fry. All he wanted was for Josie to be happy. But when left to her own devices her choices often scared him. That was why he sat down his wooden spoon, sipped his glass of wine, and looked at her. "Who hired you, babe?" he asked her.

Josie hesitated. "It's a newspaper. But not a daily. A weekly. They go to press weekly. Which is great."

He paused. He hated it when she tried to hide something from him. "Who hired you, Josephine?"

She exhaled. "No biggie," she said. "I'll tell you all about it after dinner." She said this knowing full well that he wouldn't be able to eat a thing, not an ounce, if she were to tell him now.

Dinner was quiet. Ben ate very little, anyway, and Josie ate too much. After dinner they sat solemnly on the living-room sofa, as if there was some big secret between them that could spell the end of life as they knew it. Josie snuggled so close to Ben that he had no choice but to wrap his arm around her. He was tired, another grueling day, and Josie was being cagey. He had news too, news that he just might be in line for CEO. He wanted to tell her, but he wanted to be certain first. That was why he didn't rush Josie.

She looked into his eyes. They were so brown and soft, so filled with compassion that they still made her heart melt. "I love you, Ben," she said, near tears.

He smiled ever so slightly, the lines of age appearing on the sides of his eyes, and he pulled her closer. "What's the matter?" he asked her.

Josie sighed. She took her finger and rubbed his mustache. But she wouldn't speak. "Okay, now you're beginning to worry me. What is it?" he asked.

Josie didn't know any clever way to say it. So she just said it. "I've been hired by the *Journal*, Ben."

He frowned. "What *Journal?*"

"The *Bullhorn Journal*," Josie said.

Ben couldn't believe what he was hearing. "Josephine, I know better than that."

"Nobody else would hire me."

"Then you keep pounding the pavements! You weren't so hard-up that you had to scrape the bottom of the barrel. I pay your bills. I take care of you."

"I know that. It wasn't about that."

"Then what the hell was it about? All of that biased reporting those clowns are known for, and all of those conspiracy theories. It sounds like the *Gazette* all over again. I thought you learned your lesson in Florida."

"It ain't even like that, Ben. The *Journal* is different. I'll be allowed to do my own thing, not be imprisoned by theirs. It's nothing like the *Gazette*."

"The *Bullhorn Journal* brutalizes my company, Josie. And I mean with pure lies. How are you going to deal with that?"

"I won't have anything to do with stories about Denlex. I'll recuse myself."

"Then you'll be recusing yourself from about ninety-nine percent of their stories."

"Come on, Ben. It's nothing like that. Maybe once a month they might run a piece on Denlex."

"And how do you know this?"

"I read the *Journal* every week. I read all the papers in this region. You know that."

"But the *Bullhorn Journal*, Josephine? This is not a good time for you to be cavorting with those, those radical know-it-alls. Not now."

Josie looked at him. "What's so special about now?"

He hesitated. He could see it now: his girlfriend, the woman he loves, is a staff reporter for the chief critic of Denlex, the one paper that never gave them a break, that lied on them and caricatured them to such a degree that it was scandalous. His CEO hopes would be crushed. "Nothing at all," he said, and removed his arm from around her.

Josie leaned back. "Ben, what else was I supposed to do? The mainstream media hates me. I don't fit in with their preconceived notions of what a journalist should look like and be about. I'm tired of being the oddball. But at the *Journal* I'm not. Everybody's odd. It's a collection of the unique—that's what it is. And I think I'm gonna love it."

Ben leaned forward and looked back at Josie. She was odd all

right. But his odd. And where she worked was ultimately her decision to make anyway.

"Okay," he said, and smiled. "Just don't let them hurt us too
badly."

Josie smiled. "I won't."

Ben's smile turned to a look of concern. They'd been in Minnesota
for eight months now and although Ben's circle of friends was ever
expanding, Josie had zero to claim. He didn't have the kind of time
he wish he had to spend with her, and her lack of a social life beyond
their moments together worried him.

"Will you do something for me?" he asked her.

"Of course I will."

He frowned. "You don't know what it is yet, Josephine."

Josie sighed. She hated it when she came across as such a whipped
puppy but when Benjamin Braddock was concerned, she was whipped
beyond recognition. But Ben, she was coming to realize, wasn't all
that big on truth-telling either.

"What do you want me to do?" she asked, trying to be more like
the mature, thoughtful woman he wanted her to be.

"When you start on this new job I want you to make some friends
this time."

She smiled. "What?"

"You have no friends, Josie. I want you to meet some people your
own age and with interests similar to yours. I want you to make
some friends."

"I have friends," Josie said. Ben stared at her. "I have Scotty, remember?"

"Scotty lives in Florida, and he's it. I'm talking about here and I'm
talking about now. Give people a chance, that's all you need to do.
Once they get to know you they'll love you."

Josie hesitated. "Do you love me?" she asked, and then looked at
him.

"What do you think?"

Sometimes she wondered. "Of course," she said.

He nodded. "Okay."

He had said it to her once, when they were in the Florida Keys vis-
iting his folks, and one more time after that. Now, whenever she
brought it up, he sat mute. She wanted appeasement, he felt. She
wanted him to ease her insecurity with words of affection, as if his

saying he loves her would solve all her problems. But she didn't see what the big deal was about. She didn't see where there had to be some underlying reason to want your boyfriend to say he loves you. That wasn't too much to ask, she believed. But she also believed that things would eventually change, that once she lowered the temperature on her emotions and grew up, he'd have no problem whatsoever proclaiming his love.

But the growing up part was the problem.

CHAPTER 4

There was a woman in his bed. His eyes opened and there she was. Not very beautiful. Average. He vaguely remembered her from the club. Some two-bit hoochie who was shaking her booty for whichever brother put down the most cash. Deuce apparently won out. Now it was all a blur to him.

He turned over, but as soon as he did he could feel her arm drape around him. She wanted to spoon. He got out of bed.

His naked body was bronzed and statuesque as he walked over to his wallet and pulled out fifty bucks. He could feel her stare, and she was getting heated again, no doubt, but he wasn't feeling it. He wished it wasn't like that; he wish he didn't hate every female that easily fell in bed with him, but that was exactly the deal. He loathed them. There was nothing they could do for him, except get him off and get out of his life, and he hated being that way. He was pushing thirty now, and it was bothering him even more. He was going to end up old and alone and he knew it, unless something didn't change dramatically. And soon.

"Here's cab fare," he said to the woman in his bed, the nameless, naked woman he now despised. "Lock the door behind you, will you?"

The woman was obviously hurt. Cab fare was date code for get lost, but she tried not to show it as she hurried out of his bed and slipped on her mini dress and heels. She hurried for the front door, as embarrassed as he was annoyed. When she left, Deuce hopped into the shower. And bathed hard. As if he could scrub her off. As if he could wash away the memory of yet another blurred night. After showering he wrapped a towel around his waist and poured himself a glass of juice. He looked at the clock on the wall. 7:00 A.M. *The new girl,* he reminded himself, *starts today.*

Josie was dressed and ready for work by 7:00 A.M. She was so nervous and scared that her hands were shaking. Although she was dressed in her preferred African style, she toned it down: a chocolate brown straight-legged pantsuit made from kitenge cloth, with small black earrings and one thick, black bead-bracelet. Her heels weren't flamboyant either, just high, and she seemed determined to somehow make this gig work. Two firings in one year was astounding even to her. She couldn't handle a third knock.

But when she opened her front door she felt as if things were knocking all right, but finally in her direction. Ben was there. He was walking up the steps of her townhouse just as she opened the door.

When she saw him, so gorgeous in his charcoal-gray Oxford suit, she stopped in her tracks. "Ben?"

"Good morning," he said.

She smiled, it was that unbelievable to her, and then she ran to him. He grabbed her in his arms and smiled too. "What are you doing here?" she asked him.

"Surprised?"

"Yes. Very."

"I wanted to wish you a happy first day. Looks like I almost missed you."

"I know. I'm terrified of being late. But that's so nice, Ben. A happy first day. How nice!"

"Remember what I said."

"Make friends, I know."

"Give people a chance, Josephine. They aren't going to be perfect so don't expect them to be. And if they disagree with you, let them. You and I don't agree on squat and we're still friends."

Josie smiled. She loved him so much. "Okay," she said.

"Now if you give me a kiss, I'll let you go."

"What if I don't want you to let me go?"

Ben smiled. "Come here," he said, and pulled her against him.

Josie's smile quickly dissolved as he pressed his lips into hers and nearly smothered her in his big arms. As they kissed, Josie moved them backwards, towards her front door, as the excitement of the kiss made her want a whole lot more. And Ben was feeling the heat too, moving to her pull, kissing her with such passion that he could barely control himself. But he did. Now was not the time. She had work to do, and so did he.

"Why not?" she asked. "We can do a real quickie. It won't take ten minutes, Ben."

"I thought you were terrified of being late?"

Josie, who had just that quickly forgotten the job ahead of her, smiled. "Bye, Benny!" she said as she hurried off of her porch and moved swiftly toward her car. Ben smiled as he watched her. She looked wonderful to him, in her smart pantsuit and heels, her brief-case and shoulder bag swinging lightly as she moved. Not in a million years would he have dreamed that he would end up with a woman like Josie. So high strung. So full of life. So unlike him in every human way.

She plopped down in her car, slipped on a pair of shades, even though there wasn't a hint of sunshine in the sky, then waved once again as she quickly drove away. Ben said a prayer for Josie as he stood on her porch. She was a good woman who had been knocked down on every turn, but she still wore that big heart of hers on her sleeve. And it was vulnerable. And exposed. And ripe for the using. His prayer was that it wouldn't be misused.

Deuce spent the morning introducing Josie to the staff. Everybody loved her clothing and her hairstyle and seemingly everything about her. Josie was thrilled. Her experience had always been just the op-posite. At the *Journal* it was different. The crowd was different. They seemed to accept her for who she was, not who they wished she'd be. They reminded her of Ben, who never once asked her to change her style. These were her kind of people. She felt at home already.

She ended up in Deuce's office. He removed his suit coat and took a seat in the small, metal chair next to Josie. He rolled up his sleeves and leaned forward. He had chiseled good looks, Josie thought, square jaw and slightly sunken cheeks. His smooth forehead topped off by thick eyebrows that nearly met created an almost straight line across his forehead. His hair was wilder than before, as if he'd been electrocuted, but even that was a turn-on to Josie. He had beige-brown skin and those big, sad, coal-black eyes. Although he was muscular too, he wasn't big like Ben. He was slender and angular and barely five-nine in shoes. Josie's early impression: good looking, well-built, nice. Very nice.

"We aren't the *Herald*," he said to her.

Josie nodded. "Good."

"Not so good. We can't flash our press badge and get to talk with the big boys. They don't want to have anything to do with the *Journal*. They see us, they book, you hear what I'm saying? We're the bad guys in their eyes."

"Because you tell the truth."

"That's right. Because we tell the truth. But here's the thing." He said this and moved his chair closer to Josie. From his forward-leaning position, he looked her in the eye. "The more doors they slam in our faces, the more truth we tell."

Josie smiled. "I like that."

"You like it?" he asked.

"Yes. I know exactly what you're talking about. People try to act as if truth is out of style these days. I'm glad to know I'm not the only one who disagrees."

Deuce smiled and nodded. He knew he had read her right. He knew, from the moment he laid eyes on her, that his luck had changed, that he had himself a precious stone, a diamond long since out of the rough, within his grasp.

"How long have you been in journalism?"

"All my life," Josie said.

"Yeah, I read that article you wrote when you were three."

Josie laughed. "Well, all of my adult life, how's that?"

"Better. Started in college?"

"High school actually. I was writing commentary for a small, black weekly in Alabama, for free of course, but it got me started."

"Industrious too. My my. How can the world stand you?"

Josie smiled. She'd never heard it put quite like that. "Just barely actually."

"I'm sure. Well, you came to the right place, Josephine."

"Josie, please."

"Oh, so you hate the name Josephine?"

"Not really. My boyfriend calls me that sometimes and I love it when he says it. But everybody else calls me Josie."

"Then Josie I shall call you," Deuce said, and looked down at her large breasts and perfectly proportioned body, and up at her pretty, sweet face. He knew, despite her insistence that some other man had hooks in her, that it would be just a matter of time before his charm, which had never failed him yet, made the other brother toast, a roadblock to her happiness, rather than her true love.

Josie was uncomfortable with his stare. She decided to look up, at the plaques on his wall. He noticed the smoothness of her neck. "I see you've won numerous community awards."

"I wouldn't say I won them. They gave them to me."

Josie smiled and looked at Deuce. "That's very modest of you. But one of those plaques says journalist of the year. They don't just give those away, Deuce."

Deuce smiled. "You remembered my name?"

"Of course. Or is it more a nickname?"

"Actually, no."

"No? You mean your mama named you Deuce?"

Deuce smiled. "She did. Just before she went into labor she had won a card game and the deuce of spades did it for her. So, in her mind, she had two choices: I was to be called Deuce or Spade. Deuce, thank God, won out."

Josie laughed.

"Don't laugh. If you knew my mother you'd understand it was perfect reasoning to her."

"She sounds like a trip."

"She was."

"Oh. Was?"

"She died. I was still a teenager. She promised me she was gonna straighten out her life, get herself together, leave the drugs and the alcohol alone, and the street running. She promised it, anyway. That was the one thing you could depend on her to do. Make promises. And then she overdosed that same night. So she lied. Again. But that's a woman for you."

Josie didn't know how to respond to that. It was so tragic in her view but he was talking about it as if it was just a thing.

"What about your old lady?" Deuce asked her. "She cool or a trip too?"

"Ah, she's cool. And a trip." Josie said this and smiled. "Her name is Irene. And every man wants her, let her tell it anyway. She got married a few months back, to this dude named Titus. It was good to see her settling down."

"Is she a doper? Or a drunk?"

"No. I mean, she drinks but I wouldn't call her a drunk." Josie looked at Deuce. Behind that niceness and friendliness, there was some venom there. She didn't understand where it was coming from, exactly, but it was there.

"At least your mother seems to know how to act like a mother. You're lucky."

"I'm blessed, as Ben would say."

"Ben?"

"My boyfriend. He doesn't believe in luck. That takes God out of the equation, he says."

"God? What, you got yourself a preacher man?"

Josie laughed. "No. He's just a Christian."

"A Christian?"

"Yes. Like most all black folks."

"He's such a Christian, then why hasn't he married you? Why is he laying up with a woman who isn't his wife, if he's such a Christian?"

Josie didn't care for Deuce's tone, or his topic. She decided that they had drifted into a land that had nothing to do with why either of them were there.

"About my job here," she said, "will I be able to choose my own stories or will there be assignments?"

Deuce leaned back. He had overreached and he knew it. He wasn't wooing her with his acid tongue, he was repulsing her. He decided to smile.

"Both," he said. "Mainly assignments, of course, we have to cover certain events, but I also give my reporters a lot of latitude. You find a story you want to cover, hey, we can talk."

"That's nice to know. The *Herald* didn't play that. That was the one thing I hated about working there. Assignments only. And I mean without fail."

"Not here. I would say thirty or so percent of our reporters' stories were spotted by the reporters themselves."

"Oh, I like that."

"Good. And listen, I'm sorry if I seemed a little petulant there. I guess I'm still grieving my mother's life."

"You mean her death."

"I mean her life. She did terrible things in her life. That's what I grieve. I'm twenty-eight years old and I'm still grieving. But I'm cool."

Josie smiled. "I think so too."

"That's good to know. And if your boyfriend can't see what manner of woman he's lucky, excuse me, blessed to have, then we'll just let that be his personal problem. Deal?" Deuce asked and then extended his hand.

Josie looked at his hand, and then shook it. "Deal," she said. Deuce smiled and sandwiched her hand in both of his. He did not release that hand of hers until the door of his office opened and Rain peered inside.

"They're making a little noise over on Lincoln, Deuce," she said.

"What's happened?"

"Some store owner beat up a kid, that's all we know."

"Send Demi. See what she can find out," Deuce said.

"Which will be nothing."

"She's all we can spare right now, Rain. Just send her."

"Josephine will be better. She's more experienced."

"Agreed," he said. "But I'm not sending her out there on her first day. Send Demi."

"You're the boss." Deuce looked at Josie and smiled.

"Got that right," he said.

Josie arrived on the top floor of the Denlex Corporate building tired but loaded with excitement. She could see Ben's door slightly ajar and his light still on. Every other office on the floor had long since been vacated. It was late, nearly ten at night, and Josie decided that she couldn't wait to tell Ben about her first day at work. She thought it was so sweet the way he had come by her house that morning just to wish her a happy first day, and she knew he would be too tired to come by tonight. So she decided to go to him.

She heard laughter as she approached the suite of offices, under the umbrella OFFICE OF THE VICE PRESIDENT written on top of the entrance that led to his outer sanctum. She walked past his secretary's desk and then up to his slightly opened office door. If there was a meeting going on, it was a gregarious one, she thought, as she pushed the door further open and walked inside. Ben wasn't at his desk but was slouched down on the sofa against the wall. Beside him, so close that their shoulders touched, was a beautiful sister with a short Afro and a toothy smile. Josie could tell immediately that she was exactly Ben's type: fortyish, sophisticated, mature. Her heart dropped.

The woman quickly sat erect, as if she knew she'd been found out, but Ben remained as he was, comfortable on his couch, his suit coat off, his white shirt still perfectly pressed. He took his tie, which had slanted askew, and flapped it straight against his shirt.

Josie didn't say a word. She couldn't. She was too busy imagining all the wonderful things Ben had probably done to that female. That was why the woman couldn't stop smiling, and that was why she nearly jumped out of her skin when Josie walked through that door.

"Hello, Josephine," Ben said. He wasn't smiling anymore, but had a stern look on his face, as if he just knew she had come to spy on him when that wasn't her intention at all. At least she convinced herself that it wasn't.

She wanted to lash out, but she knew Ben would hate it. And besides, she wasn't about to let some old-ass hot mama ruin her good day. "Hello," she decided to say. "I hope I'm not interrupting anything."

"No, not at all," the woman said quickly and stood up. Ben stood up too, his big, muscular body perfectly matched beside the woman's pleasing plumpness. "I need to get going anyway." She walked over by the chair and grabbed her purse and attaché case. Ben helped her get into her trench coat. She then turned and looked at him. "Ben, I'm going to ask you again. Are you sure about these figures?"

"We can live with the figures if you can."

"Oh, can I," she said, and Ben smiled. "I'll get with your budget people tomorrow and finalize everything," she added.

"Sounds good, Gwen."

"And thanks again. For everything." She gave Ben a small hug and brushed his cheek with hers. Ben placed his hands on her waist, but he did not hug her back.

"Take care of yourself," he said, and she smiled. Then she turned toward Josie as she began to leave.

"Goodnight, Josephine."

"Goodnight," Josie said. Gwen smiled and left.

Josie looked at Ben. He stood in the middle of his office with his hands in his pockets.

"What are you doing here?" he asked her.

"I'm not spying on you, Ben, if that's what you're thinking. That's not why I'm here."

Ben looked at her with mild frustration, and then walked over to his desk and sat down. Another long day, another exhausting day, and the last thing he needed was Josephine relentlessly questioning him about that woman and her smiling and whatever other nonsense she could think to ask. And he still had work to do.

Josie walked further toward his desk, her arms folded, her heels practically dragging along. "Who was she?" she asked him. Ben didn't respond. He wasn't about to. Josie figured he wouldn't. But she still couldn't help but try. "It's chilly out tonight," she said, trying to change the subject. But he wasn't buying it.

"What do you want, Josephine? I don't have time for games."

Josie couldn't believe it. "Why you got to act like that?" she asked him. "I told you I wasn't spying on you. Just because I asked you who she was, I don't see why that's such a crazy question. All I was . . ." She could feel the emotion welling up inside of her. And she hated that she wasn't stronger around Ben. "Just forget it," she finally said, and headed for the door.

Ben started to let her go. He didn't exactly have the energy for her tonight. But he couldn't. "Josie, wait," he said.

Josie stood at the door, her back to him, her eyes now filled with tears. She thought she was doing the right thing when she refused to fall in love, when she refused to let some scrub make a fool out of her. But it had crippled her, because now she was in love and had no point of reference. She had no goody bag of experiences to tell her how to behave.

Ben looked at her, and she was pitiful all right, and more than a handful, but what could he do? "Come here," he said to her.

She moved slowly to his desk, trying to regain her composure, trying to at least walk as if she had herself together. When she walked up to where he sat, he placed his arm around her waist. "I'm sorry, honey. I've been working too hard. So what's up? What did you want to tell me?" he asked her.

Josie hesitated. It didn't seem worth it anymore. "I had a good day, that's all I wanted to say."

"That's it?"

"That's it," she said.

Ben smiled. *That's Josie,* he thought. "I'm glad to hear it, sweetheart. And I'm glad you came to share it with me."

"I wasn't trying to spy on you, Ben."

"I know." There was a pause, and then Ben smiled again. "So you had yourself a good first day?" he said.

Josie's smile grew huge and she excitedly hopped up on his lap, causing him to grimace as her butt slammed down on his penis. But when she looked at him, he continued to smile. "It was better than a good day, Ben," she said. "Everybody was so nice to me. It was unbelievable!"

"Okay," Ben said, deciding to listen quietly and not feed her hysteria. He was accustomed to her inability to keep things on even keel. She didn't understand that people were by their very nature moody and fickle and could turn on her without provocation. Today they were sweet as doves, tomorrow, cunning as snakes. But Josie wasn't moody or fickle and she didn't turn on anybody. And that was why she could never comprehend why others would.

"And they loved my style, Ben," she continued. "My African clothes are cool to them. They seemed to love everything about me!" She said this and wiggled around on Ben's lap, awakening his penis once again.

"Slow down, honey," he said. "What about your work? Were they familiar with your work?"

"Oh, yes! They even loved what I was trying to do at the *Herald.* Oh, and let me tell you! Remember Mayor Keating's press conference? You remember that?"

"Settle down, Josie. Of course I remember it."

"My performance might have gotten me fired at the *Herald,* but at the *Journal* they loved it. Deuce said I won rave reviews."

Ben heard the name, took note of it, but decided to let it slide. "What did they like about your performance?"

"All of it. Everything!" As she said this Ben could feel her tight behind continue to rub against him. But it wasn't painful anymore. Now it was soothing. "They liked the questions I asked," Josie continued. "Deuce even said I asked the kind of questions he would ask if the mayor would ever call on him, which, of course, he never does. But I speak the truth, Deuce said, and that's what the *Journal* is all about. Truth at all costs. That's the *Journal*'s motto you know. Truth at all costs. It's like it couldn't be a better fit. And I'm sure to make friends there, Ben."

Ben was, by now, completely erect, which meant he was barely able to speak. He placed his hands on Josie's hips to try and position her away from his center. But she kept moving back, rubbing harder and harder against him. He leaned into her ear, the only way, he felt, that she was going to be able to hear him. "You love it then?" he asked her in a barely discernible whisper.

"Oh, I do. It may turn out to be the best job I've ever had."

Ben was still pressed up to Josie's ear and she could hear that his breathing had become more labored. It was only then that she realized that his bundle was ever expanding beneath her. Just by sitting on his lap she had managed to turn him on. But she also knew he was fighting the feeling, that he had made love to her just two days ago and no way was she getting some again. His pattern had been weeks between lovemaking, not days. Not ever.

But Josie also knew she had him where he may not be able to resist. She kissed him. When he returned her affection with an even stronger kiss, she rubbed his soft hair until she was practically scratching his skull. He wrapped his arms around her and pulled her closer to him, her excitement turning him on too, and he kissed her with hard, forceful thrusts. But Josie pressed so hard against him that they leaned back way too far, causing the chair, with them in it, to crash to the floor. Josie, now on top of Ben, looked into his eyes, certain that he would be upset by her overreaction. But he wasn't. He laughed and shook his head.

"You don't do anything halfway, do you?" he asked her. She smiled, and then laughed too.

CHAPTER 5

The assignment was an interesting one, she thought. A group of Clean Air Now (CAN) activists planned to enter the grounds of the Oxidare petroleum plant near Fergus Falls and deface as much of the building as they possibly could. Deuce, having gotten wind of this from his connections with the group, assigned Josie to tag along. She was not to participate in the vandalism, not to even go onto the property, but she could witness the reaction of the activists whose organization the *Journal* would not expose. She knew it wasn't the safest assignment and that she wouldn't hear the last of it if Ben found out, but she was too intrigued by the sheer boldness of the group to let a story like this one pass her by.

She sat in her Mustang outside the barbed wire fence at Oxidare, sipping her coffee. It was late, nine at night, and the cool chill in the air kept her anxious to get this over with. The CAN members, however, were not slaves to punctuality and arrived nearly thirty minutes late. They came with wire cutters and placards and every imaginable paint color. Josie, in a pair of jeans and an oversized jersey, grabbed her pen and pad and hurried to the main entrance. Deuce had told her to ask for Lynn. Lynn, a forty-something woman with long blond hair and full cheeks, greeted her eagerly.

"Deuce is a good man," Lynn said as she walked, her bulk making her breathe heavily as she spouted out orders to her colleagues. "And the *Journal*'s all we've got to help us get the message out."

"But why Oxidare and not some of the other, more egregious companies?"

"Because Oxidare won't get it together. The others are at least pretending to do a better job with their environmental records, but Oxidare refuses to even attempt to make amends." She looked back at her fellow activists. They were hard at work tearing through the fence that stood between them and their civil disobedience. "That's why we must resort to drastic measures."

"I understand that, Lynn. But aren't these illegal measures?"

"The cause is greater than any individual implication. The message is the point. We've got to wake these people up, and the only way we know how is to make such a stink right on their precious property until they'll have no choice but to take the message seriously."

"And what exactly is your message?"

Lynn turned around again, to keep tabs on her activists, but this time she seemed horrified by what she saw. "Ah, man!" she screamed.

"What?" Josie asked nervously, turning around too.

"Abort! Abort!" Lynn ordered the protestors, and then began hurrying away from the scene. Before Josie could fully understand what was going on, the protestors began dropping everything and running as fast as their feet could take them. Sirens immediately roared and police cars began to surround them. Josie was stunned, trying to get away with the protestors but not as experienced at this as they. She stumbled, not once, but twice, and got caught in the thick of the onslaught, and was knocked down. She laid on the ground, her hands covering her head, as those wonderful absconding activists, who would risk their lives for clean air, legalized cannabis, and humpback whales, but would kill her to avoid arrest, ran over her as if she were strategically placed as their escape mat.

The dinner party was held at the mayor's home, a massive estate on the banks of the Mississippi River, and many bigwigs in Saint Cloud and the whole of the central and Twin Cities region were in attendance. Ben was there too, along with Sam Darrow and about ten other senior executives from Denlex. Wayne Murdoch, the company's embattled and soon-to-be ex-CEO, was conspicuously absent. Ben was Denlex's chief representative and Mayor Todd Keating, who

knew more about the inner workings of Denlex than Ben felt appro-
priate, was delighted to see him.

"You the man!" Keating said jokingly as he shook Ben's hand at
the door. Ben, accustomed to the brother-man play by the mayor and
those like him, smiled mildly.

"Hello, Todd."

"Come on in. Come on in. Glad you could make it. I knew if
Wayne wouldn't be here, you would."

"He offers his apologies."

"I'm sure. But listen, Ben," the mayor said, as he pulled Ben aside,
"I heard about Murdoch. Is it true?"

"Is what true?"

"I heard it's true. I heard they're planning to ask for his resignation, which is unfortunate. Murdoch's a good man. But that's life,
isn't it?"

"I wouldn't know about that, Todd."

"His misfortune will be somebody else's good fortune, don't you
think?"

Ben didn't respond. Keating was playing that rumor-mill game
too, seeking information by insinuating that he had some. But Ben
was too well schooled for that trick to work.

"And about Josie," Keating said, quickly realizing that Ben wasn't
about to play along. "I'm so sorry about what happened. I feel horrible about the entire situation. I honestly didn't think Herb would
fire her."

"He did what he had to do."

"That's right. Because that Josie she'll . . . she'll drive you to an
early grave, that's what she'll do." Ben wanted to smile, but didn't.
"She's a handful, Benny."

"She's okay," Ben said.

"Okay my ass! She doesn't let up. You saw her at my press conference. Now I know she's your lady, Ben, but give me a break. How
do you put up with her?"

"The same way she puts up with me."

"You? Her kind should be glad to be in the same room with
you."

"How's that road improvement plan coming along, Todd?" Ben
asked the mayor, adroitly changing the subject to an even more sen-

sitive topic. "I heard you're having some problems with implementation. Some contractors not working out."

By now the mayor was no longer smiling. He had crossed the line in his criticism of Josie, and Ben was making sure he understood that.

"It's coming along beautifully," the mayor said, understanding it perfectly. "There's no problems at all, contrary to what some critics are trying to claim. Everything's falling right into place."

"Is it?" Ben asked.

"Absolutely. You heard something different?" Ben didn't respond. Keating was accustomed to that too. "Well anyway," Keating said, "I'd better spread myself around before the wife starts complaining. Hope you enjoy yourself, Benjamin. We'll talk later."

Ben smiled as Keating couldn't get away from him fast enough. Then he looked around. The ballroom where he stood was one huge open space filled with movers and shakers and wannabes galore. He unbuttoned his tux, took a glass of wine from a waiter's tray, and decided to chill. But he couldn't chill for long. His reputation preceded him as young brother after young sister kept approaching him with a business card and a smile, looking for their newly crowned idol to give them a heads up. Ben hadn't been on the Minnesota scene very long, but he already had a reputation for grooming young, talented minorities for upper-management positions. And he remained true to that reputation at the mayor's dinner party, telling each one of them to drop a resume by the office and he'd take a look at it, and they'd beam, because they knew he meant it. They didn't care for his politics and they'd heard he was a tough SOB to work for, but from where they sat he was the best they had.

"Sir, it's an honor," a soft, male's voice announced just behind him, and Ben turned around. A man with bushy red hair and dark, slanted eyes was staring deeply into Ben's eyes.

"Hello," Ben said as he shook the extended hand of Hines Lowe. He was too old, Ben decided, to be handing him a business card, but he appeared to want something just the same.

"I admire the work you're doing over at Denlex," Hines said. "You help pull that company into the twenty-first century, man, it's been impressive."

"Well, thank you. But I'm afraid I don't recall where we—"

"We've not met," he said quickly. "I read an article about you in a Minnesota magazine. I remembered your picture so I thought I'd come over and say hello."

Ben nodded. And Hines stared. *What an oddball,* Ben thought, a true wannabe who probably enjoyed hobnobbing with the big boys, as if that somehow reflected favorably upon him. And although Hines seemed to be searching desperately for something more to say, to move the conversation along, Ben would just as soon prefer that Hines himself moved along. But it wasn't until Sam Darrow approached them that he even seemed to consider it.

"Well," Hines said, as Sam began talking office politics, "I'd better see what else I can see." He said this and smiled an almost cockeyed, reptilian smile, and then slithered away.

"He's creepy," Sam said, shaking his head.

"And you're not?" Ben replied.

Sam looked at him as if he'd just been insulted, and then began to laugh. "Benjamin Braddock told a joke?" he said. "I don't believe it. That's what I call a shocker."

"What you got?" Ben asked, knowing full well that Sam didn't approach him unless he had some news to tell.

"Michael Fastower."

"Fastower? He's with Botch, isn't he?"

"Now he is, yes. And he's also, along with you, in the running for CEO of Denlex."

Ben shook his head. "Is he? Well, he's a heavy hitter."

"Heavy ain't the word, Benjamin. By far our main competition right now. Big corporate boy, from Haliburton to Worldcom, he's run the gamut. Which means he knows the game. Which means we've got to retool our strategy."

"I don't have a strategy, Sam."

"But I do. The way I figure it—"

"Not tonight, okay?" Ben said firmly. Sam, who assumed Ben was just stunned by the news, nodded his understanding. Before Sam could move on to his next bit of juicy gossip, he noticed an interesting sight across the room.

"Well damn," he said. "Who's that lady?"

Ben turned and looked too. Meredith Chambers, as radiant as ever in a long, sequined gown, was standing near the entranceway where she had managed to catch the eye of most of the males in the room. Ben's heart seemed to skip a beat, immediately captivated by her too. By her walk. Her elegance. Her grace. He remembered her as the woman at Rhonda's, the woman in the yellow suit, the woman he would undoubtedly have made it his business to get to know if his responsibilities weren't what they were. But they were what they were. That was why he placed his drink on the bar counter and decided to take a stroll alone, away from all temptation, out in the garden.

The mayor's garden was a nature preserve, filled with every genus known to man, and topped off with a glorious waterfall in the middle of the trail. Ben stood at the fountain's rail, watching the water flip up and over, up and over, and he started thinking about Josie. She was as complicated and as simple as that waterfall, a woman with a lot of opinions, a lot of passion, yet with nobody but him to share in all of those feelings. He worried about her. He worried that she was too passionate, too opinionated, and was bound to get hurt at every turn. And she relied so heavily on him, when they were as different as night and day. They rarely even went out together, mainly because she just couldn't stomach his crowd, and her circle of friends was reduced to one out-of-state best friend. So he cooked her dinner at his home, or she cooked for him at hers. They'd watch videos or talk or fall asleep in each other's arms. Ben had twenty years on Josie, yet he was far and away the more sociable of the two, accepting invitations to this dinner party or that banquet practically every week. And his friends, who never understood his devotion to Josie, who viewed her as just some temporary fling for the stately former judge, would always find some unattached, attractive female to sit at the dinner table right next to him. Josie, he felt, deserved a fuller life too, a life where she could enjoy her youth, something he didn't believe she'd ever done.

"Nice view," a voice said behind him and he knew, even before he turned, that it was *her*.

"Hello," he said as he turned and saw his suspicion realized, that the radiant Meredith Chambers was standing in front of him, her white gown sparkling against her dark skin.

"Nice view, isn't it?" she asked.

"Yes. Yes, it is."

"Certainly less cluttered out here."

Ben looked around, but didn't respond. He was too preoccupied with her beauty. She was even more graceful up close. And those eyes, those big, Lola Falana eyes, almost made his knees buckle.

"I didn't expect to encounter so many people," she said. "But I guess when the mayor throws a party, they will come."

Ben smiled. The lull in the conversation felt natural, as Ben kept staring at her and she kept staring at the fountain. But then she looked at him. "I'm sorry," she finally said, extending her hand. "I'm Meredith Chambers."

Ben shook the soft, feminine hand. "I'm Ben Braddock."

"Nice to meet you, Mr. Braddock. Or should I say Ben?"

"You should."

"And Meredith, please."

Ben nodded. She was smooth as silk. The total package. "A friend of Todd Keating?" he asked.

"Once or twice removed, yes," Meredith said and smiled. "No, I just decided I was going to treat myself tonight. So a friend of mine knew somebody who worked in the mayor's office, who knew somebody else, and here I am."

"Treating yourself?"

"Right."

"Surely you deserve better than this."

Meredith laughed, a soft, extended *ha* laugh. Then she held the fountain's railing and leaned forward, as if attempting to see the bottom of the pool. Ben watched her perfectly curved body lean over, her behind a tight, round monument to sexiness. When she turned toward him, catching him looking down at her, he pulled out a cigarette.

"Smoke?"

"No, thank you. I quit five years ago."

"Good for you."

"Not so good. I gained twenty-five pounds in the bargain."

Ben glanced down at her. "You wear it well," he said.

She smiled. "You are too nice, Mr. Braddock. Thank you."

Ben lit his cigarette. When he looked up, Meredith was staring at him, but staring in such a hard, cold way that it made his skin crawl.

"So," she said quickly, realizing her lapse, "with whom are you here?"

"Should I be here with someone?"

"I don't know if you should. You just look like you are. I'd bet the farm there's a Mrs. Braddock lurking about."

"Oh, yeah?"

"Yes. And I could see her now. She's probably a wellspring of sophistication. Easily the most beautiful woman in the room."

"And that would be Mrs. Braddock?"

"Yes. I'd bet the farm on it," she said.

"You'd lose that bet."

"You mean there's no Mrs. Braddock, or she's not the most beautiful woman in the room?"

"Both."

"You mean you're here alone? Like me?"

Ben smiled. "That's what it means."

"Oh my. That is surprising. I'm not normally this lucky."

Ben took a slow drag on his cigarette and stared at her. She didn't come across as a tease. She appeared too well schooled to be that easily found out, but there was something going on there still. "I saw you in Rhonda's once," he said.

"Did you?"

"Yes," he said.

"I go there quite often. I'm amazed that I didn't see you. Or should I have remembered?"

"Not at all. You simply walked past my table."

She smiled. "And you remembered me from that?"

Ben hesitated. It was pathetic, but it was true. "Yes," he said.

Meredith turned toward him. "Well I am very sorry I didn't notice you."

"No need to apologize. You didn't do anything wrong."

"I know I didn't. Did I say I did?"

She was feisty, the way Josie could be if he pushed her hard enough. Then Meredith smiled. Just like that.

"Oh, that song," she said as the band played the soft trumpet sound of Chuck Mangione's "Feel So Good." "I love that song." She closed her eyes and began to sway her body as the slow rhythm increased.

Ben puffed on his cigarette and looked at her, at her high cheek bones and beautiful black skin. Her neck, so thin and long, so swanlike. She seemed like too much grace in one package.

When she opened her eyes, he smiled. "You like jazz?" he asked her.

"Oh, I adore it. If you were to come to my apartment this very minute I'd astound you with my collection."

"I'd astound you more."

"What? You like jazz too?" she asked.

"Adore it."

"All right. Now we're talking. Let me guess. Charlie Parker's your favorite. Right?"

"One of them. I love me some Bird now."

"Me too. Wow. Me too," she said.

Ben smiled. Meredith appeared to him to have an anxiousness about her, as if she were trying too hard to please. Every little move he made, such as a simple smile, seemed to encourage her more.

"So," she said, seemingly excited that they had something in common, "tell me a little more about yourself, Ben."

"Is this a job interview?"

"It might be," she said.

"I work with Denlex."

"I see. And what is it you do with Denlex?"

"A little of this, a little of that."

Meredith smiled. "Okay. My bad. Let me rephrase the question. What is your position with Denlex?" she asked.

Ben hesitated. He wondered if, after telling her his title, she'd whip out a business card too. "Senior vice president, that's my official position."

"Vice president of Denlex? Oh my. Now I am impressed."

"What about you?"

"Tell me more. Did you spend your entire career with Denlex?"

"No, no. I'm the new kid on the block."

"The corporate block or the Denlex block?"

"Both."

"Oh, yeah? What did you do before?" she asked.

Ben hesitated. It was still a sore spot with him. "I was a judge."

"A judge?" She smiled. "Are you serious?"

"Yes."

"What kind of judge?"

"Criminal."

"A criminal court judge? Double impressed. For how long?"

"Almost nineteen years, actually."

"And what? You just had enough?"

"Something like that. What about you?" he asked.

"Not nearly as impressive. I've been an executive assistant most of my career. Did my four years at Sarah Lawrence, then a stint with Northwestern's B-School, where I almost got my MBA, but found it all so pretentious, you know? So I dropped out. I recently left Johnson Marketing, where I was the executive assistant to the president there."

"Why did you leave?"

She smiled. "Is this a job interview?"

"It might be."

"I left because the president was ousted. The ouster was wrong, I didn't agree with it, so I left. Now I'm weighing my options."

Ben nodded. "A woman of principle. And loyalty. I like that." Then he paused, staring at her. "I certainly could use a good assistant myself," he said.

"Is that a job offer?"

Ben hesitated. For some reason his instincts were telling him to just say no. But he looked at Meredith. And there was something about her. "Yes," he said.

"Well, thank you, Judge Braddock. That's very kind of you to offer. But I can't say yes or no right now. I promised myself that I would take my time for a change and weigh all options carefully."

Ben nodded. "Good strategy."

"Is that it? My, you don't put up much of a fight, do you?"

"If it'll be, it'll be."

"Good way to live your life. Unburdened, I mean," she said.

Ben nodded. Hardly his life. "Yes," he said.

And then his cell phone rang. He thought without checking the caller ID that it was most likely Josie wondering where he was and, more specifically, if some woman was with him.

"Hello?" he said into his phone and glanced at Meredith. She slowly moved away, to give him at least the appearance of some privacy. He liked that.

"Hello, is this Benjamin Braddock?" There was a hesitation in Ben's response. The voice on the other end, female, was a stranger's voice.

"Yes," he answered cautiously, knowing full well that precious few individuals knew his personal cell-phone number.

"This is Saint Cloud Hospital, sir. A Miss Josephine Ross asked that we contact you."

Ben hesitated. "Josephine?"

"Yes, sir. There was an accident. She's okay. She wanted to make sure I told you that. But she wants you to come."

Ben's heart fell through his shoe. An accident. Involving *Josie?* It felt like his worst fear realized. Something had happened to Josephine. He flipped shut his phone and hurried out of the garden, completely forgetting that Meredith was even there. Not until he was near the exit did he realize his error. He turned quickly toward her. "I'm sorry," he said, "but I've got to go."

"Is everything all right?" Meredith yelled after him, but he was well on his way.

CHAPTER 6

Josie was sitting on a gurney in a small room when Ben arrived. He entered in his expensive tux, a stark contrast to Josie's hospital gown and socks, and he stood without movement when he first saw her. He looked over her entire body, from her feet to the crown of her head. Except for a tiny cut on her forehead, she appeared fine. He exhaled.

"Where were you?" she asked him.

"Are you okay?"

"I'm fine, Ben. Where were you?"

He kissed her on the forehead, on her small, almost invisible cut, and looked into her eyes. She looked up at him, anxious for an answer, an answer she knew he wasn't about to give.

"What happened?" he asked, fully expecting her to answer him.

Josie rubbed his coat lapel. "You're wearing a tux."

"Answer my question."

"Nothing happened. I told them to tell you I was okay."

Ben glared at Josie. She knew him better than that.

"Oh, all right," she said. "I was working on an assignment, that's all, just a tag-along, and there was a kind of police raid. I was in the way a little and kind of got trampled on."

Ben frowned. He hated it when she obfuscated, when she chose to tell selected parts of the story to soften its impact. "What are you talking about, Josephine?"

"I was on assignment . . ."

"You said that. What kind of assignment would involve a police raid?"

"Deuce, my boss at the *Journal*, he wanted me to interview CAN—"

"Who?"

"A local group called CAN. The Clean Air Now activists. Deuce wanted me to interview them during one of their message nights."

Ben frowned and shook his head. "Their what?"

"Message nights."

"What's a message night, Josephine? Now don't play with me."

Josie sighed. "A message night is when CAN members get together with paint and posters and make their views known."

"They vandalize people's property, in other words."

Josie paused. "Yes."

"Why is this Deuce sending you to something like that? Something illegal?"

"I wasn't participating, Ben. I was just a reporter finding out why they did what they did and what they hoped to accomplish."

"Oh, that's nonsense! I could have answered those questions for you. They're a ragtag band of radical thugs who have no regard for the rule of law or the sanctity of private property. They don't like something, they destroy it. It's exactly what they did to me in Florida, Josie. It's the exact same mentality. You didn't have to go out there and practically get yourself killed to get those questions answered!" Ben's cell phone began ringing. He exhaled and angrily grabbed it from his inside coat pocket.

"I didn't practically get killed," Josie said as he flipped open his phone.

"Yes, hello?" Ben said into the phone. It was Sam Darrow.

"Hey, bud, what's up?" Sam asked lively.

"Hey," Ben said with little punch, his stomach beginning to churn.

"I was worried about you. You left Keating's place so fast I wondered if something had happened."

Ben glanced at Josie again, who was frustrating the hell out of him, and then he began pacing the room. "My lady had a slight accident. I was called away to the hospital."

"Whoa. An accident? Josie? She okay?"

Ben stood against the wall by the room's doorway, pressing the sole of his wingtip shoe against it.

"Yes," he said.

"Josie again, huh? She's an active woman, isn't she?"

Ben looked at Josie as she sighed and folded her arms. "Yeah," he said. "That she is."

The room's door opened suddenly and Deuce Jefferson, in jeans and a parka, hurried in, walking past Ben without realizing he stood against the wall. "Josie!" he said with a sigh of relief as he hurried to her hospital bed.

"Hello, Deuce," Josie said, trying to smile, trying to quickly assure him that she was okay. It seemed to her that he looked more worried than Ben.

"Ah, man, I am so sorry. I am so sorry!" Deuce said.

"I'm all right."

"You should hate me, J. You should just hate me. I had no idea the cops would show up. I would have never sent you out there if I had known that."

"I know," Josie said. He smiled and stared at her.

"Here I am putting you in harm's way on your first assignment," he said, his expressive eyes unable to conceal his grave concern. Then he placed his hand on the side of her face and rubbed it. Ben looked up from his cell phone when he touched her.

"I'm fine, Deuce, really," she said, looking at Ben and gently moving her face away from Deuce's hand, hoping that he would understand the inappropriateness and back off himself.

But he didn't. He removed his hand from her face and placed it on her narrow shoulder. He began massaging her. "It'll never happen again, sweetheart," he said to her. "I promise you that."

"I'll call you later," Ben said into his cell phone, then flipped it shut. On hearing a male's voice behind him, Deuce quickly removed his hand.

With the sole of his shoe Ben pushed himself away from the wall and walked slowly toward Josie's bed. Deuce turned toward Ben and attempted to smile. "Hey there, brother," he said, overcompensating. "I didn't see you back there, partner. I'm Deuce Jefferson." He extended his hand as he said this. Ben shook his hand, without putting on a fake smile. He stared instead at the man before him, looking deep into his eyes, sizing him up on the strength of his lust for Josie alone.

Deuce's eyes began to widen too, not from concern over Ben's stare, but from recognition. He knew the brother. He'd done too many stories on him, too many stories where they couldn't even get an interview with him. His reporters had tried to get him on the record, tried every chance they could, but hotshots like him never bothered with the *Journal*. But Deuce remembered that face, that thick mustache and those bright brown eyes, that perfect, smooth face one female reporter had said could charm a wino out of his wine. Benjamin Braddock. That's him. The asshole, big corporate boy who had the audacity to be a conservative republican too. The enemy.

"Deuce, this is Ben Braddock," Josie said, breaking both men's stares. "He's my significant other."

Ben glanced at Josie. He never liked that term. It sounded too PC for him, and Josie knew it. But he suspected that was exactly why she continued to use it.

Benjamin Braddock was the *Ben* Josie was always talking about. *Damn,* Deuce thought. *This was Ben? This asshole was Ben?* The enemy was now *his* competition?

"Nice to meet you, Ben," he said. "But wait a minute. Wait a minute here. You're Benjamin Braddock of Denlex, aren't you?"

Ben placed his hands in his pants pockets and continued to stare at Deuce. Deuce had known who Ben was the moment he'd seen him, and Ben knew he knew. Why he wanted to play some game only heightened Ben's suspicions of the man. "Yes, that's right," he said.

"Yeah, you're the VP at Denlex. I remember you. You guys are major polluters, man, don't you realize that? You're killing our babies."

"Ben isn't like that, Deuce," Josie said, but Ben cut her a look that quieted her.

"Don't you apologize for me," he said harshly.

"I wasn't apologizing for you. I was just telling him the truth. But forget it, okay?" Josie frowned and looked away from Ben.

Ben regretted immediately that he had spoken to her in such a tone, especially when he knew she meant well. But the idea of her trying to appease some left-wing, closed-minded punk like Deuce Jefferson was more than he was willing to stomach.

"You all right, J.?" Deuce, capitalizing on the breach, asked, and Josie nodded her head.

"Yeah, I'm good. Thanks." She wanted to fight back but she wasn't about to give Ben that satisfaction.

"And I'm not trying to down your boyfriend. I'm not about that and you know it. But Denlex is messed up, man. They don't care what they're doing to this environment."

"Deuce, let's just move on, okay? I'm kind of tired," Josie said.

"You're right. You've been through hell and I'm standing here preaching like some idiot. Forgive me?"

Josie smiled, then glanced at Ben. He didn't appear jealous in the least. And it disappointed her.

"I'm just glad you made it out of there okay," Deuce said. "Lynn called and told me what happened. She said her own people trampled you."

"They did. I was knocked down by absconding activists."

Deuce laughed. "That's a damn shame," he said.

"Are all of the CAN folks okay?" Josie asked.

Deuce glanced at Ben. He loved that Ben, not he, seemed to be the odd man out. "Yeah," he said, "they're all good. It's ironic, but nobody got hurt but you, Josie."

"Ain't no irony in it. Don't even trick that. It's the story of my life." Deuce laughed just as a uniformed policeman, fortyish, white, peered into the room.

"Josephine Ross?" he asked.

"Yes," Josie said, and then the officer walked into the room.

"I'm Deputy Nimoy with the Fergus Falls PD, ma'am." He said this and nodded in Deuce's direction. "Sir," he said to Ben.

"What can I do for you, Deputy?" Josie asked, already knowing full well what.

"I need to ask you a few questions about tonight."

"Shoot," she said, and she and Deuce laughed. Ben, like the officer, failed to see the humor.

"I'm going to get to the point, Miss Ross. I need some names, ma'am. I need the names of the violators."

"What violators?" Deuce asked, and both the officer and Ben looked at him.

"And you are, sir?"

"I'm a newspaper editor. I'm her boss. Now what violators are you referring to?"

"The ones who were attempting to vandalize property at Oxidare, sir. Miss Ross knows what I'm talking about."

"I don't think I do know, Deputy," Josie said, and Ben, surprised, looked at her.

The deputy hesitated. He knew it wasn't going to be easy. "What organization was out there tonight, Miss Ross? Who spearheaded the event?"

"Organization? Event?"

"Yes."

"What are you talking about?" Josie asked.

"It was CAN, wasn't it?"

"CAN?"

Ben unbuttoned the coat of his tuxedo and placed his hand on his waist. He knew better than this.

"Yes, CAN," the deputy said to Josie. "The Clean Air Now organization, ma'am."

"I don't know what you're talking about. I was hanging out on a public street, then the police came and I was trampled. That's all I know, and that's all I'm going to say."

The deputy sighed and looked to Ben. Ben, however, was staring at Josie. The policeman therefore closed his writing pad and shook his head.

"You're tired, ma'am. Perhaps we can revisit this tomorrow."

"Okay, but I'm not going to have anything further to say tomorrow or any other day."

"That's right," Deuce said, and the deputy glared at him.

"Look," the police officer said to Josie, "I know you're a journalist trying to do your job. But when they cut through that barbed wire and penetrated that property, a crime was committed. You're more than a journalist now. You're a witness, ma'am. A witness to a crime. And you're interfering with a police investigation when you withhold information."

"She said she doesn't have any information," Deuce said, knowing full well how far the police department was willing to go when a journalist was involved.

"I have a First Amendment right not to reveal my source, Deputy. And I'm not about to say anything more than that," Josie said. She knew the drill too. The deputy knew she knew it. That was why he looked at Ben one more time for some support, but he saw a man consumed by his own rage, so the deputy finally left.

"What do you think you're doing?" Ben asked Josie.

"I'm doing my job, Ben."

"Why didn't you answer his questions, Josephine?"

"I'm a journalist. I don't have to answer those kind of questions."

"Like hell you don't! Laws were broken tonight."

"I didn't break any laws. The people who were at that location tonight were my source for a story. And I'm not about to reveal my source."

"I know that's right," Deuce said, more than happy to take sides.

"They committed a crime, Josephine. You heard that officer. A crime. They aren't sources. They're criminals."

"I have a First Amendment right not to reveal my source. Not you, the police, or anybody else will force me to reveal my source. I don't care what y'all say."

Ben exhaled so harshly that he could instantly feel his stomach knotting up. To him the rule of law was sacrosanct, a necessity in all civilized societies, and what Josie was doing was just flat wrong. He was up to *here* with her inability to think her actions through. He was up to here with her inability to count up the costs. Everything was a cause that she jumped on without reflection. And he'd had it. He was so frustrated, in fact, that he felt he had to get away from her; that his anger was rising to heights he wasn't sure he could control. He started to pace the room again, but instead of pacing he left the room, and then the hospital, altogether.

They released Josie a few minutes before 1:00 A.M., and Deuce agreed to drive her back to Oxidare so she could retrieve her car. But only on one condition.

"What condition?" Josie asked as they walked out of the ER.

"You have one, just one drink with me before calling it a night."

"I can't, Deuce."

"Just one?"

"No, I can't. I just want to go home."

Deuce didn't like it, but he understood. "You're right. Sorry again. Forgive me?"

"You're forgiven," she said with a weak smile as they walked along the long hospital corridor that led to the parking lot. She kept looking around, for Ben, still not quite able to believe he could have left her like this. But he had. He was nowhere to be seen.

"Why him?" Deuce asked after she had piled into his car, an old Datsun 240Z with a loud, revved-up engine, and they began to drive away from the hospital. Josie glanced over at Deuce, and then leaned her head against the headrest, unable to feel at all satisfied with anything that had gone on in the course of the day.

"What do you mean?" she asked him.

Deuce downshifted as he pulled onto Sixth Avenue, and then he slowed down even more. Because of the lateness of the hour the traffic was practically nonexistent, so he decided to take full advantage of the sparsity and drive at a snail's pace.

"You two are so different. And I mean in every way. You're young and beautiful and understanding of people. He's a conservative tight-ass who just doesn't get it. I mean, come on, Josie. Of all these brothers out here dying to get your attention, and I mean dying, why on earth would you choose a dude like Ben Braddock?"

Josie closed her eyes. *A million reasons. A zillion.* "Because he's good," she said.

"Good?"

"Yes. He's good."

"You mean in bed?"

"No! I mean, well, he's good there too." They both laughed. Deuce also ached inside. "He's not like anybody I've ever met, Deuce. He gets mad if I cuss, can you believe it? He goes to church, like, every Sunday."

"Yeah, you told me he was this great Christian man. A Christian man who won't marry you."

"Who said I wanted to get married?"

"You do."

"How can you say that? You don't know me like that."

"I know your type, Josie. And you're pushing thirty too? Yeah, you want to be a Sadie so bad you can feel it. But old man Braddock won't budge."

"Stop calling him old. He and Denzel Washington are the same age, I'll have you know. Do you consider Denzel old?"

"Yeah, his ass is old," Deuce said and laughed. "Just kidding, girl. But why won't the brother marry you, Josie? That's the question."

Josie sighed. "He will," she said. "Eventually."

"Eventually?"

"Yes, Deuce. He's a cautious man, what can I say?"

"So that's what it's called?"

Josie looked at Deuce. "What's that supposed to mean?"

"Where I come from it's not called caution. It's called getting the milk for free."

Josie shook her head. "It ain't even like that. He's not using me, if that's what you're implying."

"Okay."

"He's not."

"I said okay."

"He'll marry me. You can bet that," Josie said with confidence, mainly to convince herself. Because after tonight, after the way he'd just left her at the hospital, leaving her in the hands of a man who any fool could see had the hots for her, made her anything but confident.

"So you think an elitist dude like Ben Braddock is good?" Deuce asked her.

"That's right."

"I don't see it. In what way?"

"In every way, Deuce. You just don't know him."

"Damn straight I don't. Don't wanna know him, either. I mean, him? With you? I took you for a different kind of lady."

He glanced at Josie when he said that. And Josie looked at him. He was a good-looking, young brother ready to sweep her off her feet. All she had to do was let him. Probably a good man who would be good to her, who wouldn't dream of leaving her in a hospital just because he didn't agree with her. But she loved Ben because of his high standards, not in spite of them. Deuce probably had a lot of good, positive things going for him too, but he was no Ben Braddock.

Deuce reluctantly stopped his car behind her Mustang. It sat alone outside the now partially ripped gate of the Oxidare Petroleum plant. She quickly thanked him for the ride and stepped out of his car. He wanted to keep talking, to keep her in his sight, but she wasn't interested.

She got in her car and waved goodbye to Deuce. He watched her leave, watched her with an ache in his heart. The more he ached, the more he knew he had to have her, and it wasn't going to be as easy a task as he had thought. Ben Braddock was the competition, not some smooth joe he'd calculated would easily leave the scene. Josie also thought the world of her precious Ben. He could leave her at the hospital, yell at her and neglect her, but he was still an angel in her eyes. But Deuce never shirked from a challenge before. He knew what he had to do. He not only had to convince Josie that he was the best man for her, which wasn't going to be as easy as he had hoped, but he also had to bring Ben Braddock down. He had to knock that halo off of Ben Braddock's head.

Instead of driving north, where she lived, Josie headed south. To Ben.

He wasn't home. And she didn't have a key. So she waited, waited on his doorstep like some stray puppy, waited and got angrier the longer she did. She couldn't believe he wasn't home. Nearly 3:00 A.M. and he wasn't home. He had some nerve, she thought, as she sat there for nearly thirty minutes longer, wanting desperately to call his cell phone and cuss his ass out. But as her anger rose the senselessness of it rose too, and she decided to forget it. She was tired too, tired of doubting Ben and trying to run down some grown-ass man. *He wants to play these games, fine,* she thought. But not with her.

Her car was parked in front of the house on the quiet street, and she began to walk down the dark driveway. Before she made it to the street, the unmistakable soft hum of Ben's Mercedes could be heard turning the corner at the end of the block, coming home.

She hurried to her car, because she couldn't bear to see his face. As his car drove up and stopped beside hers, she just stood there, unable to move, her hand tightly clutching the handle of her driver's side door.

"Hey," Ben said with little enthusiasm, as if he wished to God she weren't standing there. And she wished it too, as the tears began to form in her eyes. She kept her back to him, just to avoid a confrontation.

"When did they release you?"

She shook her head. "As if you care."

Ben sat behind the wheel of his car, staring forward at the darkness of his quiet neighborhood. Then he looked at Josie, who still refused to turn around. "Let's go inside," he said.

"No," she replied.

"Why not?" Ben said. Josie rolled her eyes. *As if he didn't know,* she thought. "Why not, Josie?" She still didn't respond. She couldn't. "Josie?" he said again, and that was enough. She turned around quickly.

"What?" she said harshly, even though she knew her anger would probably unleash his.

And normally it would have, but when he saw her pretty face, the tears in her eyes, his entire mood softened and his heart went out to her. He unbuckled his seatbelt and quickly got out of his car. He walked up to her and placed his big arms around her. He could feel her emotion well as she cried into his chest.

"Come inside, sweety," he said softly into her ear.

And she wanted to, every fiber of her being was craving to go inside and be with him, but she couldn't do it. It was still three o'clock in the morning and he was still just getting home. "Good night, Ben," she said as she pulled away from him and got into her car.

She watched him through her rearview mirror as she drove away. She watched him standing in the street as if he was stunned that she would just leave like that. But that was exactly what she was doing. She wiped her tears and drove away, deciding that she couldn't keep taking herself on these roller-coaster rides with Ben, day in and day out, always something with that man.

As she picked up speed on the highway—driving faster because she couldn't get away fast enough—she began thinking, not about Ben, but about Deuce and how she should've had that drink with him. At least she'd have somebody to talk to. At least she'd be with somebody who could make her feel that it was possible, that there could actually be a life for her after Ben.

CHAPTER 7

At work the next day Josie was bored, bored because Deuce was keeping her on desk assignments, which meant editing other reporters' work, and she wasn't allowed back in the field this soon. "Too soon," was all Deuce would say when Josie asked, for the tenth time, if she could take an assignment too. She tried to argue with him, insisting that she was fine, no scars, nothing, but he wasn't feeling it. "Give it at least a full day, Josie, all right?" he said.

So she was giving it a day. A day to heal. But it was one hell of a thing for her. Only a handful of people were even in the building, with all the reporters out doing what they do. Those still in the building were stationed so far away from her desk that conversation would have required her to move closer to them or yell. Neither option interested her, so she just tried to stay busy too. But she couldn't pull it off. She was bored to tears. Her boredom was so pronounced, in fact, that she kept finding herself dozing off at her desk. When she woke up after one such dozing, Ben was standing there.

She looked up at him, at his brown Armani suit with the predictable handkerchief ever so neatly triangulated in his top left pocket, at his predictable pure-white shirt and dark brown tie. His expensive Italian shoes were also so predictable that Josie didn't even bother to confirm their presence on his feet.

"Good afternoon," he said with his trademark cool, but Josie wasn't having it. She leaned back and folded her arms. She had decided last night after sitting on his steps, waiting for him like some damn lap dog, that a kind word from him wasn't getting him out of this one. Ben, knowing Josie all too well, smiled. "Not speaking to me, I see."

"What do you want, Ben?"

"I want to know how you're doing."

"You didn't care how I was doing last night. You didn't care how I was doing when I was sitting on your steps like some damn fool for nearly an hour, waiting for you to get back from wherever the hell you were at that time of night. You left me in a hospital, Ben. A hospital. After I was nearly killed you just left me there."

"You weren't nearly killed, Josephine, stop being so melodramatic."

"I could have been killed. You don't know."

"You said you were fine."

"I said that because I didn't want to worry you." She said this and looked at him. He hesitated, then walked around the desk and stood beside Josie's chair. He sat down on the desk's edge and returned Josie's glare. His handsome face was almost serene, as if her emotionalism was so overstated that he didn't even feel the need to dignify it with a look of concern. That only angered her more.

He took his hand and cupped it under her chin, turning her face ever so slightly to get a look at the small scar on her forehead. She wanted to jerk away from his hand, but his touch felt too good.

"It's barely visible now. That's good. I take it all of the tests were negative too?"

There he goes again, Josie thought. Minimizing her plight. That was why she jerked away from him, which she knew would anger him, but in that moment she didn't even care.

But she was right. He was angry. He sighed and stood up.

"Okay, let's go," he said, his voice attempting to remain calm, in keeping with the office atmosphere, but only mildly succeeding.

"Go where?" Josie asked, astounded that he would make such a request.

"Some place to talk. Get your purse and come on."

Josie smiled, amazed at his arrogance. "I'm not going anywhere with you," she said as she stood up, grabbing a stack of files from her desk. "I've got work to do."

"Is there an empty office around here where we can talk, Josephine?" He asked this in his best-controlled voice. And Josie was weakening, because she knew too that they needed to talk, but she couldn't weaken.

She couldn't keep letting him misunderstand how deeply his actions hurt her.

"There's no empty office in this building, okay?"

Deuce, seemingly from out of nowhere, was walking their way. Ben was the first to see him, and it appeared to him that Deuce was hurrying to Josie as if he were her rescuer. "Is there a problem here?" Deuce asked as he walked up to them.

"No," Ben said. "There's no problem."

But Deuce, in total disregard of Ben, looked at Josie. "You okay, J.?" he asked her.

Ben folded his arms and stared at Deuce. Maybe it was that ridiculous crush he had on Josie, or maybe it was the way he seemed to want to stoke Josie's grievances, but there was something about the guy Ben just didn't like. He continued staring at Deuce, as if he could stare through him, and he was amazed by the young brother's boldness. Josie had to literally insist that she was fine before Deuce would give it a break. And even when he did walk away, he kept looking back, as if Ben Braddock was some upstart punk there to make trouble, as if he wanted Ben to know beyond a shadow of a doubt that he was keeping an eye on him.

When Deuce finally had gone back to his office, Josie looked at Ben.

"Just leave, okay?"

"We need to talk, Josephine."

"I don't have anything to say to you."

"Sure you don't. Not until you decide you have a lot to say and begin calling me every hour on the hour complaining that I neglect you and how we need to talk. No. Let's skip the drama and get this done."

"So that's how it goes?" Josie asked him. "It's everything on your time now? We talk when you say we talk? Is that what you're saying, Ben? Well I say to hell with you!"

That did it. Ben, doing all he could to keep a tight lid on his anger, took Josie by the hand and pulled her along with him, moving like a man on the verge of losing it, opening every office door, every closet door, until he flung open the door of the file room, where there was just enough space for them, and pulled her into that room with him and closed the door.

"Okay, let's have it," he said, unbuttoning his suit coat and placing his hands on his waist. She wore him out, he swore to God she did.

"I told you I don't have anything to say to you," she said, her anger growing too.

"What are you so damn upset about, Josephine? And don't tell me it's because I left you at some hospital."

"That's exactly what it is. Don't you understand that? I couldn't believe you just left me like that."

He sighed and stared at her. "Josephine, you know why I left that hospital," he said, amazed that she just didn't get it.

"You left because you got upset. Because you disagreed with me, which is a poor excuse, know what I'm saying?"

"I left that hospital because you were attempting to obstruct a police investigation."

"I was protecting my sources, Ben! What do you expect from me? I'm a journalist, remember? A journalist has a First Amendment right to not reveal her source."

"Those got damn agitators don't have a right to be protected! They're nothing more than hardcore criminals defying the rule of law, Josephine, and you were more than willing to aid and abet each and every one of them!"

Josie folded her arms. As usual his argument was more powerful, more to the point, more true. And she was never good at arguing against truth.

Ben couldn't do anything but shake his head. She was almost delusional in her stubbornness.

"And that's what's got you so hot that you can hardly contain yourself? The fact that I wasn't going to uphold you in wrong? The fact that Deuce Jefferson and this rag of a newspaper has no problem whatsoever in sending you to hang out with criminals and I refuse to agree with that? Is that it, Josephine?"

"Regardless of what I did or what this paper is all about, you should have stayed and taken me home, Ben. That wasn't Deuce's job. That was your job. And then after he drives me all the way to my car and then I drive all the way to your house, you still weren't home? I couldn't believe it. I was dying in the hospital and you were out caravanning with some skank-ass female somewhere? What's up with that?"

Ben couldn't help but smile and shake his head. It was all so crazy to him that it bordered on insanity. But Josie failed to see the humor.

"Stop laughing at me," she warned him.

"Then stop being so ridiculous," he replied.

"Ridiculous?"

"Yes," Ben said.

"Okay. Fine." She said this and unfolded her arms. "So where were you last night?"

"That's none of your business."

"None of my business?"

"That's right. I'm not feeding your insecurities."

Josie shook her head and looked up, her hazel eyes rolling back with utter frustration. She was insecure—she knew she was and she hated it—but she also knew that Ben's suspicious behavior didn't exactly calm her fears. Always working late. Always in a meeting. Always gone when he should be home. Home when he said he'd be gone. Always something with Ben.

Ben watched her beautiful gray-green eyes as they rolled back, stared at the ceiling, and then looked at him. She was one of a kind. He'd never met another living soul quite like Josie Ross. She was so kind and compassionate and sweet and fresh. His heart dropped.

"You take me for granted, Ben," she finally said. "Ever since we met you've always taken me for granted. I know I'm not the kind of woman you expected to be with, I know that. But you aren't exactly who I had in mind either. But I hung tight with you and I gave it my all. I have been totally devoted to you, Ben. Totally. But what do I get in return? Nothing. Not even the time of day from you. Because you take me for granted. But you better watch out. So many men want me—you just don't know!"

He knew. God, he knew. That was why he moved up to her and pulled her in his arms. She fell against his chest sobbing, she couldn't hold it in a second longer. Ben held her tightly and listened to her cry, listened and soothed her tears, trying with all he had to not break down himself.

But then the door of the file room opened and Deuce peeped inside. Josie removed herself from Ben's embrace and wiped her eyes with his handkerchief.

"You okay, Josie?" Deuce asked her.

"I'm fine."

"Sure?"

"Positive, Deuce, what do you want?"

Deuce hesitated. He didn't exactly like Josie's tone of voice. "I'm sorry for the interrupt," he said, "but you've got an assignment."

Josie frowned. "An assignment? I thought you said I had to stay on desk today."

Deuce looked at Ben. "I changed my mind."

"Changed your mind?"

"It's okay," Ben said.

"No, it's not okay, Ben. Every time I asked him if I could get an assignment he said I couldn't. I asked him at least ten times already."

"Honey, look at me," Ben said to get Josie's undivided attention, knowing full well that she tended to go off with little thought of the consequences. She looked at him. "It's okay. I've got to run anyway."

"But . . ."

"Josephine! But nothing. Just do your job."

Josie looked at Ben. She would have been thrilled to just stay in his arms. She hated that Deuce had interrupted that, but she knew Ben was right once again.

"Okay," she said reluctantly. "You're right. Okay." Then she leaned against Ben and kissed him on the lips. "I love you," she said.

"You take care of yourself," he replied, then looked hard at Deuce once again.

He left Josie on her own to deal with her still unfulfilled heart and Deuce Jefferson.

It was a scam. At least that was the only way Josie could think to put it when she realized there was no assignment after all.

"I wouldn't go that far," Deuce said with a smile as they sat down at a table in the small cafe. "If I had out-and-out asked you to go to lunch with me, you would have turned me down cold."

"Why would you say that?"

"Because I'm getting to know you. You wouldn't even have a drink with me last night."

"I was just getting out of the hospital. Remember?"

"It wasn't exactly a life threatening injury, Josie, come on."

Josie had to smile herself. But she still didn't like the deception. "But you still didn't have to lie like that, Deuce."

"I felt I had to. I saw what that dude was doing to you. Had you all emotional and crying and shit. You didn't need that drama. You were fine before he showed up."

"That's what you think."

Deuce shook his head. "I'm twenty-eight years old so I'm not gonna try to act like I've got as much experience as your old-ass boyfriend, okay? But I've got a heck of a lot more experience than you, Josie."

"You don't know that."

"I know it," he said. Josie looked at Deuce. Did she have a sign around her neck or something? How could he possibly know that?

"But how?" she asked him, and then pleaded with him to tell her the secret, to tell why was it that everybody seemed to see it in her, but her.

"Experience, Josie, that's what I'm talking about. You're green and it shows. That's why I'm telling you that a lady like you, a real, wonderful, compassionate lady like you, deserves better than some player like Benjamin Braddock."

Josie looked out of the window, at the traffic whipping by on Division Street, and it seemed to her then that everybody was trying to get anywhere but where they were. And to Josie it was all the same. People, cars, there was no difference. Deuce wanted her, but she didn't want Deuce; she wanted Ben. And Ben, she thought, didn't know what he wanted.

The waitress came to take their orders. Ham sandwiches for both, and juice. When the waitress left, Deuce leaned forward, his large, dark eyes like glass.

"I'm not some hard-up with a hard-on, Josie, okay?"

Josie laughed. "What?"

"I got prospects, that's all I'm saying. So don't think my advice to you is some kind of play for your affections, because it ain't about that. I like you. I think you're a special lady. But all I'm looking for right now is a friend."

Josie looked at Deuce. She could use one herself. "Me too," she said.

Deuce smiled. "Good." He leaned back. "And from one friend to another, you can do better than Braddock."

Josie laughed. "You will not let up, will you?"

"Never."

"But you're worrying for nothing. I've got Ben under control, my friend. Okay?"

"Now that's funny. You controlling Ben Braddock? I'll buy anything if I buy that."

"It's the truth," Josie said, although even she knew better than that. "And why did you call him a player? He's no player."

"Okay."

"He's not."

"Cool. I'm wrong then."

"But why would you even say it?"

"Experience, baby girl, didn't I tell you about that? You can just look at him and see it. It's all over the man."

"So you're just guessing? But based on experience, of course."

"Come on, Josie, you see it too. You ain't that green. Is he always working late, got something going on where he can't spend a lot of time with you?"

"He's got a tough job. It's only natural that he works late and is busy a lot. You don't get to be where he is with a nine-to-five mentality."

Deuce didn't expect such an understanding response. "Does he tell you that he loves you?"

"He has."

Deuce didn't expect that response either. "He has?"

"Yes."

"Does he tell you at the times you want him to?"

Josie hesitated. "No."

"See what I mean? The brother is L.L. Cool B., Josie, I'm telling you."

Josie frowned. "He's what?"

"L.L. Cool B. Ladies Love Cool Ben. I'm telling you. That uptown brother's got a rep."

Josie didn't know if Deuce was playing her or telling what he knew. But either way, she didn't like it. "Do you have any proof?" she asked, and Deuce laughed.

"Proof? You mean do I have any pictures of him with the females? Of course not. That ain't my job to be compiling proof. That's your job."

Josie leaned back and sighed. She could fall into her funk once more, where all she could think about was Ben, or she could just forget Ben and get on with it. She had to be patient. Ben's true intentions would be coming out soon. He would have no choice. Josie's birthday was less than a month away. She was turning thirty in three and a half weeks. She had already marked her calendar, and her conversation with Deuce made her glad that she did. The proof would be on that day. Ben could wine and dine her and buy her all the precious stones he wanted, but if one of those stones didn't include an engagement ring, something that at thirty she felt she was more than deserving of, then she'd know unlike she'd ever known before, despite anything Deuce could ever tell her, what the real deal really was.

Meredith was late, coming home to her waterfront apartment well after midnight. Hines Lowe sat in the arched-top chair off from the foyer, sat there as if his life depended on his stillness. Meredith removed her scarf and looked at him. She knew very well her brother's problem before he even opened his mouth.

"Where were you?" he asked her, his narrow face filled with anger and grief, his cat-like eyes flush with sorrow.

"I told you I had to see a customer tonight."

"At midnight? They don't call you to come out this late."

"Yes, they do. And you know they do."

Hines leaned forward and began running his hand through his bushy red hair. "I don't know how much more of this I can take, Sis. I swear to God I don't."

Meredith hurried to her brother and fell down on her knees. "It's going to be all right, Hines. We've got to hold on. Things are looking up for us now."

"Getting calls at midnight. Anything could have happened to you. That dude, that customer, could have been a maniac for all we knew."

"It's work, Hines. It pays the bills. We have a good plan."

"I used to be there for you. They wouldn't have dreamed about calling you out at midnight when I was around. Now they don't give a damn. I'm a joke to them now. A shell of the man I used to be. Look at me. They're right."

Meredith placed her arms around her brother. "They're wrong, Hines. You're still a great man. If it wasn't for what you did for me, and for what happened, you'd know it too. Life knocked us down, dear, that's all. But things are looking up again." She looked up at her brother when she said this. "He offered me a job."

"He offered?"

"Yes. That night at the mayor's party. And I played it exactly right. Exactly as we had planned. You would have been so proud of me."

"Why didn't you just take it, Sis? Why do we have to play these games?"

"We have to stick to the plan, or nothing will work. I played it right. I told him I was still weighing my options."

"But what if he changes his mind?"

"He won't."

"How can you be so sure?"

"He won't change his mind. I see how he looks at me. There's no way he'll turn me down." There was a pause. "And when I do accept that offer of his, it'll be the beginning of the end of our troubles, Hines. I promise you that. No more midnight calls, no more crazy customers. Things will be the way they used to be. We'll get what is rightfully ours. We'll finally have it in our grasp. And the agony we had to endure will be worth every minute. Worth every blood-sucking minute."

Hines leaned back and exhaled. *She still believes in fairy tales,* he thought. *Just as she did when we were kids.* But he knew better. Dreams didn't come true for people like them, only hard luck and harder luck. That was why he worried. Not because he knew. But because Meredith, his dear, sweet baby sister, didn't.

CHAPTER 8

She was up with the roosters, but she wasn't crowing. She was showering, dressing, and making her bed. She was even singing along with old-school pros like Marvin Gaye, all before 7:00 A.M. In no way was she lively at the crack of dawn by nature. She was grooving for hopeful reasons. She was getting off on "Let's Get It On" because her day had come. Her thirtieth birthday. And she was ready.

She went downstairs and began preparing breakfast for Ben. She was no cook, but she knew he loved a down-home kind of breakfast with grits and eggs and bacon and toast and she was determined to do it up right.

The doorbell rang earlier than she expected. She nervously stirred her grits one more time, quickly removed her apron, and hurried for the door. On her way she stopped and stood before the huge mirror that hung over her living-room sofa. She looked at herself, front, side, and even tried to get a peep at her back. She was wearing longer braids now, neat and trimmed and swayed at the shoulders. Her outfit was a bright white Versace pantsuit with a feather-sheer, sky-blue scarf, and matching blue heels. She was going for sophistication this day, and looking at herself didn't make her certain that she had pulled it off. But it was too late to worry about that now, she thought, as she smiled at herself in the mirror and fluffed her braids one more time, before quickly heading to her front door.

It was, as she had hoped and expected, Ben. He stood at her front door as if he were a large gift from God, his mustache lifting up into a smile as soon as he saw her. She wanted to fall into his arms, to unleash her excitement immediately, but she held back.

"Ben, hi," she said and stepped aside. He walked in, still smiling but staring at her. She closed the door behind them, and he was still staring. She thought it was the reality of this day, as if turning thirty magically changed her somehow. But that wasn't it.

"What?" she finally asked when his stare wouldn't quit.

"You're up," he said.

She laughed. "Oh, yeah, I been up."

He nodded. "Good for you," he said, seemingly well pleased.

"Well don't just stand there," she said, "come on and have a seat." She said this happily as she took him by the arm and walked him toward her sofa. He was dressed, not in a suit for a change, but in a pair of green, pleated, dress pants, a white, dome-collar shirt, and a black, snakeskin bomber jacket. His shoes were Ferragamo wingtips. His cologne was a sweet but understated fragrance he started wearing when they first relocated to Minnesota, a scent Josie had never placed or bothered to ask about, and it made her move her body closer to his. He had a fresh haircut, and although it was his usual close-to-the-skull cut, it seemed softer and neater to her. He, in fact, looked gorgeous and youthful and so sexy that she didn't want to let go of his arm. So she didn't. She sat down on the sofa beside him with her arm still interlocked with his.

He continued to stare at her as she sat beside him, as if he was amazed by something, and she decided not to disappoint. She leaned her head back, flipped the braids out of her face, and crossed the flaired legs of her Versace suit. She wanted him to stare. She wanted to turn him on. When she looked at him, when her gray-green eyes locked onto his bright brown eyes, it was he who moved closer to her. He looked down, at her breasts, at her mouth, and then into her eyes. And he kissed her. His lips moved in a rhythmic circle, as if grooving to the beat of his own tune, and she leaned her head back and rolled with it too. She pulled on him until his big, muscular body was completely in her arms, and then she lifted her legs and wrapped them around him. She was still so in love with his taste that she always felt like coming from the power of his sweetness alone. She was in love. Fully, no doubt about it, deep down in love. And she craved more of the feeling.

When their lips finally parted, she opened her eyes. He smiled that smile of his that always made her heart flutter. She touched the lines on the sides of his eyes and was so happy to be a part of his life, of this man's life, that she wanted to cry.

"Happy birthday, Josephine," he said to her. "Or did you forget again?"

She smiled too. "Does it look like I forgot, Ben?"

He laughed. Then, after removing himself from her embrace, from what he jokingly told her felt like a death grip, he handed her a small, beautifully wrapped box.

Josie's heart wanted to leap for joy. The box was perfect. It was the right size and felt the right weight. But she contained herself. "Oh, Ben, you didn't have to buy me a gift," she said as she accepted the box, knowing full well that that was a lie.

Ben pulled out a cigarette, lit up, and then leaned back. He was so tired from having worked nonstop till eleven last night, and then having gotten up before six to keep with his plan for Josie's birthday. But just seeing her, already dressed and beautiful and ready for whatever the day may bring, made him feel rejuvenated too, made him feel like every moment of his efforts was well worth it.

But when the gift was unwrapped, it was Josie's efforts that felt wasted. It was a small, black box. It could have been an engagement ring, the size was about right, but suddenly the feel changed. She knew it could have been her nerves or just the fear of the unknown, so she decided not to focus on all of those unhelpful thoughts when opening the box. She opened it slowly and deliberately, still smiling although her hope was dwindling fast. She'd been right. It wasn't a ring. Just a pair of beautiful diamond earrings. She touched the earrings, her small hand glided over them, and she continued to smile. But the excitement in that smile had vanished.

"They're beautiful," she said to Ben, and then looked into his eyes, only tears began to appear in hers.

He crossed his legs and looked at her. "What's the matter?" he asked her.

"Nothing."

"Don't tell me nothing. I can see better than that."

"I'm sorry, Ben. I don't mean to be so emotional all the time. It's a wonderful gift, really, it is. I just thought . . ."

She couldn't continue. He placed his arm around her and pulled her closer to him. He handed her his handkerchief as she lifted her head off of his shoulders. "You must think I'm so ungrateful," she said, and then blew her nose.

"You're not ungrateful."

"I'm really not. They're beautiful earrings. They're really beautiful. But I just thought that . . . I thought . . ." Again, she couldn't say the words. She looked at him instead. He uncrossed his legs, leaned forward, and tapped off the ash of his cigarette in the ashtray on her coffee table. He exhaled and looked back at her.

"When the time is right," he said, "I'll consider marriage, Josephine. But we're not there yet, sweety. You're not there yet."

She could have been combative with him; she could have decided he just didn't want her and that was why he wouldn't marry her, that Deuce was right all along, but she refused to go there. She knew the deal. She wasn't ready by a long shot. She looked at Ben and actually managed to smile. His words were a painful reality. But he was only telling the truth. And she could never argue with the truth.

"Thanks for the gift, Ben," she said. "Despite my reaction they're really very beautiful. And it was very thoughtful of you to give them to me. Thank you." She leaned up and pecked him on his lips, and then again on his mustache. He smiled. But then she frowned.

"Oh my God!" she yelled and jumped up.

"What is it?" he asked, standing too. But she ran, ran as if her life depended on it, into her kitchen. Ben doused his cigarette and hurried into the kitchen behind her. When he saw that she was attempting to remove a smoldering pot of grits off of the stove and an equally smoking pan of bacon, he grabbed the pot holders from her and removed the burnt food himself. Then he turned on the stove's fan and lifted a window. Josie stood in the middle of her kitchen so flustered she didn't know what to do. She looked to him. He stared at her, and disappointment seemed to overtake her, and then he smiled.

"It's time to go anyway," he said.

"But what about breakfast?"

"We'll eat on the plane."

"The plane? What plane?"

"Get your purse and find out," he said.

Although she was still reeling from the morning, she got her purse.

* * *

The twin-engine jet with *Denlex* written on its tail whisked them away from the Minneapolis airstrip and flew nonstop to Florida. Josie was smiling again, because it was shaping up to be one of the most memorable birthdays she could ever recall. The prospect of going back to Jacksonville and seeing her best friend Scotty was more than she could have wished for. Ben had leaned back in the white leather seat reading newspapers and sterile business journals, but mostly he watched Josie. He watched her sip her wine and sway to the beat of his gospel music, as if she were in a church somewhere. He'd smile when she would forget the nature of the music and began, especially when songs like Kirk Franklin's "Stomp" would play, to bust a move. Then she'd remember it wasn't exactly hip-hop she was grooving to and chill again.

"Sorry," she said, shaking her head.

"Don't be."

"I keep forgetting."

"I know."

"I'm a trip like that. I just go off into my own little thing. I don't know what gets into me."

"You're okay, Josie."

"I don't know, Ben. I think I'm a little loopy."

Ben smiled. And then he laughed. "Loopy?"

"Yes! Crazy. And not like a fox, either. Just crazy."

"You're okay."

"Sure about that?"

Ben looked at her. Then he nodded. "Oh, yeah," he said.

Josie smiled and began busting a move again, forgetting again just that quickly, and Ben laughed, shook his head, and returned to his reading.

But mainly Josie interrupted him, over and over, by constantly thanking him for the unexpected trip, as if she still could not get over how romantic he could be.

"And here I was grateful for earrings," she said. "But you give me this too, a trip all the way to Florida? Damn, Ben, thanks."

Ben looked up from his newspaper and smiled. "You're welcome," he said again, for the ninety-ninth time.

The plane touched down in Jacksonville, some five hours after it took off. A limousine was waiting to whisk them off to Fleming

Island, where Fred Caldwell, Ben's best friend and a former pro football player for the Pittsburgh Steelers, lived with his wife Angela. Josie sat back and watched as the limo lumbered through quiet downtown Jacksonville, past the empty office buildings and banks and warehouses, closed for the weekend. Josie remembered this quietness well. She remembered how in Jacksonville the only downtown action most Sundays was the enormous amount of people attending church service at First Baptist Church, which took up an entire city block or, during football season to see the Jaguars at Alltel Stadium. Otherwise, like today, it was a ghostly place.

At her request the driver drove onto Forsyth Street, where the *Gazette,* her former employer, was housed. *It's still standing,* she thought, as she stared at the brown and yellow ten-story building. It was still holding itself out as the shining example of the liberal media, still willing to tell the truth, but only if that truth was convenient. WHERE THE RIGHTS OF CITIZENS DARE TO BE HEARD remained its motto, and Josie looked at those words as they drove by, still etched above the main entrance, words that were once her inspiration.

Ben took her hand as their limo lumbered by. He remembered the pain too. They had just returned from a vacation in the Florida Keys and were both hopeful that their budding romance was about to go somewhere. But then the lies came. He looked at Josie. Tears were in her eyes.

"It's over, honey," he said, and she tried to smile, to show that she believed it too, but she couldn't smile. Because it didn't feel like it was over. And she wasn't sure if it ever would be.

Fred and Angela Caldwell lived in a Tudor-style home that reminded Josie of a modern day castle, and as the limousine climbed the long, arching driveway, Fred Caldwell opened his front door and looked like the knight of the castle to her.

"There's Freddy!" Josie said excitedly and Ben looked too. He and Fred had been best friends for over thirty years, having met when they both attended the University of Florida. But it was Josie who seemed thrilled to see him. She hurried out of the limo before the driver could open the door for her, and ran toward him. Fred laughed as he ran to meet her halfway.

"Josie and the pussycats!" he yelled as he embraced her. "How are you, sweetheart?" He lifted her off her feet as they embraced. She loved Fred, loved him because he loved Ben, loved him because she always knew he'd be in her corner.

"It's so great to see you," she said smilingly as he put her down. "And look at you!"

He turned around, so she could get a good look, and she laughed. He was handsome in a mild kind of way, she thought, a man with more wit than charm, who had a youthful playfulness about him that Josie enjoyed. Although he and Ben were the same age and both businessmen of the first order (Fred ran his own electronics company), Fred was nothing like Ben. *Even in his style of dress,* Josie thought, as she looked at him. He wore a sharp pair of chino pants and a very hip Phat Farm jersey, and he even sported a little bling bling: a thick, gold chain around his neck. She also noticed, to her shock, the small, pierced earring in his ear.

"Ah, sukie-sukie now!" she said, looking at the earring.

"You like?"

"I love it, Fred. It's sharp! Does Ben know?"

"No," Fred said, leaving Josie's side to hurry toward the driveway where Ben was talking with the limo driver, "and don't you tell him either."

"Like he's not gonna see it himself."

"Look, babe, you know me. Anything's worth a try."

Josie smiled and watched as Fred hurried up to Ben and embraced him heartily. They had been friends for thirty years, ever since they were freshmen in college. It seemed almost impossible to Josie to have a friendship that could endure that long. She didn't see how she would be able to stand the sight of anybody for thirty years. Although she was more than willing to try with Ben.

Angela Caldwell, Fred's prim and proper wife, came out of the house less excitedly than her husband, but she was pleased to see Josie too.

"Hello, Josephine," she said as she walked down the steps. When Josie saw Angela she ran and embraced her too. Angela couldn't help but smile at Josie's enthusiasm. And when they stopped embracing, she touched the side of Josie's cheerful face.

"How are you, dear?" she asked, seemingly glad to know that somebody still knew how to embrace life fully.

"I'm good, Angela. How you doing?"

"I'm fine. But don't you look wonderful. I simply adore that suit. It's so attractive. So Versace. Although I must admit I was half-expecting to see you in your usual African."

"I know," Josie said and smiled. "I thought I'd give them something to talk about, know what I'm saying?"

Angela laughed. She was an attractive woman to Josie, a woman in her late forties who dressed elegantly, wearing a sleeveless, red mini-checked blouse and a pair of blue cotton pants. Her unblemished coco-brown skin, bleached-white teeth, and deep brown eyes glistened against the mild Florida sun. Josie liked Angela, admired her, but they were never able to go beyond the barrier of associate to friend even though their men were the best of friends. Most of it stemmed from the fact that she and Josie were just too dissimilar in age, style, and taste, but also because Josie had thought for a long time—and still wasn't completely convinced she was wrong—that Angela had had an affair with Ben.

"So tell me," Angela asked, "how does it feel to be back in Florida?"

"Sad, but happy too."

"Ah, yes. The *Gazette.*"

"Right."

"Were you prepared?" Angela asked.

Josie shook her head. "Not really. I had no idea we were even coming to Florida, to tell you the truth. It was all a complete surprise. Ben didn't tell me anything until we were on the plane."

Angela smiled. "Ah, you poor thing," she said and looked toward the driveway.

Josie smiled also, and looked at Ben as he and Fred made their way up the winding driveway. Ben looked gorgeous to her in his bomber jacket, so alluring and sexy as he walked toward her that even she could understand how Angela, how any woman, would want him. But that very knowledge was why her heart stayed in turmoil. Too many women wanted him. Too many well-experienced females were hellbent on having him. Regardless of her claim.

"Shame on you, Benjamin," Angela said as he made his way up to them.

"What did I do now?" Ben asked with a smile.

"You kept Josie in the dark, that's what. Shame on you."

Ben laughed. "Oh, that," he said in a tone Josie took to be yet another slight of her. Then he and Angela looked serious. He stared at her. "Hey, lady," he said, and then she hurried to him, her hands flapping as if they would incinerate if she didn't touch him. He wrapped her in his arms. She fell into him, holding him tighter than Josie thought necessary, and Ben rubbed her back and her hair as if she was his woman. Her. Not Josie. They were in their own little world.

Josie looked at Fred, and she wondered why he didn't do something. But unlike Josie, Angela's show of affection toward Ben didn't seem to faze Fred at all. Josie was astounded. She was about to show her behind; she was just that close to grabbing Angela by the hair and pulling her away from Ben, and Fred didn't even seem to care. She wished she could be that way. She wished to God she could have the kind of confidence that would make her certain that she was more than enough woman for Ben.

When they stopped embracing, Angela appeared to be on the verge of crying. She touched Ben's face and smiled. She looked older, Josie thought, with those lines of age beginning to crack through.

"You've been taking care of yourself?" Angela asked Ben.

"I've been trying."

"Don't try. Do it."

"Yes, ma'am."

"I miss you so much," Angela said. Ben smiled weakly and stroked Angela's hair. "You look great, Ben. You and Josie both." She said this and moved back, bringing Josie and Fred back into their world, although she and Ben were still holding hands.

"They look like a Norman Rockwell painting," Fred said, placing his arm around Angela's waist. "Don't they, Annie?"

"Yes," Angela said as Ben slowly removed his hand from hers. "A very attractive couple."

"Well, you two don't exactly look like an Andy Warhol," Ben replied, and they all laughed. But Josie could see the anguish on Angela's face, as if seeing Ben again brought back some heavy memories, and the way their hands had interlocked, even after they were no longer embracing, didn't help Josie's suspicions at all. But she decided to keep it to herself. She decided that if she didn't do something about that rampant insecurity of hers, even if she had every reason to be insecure, she could forget getting what she had determined she had to have.

"We're waiting," Angela said.

"Waiting for what?" Ben asked.

"For you to tell us what it feels like to be a Minnesotan."

Ben laughed. "Different, to be sure. But we're adjusting."

"He's more than adjusting," Josie said. "Ben's taken the place by storm."

"I'm not surprised. That sounds like Ben."

"What about you, Josie?" Fred asked. "How's it been for you?"

Josie hesitated. Not great, she wanted to say. "Okay," she said instead.

"Just okay?"

"Just okay."

Fred nodded and was about to tell her to keep her chin up, it'll get better, some advice like that, when he noticed the car. "Uh-oh," he said. "Here he comes!"

Everybody looked toward the street. Josie saw Scotty's little silver and blue Miata swinging into the driveway, moving fast up the incline because that was the only way he knew how to drive, and the biggest smile she had yet to display came over her face. Scotty Culpepper, the long-haired, humorous, forty-two-year-old art-gallery owner, was her best friend. And her delight rose exponentially. Before his car had even stopped, she was running toward him.

"Be careful, Josephine!" Ben yelled after her. But she couldn't respond. She was too busy opening Scotty's car door before his car came to a complete stop. Fred laughed out loud.

"Now she's what I call a wildcat!" he said.

Ben looked at that wildcat of a girlfriend of his and how she was falling all over Scotty as soon as his car door opened. They fell back onto the front seat, hugging each other and in tears with happiness. It was that kind of passion, that kind of trusting, uninhibited, no-holds-barred, childlike delirium that Ben loved most about Josie. But that same passion of hers, that same high-strung emotionalism she was never quite able to control, worried him too. She was full of life, full of the promise of life, yet still idealistic in the face of the harsh realities of life. It was a balancing act, how to keep your gusto and grow up too, and Ben had yet to see it successfully done.

"She is so excitable," Angela said, who wouldn't in a million years sanction such a display. "She's going to break Scotty's neck if she's not careful."

But Ben smiled. "I'm sure he won't mind," he said, and Fred and Angela looked at Ben and laughed.

In the backyard patio, dinner was over and it was time for Josie to open gifts. Scotty's gift was a muzzle. Everybody laughed.

"What in the world is this supposed to be, Scotty?" Josie asked, smiling too.

"Just a reminder," Scotty said, swinging his long, wavy hair out of what Josie could only describe as his gorgeous, whimsical-looking face.

"A reminder?"

"Yes, girl, a reminder. A reminder for you to keep that trap of yours closed sometimes."

"Very funny," Josie said, and threw it at him. He laughed, and then pulled out his real gift, a beautiful African mud cloth painting from his gallery.

"Oh, Scotty, it's precious!" she said, smiling, and then hurried to him to hug his neck. But he got up quickly and had her chase him around the backyard. It was cool in Florida, but Scotty still had on a pair of Bermuda shorts, a hot pink polo shirt, and Reeboks, and catching him was out of the question. Josie enjoyed the chase, anyway, enjoyed it because it reminded her of how much fun life used to be before she relocated with Ben to that slow behind Minnesota. She wasn't about to trade in her new life, being with Ben was the point to her, but seeing Scotty again certainly made her miss some of her old Florida days.

Fred and Angela's gift was far less dramatic, an expensive leather attaché case with *Josie Ross,* Saint Cloud Herald, engraved on top. Josie glanced at Ben when she saw the engraving.

"What's the matter, Josephine?" Angela asked.

"I told her it was too stuffy," Fred said. "A young girl like you don't want some briefcase. But who am I except the breadwinner around here?"

"I thought it was a charming gift," Angela said.

"It is," Josie said. "Oh, it's wonderful. It's just the engraving."

"What's wrong with the engraving?"

Josie glanced at Ben again. He took a slow drag on his cigarette, and then sipped from his glass of beer.

"I'm no longer with the *Herald,*" Josie said.

Scotty looked at her. "No longer with them? Damn, Josie. They just hired your butt."

"I worked for them for almost a year, thank you very much, Mr. 'Don't Know Squat' Culpepper."

"What happened?" Angela asked. Again, Josie glanced at Ben, which caused Angela to do so too.

"I apparently said something that offended the mayor."

"The *mayor?*" Scotty asked, astounded, and then he started laughing. "That mouth rides again!"

"I personally don't think I said anything offensive, okay? But the mayor thought I was offending him and the managing editor of the *Herald* agreed. So they fired me."

Angela frowned. "But I thought the managing editor was a friend of Ben's. I thought that was why you got the job so quickly in the first place."

"He is Ben's friend. I even asked Ben to talk to him for me. But he wouldn't."

"I don't know why y'all even going there," Fred said. "Y'all know Benjamin doesn't play that. If you get yourself into some mess, you'd better get yourself out. That's his motto."

"But I didn't do anything wrong, Fred. All I did was question why the mayor's road improvement plan didn't include more minority contractors, that's all I said."

"But why you even had to say that, Josie?" Scotty asked.

"What you mean why?"

"Why. As in what is that your business? Let them minority contractors worry about why they ain't included in the plan. And if they don't care to look into it, why should you?"

Josie rolled her eyes. Scotty was always protective of her, always worried that one day she was going to say the wrong thing or jump on the wrong crusade and was going to lose it all, including Ben. But she just couldn't sweat that. The truth was the truth and she wasn't about to sit back and pretend that it was something else. A reporter's job is to question, and that was all she did.

"In any event," Angela said, "give me back the case and we'll have the engraving changed."

"No, Angela, thank you, but this is fine. It'll be a nice reminder."

"Of what?"

"Of what happens when you tell the truth," she said, and just as she said it Ben slammed his glass of beer down on the table, causing everybody to react. He pointed his cigarette at Josie.

"You know you need to cut that shit out," he said to her.

Josie shook her head. *He still just doesn't get it,* she thought. "I told the truth, Ben. I don't know why you keep trippin'. All I did was tell the truth."

"And what truth was that, Josephine? What magnificent truth were you revealing that was so profound that it was worth losing your job? Tell me about it. Please let me in on this remarkable truth you alone can see and you alone must tell!"

Josie folded her arms and began shaking her leg. *Here we go,* she thought. Another one of his sermons.

"There are balances, Josephine. Pros and cons. You can't jump on every bandwagon, you have to be smart enough to understand that. You have a job, a job you wish to keep, then you have to be in tune with what that job requires. And you know good and well the *Saint Cloud Herald* didn't send you to that press conference to advocate for anybody or to confront Todd Keating about his lack of diversity or whatever point you were trying to make. They sent you there to ask him sweet little nothings about his sweet little plan, and then get the hell away from there. If they wanted you to do commentary on the plight of the Minnesota minority contractors, then they would have hired you as their commentator. But they didn't. They fired you instead. Now you're working for some obnoxious tabloid newspaper that wouldn't know honest journalism if it bit 'em in the ass, and you're talking to me about truth?"

Momentary silence engulfed them as Ben's anger, which always seemed to come out of nowhere, had caught them all off-guard. Josie most of all.

"So what you're saying," she said, trying her best to keep her anger in check, "is that I'm supposed to go along and play the game. If the game is crooked or rigged or wrong, then too bad. Play it anyway? Is that what you're saying to me, Ben?"

Ben's stomach began to rumble. He paused, to settle down. "There are consequences, Josephine," he finally said, his voice far more measured. "Count up the costs and think about the consequences before you decide to put it all on the line in the name of truth."

"I do think about the consequences."

"No, you don't," Ben said as he shook his head and tapped the ash off of his cigarette. "You're a crusader to your heart and deep in your heart. But deep thinking isn't part of your make-up."

"I try to do the right thing, that's all I try to do. Is that supposed to be wrong now?"

Ben looked at Josie, at her soft gray-green eyes once again on the verge of tears. She was wearing him out. "No," he said to her, giving up, but meaning what he had previously said.

"Then why are you so upset?"

"I'm not upset. Not anymore."

"Yes, you are," Josie said.

"I'm not."

"Yeah, whatever." Josie looked away.

"Josie?" Ben said, and after a moment of hesitation, she turned and looked at him. "I'm not upset."

"Yes, you are."

"I'm not."

She smiled. "Cross your heart and hope to die?"

He laughed and shook his head. "I cross my heart and hope to die," Ben said.

Scotty sighed relief. "Good," he said. "Because that was too much emotion for me. And if you weren't upset, Ben, I hate to see you when you truly are. But Josie, I'm gonna be honest. He told you the truth, girl."

Josie looked at Scotty and smiled. "And what is that your business?" she asked, to coin his phrase.

"All right now," Scotty said. "You better watch yourself. Just because you thirty now don't mean nothing to me. You still aren't too old that I can't put you across my knee, sweetheart."

"I don't think that'll happen, Scotty," Ben said as he put out his cigarette without looking up. Everybody, including Scotty himself, laughed.

Later that afternoon, as the laughter died down into small conversations, Angela invited Josie to come with her. "I want to show you this marvelous sculpture we purchased during our last pilgrimage to Africa."

Josie stood from her seat quickly. "What part of Africa did you guys hit this time?"

Angela smiled. "Zimbabwe," she said. "Come."

Josie followed Angela off the patio and into the house. Ben sipped from his glass of beer and watched them leave. Then Scotty stood up.

"Mind if I look around, Fred?" he asked. "I've been adoring from afar your beautiful lawn and garden. It's so picturesque back here. I want a more personal look."

Fred smiled. "Help yourself, my man," he said eagerly, and Scotty, with a glass of beer in hand, began walking around the expansive backyard. Fred leaned back in his chair and rubbed his belly. "I am too full, you hear me? Those were some good ribs, boy."

"Yeah, I'm pretty stuffed myself." Ben said this, and then he looked at Fred.

"What?" Fred asked.

"An earring," Ben said, as if it were a statement.

"That's right. You like?"

"No."

"Tough."

Ben smiled. "There ya go," he said.

"Josie would love you in an earring," Fred said.

"No, she wouldn't."

Fred laughed and then shook his head. "Yeah, that kid is a burst of energy, ain't she? And did you see the way she ate? Where the hell does it all go? I tell you she pigged out." He shook his head again. "She's got to be a lot to handle, Benjamin."

Ben stared at his glass of beer. He knew what Fred was trying to say, and it was true. His life would be infinitely easier if he broke it off with Josie—if he told her once and for all that it wasn't working, that it couldn't work, and they needed to stop kidding themselves. Then he could settle back into a "normal" relationship with a lady not unlike himself, somebody of stature and maturity who'd been there, done that, and was at a point in her life where she had no more points to prove. His existence would calm down considerably if Josie wasn't a part of that picture. He knew exactly what Fred was talking about.

"I didn't think you went for that," Fred said to Ben, smiling.

"Went for what?"

"The younger crowd. I didn't think they turned you on."

"They don't."

"Josie does."

Ben nodded. "Yes."

Fred paused and then he sighed. "Benjamin, everything okay?"

Ben looked at his old friend. "It's okay."

"I don't mean to pry."

"You aren't prying."

"I just don't want her driving you nuts, that's all," Fred said.

Ben smiled and ran his hand across his cropped-short, soft hair. "Too late," he said.

"Of all the women I would have guessed you'd end up with, all those beautiful, sophisticated ladies, it turns out to be Josie. Now, I like her, don't get me wrong. There's something genuine about her. Something fantastic, actually. But she's the one, huh?" Ben didn't respond. "Maybe it's love that keeps her so hyped up, I don't know. Maybe this is how she behaves when she's in love," Fred said.

"Impossible to know," Ben said, "since this is her first shot at it."

At first Fred smiled. Then, as if realizing what Ben had actually said, he fell back in his chair. "What?" he asked, stunned. "Get the *f* outta here! You're her *first* love?"

Ben nodded. "I'm her first and her only."

Fred laughed. "This is unbelievable. Unbelievable! How could that happen, man? It's like becoming the starting pitcher in the World Series without having ever thrown a pitch. She gets you on her first try out? You? This is too much. You have succeeded in shocking me, my friend. I am truly, without question, shocked."

Ben looked over at Scotty, who was trying to outrun the automatic sprinkler system. As it began to water Scotty down, Ben exhaled. "Yeah, I hear what you're saying," he said to Fred. "I'm still getting over the shock myself."

It was a sculpture of a mother and child, and the pure artistry of it astounded Josie. She sat on the edge of Fred and Angela's bed, in their huge, peach-colored bedroom, and stared unblinkingly at the wonderful piece. Angela sat beside Josie and pointed out the detail.

"Down to the whites of their eyes," she said. "I think it's remarkable."

"Oh, it is," Josie said. "I can just feel that mother's grip on that child."

"Protecting her."

"Right."

Angela smiled, and then she looked at Josie. "And what about you?" she asked her.

"What about me?"

"How are you doing?"

"I'm good," Josie said.

"Sure?"

"Positive."

"Everything's positive?"

"Yes."

"Including your relationship with Ben?"

Josie sat erect. She had already concluded that there was more to Angela's invite upstairs. "What do you mean?" she asked her.

"There appears to be a little tension between you and Ben."

"There's no tension." Josie said this too fast, and too defensively. "Not really," she added.

"You know, Josie, you can talk to me."

"Talk to you about what?"

"Your relationship with Ben. I've known the man for a very long time."

"I know that, Angela." She knew that well. Too well.

"I thought it was settled, Josie. When Ben's name was ultimately cleared against those sexual-harassment allegations and you agreed to leave Florida with him, I thought your days of doubting him were over."

Josie looked at Angela. Where was she going with this? "I don't doubt Ben," she said. "I don't know what you're talking about."

"Yes, you do."

Josie hesitated. She did need somebody to talk to. Somebody who would know. She wasn't thrilled that it would have to be Angela, because she still wasn't a hundred percent certain about her standing in Ben's life, but there was nobody else. "He doesn't open up to me," she said. "That's why I—"

"That's why you have your doubts?"

"Yeah. Why won't he just open up a little? I can't even ask him where he's been without him yelling at me or getting upset. And he doesn't . . . All this time me and Ben have been together, he's only told me he loved me once." There was another time, but he was anguishing over those sexual harassment allegations, so that time, in her mind, didn't count.

Angela nodded. "I believe it. You should know Ben by now, Josie. He's not going to reconfirm his love for you every time you feel insecure. He's not going to do that. He told you he loved you once. Once is enough for a man like him. He expects you to take him at his word."

"But that's not the way the world works and he knows it. What's wrong with being reminded? I don't see where there's anything wrong with that. I tell him I love him all the time and all he says is he knows. Not even *me too*. Just he knows. What kind of reassurance is that?"

Angela took Josie's small hand and placed it in hers. There was so much she could tell her, to help settle her down, but she also knew that words were never going to be enough for somebody like Josie.

"You've got to be patient with him, Josie," she said. "Just a year ago you had written him off just like everybody else. Remember? You were declaring him guilty of sexual harassment too. Your doubt broke his heart, a heart that had been broken too many times before. He can't take emotionalism the way he used to, dear. You've got to understand that."

"But I made it up to him. I investigated. I got the facts together, and I even lost my job when I gave my story to the competitor. Just to clear Ben's name. How can he think I would hurt him again?"

"He's a cautious man, Josie. I'm sorry, but he is. He's still getting used to a woman like you, just as you're still getting used to a man like him. You've got to be patient."

Josie wanted to ask her. She wanted to come out and ask her point blank if she ever had sex with Ben. But she couldn't do it. This showed, she felt, either a lot of growth or a lot of fear.

"Ben has a lot on his mind these days, Josie," Angela continued. "Between worrying about you and trying to handle the pressures of a possible presidency—"

"Presidency? What presidency?"

Angela looked at her. "Denlex, Josie."

"What about Denlex?"

"Ben may very well become the next head of Denlex. I thought you knew."

Josie was stunned. She had no idea, but she couldn't let Angela see just how in the dark Ben really kept her. "Oh, yeah," she said, as if she had known all along. But how did Angela know? "I just didn't realize you had been told. You know Ben. He likes to keep things under wraps. Fred told you about it?"

"Ben told me."

"Ben? I didn't know you had been talking to Ben."

Angela smiled. She seemed to relish this role. "Oh yes. Benjamin and I talk on the telephone practically every week."

"Every week? Why would you need to talk to Ben every week?"

"We're friends, Josie. Very old and dear friends. It's only natural that we would speak on the telephone often. Just as you and Scotty would."

"Not every week we wouldn't. Why would Ben be calling you up every single week?"

"Okay," Angela said, "let's back up a moment. Thirty-one years ago—that's right, me, Ben, and Fred have been friends just that long."

"I know all of that."

"And we have always been close. When one of us goes away we check on him every chance we get. Ben is a part of our family, Josie, you know he is. So don't act as if there's something strange or wrong going on here because you know there's not. Okay?"

Josie sighed. "Okay," she said. "And I'm sorry. I'm just so . . . I don't know what's wrong with me."

"You're insecure. And you're in love. My advice: stop worrying about it. Because I'm telling you, you will drive Ben away."

Josie looked at Angela. The idea of Ben leaving her was unbearable. "Did he ask you to talk to me?"

Angela hesitated. "Yes."

"Why?"

"You know why, Josie. You're a tough lady who stands her ground on every cause imaginable and Ben, although he worries about some of your positions, he loves your conviction. But sister, in the love department . . ." Josie smiled.

"I'm a mess."

"You're a mess. And I'm going to be blunt with you. Ben is of an age now, Josie, where he isn't sure if he wants to take on that mess."

Josie's heart dropped. "That's what he told you?"

"Give him a reason to want to stay, Josie. Prove to him that you still have room for growth. You're very fortunate, dear. I don't think you realize just how blessed you are to have a man like Benjamin in your life."

"Especially when there's a thousand women out there ready to take my place in a heartbeat," Josie said.

"Or sooner."

"Women like you?"

Angela laughed. "You are hopeless, you know that? I'm telling you what the problem is, and you declare you understand, then you fall right back into that insecurity trap, right back into it. You've got a long way to go, my dear."

Josie sighed and looked at the sculpture again. It was all so together. Why was it so hard for her to get there? She looked at Angela. "He gave me a pair of beautiful diamond earrings for my birthday this morning."

"That was nice."

"Yeah, it was. Of course I was expecting an engagement ring."

Angela nodded. "I see."

"Yep. But you know what's crazy? I honestly believe that if Ben totally commits to me, I mean, without a doubt, totally, then all of my insecurities will just vanish."

Angela shook her head. She couldn't disagree more. "You're kidding yourself, Josie."

"I know, but that's how I feel." She said this and paused. Then she looked at Angela. "You've known him for a long time. And as you said, you know him well. Can I ask you a question?"

"You can ask."

Josie exhaled. "Do you think Ben will ever marry me?"

Angela hesitated. She wanted to shirk the issue, but she couldn't. Josie was always holding herself out as this great seeker of truth, so she decided not to disappoint. She decided to give Josie a quick dose of her own medicine. "Unless you get it together," she told her, "no."

*   *   *

Deuce sat in the back of the club on purpose, deciding that he wanted the feel of hanging out rather than the reality. Females were all over the dance floor, and the males just couldn't keep up. He leaned back and shook his head. *Men never kept up, and those females love it,* he thought. Control freaks, every one of them. Got to have that control. But that was why he loved Josie. She was different. *She isn't like these freaks up in here,* he thought. She allowed a man to be a man, and she had much love for that man and was committed to him. All the other women he ever met didn't want a man. They wanted a robot, a child, somebody to boss around, to tell what to do, to control.

"Hello, Deuce," a female voice said. Deuce reluctantly looked her way. He recognized the face, the fat cheeks and big eyes, but not in a million years would he place the name.

"Hey there."

She smiled and moved toward his table. "I thought that was you. What's up?"

"Just chillin'."

"All you can do in this hole. They ain't even playing hot songs. I said, *damn.* This place is not the place to get your groove on."

"I hear that."

"May I?" She was asking if she could take a seat. It was the last thing Deuce wanted, but he didn't object. "I'm here with my girl Rae," she said as she sat down. "She was all up in some man's face so I started feeling like an extra couch, know what I'm saying? Then I saw you. Or, at least, I was hoping it was you."

"How you been?"

"I been all right."

"Been a good girl?"

She laughed. "I can lie to you now."

Deuce smiled. "Just say no, that's what I always say."

"No."

Deuce held his drink up to her.

"What about you? Been a good boy?"

He sipped from his glass of wine, then sat it down on the table. "I been aw'ight."

"That's what I'm saying. Too much goodness and you get played. And me and you, Deuce, we ain't never been that kind of person."

She pulled out a cigarette and offered him one. He shook his head and watched as she lit up. She wasn't a pretty woman, just average in the face, and the way she inhaled, like a smoker from way back, kept him uninterested. She didn't have a whole lot going for her at all, Deuce thought, looking at her, at her husky hands and chunky arms, but her fat behind and big boobs kept the brothers coming. Some brothers couldn't live without the back. Josie had back too, Deuce thought, but it was all proportioned. Everything exactly where it should be. But this hot mama sitting next to him had, he felt, a little too much of everything.

Deuce also figured her to be the hit-and-run type like him, somebody accustomed to getting exactly what she wanted, and that was why she was so confident sitting there. She just knew she was going to get her ram on tonight.

She took a slow drag on her cigarette, and then leaned back. "I take it you're here alone," she said. She looked like she was already nodding, which astounded Deuce.

"I'm always alone."

"Good-looking brother like you. Shit. I could have gave you a taste here and there. Why didn't you call me?"

Now it begins, Deuce thought. He didn't call her back. That was the rub. They'd had a thing together, although he still couldn't remember what, and he hadn't called her back. Her sudden visit to his table was no accident. It was as calculated as she was. Sistergirl was out for revenge.

"Not that it matters," she added, as if she could read his sudden air of cautiousness. "You didn't exactly promise me no rose garden."

Deuce nodded. "I'm glad to hear that."

"So," she asked, looking Deuce over, at his wild Afro and cute, oval-shaped eyes, "you seeing somebody now?"

Deuce hesitated. They always tried to play tough but as soon as you sleep with one of them they try to lay some claim. "Yeah, I am," he said. It was a lie, but it was protection.

"Who?"

"You don't know her."

"You don't know who I know." Now she was defensive. It was all he needed.

"Her name is Josie," he said and smiled. He wished.

"Josie? You talking about that stank-ass female over in Brainerd? Josie the dominatrix?"

Deuce laughed. Josie a dominatrix? Not on his life. "No, not her. Not *that* Josie. She's nothing like that."

"How good is she?"

"Sorry?"

"What is up with you, Deuce? You know what I'm talking about. Why you trying to front, trying to play so standoffish all of a sudden? I bet she ain't better than me."

Now he remembered her. Martha. No, Margaret. Or something with an M. They had spent a night together, not all that long ago, either. *And she was right,* he thought. She was good.

"No," he said, "she's not as good as you."

She smiled. "Don't you know I know it. Josie. Sound like some white chick. She a white chick?"

"No."

"And she ain't as good as me?"

"That's right."

"Then lets go," she said. "Unless you scared of this Josie?"

Deuce looked at her. *Yeah,* he thought, *I'm terrified of Josie.* But he left the club with her anyway.

Back at his place, M went to freshen up. Deuce stood behind his bar thinking, not about the woman in his home, but about Josie. As soon as he heard the bathroom door clang shut, he pulled out his cell phone and called her number, a number he had committed to memory, a number he called most every night since the first day she started working for him—in his dreams.

It rang and rang. The answering machine picked up, and he heard her soprano, upbeat voice. "This is Josie. I'm not available. Please leave your name and number and I'll holler." He smiled. It was so her. She'll holler. Then he looked at his wristwatch. It was closing in on one A.M., and that depressed him because he knew. Because wherever Josie was, he was certain that Ben Braddock was right there too.

They both were happy and exhausted as they walked slowly to Josie's front door. "Come in for a nightcap," she said with a smile as Ben unlocked her door.

"Can't. Got to get an early start in the morning."

"Ah, come on, Ben. Just a nightcap."

Ben looked at Josie, his exhausted eyes barely able to focus. "Not this time, sweety."

Josie exhaled. She wanted him to make love to her so bad she could hardly contain herself. But he was tired and she knew it, so she decided to just be grateful for the day, a glorious day, and stop tripping.

"Okay," she said. "I'll let you slide this time, since you've been so good to me all day."

Ben smiled. "That's my girl," he said, and kissed her on the forehead. But the question Josie had asked Angela was still burning deep inside of her. And she knew the night could not end without Ben answering it for himself.

"Thank you for a terrific birthday, Ben," she said. "It was so great seeing Scotty again, and Fred and Angela too. Thank you from the bottom of my heart."

Ben nodded. He loved it when she was like this. "You know you're welcome, babe."

"But I've just got one question to ask you."

He sighed. No clean getaways for him. "Sock it to me," he said.

"Don't say it like that. Why did you have to say it like that?"

"Because I know you, Josephine. You've never been able to let well enough alone. There's always got to be some philosophical discussion at the end, even though you know I'm so tired I can barely stand up. So let me have it."

He was right. She had to learn to pick her moments. And right here, right now, at this time of night, wasn't one of them.

"I just wanted to ask you a question, Ben, that's all."

"Ask it."

She paused. She now didn't know what to ask.

"I'm very tired, Josephine."

"What's the name of that cologne you're wearing?" she asked.

Ben smiled, and then he laughed out loud. "You are something else, you know that?"

She smiled. "I've been told."

"Goodnight, darling," he said, kissed her one more time on the forehead, and then walked away still smiling, still happy to know that somebody was still able to make him laugh.

CHAPTER 9

Josie's Mustang sped toward the east end of Saint Germain, as if she didn't know what a speed limit meant. Even after parking on the street a block from the *Journal* and running like a mad woman for the entrance doors, she was still nearly three hours late. She dropped her purse and keys at her desk and hurried into Deuce's office ready to hear his wrath. But he smiled.

"Stop being so predictable, Josie," he said. "Sit down."

"I overslept big time," she said, sitting down in the chair beside his desk. "It was nine o'clock when I woke up. I said *damn*, Deuce is gonna have a fit."

"Was your boyfriend late too?"

"Ben? I don't know. I doubt it. Why would you ask about Ben?"

"I just thought he would have woken you up."

"We don't live together, Deuce. Remember?"

"That's right. My bad. You did tell me that. Nice suit."

She looked down at her red dress pants and sleeveless vest, her black suit coat to top it off, and she looked back up at Deuce.

"Thanks."

"Do you make your own clothes?"

"Now that's funny. No, sir, I do not. I buy my own clothes. What about you? Make your own clothes?"

Deuce laughed. "Oh, you're good. Quick. I like that."

"Well, anyway," Josie said as she slowly rose to her feet, "I'd better get to work. I'm late as it is."

But Deuce motioned her to sit back down. "Just sit down and relax, Josie, come on," he said. "What's the rush, anyway? I'm the boss, remember? And I haven't seen you all weekend."

It sounded like an odd thing to say, Josie thought, since he never saw her on weekends. But she sat back down. "So what's up?" she asked.

"Happy birthday."

"Well, thank you, Deuce." She didn't realize he would even know her birthday.

He pulled a long, rectangular-shaped, gift-wrapped box out of his desk drawer and handed it to her.

"I had hoped to give you this on your birthday."

"Now isn't this nice? You didn't have to give me anything, Deuce."

"I know I didn't have to. But I thought it might cheer you up."

"Cheer me up?"

"Yeah. You seemed down in the dumps the last couple weeks."

"Did I?"

"Others noticed it too."

Josie began unwrapping the box. She didn't recall being particularly depressed lately, especially where people would notice it. She loved her job and her coworkers were all right by her, although she wasn't especially friendly with any of them. Except maybe Deuce. But if anything, life was looking up.

"I called you this weekend," Deuce said. "Was gonna ask if I could come over."

Josie looked at Deuce. "Come over for what?"

"To wish you a happy birthday. That's what friends do. Remember?"

Josie smiled. "Oh, yeah. But you didn't have to make a fuss over my birthday."

"It was no fuss. I called you really late, something like one in the morning. But I didn't get an answer. You probably don't answer phone calls that late at night, huh?"

"I answer. I just wasn't home."

"Where were you?"

Josie smiled. It was still sweet to her. "Florida."

Deuce nodded. And then smiled. "Damn."

"We visited some old friends. It was great."

Deuce sat there, glaring at her.

"What?" she asked, uncomfortable with that odd look of his he sometimes had.

"Nothing."

"Come on, Deuce. One friend to another. What's up?"

"Nothing's up. Finish opening your gift."

Josie hesitated. Deuce's crush on her was so obvious sometimes that it was almost unbearable. She would just as soon hand him back his gift than lead him into believing that she shared his affection. But she looked at him, at his droopy clown eyes, and she couldn't do him like that. He was a good guy. She opened the gift.

It was a heavy black box with Pierre Cardin scribbled on it. Inside was a nice gold-plated pen and pencil set. She was so relieved that the gift wasn't something personal, like a necklace or watch, something she would have a hard time explaining, that she smiled greatly.

"Oh, Deuce," she said, "it's lovely. You shouldn't have."

"It was less than twenty bucks, Josie. It's no big deal."

"Don't say that."

"I mean, hey, if I could fly you to Florida, Paris, or anywhere your heart desired, I would have. I didn't know the game. I didn't know your boy swung like that."

"Swung like what? What are you talking about?"

"I would have done better if I would have known."

"Deuce, just stop it, okay? This is great. It's practical."

"That's what I said. You can go to Florida just so many times. But that pen set is a gift that keeps on giving."

Josie laughed. "Exactly."

"In a lot of ways it's better than some lousy trip to Florida."

"I'm not gonna go that far . . ." Josie said.

Deuce leaned back, pretending to be genuinely hurt.

"Deuce! I'm kidding. I like this. Thanks."

Deuce smiled. "I was kidding too, friend. And you're welcome. I just wanted to let you know how grateful I am to have you on my team—and in my life."

Josie stared at the pen set instead of her boss. The story of her life, she thought. She would give a million bucks if Ben would be as attentive to her as Deuce tried to be, but Ben, unfortunately, didn't roll like that. So she was stuck hoping that her fortunes would reverse, that Ben would crave her more and Deuce would just ease up. She looked at him. "I'm grateful to be on your team too, Deuce," she said, "but I think you need to understand something."

"I understand. No need to even go there, J. You got you a sugar daddy and you aim to keep him. I know the deal."

"A sugar daddy? Now wait a minute."

"Let's keep it on the real, J. Let's do that much. That's what friends do too. Benjamin Braddock is, let's face it, your sugar daddy."

"That's ridiculous. He ain't nobody's sugar daddy, okay? Every female in America would want him, are you kidding me? Women would pay to be with him, he don't have to give up anything. Trust me on that."

"All right. Damn. I was just kidding around. Don't take my head off."

Josie exhaled. "I'm sorry. But let's not play about Ben, if you don't mind."

Deuce nodded. "Okay, I can respect that."

Josie stood up. "And thanks again for the pen set. It was very thoughtful and, yes, practical. I appreciate it, Deuce."

Deuce smiled his gorgeous white smile. "You're welcome. Now get to work."

Josie laughed. "Two-face."

"Takes one to know one, baby."

Josie smiled and left Deuce's office. Deuce leaned back in his chair and shook his head. Braddock was like a mountain in Josie's eyes. A got damn Everest. *How in hell,* Deuce thought, *do you knock a mountain down?*

When Josie walked out of Deuce's office, Ben was on her mind too. But her coworkers didn't think so. They stared as if she had a story to tell when she stepped out with Deuce's unwrapped gift in her hand. They just knew she and Deuce had it going on like that. They just knew the gorgeous brother and the good-looking sister were hitting the heights as often as they could. It used to bother Josie when she first came on board, and many times she wanted to open her mouth and set those sisters straight. But now she didn't give a damn.

It was turning out to be a slow day for Josie, as the hours seemed to lumber by and no assignments had yet to come up that required her expertise. At least none Deuce wanted her to bother with. "You'll be wasting your time on that story, Josie," he would say. Or, "I'm not about to send my best reporter on something that lame." It was always something. Always an excuse to keep Josie right under his nose. She wanted to confront him about it, to tell him to hold on, he needed to get a life if he thought for a second he'd be controlling an inch of hers. But, she didn't even go there with Deuce. He was just trying to help a sister out, just trying to show her a little favor here and there, and she could appreciate that. But she could also appreciate the line. And if he crossed it, favors or no favors, she'd have no problem putting the brother right back where he belonged.

So she didn't sweat Deuce, either. She accepted the slowness of the day and got to work. She had no pressing assignments so she was forced to work on rewrites, which she hated, but she knew she had to do something. By mid-afternoon, when she was finally in what she considered to be a good working groove and had practically cleared her desk of all her backlog, the pace of her day changed dramatically.

"Josie Ross, may I help you?" she said cheerfully as she picked up line two on her desk phone.

"Is this Josephine Ross?" the voice on the other end of the phone asked.

"Yes, may I help you?"

"How are you, Josephine?" The voice was a slow, soft, female's voice, a voice unknown to Josie.

"I'm fine," she said. "May I help you?"

"It won't work. You've got to understand that."

"What won't work?"

"He said you was just a friend of his. I asked him repeatedly and he told me you was just his friend. Now this new shit."

Josie frowned. "Who is this?"

"He's my man, you understand that? Ain't no bubblegum ho like you taking my man away from me."

Josie could feel her heart racing. Who was she talking about? Deuce? *Ben?* "Look, lady, I don't know what you're talking about. What man?"

"I know your type. Think you all that. But your little magical charms will not be working this time, sister. I love him, you understand me? We were trying to make our relationship work, and it was working. He was getting you out of his system once and for all. And now this Florida shit. But it won't work, not this time."

It was Ben. She was talking about Ben. Josie held onto the phone with both hands, as if she needed the support.

"Who are you?"

"None of your damn business, that's who. Don't worry about who I am. Just leave him alone."

"Leave who alone? Ben?"

"Who do you think?"

"You have a relationship with Ben?"

"We love each other, that's what kind of relationship we have. We met during a conference at Denlex four months ago and we've been lovers since. He wines and dines me and makes love to me almost every night. That's why he don't never be with your ass, because he's always with me. He loves me. You got it? He loves being with me."

Josie swallowed hard. It couldn't be true. "I don't believe you," she said.

"And? Don't believe me, then. But you better stay away from Ben!" The phone went dead.

"Wait!" Josie said so loudly, so desperately, that others in the newsroom looked her way. She paused, and hung up too.

She sat back, reliving every word: how they shared the same interests, how he wined and dined her, how he made love to her almost every night! And suddenly she had to get away, to get some air. She pulled her purse out of her desk drawer and began grabbing items out of it, from combs to compacts to her wallet, until her cell phone turned up. She rushed out of the newsroom like she'd pass out if she didn't hurry, then out of the heavy doors of the converted warehouse building.

She stood like a spooked basket case on the sidewalk of Saint Germain. Her suit coat was back inside the building, which meant she was wearing only her red pants and sleeveless vest, but the cold didn't bother her. She was too excited. She was too devastated by the revelation that there could be another woman in Ben's life to pay any attention to the whip and whirl of the wind.

She phoned him, pressing the numbers so fast that she pressed the wrong numbers twice, causing her to redial both times. When she finally got through and Whitney told her that Ben was unavailable, her anger replaced her fear.

"Listen to me, Whitney, and you listen good. I am not asking you to put Ben on this phone, I am telling you. I don't care if he's in a meeting with the president, you get him on this phone! And you tell him that if he does not take my call he'll be sorry, because I'll come to his office and show off my natural ass—you hear me? I've got to talk to him!"

There was a pause on the line as Whitney, Josie was certain, was digesting all she had just said. Then she asked her to hold on. Within seconds Ben was on the line.

"What is it, Josephine?" he asked. And as soon as she heard his voice, that firm, hard voice of his, tears came to her eyes.

"Josephine?"

"She called me," Josie said, her voice emotionally hoarse already.

There was a hesitation in Ben's voice as well, which didn't help. "Who called you?"

"She said she was your lover. She said y'all been together for four months. Four months, Ben!"

Ben didn't respond. And his silence spoke volumes to Josie.

"You make love to her almost every night. But you can't be bothered with me but once every few weeks like I'm the other got damn woman!" The realization caused Josie to close her eyes, as if truth could disappear that easily. "It wasn't true, Ben. What you were telling me wasn't true. It wasn't because I was young and inexperienced and too emotional. It was because you were gettin' yours somewhere else! How could you do something like that to me? You know how much I love you!" There was no response from Ben, not even a denial, and it angered Josie. "Answer me, dammit!" she yelled.

"Not until you settle yourself down," he replied.

"Settle down? What the hell do you think this is? Some woman calls me and tells me she's playin' bed-rock with my man and I'm supposed to remain calm? I guess I'm behaving childishly now too, is that what you're trying to say? I'm too damn emotional again? Well you kiss my ass, Ben! You hear me? You and your women and every man that's ever been born can kiss my emotional ass!"

As soon as those words dripped from Josie's mouth, the connection was gone. At first she didn't believe it. She even said his name again, but it was true. He had hung up in her face. She shook her head and turned off her cell phone.

The heavy doors of the *Journal* building crept open and Deuce, as if on cue, stepped out. Josie had by now drifted away from the front door. She stood there, her back to Deuce, her behind round and firm underneath her tight red pants. Deuce walked slowly toward her, cautiously, until she turned his way. He smiled.

"You okay?" he asked, but Josie didn't respond. "You looked pretty upset when you left. I was just checking." Still nothing from Josie. "Okay. I know when I'm licked. Didn't mean to get up in your business." He said this, and then made a slow move to turn around and leave.

"He's got another woman," Josie said, but without emotion, and Deuce turned back toward her.

"She called and told me. He loves her, according to her."

"He denies it, of course."

Josie hesitated. He hadn't even bothered. "Yes," she said. "I guess. I don't know. I don't care. I can't believe this, Deuce! How could I have been so dumb?"

"Now hold on, Josie. Don't start beating yourself up. Just because some woman called doesn't mean it's true. She could have been lying."

Josie frowned. "She wasn't lying." She turned her back to Deuce. He wanted to reach out and touch her, but he knew he couldn't. He was winning. She was finally seeing Braddock for the bastard he really was, and good fortune was beginning to turn his way. But he had to tread lightly.

"I know you're upset, Josie. But you can't let something like this devastate you."

"She knew about us," Josie said. Deuce waited for more. But Josie only exhaled.

"Us?" he asked.

"Me and Ben. She knew."

Deuce hesitated, then he walked around Josie until they were face to face. "I'm not following you, kiddo."

"He doesn't make love to me, Deuce."

"He . . . *What?*"

"He doesn't make love to me. I mean, he does. But hardly ever. And she knew about that. She said he's never with me because he be with her all the time. How could she say that unless she knew he wasn't with me all those nights, Deuce?"

Deuce paused. He knew he had to play devil's advocate; he knew he had to convince her that he was disappointed too. "I see what you're saying, Josie," he said, "but let's think about this. A phone call from some anonymous woman isn't what I'd call compelling evidence of infidelity."

"You said yourself he was a player. L. L. Cool Ben? Remember? You said that. And you were right." She hesitated, waiting, unsure if she should say more but unable to remain silent. "Remember that night I was in the hospital and you drove me to my car?"

She wouldn't have a drink with him. He remembered it well. "I remember."

"I went by his house after I left you. Just to talk to him. And he wasn't even home. Then he comes driving up when I was leaving like it was no big deal to him. No big deal? What man is out at three o'clock in the morning unless something's undercover? Now you tell me that. He was taking me for some kind of fool. Like I was so in love with his ass that I'd be glad to sit back and take it. Like hell I will! I'm not about to bury my head in no sand for nobody, okay? That woman wouldn't be wasting her time calling me if something wasn't up!"

She looked at Deuce when she said this, looked into his understanding eyes, and she couldn't contain her emotions any longer. The tears returned. And she fell. She fell right into Deuce Jefferson's arms.

She spent the afternoon trying her best to stay busy. She covered a pro-abortion rally, interviewed the sister of a murder victim, and then sat behind her desk writing up both stories. Deuce had told her long ago to take her behind home, but she wasn't about to do that. She wasn't about to go home and sit around crying her eyes out over some man who couldn't even be faithful to her. No way, she thought. She wasn't even trying to deal with that craziness right now. At least at work, she thought, she could focus on other people's problems; at least at work she was too busy to worry about just how pitiful her life really was.

But Ben showed up. It was late, after six, and Josie was one of the few reporters still hanging around the *Journal*'s offices. She was at her computer, pecking away feverishly, when she became aware of somebody approaching her desk. She glanced up from her computer screen to see who it was, but when she realized it was Ben she did a double take. He was in a black suit and tie, and moved slowly. His eyes looked at her with a hard, cold stare and they didn't so much as glance away. He was upset and she could see it all over his face. He was the one with the bitch on the side, but he was upset? Josie wanted to puke.

Deuce saw him too. He saw him from the prism of his office glass. He stood up, when Ben walked in, and moved up to the window for a better view. He never figured Braddock to be the type to show up. A woman bust a brother like that, Deuce figured he'd just accept his fate and move on to the next conquest. But Josie was involved. Braddock may have been a lot of things, Deuce decided, but a fool wasn't one of them.

Ben stood at Josie's desk without saying a word. He had both hands in his pants pockets and was staring intensely at her. He looked drained and angry at the same time, she thought, a man just one wrong word away from losing it, and she tried to stare back. He wasn't about to lay some guilt trip on her, as if she had done something wrong, but looking into his eyes made her too upset. She decided to get on with it.

"Did you come here for a reason or just to stare at me?" she asked him. He remained still. He didn't so much as bat an eye. "Which is it? To stare at me? Because if it is I can tell you now that it won't work."

"What's wrong with you, Josephine?" he asked her, his face seemingly pained from trying to understand just what drives this woman before him. "You receive a phone call from some woman you know nothing about, some anonymous phone call, and that's all it takes?"

"You can minimize it all you want. You can act like it's no big deal all you care to. But I know better."

"You don't know a damn thing!"

Josie hesitated, surprised by Ben's tone. But she couldn't keep giving in so easily.

"I know more than you think," she finally said.

"You need to stop it, Josephine, you understand me? You need to stop this nonsense right here and right now."

"What nonsense? All I did was finally face the truth."

"What the hell kind of truth do you keep talking about? That same truth that nearly destroyed us in Florida? That kind? Truth based on half-truths and innuendo? That's all it takes with you, isn't it? If it has the least plausibility, then you're off and running. That's all you need."

"Right. That's all I need. You don't do a damn thing. It's all in my imagination."

"Don't you talk to me that way."

"I'll talk to you any way I damn well please! Who the hell are you?"

Ben sighed and folded his arms. If she didn't wear him out he didn't know what could. "I don't have a lot of patience, Josie. And you're pushing it."

"Then leave, damn it. I ain't got no patience, either!"

"All right, that's it," Ben said as he unfolded his arms. "Get your things and let's go."

Josie smiled. "What?"

"Get your things and let's go."

"You must be out of your mind. I'm not about to go anywhere with you!"

As soon as she spoke those words, Deuce came out of his office as if he were some Superman coming to the rescue. That only made it worse.

"I think you need to leave this building, partner," he said. Deuce couldn't seem to get to Josie's side fast enough. Josie quickly stood up as Ben turned toward him.

"It's all right, Deuce," she said to head off his advance.

"We're leaving now."

"You don't have to go anywhere with him," Deuce said, staring at Ben. Ben exhaled, his stomach boiling in pain.

"Deuce, it's okay," Josie insisted. "Just go on back to your office. I'm fine."

Deuce stared at Ben, checking the brother out from head to toe, and then he looked at Josie. "You certain about that?"

"Yes."

"You don't have to be afraid of him around here."

"I know that, Deuce. I'm not afraid."

"Okay, but call me if you need me."

"I will."

"I mean no matter what."

"I will, Deuce."

Deuce nodded. "Okay," he said. Then he looked at Braddock one more time, looked at Josie, whom he just couldn't read sometimes, and went back to the cold confines of his small office.

Ben stared at Deuce as he walked back to that office, and he could only shake his head. The way Josie got him so crazy sometimes he wondered why he didn't just let Deuce have her. They matched. They were both impulsive and excitable and ready to jump to conclusions at the drop of a hat. But then he looked at Josie, at the woman who soothed and angered him to heights he'd never experienced. And he knew it was easier said than done.

"Where are we going?" she asked as she grabbed her purse from her desk drawer.

"Away from here."

"I know that, Ben. What about my car?"

"We'll get it later."

Josie paused and stared at Ben. Why she didn't tell him to take a hike with all of his demands she'd never know. But she didn't tell him a thing. She went right along with him. She grabbed her briefcase with her purse, and then led him toward the exit doors.

Deuce remained in his office, watching them as they hurried out. Watching that smooth Braddock take Josie away to fill her up with lies of his fidelity. Josie was so in love and so naive that she would believe anything he told her. Deuce would give an arm to be right where Ben Braddock was, to have Josie's complete and seemingly unshakable loyalty. Someday he would be there. Deuce believed in his soul that one day very soon the tables would turn and he would take Ben Braddock's place. Josephine Ross would still be loyal, but she'd be completely and unshakably loyal to him.

Josie leaned back against the headrest of Ben's Mercedes and watched the dark road ahead. What she thought was going to be a short drive to Ben's place turned out to be an hour-long trip up Highway 23. She turned and watched him as he drove. He'd drive slowly, then faster, as if he was distracted, as if he was thinking about some heavy-duty issues and had forgotten that she was even in the car. He took slow drags on his cigarette, listened to his jazz, and stared straight ahead. Josie had so many questions to ask him. She could burst if she didn't get some answers soon, but she also knew she had to hear him out first. Was that woman telling the truth when she called and told her story, or was it a pack of lies? If there was indeed another woman, was it all true? Was he really in love with her? Did he really sleep with her?

They ended up in Willmar, Minnesota, a small, wooded, lakeside town some fifty miles out of Saint Cloud. Ben turned down a long, dark road that led to a small cabin by the lake. The lake was beautiful to Josie, so peaceful that just seeing it helped to calm her down. Ben looked out at the lake too, as if he needed its calming force just as badly as Josie. Then he got out of the car.

Josie leaned back and watched as he walked slowly around the front of the car, his suit coat flapping wildly with the heavy winds, his every step appearing to confirm just how gut-wrenching and methodical his thought process was. She kept watching him as he opened the car door for her and reached out his hand. She stepped out of the car, but she did not touch his hand.

Ben glared at Josie as she stepped out, but he was determined to keep his cool. He closed the door behind her and did not hesitate. He walked toward the lake. Josie stood by the car, but then felt foolish and followed him.

He stood at the shoreline, where the water lapped over his dress shoes, then backed off. Josie stood beside him. He looked at her, her arms folded and her braids blowing back in the wind, and he took off his suit coat and placed it across her shoulders. She wrapped herself in the coat that seemed to swallow her, and then she looked at Ben.

"Was that woman telling the truth?" she asked, desperately seeking some special words that could take away the ache that had settled deep inside her. But Ben, as she should have expected, wouldn't cooperate that easily. He seemed less concerned about some woman calling Josie, and more concerned about Josie's reaction to that call.

"You've got to learn to trust me, Josephine," he said almost as if it were a warning. "You have got to have enough confidence in me to know what I will and will not do."

"But is it true?" she asked.

Ben frowned. "Did you hear me? Did you hear a word I just said? Your behavior is destroying our relationship, lady, and you'd better understand that."

Josie looked out across the dark lake, as the wind caused it to ripple, and she knew she couldn't do it anymore. Somebody called and told her either the truth or lies today. Ben telling her to just blindly trust him, without even bothering to tell her what was going on, wasn't enough for her. Not anymore. She lived her life believing in truth, in following the facts, not the emotion, not the fiction, not that blind kind of lovesick loyalty she'd been displaying ever since they moved to Minnesota.

"Tell me what's going on, Ben," she said to him. "Tell me what's happening."

He released a heavy sigh, as if he'd had it up to here. "Nothing's happening, Josephine."

"But why would a woman call me, out of the clear blue sky, if something wasn't up? Why would she just call me like that, Ben?"

"How am I supposed to know why some woman would call you?"

"But she knew about us. She knew you didn't make love to me that often or she wouldn't have said what she said. How would she know that? When she said you were with her most every night, I could have called her a liar. But she knew I wouldn't, because she knew what she was talking about."

Ben shook his head. "Right. She knows. Just like those women in Florida knew. You believed them too. Didn't you, Josie?"

"Yes, I did. Until the truth came out. I'm sorry if I don't measure up to what you want me to be, but you need to quit trying to act like you don't understand me yet. You knew what you were getting when you asked me to move to Minnesota with you. You knew how I was, Ben. I feel I've changed in a lot of ways, in a lot of good ways. But I'm still me. That ain't gonna change. And just telling me you don't know what's going on ain't gonna cut it this time. I'm not like you. People can't just tell me something and I just—"

"And you just believe it? Is that what you were going to say, Josephine? That woman told you something. You believed her."

Josie almost fell back in the sand as she realized what she was doing. It was just like Florida all over again. A woman called her on the phone claiming to be Ben's lover and she believed her. Just like that. That was all it took. Words. Words from a stranger's mouth. Yet every word this man beside her had spoken, this good man, a man who cared enough to have driven her far away to a place of calm, was questioned by her. She believed a stranger, some woman she'd never even met, and doubted her good man. The anguish she felt, that she had so easily fallen into that same trap again, caused her to suddenly feel lightheaded, foolish, so damn green, and she couldn't deal with it anymore. She looked at Ben. And collapsed at the shore.

* * *

The cabin was warm. Wood crackled in the fireplace, and Josie was lying in a soft bed. It was a quiet, rustic place, she thought, with brick-lined walls and a big bear's head hanging over the fireplace. Hunting rifles were in a large glass case, and a set of golf clubs were in a corner. Most of the furnishings were leather, all grayish brown and overstuffed. The music in the background was jazz of course, which relaxed Josie beyond what she'd earlier thought possible.

Ben came to her with a cup of hot coffee. She sat up against the headboard and gladly took the coffee from his hands. He sat on the edge of the bed, and then leaned his body over her legs, his arm resting on the other side, and smiled. "Still cold in here to you?"

"No, not at all. It feels great."

"I'm glad you're feeling better. You had the chills at one point. I don't know, sometimes that fireplace is enough. Sometimes it's not."

"It's plenty tonight. But how did you find out about this place? This is really cool. Who owns it?"

"I found out about it through my realtor. I own it."

Josie stopped sipping her coffee and looked at Ben. "You? You own this?"

"Yes."

"You? Own *this?*"

Ben smiled. "Yes."

"Since when?"

"Since about ten years ago."

"Ten years? You've owned this beautiful, peaceful cabin for ten years, Ben?"

"Thereabouts, yeah."

"Why didn't I know about it?"

"You've been in my life for less than two years, honey. You can't expect to know everything about me in that short span." Josie nodded, but Ben could tell she was disappointed. "I used to spend my summers here. Just a place to get away from Florida, Josie. Nothing more than that."

Josie smiled, although she was sick and tired of surprises. "Well, I like it. Even though I'm sure I'm not the first female you've brought up in here."

Ben smiled. "Glad you like it."

"But I'm not the first. Am I right?"

"Josie."

"Okay, forget it. But just so we're clear: you've had other women here before, haven't you?"

"You will not let up."

"I just wanna know, Ben, that's all. Have other women been here before?"

"Yes. Before I met you, yes. Satisfied?"

Josie nodded. "That's all I wanted to know."

Ben shook his head and sighed. His hope, that they could actually get on the same page for once and stay there, seemed more hopeless as the days drifted by.

"Let's stay here tonight," Josie said, as if she had something more to prove. "We may as well."

Ben looked at her, at the way her entire face lit up when she was excited. The idea of curling up in that soft bed beside her, with the fireplace going and the music soothing, was tempting. But he decided against it.

"We'll stay another hour or so but then we'll head on back."

"But why?"

"Because I don't want to make that drive in the morning."

"Then I'll drive."

"Josie," he said. "We're going back tonight." She knew that tone.

Josie rolled her eyes. She felt as if he was rationing himself out to her, a little at a time, and that wasn't good enough for her tonight. She had tension she needed to work off, and emotions that had already overtaken her, and Ben, she felt, was just the man for the job. They had problems—that woman's call would never be easily dismissed by Josie—but she couldn't worry about that now.

"Will you refresh my cup, please?" she asked him as she handed him her half-empty cup of coffee.

He gladly obliged her, and went out to the kitchen to pour out her old coffee, replacing it with a fresh fill-up. When he returned to the bedroom, with the cup in hand, he nearly stopped in his tracks. Josie had completely disrobed and was sitting in bed with the covers pulled back. Ben stared at her, at her face first and then her attractive, naked body, and he could feel his heartbeat quicken. He slowly sat the cup on the night stand, and then he exhaled.

"Josie," he started saying, but before he could complete his thought, before he could remind her that his plan didn't include *this,* she lay down and turned her back to him. She knew he was an ass man—a lover of back from way back—and he could never resist hers.

She lay there quietly, certain that he was standing behind her thinking long and hard about the implications of it all, as if making love to your woman required all that forethought, but she also knew he was staring lustfully at her.

But he was taking longer to make up his mind than she had hoped. She decided to lie on her stomach and give him the full effect of what he was missing, to make sure he clearly understood what her body language was trying to say. But he still didn't make a move. She was about to tell him a thing or two, like what was his damn problem, but before she could open her mouth, she felt the bounce of the bed and his fully clothed body lying down beside her. She turned and looked at him, as he began to rub his hand along her back and then her backside, and the inexplicable guilt on his face, a guilt so pronounced, put a smile on hers.

"It's okay, Ben," she said, finding his hesitation almost adorable. "I trust you."

Ben smiled too, as he sometimes loved her ability to take life as it comes, and then he looked into her eyes. Nobody turned him on the way Josie did. Nobody. And by the time he took her into his arms and began kissing her, he was completely turned on. He pulled her on top of him, his warm hands still massaging her plump behind, his lips refusing to give hers a break.

And she was turned on too, as she rubbed against him, the warmth of his hands causing her to want to rip every shred of those clothes of his off and do him until the break of day.

But the most she could manage was undoing a few buttons on his shirt. For before she knew what was happening he had unzipped his pants and was entering her, sliding in slowly, and then moving in and out of her with the kind of forceful thrusts she loved. And although she still felt the scars of that woman's phone call, although she still wasn't completely satisfied that she knew the real deal, she hollered with total elation as he did her, because she loved him, and because she knew at times like this how any woman, including herself, would resort to some damn drastic measures to get her hooks in a man like Ben.

CHAPTER 10

Ben was back at work and swamped in site audits when Sam Darrow hurried into his office.

"Got a minute?" he asked excitedly.

Ben glanced up over his reading glasses, and then looked back down at the papers before him. "Just barely," he said.

"You break my heart, Ben. And all I do for you."

"What's up?"

"You aren't going to invite me to sit down?"

"Sit down, Sam, but I've got a lot to do."

Sam sat down. "That's more like it."

"Okay, what is it?"

Sam smiled. "A man of action. Every minute counts. I like that."

"The point?"

"All right already. I just thought you should know that the board of directors of the Denlex Corporation will officially ask for Wayne Murdoch's resignation today." Ben looked up. Sam smiled. "I thought that would get your attention."

"Today?"

"Today."

"You've confirmed this?"

"Yes sir, I have. But there's more. Much more. The board will then, later this same day, ask one Judge Benjamin Braddock to become interim President and CEO pending a replacement search and final decision."

Ben removed his glasses and leaned back. "Well," he said. "My goodness."

"My goodness indeed. It'll be your trial run to the permanent appointment, and you will bowl them over as usual."

"But no announcement has been made?"

"My spies are always right, Ben."

Ben shook his head. "This is some news, Sammy."

Sam smiled, and his enthusiasm was contagious. "I told you it was coming. Didn't I? I told you we were in. They never did it this way before. They usually wait and let the chairman's people handle the CEO duties until they name a permanent head. This interim stuff is new for Denlex."

"I've got to prove myself."

"You've already proved yourself. Our earnings are at record highs since you came on board and those plants, even that antiquated Portland plant, are finally coming together. Who do you think the board credits for this sharp turnaround? Murdoch? Please. The chairman knows what he's doing. He wants you already in place should some rogue director try to sabotage your ascension. You've got it made, Ben. I know what I'm talking about."

It sounded wonderful, and it was exactly what he wanted, but Ben wasn't laying bets on any of it. Not yet.

"Mr. Braddock?" Whitney said and Ben pressed the button of his desk intercom.

"Yes, Whitney?"

"Excuse me for disturbing you, sir, but the chairman is on line one." Ben looked at Sam. Sam leaned forward in his seat.

"Thank you, Whitney," Ben said, and picked up the phone.

Sam listened too carefully, waiting to hear something that would finally change that stoic expression on Ben Braddock's face. But nothing changed. Ben spoke and listened and spoke again, and then hung up the phone.

"Well?" Sam said as soon as he did. "What did he say?"

"He said there's going to be a reorganization."

"But what did he say about Murdoch?"

"Murdoch's out."

Sam fell back in his chair. "And?"

"And he's called an emergency board meeting."

"Ah, man. That's beautiful. That's perfect. When's the meeting?"

"This afternoon."

"Yes!" Sam said, and then he braced himself. "Did he say what the meeting would be about?" he asked. Ben's expression went unchanged, although his heart was trying to leap with joy.

"Me," he said.

Josie stood in the middle of Deuce's office with folded arms. It had been their first contact of the morning after yesterday's fireworks, and she was determined not to let him get personal with her again. It was a mistake, she now believed, to tell Deuce all her business, especially where it concerned her relationship with Ben. Deuce was an opportunist if he was anything, and she knew it. Now he had to think that there was a possibility, an opening, a little trouble in paradise ripe for him to exploit. But he was wrong, Josie thought. There was no daylight between she and Ben, especially after their hot 'n' heavy romantic evening together at the cabin. They had their problems, she'd be the first to admit it, but it was between him and her, and it was going to stay that way.

To her surprise, Deuce wasn't calling her into his office to discuss her love life or that anonymous phone call or why she didn't tell Ben to take a hike last night or anything like that. He had an assignment for her.

"Lincoln Avenue?" she said, after he told her where.

"Yes."

"What's up on Lincoln?"

"Apparently there's a friendly, neighborhood riot going on."

Josie smiled.

"A riot?"

"That's the info we're receiving. You remember that story Demi did the week I hired you, about that store owner who beat a kid with a pipe?"

"Just for stealing a bag of chips? Of course I remember it. The *Journal* was the only paper to even mention it."

"Right. Well, the kid died today."

"Oh, no."

"Yep. And that's the reason for the season. So go check it out. And take a click man with you."

Click man was Deuce's term for a photographer, which meant it was big news. Josie was ready for a little action herself and quickly hurried to it.

*   *   *

They could hear the noise a mile away. Even the police had con-
structed a barricade, although the barricade was on Division Street
and nearly half a city block away. Josie looked at Avery, the photographer, who was driving the car.

"They're kidding, right?" Josie asked him, and then looked again
at the cops as they stood around and drank coffee and laughed at
each other's jokes.

"It must be serious up in there, JoJo."

"Serious my behind. They just don't care. What's the purpose of a
barricade this far away?"

"To prevent spillover into our more respectable westside commu-
nities," Avery said.

"Exactly. Forget those brothers and sisters on the East End. They
could kill themselves for all they care. Containment is what this is
about. Let me out."

Avery looked at Josie. "Let you out? For what? They aren't gonna
let you through that barricade."

"We can cut through that alleyway by the Chicken Coop. That'll
get us close to the action. But we've got to walk."

"Now you're the one who's kidding, right?"

"Pull over, Avery."

"You think I'm going up in there when the police are scared to
go? And they got guns?"

Josie shook her head. "Just let me out."

"No, Josie. Deuce ain't taking my head off. Let's just back off,
okay? Things sound rough out here."

Josie rolled her eyes. "Just stop the car," she said.

"Why you got to be like this? We'll get a story eventually."

"Stop the car, Avery, I mean it."

"Josie!"

"Stop the car, dammit! You don't wanna go, don't. But let me
out!"

Avery shook his head. He'd heard about her before she even came
on board. Josie Ross, the slash-and-burn queen. You couldn't tell her
a thing, because she was too busy telling you. Avery wasn't about to
mix it up with her. He stopped the car.

*   *   *

The outer sanctum of the vice president's suite of offices was abuzz. Whitney and a group of fellow office workers were glued to a small television that sat on top of a large file cabinet. The east end of Lincoln Avenue appeared to be in chaos as people were running and flailing fists in the air and trashing the entire street. The workers, many of whom had grown up in that very area of town, were shocked by the display.

Ben arrived back into his office suite and was at first surprised that a crowd had gathered. Whitney, upon seeing him, quickly and nervously moved to turn off the TV.

"You don't have to do that," Ben said, and the workers, who could always depend on Ben, were relieved. "What's going on?"

"Looks like a riot on Lincoln."

"Really?"

"Yes, sir. They're protesting what happened to that little boy."

Ben had no idea what little boy she was talking about, but he decided not to pursue it. He looked at the television instead. The scene was filled with aerial video of East Lincoln and what appeared to be a thousand or so people going nuts, running and breaking store windows and setting parked cars ablaze. The police were nowhere to be seen, which astounded Ben given the horrific look of the scene. He considered calling Todd Keating to find out why law enforcement had not taken charge of the chaos. Even he could see that this was no penny ante protest, that those people were hellbent on destruction. The local TV station had even interrupted programming, that's how big of a deal it was. And then, as he should have done so much sooner, Ben suddenly thought about Josie. He turned to his secretary.

"Get Miss Ross on the phone."

"I already tried, sir."

Ben hesitated. "You already tried?"

"Yes, sir. I knew you would be wondering if she was caught in that mess."

Ben's heart knotted up. "Is she?"

"I asked where she was but they wouldn't say, against their policy to divulge their reporters' whereabouts. The only thing they would confirm was that she was out on assignment."

Ben remained cool, although his heart was beginning to pound. "Thank you, Whitney," he said, and went into his office.

*   *   *

Everything was crazy. Josie had taken out her reporter's notebook but she was too fascinated to write. *A thousand people have gone mad,* she thought, as they tossed bricks through anything glass and torched cars and buildings galore, while still others robbed and looted store owners blind. Then there were the sound of police helicopters, buzzing like war-zone spy planes across the sky. No cops on the ground, but plenty of them safely up and away. Most of the rioters were young men, all African American and Hispanic, all running so fast from one hot scene to the next that Josie could barely get a single one to answer her questions. So she started running too, right along with the crowd, asking *why,* over and over.

"We're tired, that's why," one young brother answered as if offended by the question.

"Tired of what?"

"Everything, dawg. They treat us like we animals. Like we don't matter. That boy's dead. Over some damn potato chips."

"The boy who stole the potato chips?"

"Right. He's dead because of that. And for what? 'Cause he black, that's what. 'Cause he poor. We ain't taking it no more, that's why we here!"

Josie got another view, from an older participant who was walking fast, his long, thick dreads pounding fiercely against his neck as he moved.

"He had no business stealing, okay?" the man said. "We understand the little brother was wrong. We understand that. But it was just some chips. That's nothing to kill somebody over."

"And that's why you're here?" Josie asked.

"That's exactly why. There comes a time when you've got to run through the fire or start your own. They'll never hear anything we say until we start our own."

His walking pace overtook Josie's slower stride and she had to let him go. She was about to join another group of rioters, but her cell phone started ringing. She was amazed she even heard it.

"Yes, hello?" she said loudly, pressing a finger to her outer ear. It was Ben.

"You better not be anywhere near Lincoln Avenue, Josephine."

"Ben, you should see this."

"Got damn it, Josie! Are you trying to get yourself killed?"

"No. Of course not. But you should see this. It's incredible. These people are fed up. That's what this is about. They're tired of being treated like animals."

"So they behave as animals, is that how it goes?"

"It ain't even like that. You just don't understand. A little boy was killed over a bag of potato chips. Potato chips, Ben. That store owner beat that poor boy down with an iron pipe over a bag of lousy potato chips. These people have had it."

"Maybe that store owner was fed up too, Josephine. Maybe that poor little boy you're so in sympathy with was the last straw for him too."

"How can you take his side?"

"Just get out of there now."

"I'm doing my job. I'm not going anywhere."

Ben sighed. When Josie was passionate like this he knew his influence over her was nil. "Where're the police?"

"Far away from here, that's for sure. They're setting up perimeters to keep it contained in this community—which is a pathetic response."

"And what do you suppose they do?"

"What do you think? They need to put on some riot gear and get in here before somebody gets hurt. I mean it's crazy up in here, Ben. It's like—"

A gunshot went off.

"Jesus!" Josie yelled as she ducked and turned toward the sound. The crowd, which heard the gunshot too, was running toward her as if she was the way to safety. Josie turned to run too, but the sheer onslaught caused her to drop her phone. She reached to pick it up but it was kicked away in the stampede. So she just ran. Ben's voice was yelling one word into the trampled phone, over and over. "Josephine? Josephine? *Josephine?*"

The aftermath shocked even Josie. It looked like Rwanda during its civil war, or Beirut. Trash like confetti littered the streets. Buildings still smoldered. There was broken glass, torn-down fences, and torched cars reduced to rubble. It was all over now, the damage was done, and the cops and paramedics were everywhere. Three people died, one from a gunshot wound, two others trampled to death.

Josie could have easily been one of the dead, and she knew it.

That was why she was stunned. She sat on the sidewalk near a burned-out liquor store, waiting for the paramedic to take a look at her. She had no cuts, no bruises, just fear. Just memories forever etched in her brain. The seriously and critically wounded were long since carted away. Now the walking wounded and the stunned were getting a look over. Josie had wanted to leave an hour ago, but they wouldn't let her. She just didn't look right to them.

The last thing she remembered was a young man grabbing her hand and pulling her into a building. She thought he was her guardian angel. She couldn't run fast enough and the crowd was just pulling her along—a sure recipe for a stumble, fall, and being trampled. Then the building the young man had pulled her into was fire-bombed. Before she knew it, they were running again, and the crowd was pushing her along again until they ran one way and she another. What she just knew was the grace of God Almighty forced her to give up and fall against the wall.

The paramedic was just about to come to her next to take that good look at her that they had insisted on, but she saw Ben. He was cleared to enter by a police sergeant, and Ben began walking through the war zone, his brown suit coat flapping as he moved cautiously, looking at all the destruction. He looked amazed by what he was witnessing.

Josie left the medic's side and began, as if on autopilot, walking toward him. When he saw her he stopped and sighed relief. And she ran to him, ran with energy she thought she no longer had, ran with determination she thought had died in the crowd. She ran knowing that he'd told her not to stay, and she jumped into his arms, certain that he wouldn't hold it against her now.

Ben unlocked the door to Josie's townhouse and followed her upstairs. She was so emotionally exhausted that she stumbled back, causing Ben to clutch her around her waist and push her forward. He kept asking if she was okay, and she kept insisting that she was fine.

"You don't look okay, Josie," he said as they entered her bedroom.

"I'm fine, Ben," she said. "I just need to take a shower."

"I want Doctor Scott to have a look at you anyway."

"I don't need a doctor."

"You don't know what you need."

Josie rolled her eyes as she took off her earrings and bracelet and tossed them on her dresser. She looked through the mirror and saw Ben picking up her telephone, and then lying down on her bed. She smiled.

"I need to be doing that."

"You need to take a bath," Ben said, and Josie managed to laugh, although the memories of the day were still haunting her.

Ben dialed the number to his office and then placed his hand inside his coat lapel. Josie stood at the mirror looking at herself, picking up her braids and dropping them down, placing her hands on her cheeks as if she too could see the look of terror that still had not left her face.

For Ben it was a different feeling. Ben was grateful that she was okay, but he was still worried because he knew her; he knew that as long as there was some perceived injustice somewhere, Josie would find a way to forget about the danger and run to the cause.

"Denlex Corporation," the voice on the other end of the phone proclaimed. "This is the office of the vice president. How may I direct your call?"

"Yeah, Helen, this is Ben Braddock. Put Whitney on the phone."

"Mr. Braddock, yes sir. One moment, please."

Josie began undressing, slowly, removing her shirt and then her bra and slowly slipping out of her pants. Ben's heart fluttered as he watched her, her brown, juicy breasts and black nipples, her soft, flat stomach. As she slid out of her panties and turned away from him, her ass a perfectly rounded ball of tight plumpness, he crossed his legs. Her body was about the most perfect specimen he'd ever seen, and he craved it constantly. But he kept the contact to a minimum, refusing to fall prey to her flirtations because he still wasn't convinced that Josie was ready to take it higher. He still felt caught in too many unnecessary situations with her, where he was left dangling in the balance, like a piñata, waiting for her to get it together, fearing that she was about as together as she was ever going to get.

He looked away from her just as she glanced over at him. She was completely naked now, and she had hoped he would be burning with desire when she turned his way. But he wasn't even looking at her. She felt disappointed, wondering why he wouldn't be turned on, but she sighed and went on into her bathroom. *Forget him,* she thought, although she knew that was impossible.

Whitney's voice came onto the phone and quickly informed Ben that Sam Darrow had been calling all afternoon.

"Sam?" Ben asked.

"Yes sir. All afternoon."

"Get him on the line."

"I'll connect you, sir." And she did. Ben had a good idea what the problem was, but he didn't realize the gravity until Sam's high-pitched voice came onto the line.

"I can't believe you, Ben! Where were you?"

"Just slow down, Sammy. Now what happened?"

"It was a done deal. All you had to do was show up and accept your ordination. But not Ben Braddock. That was too easy for him. He's got to make good old Sammy look like a pure idiot in front of the board of directors!"

"I missed a damn meeting. I had Whitney inform them that I wouldn't be able to attend."

"But why the hell not? This was vital!"

Ben hesitated. He wasn't about to tell Sam a thing, especially something as lame as the truth, that he couldn't make perhaps the biggest meeting of his career because he had to pick up his girlfriend from some riot.

"Just tell me what happened," he ordered.

Sam paused, probably to calm himself down, Ben believed. Why Sam was so certain that Ben's success somehow automatically translated into success for him was beyond Ben. He never promised him a thing.

"They won't admit this but they changed the game plan in the middle of the game," Sam said.

"English, Sam."

"The board has decided not to name an interim replacement for Murdoch after all."

Ben sighed. It was a huge disappointment. "I see."

"The chairman will handle the duties of the CEO's office until a permanent replacement can be named. They're compiling names now, but it could take months. Surprised?"

Ben paused. "Yes."

"But not disappointed?"

"Of course I'm disappointed, Sam. I had no idea they would react this way."

"I don't know why the hell not. You slighted them, Ben. Having your secretary tell them you couldn't make it. And no explanation. Nothing. You know better than that. Tell 'em your mother died, your daddy was in a car wreck, something unavoidable. But, oh, no. Not Benjamin Braddock. He doesn't sweat the small stuff. Well the small stuff just sweated you, my man."

"I'm out of the loop completely?"

Sam exhaled. "We'll have to see if your name makes the final cut. My hunch is that it will, but I can't be sure about that. I'm not hearing anything right now. They were highly pissed with you, Ben."

"And I'm sure you, our great PR man, have a recommendation?"

"Call for a private audience with the chairman. Apologize. Explain to him why you couldn't make the biggest meeting of your life. Even if he doesn't understand, he'll at least forgive you. He's your biggest supporter. He views your absence as a personal affront to him."

"Okay."

"So you'll do it?"

"I'll see."

"I know you, Benjamin. That means no. It won't be groveling."

"Sounds that way to me, kid."

"But it won't be. You're just playing the game, that's all."

Suddenly a loud, agonizing cry was heard. Ben, startled, looked toward the bathroom. "I'll talk to you later, Sam," he said, and hung up the phone as Sam shouted his name.

He got off the bed and hurried into the bathroom. It was Josie. He could hear her even above the sound of the running water. His heart pounded as he slung open the shower curtain. Josie was dropping to the floor sobbing, the water splashing down upon her narrow, brown back. She looked up at Ben. The tears in her beautiful eyes made him shudder.

"People died today, Ben," she said through her sobs. "People died. And for what? It was awful!"

Ben's heart melted. She was so tough in a lot of ways, the queen of mean when she wanted to be, but she was also inexplicably vulnerable too. Emotion overtook him as he stepped into the shower, the water pelting against his expensive shoes and suit, and got on his knees. He reached out to her trembling naked body, and pulled her into his arms.

CHAPTER 11

He arrived to work early the next day expecting all kinds of fire-works. He had missed an important meeting yesterday afternoon and he expected everybody to have an opinion why. He also expected Sam Darrow to drop by with what would probably amount to hourly updates on the horse race to become CEO of Denlex. But he didn't expect to see Meredith Chambers.

She was sitting primly in his secretary's office, her conservative, blue business suit topped off with a nice, red, sheer scarf around her thin neck, just enough hint of color, he thought, to bring out even more of the beauty of her dark skin. She stood up when Ben walked in, and her great smile and large, dark eyes almost necessitated that he smile too.

"Well, hello there," he said, remembering her well, first from the restaurant and then from the mayor's dinner party. He also remembered how when they talked he had had to run off to see about Josie, failing to give her a proper good-bye.

"Hello, Mr. Braddock," she said, extending her small, soft hand. "Meredith Chambers. I was hoping you'd remember me."

"I do indeed," Ben said as he placed his hand in hers. She seemed to give him an extra squeeze, upon which he immediately let go.

"You left so abruptly when we met, I wasn't sure if you'd remember."

"I apologize for that."

"No need for apologies, none at all. You gotta go when you gotta go."

He smiled. "That's very understanding of you."

"Oh, I don't know if it's so much understanding as experience. I've been left hanging by the best, sir, so don't you worry about me."

Ben laughed. "Yes ma'am."

There was a slight pause, as Meredith could tell that Ben was genuinely pleased to see her.

"I was hoping to have a few minutes of your time," she said.

"Certainly. Come on in my office," he added, and then he looked at Whitney, who was staring at them. "Hold my calls," he said to her, and Ben, still smiling, escorted Meredith into his office. Whitney watched them as they disappeared behind closed doors, and then she shook her head.

Meredith sat in the wingback chair in front of Ben's desk and accepted his offer of coffee. She watched him as he stood at the table pouring her coffee, looking gorgeous even in his black business suit and white shirt, perfectly tailored to fit his fine body. Here was a man invented for women to desire and men to envy. It was easy to fall into the trap of Ben Braddock's charm, easy to get swept away by his elegance and good looks and wealth, and Meredith knew it. She had to be careful. She and Hines deserved to have Ben Braddock's head on a platter, stewed if possible, and she was self-appointed to make it so. But watching him operate, so smooth and experienced, made her less confident; it made her ever more aware of the fact that she had some serious work on her hands.

"Here you are," Ben said as he handed her the coffee, and then he leaned back against the front of his large desk.

She accepted the cup graciously, thanking him in an almost whisper. And then, when she was certain she had his undivided attention, she crossed her legs—her skirt as short as possible without revealing all. "There's nothing like a good cup of coffee in the morning," she said.

"Yes," he said, sipping from his cup too, studying the beautiful curves of her long, shapely legs going up into a skirt hem that barely covered her undoubtedly warm inner sanctum.

"So," he said, putting his coffee cup down on his desk, "to what do I owe the pleasure of your visit this morning?"

"I've decided to accept your offer, sir."

Ben hesitated. "My offer?"

"Yes. Oh, my, you've forgotten."

"No, I just . . . don't remember." Ben said this with a smile. Meredith smiled too.

"At the mayor's party you seemed to hint at a job offer. You said you could use a good executive assistant."

"Oh. Yes. I remember that. But I thought you were weighing your options?"

"I was. And I did. But your offer seemed to appeal to me most. Don't ask me why. It just did."

Ben nodded. "Okay. Good."

Meredith reached into her briefcase and pulled out a thick manila folder. "I have my résumé and my references all here," she said as she handed the folder to Ben. "I also included information on awards that I've received and articles I've written, in business journals and other germane periodicals, just to give you some idea of what I'm about."

Ben accepted the papers without opening the folder. He set them down on his desk.

"I'll have my people down at human resources take a look at it."

"All right. Okay, understood. But this is the deal. Am I wrong to be hopeful?"

"No, no. Not at all. My offer to you is still on the table. If the background check turns out all right, then I don't see why we can't work something out."

Meredith smiled and then exhaled. She was careful. The background check, she was certain, would not pose a problem whatsoever.

"Wonderful," she said. "I was worried there for a minute."

"Worried? Why?"

"It's been a little while since your offer. I wasn't sure if it still stood, or if you would even remember it." She took her slender finger and slid it slowly along the under part of her skirt hem. Ben unbuttoned his suit coat.

"Hopefully I have put your fears to rest."

"You have. Oh, have you. Thank you so much, Ben." Meredith said this with a smile, and Ben, unable to resist the pure magnetism of her charm, and how delightful it was to talk to her, smiled too.

* * *

Deuce ordered a beer and leaned back in his booth at Rhonda's. The lunch crowd was animated. Everybody was laughing and talking and not giving a second thought to the three young people who had lost their lives yesterday on Lincoln Avenue.

Deuce was horrified by the scene, and when Avery called in with the news that Josie had managed to get through the police barricades and enter that war zone, his heart dropped through his shoes. He spent ten minutes yelling at Avery for letting her do it, realizing as he yelled that nobody stopped Josie Ross from doing anything. But the idea of it, of that beautiful sister running for her life, of nearly losing it, brought chills to his spine.

Those chills kept rolling when Josie entered Rhonda's. She was wearing a pair of tight jeans and an oversized jersey, looking more like a college kid than his thirty-year-old ace reporter. To Deuce she was still, even dressed like that, the prettiest human being in the joint. And as she walked toward him, as her small hips swayed, he wanted her so badly that he could taste it. If it wasn't for that damn Ben Braddock, he believed, he would have had her a long time ago.

"There's Miss America!" He stood up as Josie arrived at his booth.

"Hey, Deuce," she said, sitting down. "Were you waiting long?"

"Just a couple hours."

"What?"

"I'm kidding, J, come on." He said this and sat down too.

She smiled. "I'm sorry. I'm just—"

"You're just still getting over that horror show from yesterday. And you still showed up for work this morning. I couldn't believe it."

"I know, but I'd go nuts if I stayed home. Staying home is not an option."

"Thanks for coming to lunch with me."

"You didn't have to do this, you know."

"Oh, yes, I did. Two near-death experiences since you've been on my payroll? This is the least I can do."

Josie laughed. The waitress came up and she ordered sherry. When the waitress left, Deuce smiled.

"Sherry for the lady," he said.

"I'm sure your pocket can handle it."

"I don't know now. I'm no millionaire like Ben Braddock."

"He's no millionaire."

"He's something. I heard he's got holdings in companies as far away as Switzerland, and you know what that means. Switzerland? Swiss bank account? He's got something."

"Whatever," she said. Ben had never discussed his financial standing with her and she never bothered to ask. He had money—she knew that, but the extent of which, given Ben and his high privacy issues, would probably always be a mystery to her. "We can go Dutch if you like," she said, hoping that such a comment would force Deuce to change the subject.

"Not on your life," he said. "A man who makes you pay for a drink is a sick man."

Josie laughed. "What is this? Flatter Josie day?"

"Yeah. Why not? You got it going on like that sister, I ain't even gonna lie. From the first moment I saw you I wanted to . . ."

"To what?" Josie asked. She, like Deuce, was in a playful mood. Something about surviving, where the day after was so refreshing, where she was still standing and still alive to talk about it, made her giddy. "Go on, Deuce. And tell the truth. From the moment you first saw me you wanted to what?"

"To tap that ass. All right? There, I said it."

Josie laughed. "You are so diplomatic."

"I'm kidding, J. I didn't mean to be disrespectful."

"Come on. I know you didn't. And you weren't kidding, either. You were just being honest, which is always cool with me because I'll take truth any day of the week. A friendship can only thrive if truth is there. And you did say you wanted to be my friend."

Deuce smiled. She almost seemed flirtatious, which he didn't quite know how to take. "That's right," he said. Josie's glass of sherry arrived and she and Deuce made a toast. "To the victims," he said, and Josie quickly concurred.

"You did good, kid," Deuce said after gulping down half of his beer. "The way you went into that war zone when even the cops wouldn't penetrate it said a lot about your courage. You've got that crazy kind of courage, babe, that turns me on, you hear me? I mean, life is a risk, anyway. And when it's your time to go it's your time to go. So why be a tight-ass?"

Josie nodded. "That's what I'm saying. Like Avery. You should have seen him, Deuce."

"The boy was scared?"

"Oh, man," Josie said, and laughed. "Your boy was terrified. He wouldn't even let me out of the car at first. He was pathetic."

Deuce laughed. "And I'm gonna tell everybody too."

"Don't you dare."

"Why the hell not? He think he's the mack daddy anyway, so why the hell not? It'll bring his scared ass back to earth a little."

"Don't do it. Most people aren't like us, Deuce. Most folks would do exactly as Avery did and keep their behinds in the car."

Deuce nodded and watched her sip from her glass of sherry. They did have a bond, he felt, a kind of devil-may-care attitude that both of them have had to suppress. He suppressed his when he agreed to run a newspaper, and she, he believed, suppressed hers when she agreed to hook up with king tight-ass, Benjamin Braddock.

"I wanted to come over to your crib last night," he said. "Not to hit on you or anything like that. I wanted to make sure you were okay."

"Why didn't you come? I could have used the company, to tell you the truth."

"That's why I didn't show. I figured you had company. I was certain Braddock would be right there by your side lecturing you on why you need to quit that crazy job of yours and return to the mainstream. I figured he wouldn't take too kindly to the man who sent you into the fire in the first place dropping by."

"He was there, but he didn't stay very long. He never does." Josie said this but she didn't feel sorry that she was once again letting Deuce get in her business. She decided last night, when Ben left and she was sitting alone in her house, that Ben was right. She needed a friend. She needed somebody she could talk to and unload on. Scotty was too far away—he was in Florida. And she and females never seemed quite able to make that connection. Deuce, she decided, would have to do.

"Let me get this straight," Deuce said, more than willing to get in her business. "Your man never stays the night with you? Is that what you're saying?"

"That's what I'm saying."

"What is that man's problem? Damn, Josie. If I had you I wouldn't be able to stand to be away from you. I'd want to stay with you every night of the week if you'd let me."

Josie smiled. "That's sweet. Thanks."

Deuce hesitated. He was treading on dangerous waters, and he knew it. "He's still the one, then?"

Josie paused before answering. She didn't want to hurt Deuce, but she also didn't want to lead him on. "Yes," she said. And then she looked into his doleful eyes. "You know he is."

"Good."

Josie smiled. "Oh it's good now? Me and tight-ass together is a good thing now?"

"Yes, it is, as a matter of fact. Not because of him, but because of you. It's what you want and I'm glad you have what you want. Besides, I like your certainty. I'm not certain about anything anymore, so it's good to see that everybody hasn't given up." Josie nodded, although her certainty was as fragile as a loosening rope. "Listen," Deuce said, "why don't you come over to the house next Thursday night? I'm having a little get together."

"A get together?"

"Yeah. Just a few friends. I think you'll like it."

Josie sipped from her glass of sherry. She was tempted to just say yes. He was, after all, a friend of hers now. But she couldn't. Deuce wanted more than a friendship, even as he was pretending to understand that she was eternally yoked with Ben. She declined.

"Come on, Josie. Why not?"

"I don't think it's a good idea."

"So you don't want to be buddies, is that it?" Deuce asked.

"Of course I do. But . . ."

Deuce hesitated. Maybe she wasn't flirting after all. "But that's all you want," he said.

Josie looked at him. "Right."

He nodded. "I can dig that. That's fine. Hey, why don't you bring Ben along, if that'll make you feel better."

Ben at Deuce's house? Josie wanted to shake her head. It seemed impossible. But Ben was the one who so desperately wanted her to make friends this time. He was the one who wanted her to stop being so damn demanding and give friendship a chance. So she nodded. "Okay," she said. "We'll come." She said this as if she were certain they would be there, as if she didn't expect Ben to laugh in her face when she told him the deal, that Deuce Jefferson of all people wanted to break bread with him.

*   *   *

Whitney smiled when Josie walked into her office. She liked Josie, although she also knew how aggravating she could be sometimes. "Hello, Miss Ross," she said.

"Child, please," Josie said as she walked in. "You better call me Josie. That's my name."

"I'm hearing ya, girl. But you know how Mr. Braddock is."

"Is he in?"

"He's in a meeting."

"Damn."

"But it won't be long. They've been meeting all morning and the judge has to be somewhere in less than an hour."

"Where?"

"He's got to speak at some conservative something or other downtown."

"Conservative? Never mind. I was actually considering going with him," Josie said.

Whitney laughed. "You don't be about nothing good, you know that?"

"I know. It ain't easy being me."

"You were over on Lincoln yesterday, weren't you, girl?"

Josie hesitated. "Yes," she said.

"I thought so. The judge looked mortified when he came out of his office and told me to notify the board that he wouldn't be able to make that big meeting. Then he just took off."

"What big meeting?"

"He didn't tell you?"

"No."

"They were gonna name him something like the temporary CEO or something until they could find somebody permanent."

Josie was stunned. "Really?"

"Yeah. It was a big deal around here. But they changed their minds when he didn't show. He couldn't attend the meeting. He had to go see about you." Then Whitney smiled. "He's getting too old to be running behind you, Josie."

"Sounds like a personal problem to me," Josie said, and Whitney laughed again.

Josie sat down beside Whitney's desk and her upbeat, playful mood turned somber. He had missed an important meeting because of her mess. A meeting that would have officially put him at the top of the largest corporation in town. Then she wondered why he didn't even mention it to her, a meeting that important. But that was Ben.

Whitney left the office to take some copies of some important fax to other senior people, but when she returned some ten minutes later, Josie was still sitting beside her desk.

"He's not out yet?" she asked her.

"Not yet."

"I would let him know you're out here, Josie," she said as she sat back behind her desk, "but he told me to hold everything."

Josie nodded her understanding. "I know," she said. "But you said he's been meeting with this person all morning?"

"All morning, girl," Whitney said.

"Who is it?"

"I don't know. Never saw her before."

Josie nodded. A female. That figures. But she wasn't going to let it worry her. Besides, she reasoned, she was probably one of those stuffy business types who wouldn't know style if it bit her on the lip. And Ben liked a woman to have some style, if nothing else. But when his office door finally opened and he and Meredith stepped out, Josie could not believe her eyes. She could not have been more wrong. Meredith was no styleless windbag of a business woman, but a gorgeous, solid-packed seductress.

Whitney looked at Josie.

"I forgot to tell you," Whitney said. "I really don't know a thing about the woman. But I know a hoochie when I see one."

Josie glanced at Whitney and then stared at Meredith. She and Ben appeared to be so friendly together, as they continued to talk and shake hands, and it seemed to Josie that they were holding hands the way neither one of them seemed able to let go. Josie stood up quickly to make her presence known immediately, and moved toward them. When Ben saw her, his smile didn't disappear, but it did weaken. He slowly slipped his hand out of Meredith's.

"Well, hello, Josephine," he said, as if he was more surprised by her presence than thrilled to see her.

"Hey," Josie said, and although she was disappointed, she decided not to show it. "I've been out here waiting for you."

"Oh, I'm sorry," Meredith said, realizing almost instinctively that this young, abrasive sister could very well be her main competition. "It's my fault. I have a tendency to go on far too long."

"And you are?" Josie asked, unable to wait for Ben's slow-in-coming introduction. Meredith glanced at Ben and then looked at Josie. She extended her hand.

"I'm Meredith Chambers. It's nice to meet you."

Josie reluctantly shook Meredith's hand. "Nice to meet you. Who are you?"

"Meredith will most probably be joining the Denlex family very soon," Ben said, knowing full well that Josie was ready to pounce.

"She'll be working here? As what?"

Ben glared at Josie. "As my assistant."

"I see. So y'all were in there all morning having a job interview?"

"Excuse me?" Meredith asked, glad to see the tension. Ben continued to glare at Josie.

"You heard me. I never heard of a four hour job interview. Unless you were interviewing for more than an assistant's job."

Meredith looked at Ben as if she were completely confused. Ben, however, didn't take his eyes off of Josie.

"I don't understand what you're insinuating," Meredith said to Josie, inwardly hoping that such a jealous, uninhibited individual would indeed be her main competition.

"Were you the female who called me at work?"

Ben's mouth nearly gaped open. He could not believe Josie would ask that woman such a question. He looked at Meredith. "Someone from personnel will be in touch with you shortly, Meredith," he said, and Meredith smiled.

"Thank you. But I don't understand what's going on." Then she looked at Josie. "Why would I call your job? I don't even know you."

"It's nothing," Ben said with a shake of the head, as if to assure her not to worry at all. "You have a nice day."

Meredith, still appearing confused, smiled. "Yes, and you too, Ben." She looked at Josie one more time, at this woman in jeans and a jersey. As she left the office of the vice president, she just knew that if it was true and this impulsive female was indeed her main competition, her job had just gotten easier by leaps and bounds.

As soon as Meredith had cleared the entranceway and was gone from view, Ben looked at Josie in such a way that she couldn't help but regret her behavior. He stared her down, as if to make it perfectly clear just how upset he really was, and then he turned and went back into his office, slamming the door behind him.

Josie stood there, not really knowing what she wanted to do. Stay. Go. Beg forgiveness. Cuss him out. But she could not forget that look on Ben's face. She looked at Whitney, who was staring at her.

"I overreacted, didn't I?"

"Hun!" Whitney said. "Not to me you didn't." And then she added, "Four hours for a job interview?"

"Okay!" Josie said with a smile, although her heart was a mangled mess, which was why she knew she couldn't leave. She went into Ben's office, without knocking, without obeying all of those annoying rules and regulations that seemed to govern every inch of his life.

He was staring out of the window, his back to Josie, his tailored pants tight across his tight behind, his white dress shirt appearing freshly pressed. She slowly walked toward him.

"I'm going to just say it, okay? I was out of line. I don't know what gets into me sometimes." He didn't turn around. He didn't respond to her plea. He just exhaled. "When I see you with these females I just get mad. I don't know why." She said this and waited for some response from him, but he still said nothing. "I know I have trust issues, Ben. And I know it started in my childhood when my dad died on me and my mother just didn't know how to get it together. Then she started fooling around with all of these guys who were just using her. But she—"

Ben sighed loudly. "What is it you want, Josephine?" he asked her. And then he turned around. "Because I absolutely do not wish to hear your life story right now."

Josie's basic instinct told her to fire back. But she didn't. "I was trying to apologize to you."

"Is that it? Is that why you came to my office in the first place? To do what you do? To start a scene and then apologize for it?"

"I'm no fool, Ben. It doesn't take no four hours for a job interview."

"No, it doesn't. I didn't say it did."

"Then what were you doing with her for four hours?"

"What do you want, Josie?"

She paused. Folded her arms. It seemed useless. "We've been invited to a dinner party."

"Can't."

"You don't even know who invited us."

"Who?"

"Deuce."

"No thanks."

"Then I'll go by myself."

"That sounds like a good solution to me."

"He invited me by myself at first anyway. But I turned him down. I didn't want him to think that I was available or anything." She said this and looked at Ben. "I only accepted when he invited you too. But I knew you wouldn't come. You are so elitist."

Ben looked at her. "What?"

"You heard me. Deuce isn't well connected enough to have the senior vice president of Denlex in his home—is that it?"

"Right. That's it. That's exactly it."

Josie frowned. "Stop patronizing me," she said.

"Stop patronizing yourself. You know my nights are seldom free, Josephine, so stop trying to act as if I have this mountain of time I can spend with your boss."

"I said I was sorry," Josie said.

Ben looked at her. "Are you really, Josie?"

"Yes. I was rude to your friend and I'm sorry. But she just seemed so . . ."

"So what?"

"So . . . So perfect for you." She said this and looked at Ben.

Ben stared at her. And he and she both knew that a woman like Josie was anything but perfect for him. But Josephine was the one who tugged at his heart. She was the one who had him awake at nights staring at his ceiling. "I can't make it to anybody's dinner party," he said. "I'm swamped."

"You could go if you wanted to."

"Didn't you hear what I just said? I told you I have too much work to do."

"So much work to do," Josie said derisively, "but you spend four hours doing nothing with a stranger?" Then she added, as if she couldn't help herself. "Or were you doing the stranger?"

Anger rose in Ben like a surging tide and he wanted to tell her about her natural self. But he didn't say a word.

Josie, too, could sense his changing mood, because she knew within herself that she had gone too far. That was why she decided to just leave. She'd done enough damage for one day, she thought, and she quickly headed for the out.

"When is this dinner supposed to take place?" he asked her, reluctantly, driven more by his own sense of guilt over his temper than any interest in some dinner party of Deuce's.

Josie turned toward him. She was astounded that he would even want to say another word to her.

"Next Thursday," she said.

He exhaled. "Okay," he said, and then he looked at her. "We'll go."

She wanted to smile. But she just nodded her okay, and left.

The apartment door flew open and Meredith pushed Hines inside. Hines stumbled forward, in dirty pants and T-shirt, his face sporting a day old beard and other elements of the streets. Meredith hurried in behind him and slammed the door.

"What do you think you're doing?" she said immediately as Hines stumbled again.

"I don't wanna hear it," he said and Meredith couldn't believe he'd said that.

"You don't *what?*" she asked, and then she rushed toward him and pushed him until he landed on the sofa. She then sat beside him, the very urgency of her movements causing Hines to just close his eyes.

"You can't do this to me, Hines. You can't self-destruct on me."

"I'm not self-destructing."

"You've been gone for almost two days. Two days! And I'm roaming the streets searching for you. Wasting my valuable time searching for you when you have no business out there anyway!"

"Why didn't you just leave me alone? I can take care of myself."

"Then I find you, with these . . . people. Roaming the streets like some bum. I could not believe it. Mother would have cried from her grave if she would have seen her precious son like this."

Hines opened his eyes. He once loved his sister. There was nothing in this world he wouldn't do for her. Now he couldn't bear the sight of her.

Meredith angrily pushed him again.

"Do you understand me?" she repeated.

"Yes!" he said unconvincingly. It was just a word, a robotic sylla-ble, whatever it took to get her off his case.

She smiled. "Good. Now, no more of that. No more desperation. Desperation devastates. It destroys good, sound plans. And we will stick to the plan."

"The plan. That's all I hear about. The plan."

"That's right. It's working beautifully, Hines, better than I'd imag-ined. I'm about to become Ben Braddock's right-hand woman. I'm about to become the closet thing to him on the face of this earth. Me. Your sister. We're going to do it, Hines. We're on our way. All those wasted years . . ."

"Why do you keep talking about that?" Hines asked, his face be-traying his inner anguish. "I don't wanna keep hearing about that." He was tired of living in the past, where life for him was as dismal as it comes and, contrary to what his sister believed, the future didn't hold out much promise either. He looked at her. He pleaded with her: "Why did you come for me? Why couldn't you just let me be, Sis. I'm not worth it, don't you see that?"

"Stop it," Meredith said. "You just stop that. We did not come this far to give up. You hear me? You're talking nonsense, Hines. Of course I came to get you. I will always be there for you. The past is painful, I know it is. But we can never forget what happened. That's why we rejoice now. Because we haven't forgotten. We're moving forward, Hines. We're winning. And it'll be a cold day in hell before we ever lose again."

CHAPTER 12

"They're here!" Rain shouted, and Deuce and his house guests hurried to the living-room's front window. It was a gathering of friends, all of whom worked at the *Journal*: Rain and her boyfriend Malcolm, Demi and her beau Ralph, and Deuce. Deuce flew solo, mainly because Josie was coming, mainly because his hope was that she'd come solo too.

"What's he driving?" Demi asked as she hurried to the front of the pack.

"A Benz, girl, what else?" Rain said.

Ben's Mercedes stopped in front of the small, clapboard house on Thirty-fourth Avenue, but the tint of the car's window and the darkness of the night made it impossible to see who was inside.

"A Mercedes Benz," Demi said. "He is so unoriginal."

"He may be unoriginal," Ralph said, "but that's a bad-ass ride."

"That car cost more than your house, Deuce," Rain said, and the others laughed.

"I'm not pretentious, what can I say?"

"You ain't got no cash flow, that's what you can say." Laughter again.

Deuce, hoping that it would be Josie driving that Mercedes and that Ben had decided to stay away, looked out of the window and waited for the confirmation.

Outside, three cars were bumper to bumper in the driveway and every light in the house appeared on. Ben, who was sitting behind the steering wheel staring at the house, leaned back and looked at Josie. She wore a short, rib-tight, low-cut, red dress with spaghetti straps, looking gorgeous, he thought.

"I can't stay late, honey," he said, to warn her. "I've got a long day tomorrow."

As always, she thought. "I know," she said. "Thanks for coming anyway."

Ben nodded and looked down at her legs. "That's a very pretty dress, Josephine."

"Thank you. I like it."

"It's short." Ben said this and looked at Josie's face. Josie smiled.

"Yes, it is," Josie said. He nodded and stared deep into her eyes. Then he leaned over and kissed her on the lips.

"What was that for?" she asked with a smile. He looked at the house and then back at her. *Insurance*, she was hoping he'd say.

"Come on," he said instead, removing his seatbelt. "Let's get this over with."

Inside, Rain was the first to see Ben as he stepped out of the car.

"Here comes the judge!" she said loudly, and Deuce, seeing him too, exhaled. His hope dashed.

Ben was impeccably dressed in a dark brown suit, white shirt, dark brown tie, and brown fedora. He walked around to the passenger side of his Mercedes and opened the door for Josie. Deuce's heart began to race as Josie took Ben's hand and stepped out of the car. He had never seen her in a dress before, and her legs were even more shapely than he had imagined. He looked down at his clothes, and at the clothing of the others in the room, and all of them were in jeans and T-shirts. Ben and Josie looked liked the cover of *Esquire*; Deuce and his gang looked more like *Field and Stream*.

"Let's get away from the window, folks," he ordered, moving away himself. "Let's act like we at least know how to act."

"Even though we don't," Rain said.

"Now you're feeling me," Deuce replied.

Ben placed Josie's hand in his as they walked slowly toward the small house. He dreaded this night, and could only imagine the liberal onslaught that was sure to come, but he was doing it for Josie.

"Come in, come in," Deuce said as he opened the door and gestured for them to walk on in. "Welcome to my nightmare!" Josie smiled but Ben failed to see the humor. He removed his hat and walked in slower, looking carefully at everything and everybody, as if he were entering some rival gang's territory. Deuce glanced at Josie and shook his head. His reaction to Ben, a kind of eye-rolling, will-the-brother-ever-get-it look, was matched only by the looks on the faces of his fellow guests. Ben was Mr. Insider and they knew it, which made him, in their idealistic little world anyway, the outsider.

"Josie, you already know everybody," Deuce said, standing between his two new arrivals. "Judge Braddock, since you don't, I would like you to meet my guests."

Ben looked at his guests. They stood as if in an inspection line, with one woman saluting him. It was Demi.

"It's an honor, your honor," she said, and then laughed. Ben smiled too, and shook her hand.

Then there was Rain, who curtsied before Ben. But she was a woman of some bulk and found herself losing her balance. Ben quickly assisted her.

Ralph was Demi's beau and he, like her, found everything humorous, including the way Ben said hello. "You know how to work that word, don't you?" he asked and laughed. Ben, completely lost, smiled anyway.

Finally, he met Malcolm. Malcolm was Rain's guy and he was immediately territorial, checking Ben out as if he were a competitor.

"I know guys like you," he said, nodding his head. "Think y'all got it going on. The money, the women, but I ain't no chicken shit myself. Remember that."

"Whatever, Malcolm, okay?" Josie said with frustration. Then she looked at Ben. "Just ignore him, Ben. He's a show-off."

"That's right," Malcolm said. "And don't you forget it."

"They are all *Bullhorn* veterans," Deuce said of his guests. "All with at least five years of experience in the trenches. Rain's my assistant editor."

"Is she?"

"I am. I'm his ace and Josie's his ho. I mean hole!" Demi and Ralph laughed. "I find the good assignments and she works 'em into the ground. That's what I mean."

Josie sighed. It was turning out exactly the way she had hoped it wouldn't. But Ben, she thought, was a trouper. He easily ignored a lot of the *Bullhorn*'s bull.

They sat down in the small living room, with Ben and Josie seemingly the center of attention. All questions seemed to be directed at them and all conversation somehow seemed to be about them. Ben was surrounded, by Rain on one side and Demi on the other, leaving Josie to find a seat in the chair across from the sofa. Ralph and Malcolm sat on the floor, while Deuce fumbled around in the tiny kitchen that could be seen from the living room, putting, Josie assumed, the finishing touches on dinner. Neither Ben nor Josie were particularly comfortable with the arrangements, especially Josie, who wondered why those two females felt it necessary to hover beside Ben as if he was a piece of meat.

"I'm gonna be honest with you, Ben," Rain said, striking first, Josie thought. "I'm not a republican."

Josie laughed. "No, shit," she said, and Ben glared at her.

"And I don't have anything against republicans, Ben, I don't. It's a free country. I just can't see how an intelligent brother or sister can be down like that. Republicans aren't righteous, that's what I think. They're all about keeping the status quo, not rocking the boat, *I got mine, tough luck to you.* Why would any conscientious person want to hook up with a party like that? I just don't see it." Ben crossed his legs, but he didn't respond to Rain. "But I guess you disagree?"

"Does it matter?"

"Excuse me?"

Ben didn't respond.

"Of course it matters," Rain said.

"Why's that?" Ben asked.

Rain smiled. "Because it does. Debate is good. It's healthy."

"It's a waste. My opinion won't change your opinion. Your opinion won't change mine. It's a waste."

Rain looked at her liberal colleagues. Nobody else seemed willing to take up the torch. "Malcolm," she said to Ben, in an to attempt to steer her conservative nemesis another way, "is my boyfriend. That's Malcolm." She said this and pointed to the youngest-looking brother in the room. "He believes marriage is for those who are afraid of commitment, not the other way around."

"I didn't say that," Malcolm said.

"That's what you implied," Rain said. "What do you think, Ben?"

Ben didn't say anything.

"Of course you would know more about it than Malcolm," Rain said. "Nobody in this room has ever been married before, isn't that interesting? Except you, I'm assuming. You've been married before, haven't you, Ben?"

Josie shook her head. "What difference does it make, Rain?"

"I'm just curious, Josie. Am I not allowed to ask the man a question?"

"She doesn't even want to get married," Malcolm said, "so I don't know why she's trippin'."

"I'm just asking the man a question. Damn."

"Yes," Ben said, "I've been married before."

"Just once?"

"Just once."

"Why didn't it work out?"

"Rain!" Josie yelled.

"He don't have to answer it if he don't want to. It's a free-ass country," Rain said.

"I'm curious myself," Demi said.

"Thank you!" Rain replied.

"My wife passed away," Ben said, and everybody looked at him. There was a hush in the room.

"For real?" Demi asked.

"For real."

"What happened?"

"She was ill."

"I'm sorry to hear that, Ben," Rain said. "I'm sorry. I wasn't trying to be smart or anything. I just thought you might have some insights, that's all."

"How long were you guys married before she . . . ?" Demi asked. "You know."

Ben exhaled. "Eighteen years."

"Damn!" Ralph smiled. "That's a long-ass time, bro," he said.

"Yes. Yes it is," Ben said and the animation of the conversation died right there. Josie, in a lot of ways, was glad for the silence. They were probing, trying to create controversy, to get some heat in the room, and she knew it. Silence kept their acid tongues at bay. But not for long.

"Josie doesn't talk to me at work," Demi said to Ben, finally breaking the peace. Josie couldn't believe she would even go there.

"Is that right?" Ben replied.

"That's right. But why, Ben? I try to be civil with her. I try to treat her with respect. But she always got to be rolling those big-behind eyes and holding up her hand like I'm so annoying to her."

"She don't have time for you, Dem," Ralph said with a smile. "She's a crusader, remember?"

"We're all crusaders. She ain't no more than the rest of us. She just thinks she is," Demi said.

"She don't be talking to me either," Rain said. "So don't even sweat that. But that's the difference between you and me, Dem. You worry about it. I don't give a dang."

"I don't either," Josie said, trying to stop the cats from scratching each other. Everybody looked at her. "Damn right I don't be talking to y'all. Y'all too petty for me."

"Was I talking to Josie Ross?" Rain asked the group in general.

"I don't know," Josie replied. "Were you?"

"No, I was not. So excuse me if I tend to my own business, unlike some people I know."

Josie rolled her eyes and glanced at Ben. He had that disapproving look going big time, as if just by responding to Rain's pettiness made it all her fault. She crossed her legs. *To hell with it,* she thought, as Demi and Rain wouldn't let up, but continued to talk about how standoffish and generally unfriendly Josie could be.

Deuce arrived back in the living room with a tray of hors d'oeu-vres. He set them on the coffee table and, while a few of his guests helped themselves, sat on the arm of Josie's chair.

"You all right?" he asked her.

"Yeah, I'm good."

"I heard the little back and forth."

"I didn't realize they held such hatred for me."

"It's not hatred. They don't know how to hate. They talk too much, that's all. Don't sweat that. You know how they can be."

"I know."

"I just want you to have fun. You deserve a little fun sometimes."

Josie smiled. "Thanks," she said.

"Oh, I love this necklace," Deuce said, touching the heart-shaped, diamond necklace around Josie's neck. "Is it real?"

Josie laughed. "Of course it's real."

"It's gorgeous."

"Thanks, Deuce," Josie replied, trying to get another look at it herself.

Ben looked at them, looked at the way Deuce's hand rested on the bare part of Josie's chest, but he didn't say anything. He pulled out a cigarette instead and interrupted Rain and Demi's conversation, which had shifted dramatically from Josie to the war on terror. "Does anyone mind if I smoke?" he asked. Everybody looked at Deuce. It was his house after all.

"Smoke?" Deuce asked.

Ben looked down at the cigarette he was tapping on his gold cigarette case, and then he looked back at Deuce. "Yes," he said.

Deuce smiled. "We believe cigarettes are perhaps the worst drug there is, Judge Braddock. They're addictive. Their second-hand toxins are deadly to innocent nonsmokers. And they wreak havoc on our environment. So, yes, we all mind if you smoke."

The others in the room looked at Ben, as if expecting some confrontation. Ben, however, wasn't game. He slipped his cigarette back into his shiny case.

Josie was less gracious. She thought Deuce's tone was unnecessarily harsh to a man he should be honored to have in his presence. He didn't have to come after all. But he did. He walked into this lion's den knowing full well that they were going to try and eat him alive. But he did it for her.

"You can go outside and smoke, Ben," she said to him.

"No, he cannot," Deuce corrected her. "I don't want those harmful pollutants anywhere near my home."

"You can't stop the man from smoking outside, Deuce, now come on."

"It's all right," Ben said quickly, and firmly, and that was the end of it. Josie looked at him.

"Guess who I saw the other day?" Demi said to the group in general.

"Who?"

"Prince."

"You mean the artist formerly known as Prince," Ralph corrected her.

"You mean the symbol," Rain said, correcting Ralph. "He became the symbol, remember?"

"I mean Prince," Demi said. "I saw Prince."

"Quit lying."

"I did."

"Where, Dem?" Rain asked her.

"Right in Minneapolis. He is from Minneapolis, you know. I was coming out of a supermarket and he was going in."

Ralph laughed loudest. "You're a liar, girl! You are such a liar," Ralph said. "You're going to hell."

"What's so big about seeing Prince?" Rain asked. "I see Usher all the time."

"In your sleep," Deuce said.

"Forget you. He and Michael Jackson were walking down the street together," Rain said, and they all laughed.

"I'm telling the truth," Demi said. "If I'm lying I'm flying."

"Get her a broom, y'all, so she can fly," Ralph said, "cause she most definitely is telling a lie."

"I saw what I saw. And I know what I saw."

"I saw Tupac day before yesterday," Malcolm said, and everybody looked at him.

"Tupac?" Ralph asked.

"Yes."

"What? On video?"

"Right here in Saint Cloud. What video? It was Tupac, P. Diddy, Ja Rule, and Dre. All right here."

Malcolm, like Rain, was normally so off the chain that he was more often than not ignored. But it was difficult to ignore him. Deuce looked at Ben. He didn't know a name Malcolm mentioned, he would guarantee it.

"What about you, Ben?" Deuce asked him, seizing an opportunity. "You into Dre?"

Ben stared at Deuce before responding. "No," he said.

"What you got against Dre?"

"I don't have anything against him. Particularly since I've never heard of the individual." The sighs and laughter were deafening. Josie rolled her eyes.

"You never heard of Dre?" Demi asked with wonderment in her eyes. "I'm talking Dr. Dre, Eminem's mentor? You've heard of Eminem, haven't you?"

"I've heard of him."

"You heard of the white boy," Malcolm said.

"What about Ja Rule?" Demi asked. "I know you heard of him."

"What difference does it make?" Josie asked.

"Nobody's talking to Josie Ross," Demi said.

"But getting back to Tupac," Rain said. "I wanna know how this brother saw Tupac."

"What about Nelly?" Demi asked Ben. "Everybody knows Nelly."

Ben glanced at Deuce as he whispered something in Josie's ear. Then they both stood up and walked into the kitchen.

"You heard of Nelly," Demi asked again. "Haven't you, Ben?"

"No," Ben said.

"You jiving?"

"Ah, Dem, drop it," Ralph said. "That brother ain't down like that. I don't know why you trying to front. Look at him. His shoes cost more than what you make in a month. And you think he's gonna know who Nelly is? Ask him about MC Hammer. Now he might know Hammer. But he ain't gonna know no Nelly."

"Anyway," Demi said, "I still say a black man in America should be acquainted with the black art form. And rap is the preeminent black art form in this country today. It's poetry, literature, and music all wrapped up in one. It's our heritage now. And I'm proud to know my heritage. So I don't find it humorous when a brother supposedly of all this esteem don't know a damn about his own heritage. That ain't funny to me."

"Back to this Tupac sighting," Rain said.

"Will you quit with that Tupac nonsense?" Ralph asked. "You know Malcolm's full of shit."

"I may be full of it," Malcolm said, "but I saw Tupac Shakur."

"Even though he's dead?" Rain asked.

"Man, you can believe them folks if you want to. They'll tell you anything. I guess Elvis is dead too."

Ralph and Rain looked at each other. Ben looked into the kitchen. Through the cut-away he could see Deuce and Josie. They were laughing at some private joke, and they'd lean against each other as if it was the funniest thing they'd ever heard. They'd called themselves preparing the meal for serving, but they were laughing more than they were preparing anything. It had been a long time since Ben had seen Josie so gay.

But he was more interested in Deuce Jefferson. He did not miss an opportunity to lay his hand on Josie, on her bare arm, or ever so lightly touch her small waist. And when she turned from Deuce and bent down to open the oven door, his eyes were fixed on her ass. He had the hots for Josie in a way that made Ben's skin crawl. It wasn't as if he was jealous of the brother. It took two to play that cheating game and Ben trusted Josie with his life. The problem was that Deuce Jefferson. He trusted that brother only as far as he could throw him.

The party broke up around eleven, after dinner and more talk of celebrity sightings, and Ben couldn't get away from that crowd fast enough. Josie, however, seemed reluctant to leave. She enjoyed the party, even laughing it up with the ladies by night's end. When they began dancing to some loud, hip-hop songs whose words Ben couldn't even understand, she was dancing and getting down like the young, carefree woman she should be. Ben was pleased, pleased that she was finally having herself some fun. But he was worried too.

He tapped his cigarette in his car's ashtray as he drove the long road home. Josie was talking up a storm, about Deuce and Rain and Demi and Ralph and even that "crazy-ass" Malcolm. But mostly she talked about Deuce.

"Did you see the way he danced? He doesn't know how to dance."

"He did okay to me."

"That's because you don't know how to dance, either. He had no skills. Even something simple, like when we waved our hands in the air and danced like we just didn't care, he was bouncing around like some uncoordinated scarecrow. It was so funny!"

Ben glanced at her. "I'm glad you enjoyed yourself."

"Oh, I did. Oh, Ben, you just don't know. For the first time in my life I felt as if I was a part of a group, you know? And Deuce. Dang. Wasn't he great? I mean, he was the one who made it all work. He was gracious and funny and he kept the party jumping. I never thought he could be so . . ." She glanced at Ben, and then looked at the road ahead. "I had a wonderful time, Ben."

Ben nodded his head. "Good," he said. He was genuinely happy for Josie. She deserved to have some fun. Even her obvious infatuation with the good-looking, young brother, Deuce, didn't rile him. At least he didn't think it did. But when they arrived at Josie's townhouse, and he walked her to her door, his usual routine of not even bothering to come in for a nightcap changed. He accepted her invitation. Even she was surprised.

"Really?"

"Yes."

Josie smiled. "But you usually say no."

"Okay, no. Does that make you feel better?"

"Too late," Josie said as she took him by the arm and pulled him in. Ben smiled and moved with the pull, and they ended up in her living room. Josie immediately kicked off her heels and headed for the bar, telling Ben to make himself comfortable.

Ben removed his hat, tie, and suit coat and slouched down on the sofa. He leaned his head back as fatigue overtook him. He had so many meetings ahead of him tomorrow that he was getting dizzy just thinking about them. He knew he should be home in bed getting his behind some rest. But he looked at Josie in that tight, red dress, bringing him a drink and smiling as she came, as if it was her pleasure to serve him. She was why he stayed. She was always the reason.

When Josie saw him so relaxed in his shirt-sleeves, she felt at ease. She was worried that he was going to complain about her behavior, about the way she danced and carried on as if she'd never had such a time. But he didn't appear to be in the complaining mood at all. And that was why she smiled. She handed him his drink and turned to sit beside him, just happy to have him with her, but he took her by the wrist. She looked at him as he gently pulled her closer to him and sat her on his lap. The surprise and delight that came over her, as if it was the most uncommon thing in the world to have her boyfriend show her some affection, caused her smile to leave. This was serious. *He* was serious.

He leaned forward and sat his drink on the coffee table, and then he pulled her into his arms. She leaned against his chest and held him tightly too. And when he cupped her chin in his hand and kissed her, her body trembled with desire. She looked at him, at his mustache first, and then his eyes, and that look of quiet desperation that pierced his once cool exterior stunned her. She wanted to ask if he was all right, but she couldn't. There was no time. He kissed her until her mouth opened, and his tongue slid in.

They kissed each other and pulled each other closer until their breathing became labored, and then it was time. He did not carry her upstairs. They would not have made it, so he did her there. Right on her sofa. Her legs opening wide and letting him in. And he knew what she needed. Knew it as soon as he touched her. Her need was as soft as a pillow and as loud as a striking cymbal, and as he entered her—as his tip touched her tip—and moved further in, she screamed.

It was the force. The force of his fullness alone had overtaken her. And relaxed her. And tensed her up so euphorically that she screamed again. He needed her to feel him tonight, every inch of him, greater than she had ever felt him before. And he pushed and he pushed, trying to slide into her deepest pocket, where the intensity alone would leave her speechless. And that feeling, so full and perfect, would wipe every memory of Deuce Jefferson from her mind. He had to reassert his claim. That was why he pushed. Harder and harder. Deeper and deeper. He could not lose her. Not to Deuce. Not to anyone. And he had to let her know.

CHAPTER 13

She browsed for hours and then settled on a silk smoking jacket, ocean blue and tangerine orange in color, with large, gold, hexagonal designs splattered across the middle and back. And it was extra large, which, to her, was more the reason to buy it. It was exactly Ben's size. Although it wasn't exactly his style, and she knew it, she felt cornered. She had to get him something. Although his fiftieth birthday was almost two months away, she wasn't one of those "shopaholics" who enjoyed mall hopping. It was a major undertaking for her. A big-ass headache was how she viewed it. So she shopped when she was in the mood to shop. And after last night with Ben—when he'd satisfied her beyond her wildest dreams—she was definitely in the mood.

The mall was crowded on a Friday night, as teenagers walked around as if they were in some museum, pointing out this style and that style and giving their unintelligible but loud opinions about taste. The older set, the thirty-somethings and older, hurried to the movies with their popcorn and three-year-olds as if those cinemas weren't showing more of the same crap they showed every week. Josie laughed as one kid tried to break free from her mother's clutches just as they were about to enter the theater. She pulled away and pulled away, crying not to be forced to sit through yet another one of those annoying-ass computerized cartoons. But the mother was bigger and stronger, of course, and the little one lost again.

Josie placed the receipt from her purchase in her wallet and then turned to head for the exit. And that was when she saw Deuce. He was sitting just a few feet in front of her, on a bench, sipping a Vanilla Coke and waving at her. At first she couldn't believe it was him. And then she smiled and walked toward him.

"I didn't know you did malls on a Friday night," she said jocularly as she sat down.

"Oh, yes," he said, sitting erect, his jeans and Nike tennis shoes a perfect fit with the younger crowd. "This bench is my second home."

"If that's true, that's pitiful."

Deuce laughed. "Okay, it's not my second home." He started to admit the truth to her, those wonderful, sincere eyes of hers always made him feel as if greater things existed inside of him, but he couldn't get himself to do it. He followed her; he watched as she stepped into her car at work in her beautiful kitenge pantsuit and heels, and he followed her to the post office, first, and then the mall. He felt they made a connection last night and he had every intention of following up today. But work was hectic, as breaking story after breaking story kept both of them jumping and almost completely out of each other's sight. He wanted to ask her to go for a drink with him after work, but when he approached her, she was on the phone with Ben. *The bastard wouldn't even take her calls before,* Deuce had thought, watching her talk with Ben. Now he couldn't leave her alone. That was why Deuce tailed her like some sick, pathetic stalker. He couldn't let the day end without seeing if she, too, still felt the heat they generated the night before.

"That's what I like about you, Deuce," Josie said. "You're honest. And I'm glad some bench in this mall isn't your second home."

"What were you doing in that artsy-fartsy store so long?"

Josie smiled. "Getting a gift."

"For me?"

"You wish. For Ben."

Deuce folded one leg over his lap and hesitated. "Is this something you jump up and do just for the heck of it, or is there an occasion for the gift?"

"It's his birthday. Or it will be in a couple months."

"A couple months? And you're buying the gift this soon?"

"While I'm in the mood, yes."

"You're good."

"Thank you."

"So how old is the old geezer?"

"Very funny."

"But for real. How old will he be?"

Josie hesitated. "Fifty," she said.

"Damn!"

"It's not that old."

Deuce laughed. "If you say so."

"It's not. He's the same age as—"

"Denzel, I know. You told me, already." Then he laughed again.

"Ah, forget you."

"I'm sorry, Josie. I'm just playing. Forgive me?"

Josie looked at Deuce. He was truly becoming a good friend. "You're forgiven."

"Thank you. So, what did you get pops, I mean, Ben?"

Josie smiled. "Keep on, Negro, okay?" Then she handed him the bag.

Deuce looked into the bag, a bag that smelled of perfume, and pulled out the jacket. His heart sank as he ran his hand across the expensive silk material. She bought this for her man, a man who didn't deserve the time of day, a man who would probably toss this gorgeous gift aside as if it were nothing. But that was Josie.

He glanced at the price tag hanging from the sleeve. And then he looked at Josie.

"It was on sale. Right?"

"Wrong."

"These are serious digits, lady. Almost a week's pay for you. How could you afford something like this?"

Josie laughed. "I'm not stupid, okay? You may as well say Ben bought it. Every time he spends any appreciable time at my house he's always leaving a wad of money on my dresser or on my night stand or stuffed down in my purse. It never fails. And I'm talking hundreds of dollars, okay?"

"Why would he be tossing you cash like that?" Deuce asked. Then added bitterly, "Like you was his ho?"

"I'm not his ho."

"I know you aren't. But does he know you aren't?"

"What are you talking about? He just gives me money, what's wrong with that?"

"Because he doesn't give it to you. He leaves it for you. I've been around, J. When I'm leaving cash for a female, I know what time it is. She done gave me the *wham-bam,* and now I'm giving her the green, the *thank you ma'am.*"

Josie put the jacket back in the bag and removed it from Deuce's grasp. *Sometimes he's great but sometimes he just doesn't get it,* she thought. "It ain't even like that," she said.

"Good," he said, to bring her back on his side. "I know it's not. But not because of him, but because I know you. And Josie Ross don't play that."

Josie smiled. "Got that right." She said this and then silence overtook their conversation.

Deuce took his arm and placed it behind the back of the bench, effectively hugging Josie without touching her, and he knew he had to slow his behind down. He would be *that close,* and then his mouth would drive her away once again. The way to her heart was going to be through her friendship and trust, not by trying to make Ben Braddock look bad.

"I'd better get going," she said.

"Where're you headed next?"

"Bookstore. I thought I'd get Bob Woodward's book for Ben. I heard him mention it a few times."

"Which book?"

"*Bush at War.*"

"Good Lord."

"I know. But I think he mentioned it because he knows I have such a hard time finding gifts for him. He was probably trying to help me out." Then she looked at her current gift. "And he's probably gonna hate this jacket."

"No way."

"Really? You really think he'll like it?"

"Man, will he. I love it."

Josie smiled. "And you hang out in a mall in jeans and tennis shoes."

Deuce nodded. It was one of those true "face it" statements, although it felt to him like a slap in the face. "Point taken," he said. "The brother is hard to please."

"He is. Especially with clothes. I once bought him an African safari shirt, you know, just to mix up that wardrobe of his a little."

"And he never wore it?"

"He wore it. Once. And the whole time he was pulling on it and looking at it and acting like I gave him a leopard suit to wear or something."

Deuce laughed. "That tight-ass," he said, and then quickly caught himself. "But at least he wore it."

"Right."

"So life in paradise is good?"

Josie glanced at Deuce and then looked away, unable to conceal her smile. "Yes," she said.

Deuce looked at her. "Maybe better than good, hun?"

Josie nodded.

"Come on, Josie. No secrets between us. I'm your buddy, remember? You can tell your old buddy here."

"Tell you what?"

"Why you can't wipe that smile off your face. And don't tell me it's nothing."

"It's not."

"Josie!"

Josie looked at Deuce. She had to tell *somebody*. "Let's just say Ben and I had a wonderful time last night."

"At the crib, I know."

"No. After your party," she said.

Deuce's heart dropped. "A good time?"

"A wonderful time."

"I see," Deuce said with a forced, clenched smile. "So y'all made the hook-up last night?"

Josie's smile expanded. "That's one way to put it."

"I see. Hey, that's great, Josie. I . . . wish I was there, what can I say?"

Josie laughed. "Now, I'm not saying that it's perfect in paradise, okay? But it's good. And it's getting better."

"So no more doubts about Ben's fidelity?"

She hesitated. "Sometimes I have my doubts about him. Yeah, I ain't even gonna lie. There's a part of him I still don't feel I know and I wonder about it. But in the end I think he loves me."

"You think?"

"I know, okay?"

"Okay, babe. And I'm glad for you. All I want is for you to be happy. But remember this, Josie, if there is ever trouble in paradise and you need a friend, you can count on me."

Josie smiled. And thanked him. It felt good, she thought, to have somebody like Deuce on her side.

CHAPTER 14

She was dressed beautifully in a black and white pantsuit made of African kente cloth, with black leather matching heels. She wore her hair in longer, thicker, smoother braids coming down out of a black and white cloth hair band that centered her small head. She grabbed her two gifts for Ben, got into her Mustang, and then drove hurriedly up Cypress Road. It was a nice May day in Minnesota, without even a hint of an overcast sky, and she drove expectantly. It was the morning of Ben's fiftieth birthday, a milestone if ever there was one, and she wanted to be the first to congratulate him.

But her cell phone began ringing. She grabbed it from her purse as she turned onto Rolling Ridge, where the traffic was faster and more contemptible, and she had to adjust to the faster road before she could answer. She glanced at her phone's caller ID. An unknown number.

"Yes, hello?" she finally said into the phone.

"Hello there, Josephine."

She hesitated. Although it had been months since the last call, she still remembered that voice. "What do you want?"

"That's no way to talk to a lady. I'm trying to help a sista out. But hey, I can hang up."

"What do you want?"

"What did he tell you?"

She paused. "Who?"

"Don't play games with me, Josephine. What did he tell you?

That I was a figment of your imagination? That he's faithful as a bird dog and you're out of your mind believing for one second that he could want anybody else? Is that the gist of it?"

Josie hesitated. "Something like that."

"And you believed him?" She laughed. "Girl, you're not even competition for me. I don't know why I'm even bothering with your silly ass."

"I don't either."

"How's your sex life?"

Josie paused. "None of your business."

"Mine is great. You get quarterly hits. I get nightly hits. And if my memory serves me correctly, you got your hit just after your boss's party. You got your holler on then. Two months ago. And he hasn't touched your ass since."

Josie couldn't believe her ears. How would she know, she thought, as she quickly pulled her Mustang over to the side of the road and parked. "How did you . . . ?" she said into the phone. "Who told you . . . ?"

"He told me about it. All about it. He told me how you was crying and acting a fool and pulling all on him. So he gave you a taste. Yeah, he told me. See Ben is my man. He's completely honest with me. He even told me why he did it. To keep you quiet. He makes love to you every blue moon just to keep you quiet."

"What are you talking about? Keep me quiet about what?"

"He feels sorry for you, Josephine, don't you understand that? That's what this is all about. You got him out of that jam in Florida and he feels indebted to you. That's why he hasn't kicked you to the curb, yet. That's the only reason why. But he told me not to worry about a thing. Not one thing. As soon as he sees when you can handle the truth, he'll come clean. And that'll be the end of you with my man. Okay, bitch? So don't even try to act like you own some special place in his heart because you don't own shit. You're his quarterly ho. That's all. His bitch on the side. And that's all you will ever be to him."

"Why are you doing this?"

"Wake up, Josephine. Stop being so dumb. Ben is not your knight, girl, you need to wake up and accept it."

"Why don't you give your name? You bad. You're so tight with Ben. What are you afraid of?"

"You just don't get it, do you? You just don't wanna wake up and smell the coffee. Then don't, bitch, okay? I'm tired of playing with you!" She said this and hung up the phone. Josie stared forward at the traffic whipping past her, passing her by, and then she hung up too.

She thought about turning around. She didn't know if she could face him right now. But she knew she had to resist that urge to quit. She kept driving, slowly, methodically, trying with all she had to dismiss the woman on the phone. That woman was a stranger to her and could have been anybody, and she must never forget that, she decided.

But it was still troubling to Josie. That woman knew too much. She knew things about her relationship with Ben, personal, intimate details, and that wasn't easy to overlook. But she could be anybody. She could even be a friend of Ben's, somebody he told his problems to, and who was using that friendship to her own advantage. But the point Josie decided to keep in mind was a simple one: the woman was a stranger. And she wanted Ben. Only she needed Josie to play along, and Josie wasn't about to fall for that game again. The woman, she had to keep reminding herself, was a stranger.

But Meredith was no stranger. That was what Josie thought when she finally made it to Walden Woods and parked her car in front of Ben's brick home. Meredith's dark blue Corvette was parked alongside his Mercedes in the driveway, parked as if it belonged there. All Josie could do was shake her head, because it was quickly shaping up to be one of those days. One of those crazy, awful, *enough already* days.

Two months ago Meredith Chambers became Ben's executive assistant and Ben was rarely seen without *Mal,* as he called her, by his side. It wasn't even nine o'clock yet on a Saturday morning, Josie thought, as she got out of her car and pulled out her gifts. The idea of it, that Meredith had beaten her to the punch or, even worse, had never gone home Friday night, caused Josie's suppressed anger to slowly emerge. Enough was enough. She already didn't trust her. Just the way she behaved around Ben, all smiles and all in his face all the time, kept her suspicious. Josie had enough sense to know that a female like Meredith Chambers, the personification of the cunning seductress, wasn't about to go through all of that skinning and grinning just for the fun of it.

But as Josie stood in the calm of the morning, walking slowly toward Ben's front door, she decided to check herself. Females wanted Ben and would stop at nothing to take him away from her, and she had to remember that. And although she didn't trust Meredith, she was learning to trust Ben. She couldn't keep jeopardizing her relationship every time some woman had a story to tell. Their relationship depended on trust, even in the face of so much contradiction. Unconditional, blinding trust. The kind Josie always had a problem with. The kind Josie knew she had to learn to have.

She rang his doorbell twice. After what seemed to her to be too long a time, Ben finally answered the door. He was dressed comfortably, in a pair of painter pants and an undershirt, and the whiff of his sweet cologne as the door slung open caused her to relax.

"Good morning," she said with a smile, the two gift boxes nearly covering up her entire face.

"Hey, there," Ben said cheerfully, and then immediately removed the boxes from her grasp. "What brings you over here?"

Josie laughed. "It's your birthday, Ben. Remember?"

Ben looked at her, looked her up and down. Then he smiled. "Just kidding," he said and took her by the hand.

She looked at Ben as he closed the large door of his home. He gave her a peck of a kiss on the lips, and then told her to come on in. She followed him across the foyer, down the steps, and into his huge, quiet living room. Her hope was that she'd find Meredith Chambers busy at work instead of lounging around, thus explaining why she felt it necessary to be at Ben's home so early on a Saturday morning, but her hope was quickly dashed. Meredith was in the living room, and she wasn't working. She was reclining on Ben's sofa with her plump legs crossed, a cup of coffee in her hand, wearing her tight, up-her-behind skirt and a strapless tank top only confirming Josie's suspicions. Any woman who would dress that provocatively in the presence of her boss had a lot of things on her mind. And work, Josie decided, wasn't one of them.

"Well, hello, Josephine!" Meredith said gaily. "Come on in, girl!"

The nerve of the chick astounded Josie. She looked at Ben, as he sat her gifts on the side table, but he didn't appear interested at all in putting Meredith in her place.

"Have a seat, Josie," he said. "Would you like something to drink?"

"No," Josie replied, as she sat down.

Ben sat between his two guests and Meredith quickly seized the opportunity—not to leave as Josie had hoped—to push as many of Josie's buttons as she possibly could.

"So, Josephine," she asked, "what are you doing here this time of morning? I thought you weren't an early bird. Especially on Saturdays."

Josie looked at Meredith, at that ridiculous smile on her face, and a sense of uselessness overtook her. *I can't play the game, so why bother,* she thought.

"I'm here because it's Ben's birthday," she said in an almost defeated tone. Ben looked at her.

"Yes, it is," Meredith said. "That's certainly why I'm here too. I wanted to be the first to congratulate Ben on his glorious day. And I was." Meredith said this with some degree of satisfaction.

"You okay?" Ben asked Josie, but she didn't respond.

"So tell me, Benjamin," Meredith said, "how does it feel to be fifty big ones?"

Ben continued to stare at Josie. He had never seen her so subdued. "The same way it felt to be forty-nine big ones," he replied to Meredith, and Josie smiled.

"Now that's better," Ben said in response to Josie's smile, and then he gave her a soft slap on the thigh.

Josie smiled. She was a survivor, she figured, because the morning's events didn't cripple her. She didn't fall to pieces, anyway.

"Open my gifts," she said to Ben.

"I thought I'd wait until later."

"Why?"

Ben smiled. "Just kidding, sweety. Of course I'll open your gifts."

Josie handed him the smaller gift first, the book, and he unwrapped it. When he saw that it was indeed *Bush at War,* he smiled. "I see you caught my hint," he said.

"I knew that was why you mentioned it. I even told Deuce that at the mall. I told him you kept mentioning that book so I could buy it for your birthday."

Ben hesitated, and then pulled out a pair of reading glasses and put them on. "At the mall?" he asked, as he flipped over the book to read the jacket cover.

"Yes. That's where I bought the book."

"And Deuce was there?"

"He was there that night, yeah. Just hanging out. I told him you wanted me to get it for you."

"You told him this last night?" Ben asked, and looked at Josie over the top of his reading glasses.

"No. When I bought the book."

Ben continued to look at Josie. She, at first, didn't get it. Then she realized he was fully expecting an explanation.

"We were at the mall. I mean, not together. I was at the mall and I saw him there. And we talked for a little while." She felt defensive, and she didn't know why. "That was two months ago."

Ben nodded. "Okay," he said, stared at her a moment longer, and then continued looking at the book. "I'm glad you caught the hint."

"Don't forget my other gift," she said.

Meredith smiled. "How can he forget that massive box before us?"

"Now isn't that the truth?" Ben said to Meredith and they both laughed. Although Josie didn't like that, she refused to stop smiling.

He unwrapped the bigger gift just as quickly. And when he pulled it out, when he pulled out the loud-colored, silk smoking jacket, Meredith laughed. Ben, at first, shook his head. He could not believe it.

"Josie, what is this?"

"You don't like it?"

Ben stared at the jacket. "It's not exactly my style, sweetheart."

"I thought you might wanna switch up a little."

"Why would you think that? Have I ever given you a reason to think that?"

Josie was shocked. "It's a gift, Ben, dang. You're supposed to say it's nice and be grateful, not criticize it."

"So you don't believe in truth at all costs after all?"

"That's not what I'm saying."

"That's what it sounds like to me." Then he looked at the price tag. "Josephine?" She didn't respond. "Josephine?"

"What?" she replied harshly.

"You paid eight hundred dollars for this thing?"

Meredith began laughing again, successfully pushing Josie's buttons again.

"What's so damn funny?" Josie asked angrily, and leaned forward to get a good look at Meredith. Ben pushed her back against the sofa, which only angered her more.

"You know what," she said angrily, rising quickly, "I don't care what you do with that jacket. You don't like it, then fine. Burn it for all I care!"

Ben frowned. "What's the matter with you? Sit down."

"What did Meredith get you?" Josie asked, totally ignoring his order. "What did she get you? Something perfect, I'm sure. Just give me my jacket anyway!" She said this, then snatched the jacket from Ben's grasp. "And you're right. I don't know why I would spend eight hundred dollars on your sorry ass, either! Meredith is enough warmth for you, I'm sure! All these women calling me, knowing all about my business, and my dumb behind overlooking it. Yeah, that's Josie, always looking on the bright side. Those women are just jealous, that's what I told myself. Yeah, right. My ass was just stupid, and blind as a bat. My eyes were just completely closed to all this bullcrap you've been doing. Completely closed. But they're wide open now!"

She said this as she moved swiftly toward the front door, her anger so pronounced it was surprising even to her. As she walked out the door, as she couldn't seem to get out fast enough, she tossed the loud, colorful smoking jacket on the floor of the foyer behind her.

Meredith smiled. She could not have hoped for a more perfect scene. Ben, however, leaned back. There was nothing perfect about the scene to him. And he wasn't smiling, either. He was stunned.

CHAPTER 15

Seven days. That was how long it had been since Josie had last seen or heard from Ben. Seven whole days. She'd called his office by the middle of the week and left messages, but he hadn't returned her calls. Whitney, who was becoming more up front with Josie than had previously been the case, had admitted that Ben was getting her messages and wasn't all that busy. He just didn't want to talk to her.

She even called Meredith to see if she'd give up some clues, but Meredith had her own agenda. She even intimated that Ben had gone on with his life, and Josie should do the same. Meredith had acted as if their separation was permanent, as if there wasn't going to be a day, any day now, when Ben would come walking through Josie's front door.

Josie thanked Meredith for her so-called advice but told her not to worry, that she and Ben were merely having a disagreement, that was all.

But Meredith's words stayed with Josie, as she worked, as she came home and sipped sherry in her living room. *Was it possible,* she thought. Could Ben really just leave her like that and go on with his life? She never thought it was even a possibility. Even when Angela Caldwell warned her once, as Scotty had many times, that her antics were driving Ben away, she never fully comprehended the reality of what they were saying. Drive Ben away? For a day, maybe. A few days tops. They had those kinds of separations all the time. But forever? *Never,* she thought. But that was before his birthday. That was before she couldn't even contain herself on the man's fiftieth birthday.

And it had been seven days. The longest separation of their entire tumultuous time together. As Sunday morning rolled around—day eight—and she still hadn't been able to get any sleep, and the clock on her night stand moved from 3:59 A.M. to 4:00 A.M., a sense of panic began to grip her. What if it was true? What if all those predictions had finally come true and she had succeeded in driving Ben away permanently? What if he had decided eight days ago, after she had left his home in defiance, all but telling him that he and his birthday could kiss her ass, that enough was enough? She knew he had been upset and disappointed once again, but what if she had driven the man to his breaking point? Everybody, she knew, had a limit.

She threw the covers off of her, and got out of bed. She was in her nightgown, a long shirt with a big, pink bear on the front. She put on her overcoat, slipped in her pair of tennis shoes, and grabbed her keys as she hurried out of her bedroom, down the stairs, and out of her front door. It may be too late. He may well have given up on her and was already going on with his life. But she wasn't ready to give up on him. Not Ben. Not without a fight.

She drove to Walden Woods so fast she was astounded that a cop didn't ticket her. She got out of her car and hurried to his front door. She could have rung the bell and awakened him, but she decided against it. It would take too long for him to get downstairs. She, instead, decided to use the spare key he now kept under a flower pot. She unlocked his front door and flicked on the light. The house was so quiet that the sound of her feet moving across the foyer was deafening. But she moved lightly and quickly, down the steps, across the living room, up the stairs, and onto the corridor that led to his bedroom, a huge room at the end of the hall.

Her walk slowed as she turned on the hall's light. She hesitated and stopped, but then kept walking toward Ben's bedroom. He was either going to welcome her with open arms or insist that she leave his home at once, and leave the key while she was at it. What if he wasn't alone? What if another woman was snuggling next to the man Josie loved, and she just couldn't handle it?

That was all the more reason, she felt, to come. Because if he wasn't alone, if some female was in bed with him, then no further discussion would be necessary. Time would be out for talking, and all Josie would have to do was leave. That was why she pushed the bedroom door open quickly, to get it over as fast as possible. When she walked around the side wall and saw him alone in bed, she exhaled. Inwardly, she rejoiced. She never realized just how much she had missed him.

He was asleep, lying on his back, his face perfectly serene in the quiet room. He had on no shirt (Ben wore only a pair of boxer shorts to bed), and as Josie moved toward him she didn't know whether to wake him or just get in bed with him.

She got in bed. She removed her overcoat and tennis shoes, and laid in his bed beside him. For nearly five minutes she just lay there, afraid to make the next move, afraid that he would wake up and tell her to get lost once and for all. So she lay still, watching him as he slept, wondering if he was still working too hard, if he was taking care of himself properly, if he missed her at all.

But sooner or later, she knew she had to act. So she did. She moved closer to him and touched his bare chest with her hand. His eyes opened as soon as she touched him. Her heart raced as his eyes finally realized that it was her.

"Hi," she said, trying to smile, but still in too much pain. He hesitated, still trying to wake up, still trying to understand what was going on.

"Where did you come from?"

"The moon," Josie said. "I finally got off of it."

Ben sighed and closed his eyes once more, still battling sleep and the emotions that seeing Josie again evoked. Josie was disappointed that there wasn't a more definite reaction from him. She was, after all, expecting fireworks, but she was also pleased. He didn't throw her out. He didn't have any bad visceral reaction to her. That, at least, was good news.

She lay her head on his chest and closed her eyes. She could feel his arm move around her and begin stroking her hair. She relaxed to the feel of his stroke, and then looked up into his face. His eyes were open now, wide open, and he was staring without blinking at the wall just above their heads.

"I'm sorry, Ben," she said. "And I know you're tired of hearing it, but I mean it this time. I didn't realize my behavior would affect you like this." Ben didn't say anything. He just lay there. His stare was like steel, hard and cold. Josie knew she had to plead her case, or risk losing him forever.

"It was a bad day, Ben," she said. "And it was your birthday. It wasn't supposed to be a bad day. But when I got that call first thing that morning, and then I saw Meredith Chambers already at your house . . ."

"What call?" Ben asked her.

Josie hesitated. She had promised herself to never tell Ben about it, to just suppress it, but she also knew that he had to understand what she was going through.

"That woman called me again. The one who claims to be your girlfriend." She said this and looked at him. He was still staring at the ceiling. "She wanted to know what you told me about her. She said you was just waiting for the moment to kick me to the curb, but you didn't know how to break it to me without breaking my heart." Josie waited for a denial. She waited for him to reassure her. He didn't do either. "So I was already not feeling it, you know what I'm saying?"

Ben almost shook his head, seemingly in disgust, but Josie wasn't sure. Although he continued to stroke her hair, he seemed to her to be a million miles away. She had to do something, she thought. Her desperation was like a noose around her neck, and choking her. The harder she pulled against the rope the more she choked, but she kept pulling anyway.

She slid her body on top of Ben. It got his attention. He looked at her. But the look in his eyes scared her. Maybe it was the fact that he was fifty now. Maybe it was the fact that she had crossed some line he had drawn but didn't tell her about. Maybe it was true what the anonymous caller had told her and he was looking for the first opportunity to get rid of her and this was it. Josie didn't know for sure. But she did know that his patience with her, which wasn't very strong to begin with, was gone.

She slid her body further up on his stomach until her lips were parallel to his, but when she moved to kiss him on those lips, he turned his face away. He placed his arm around her and slid her back down.

"Get some sleep, Josie," he said to her.

She choked again, but she didn't show it.

"Okay," she said, as if that were all right with her, and then she lay her head against his chest. Her fear was as real as the ache in her heart. It was a pounding, unrelenting fear. *Am I losing you?* she wanted to ask him. But she couldn't. Her fear of what he might say crippled her. *No, Josie*, he might have said. *You're not losing me. You already have.*

Meredith was up at 6:00 A.M. She wanted to get at least an hour in at the gym before Sunday school, and she didn't want to feel rushed. She hated to rush. Inevitably something was forgotten, or misplaced, or permanently affected when she rushed.

She got out of bed and moved slowly along the hall. She was yawning and stretching as she walked, ready to take on whatever the day might bring. She glanced into Hines's bedroom, a regular routine of hers. She actually walked past, and then back again because she couldn't have seen what she'd thought she had seen. When she looked in again and saw him there, on the floor, his covers askew as if he had fallen out of bed, she hurried to him.

"Hines?" she asked. "What are you doing?" He lay stiff as a board, his face squashed down in the carpet, his arms underneath his lifeless body. Meredith's heart dropped.

She looked around, at the bed, at the night stand, and that was when she saw the pill bottles. His sleeping pills, which only marginally helped his nightmares. One bottle was empty, one bottle almost. Although she was terrified, she refused to succumb to that anxiety. She got busy. She called 911 with his cordless phone, and then tried with all she had to lift him up and walk him around. But he would not budge. She turned him over, checked his pulse. Nothing. She checked his heartbeat. Not a sound. She tried to give him CPR but he was cold as ice. She tried again, and then again. Then she sat, resigned and disgusted, beside her brother. She looked at him. It wasn't possible. He could not have given up. He was Hines. He was her brother. He would not have given up.

She placed him in her arms. He lay beside her like a rag doll. "Come back, Hines," she said to him. "I need you to stop this and come back to me. You understand? You've got to hold on a little longer. Just a little longer. We're so close. They can't win. You hear me? We can't let them win." Then she paused, as emotion overtook her. "We're all each other has. Hines? Come back, Hines. *Please* come back."

She rocked him and held him, but she knew there would be no coming back. Her sorrow would be brief, because it was unproductive. Vengeance was sweeter to her. And that was what she decided to latch onto. Sweet revenge. She looked at her brother, at her weak, helpless, now lifeless brother, and she smiled a slow, unnatural smile.

The sound of sirens could be heard on the street below. The men of the hour were ready to come and take away a man Meredith swore was alive and well and thirsty for revenge too, a man who had known he'd already died years ago, died when life itself had lost its flavor. But he had been too afraid to admit it. Until now.

Josie was still lying on top of Ben, still wide awake while he had long since fallen asleep, when the phone rang. She looked at him. He slept serenely and showed no reaction to the sound. So she sat up, straddled him, and answered the phone herself.

"Hello?" she said in a low voice. There was a definite hesitation. It was Meredith.

"Put Ben on the phone," she said, and as soon as she said it, Ben's eyes opened.

"It's for you," Josie said, handing the phone to him.

He placed his hand on the back of his head and tried to adjust his body to Josie's weight. He glanced at the clock. It was 7:22 A.M. "Hello?" he said into the phone.

Meredith paused.

"Hello again?"

"Hi," she said.

Ben paused. "Hey, how are you?"

"Not so good."

Ben glanced at Josie. "What's wrong?"

"Could you come over?"

"What's happened, Mal?"

Another pause. This one sincere. "My brother is dead, Ben."

Ben tried to sit up, but he couldn't with Josie straddling him. "Good Lord."

"He committed suicide."

"Good Lord, Mal."

"Can you believe it? A brother of mine committed suicide." She sounded more angry than sorrowful, but Ben didn't judge her.

"I'm on my way," he said. After she thanked him he hung up the phone.

"Get up," he told Josie, and she quickly moved out of his way.

"What's the matter?"

"Meredith's brother died," he said, hurrying for the bathroom.

"Oh, my God. My God, Ben. I didn't even know she had a brother."

"Me either," Ben said.

Josie could hear Ben peeing, and she knew if she didn't dress in a hurry he was going to go to Meredith's without her. She hurried to his closet, hoping that she had left a change of clothes there before. But there was nothing, not a thing. She looked at Ben as he peered out of the bathroom.

"Come shower with me," he said.

"I don't have any extra clothes over here."

"Yes, you do. They're in that bottom dresser drawer. I put them away. But come on, we need to get a move on." Ben said this and hurried back into the bathroom, with Josie close on his heels.

CHAPTER 16

The funeral was held on a balmy Tuesday afternoon. Ben held Meredith's hand as they walked across the graveyard to her brother's final resting place. Josie walked behind them, her dark dress and dark shades keeping her somber. There was something devastating about it all to her. She watched Meredith, who moved as if she could barely walk, leaning against Ben as if he were all the strength she had. When Josie and Ben had gone over to Meredith's that Sunday morning, Josie thought for sure the woman was going to follow her brother down the road to self-destruction. She would get too busy, almost manic in her drive, then she'd become catatonic, staring at the wall, unable to eat or talk or, at one point, move. Ben had been so worried about her that he and Josie had stayed with her that entire day and night. According to Meredith, she had no family, and her brother had no friends.

Now, just like that, and by her brother's own hand, her entire family was gone. Josie stood on the opposite side of the grave and watched Meredith as she squeezed Ben's hand. She had on a fashionable black dress and hat, almost too fashionable for the occasion, and she appeared to Josie to still be in a daze. No tears were shed; no emotional outburst came; and she never, not once, looked down at her brother's grave. The few other attendees, all Denlex executives, seemed surprised by this, some even whispering amongst themselves that Meredith was holding up well. Josie didn't see it. Something was wrong with this picture, she thought. She was too together, too calm, and way too reliant on Ben to be anywhere near "holding up well." As Ben took his arm and placed it around Meredith's waist, and she leaned into him as if she didn't know what she would do without him, Josie looked away. The last thing Ben needed was for her to show any outward manifestations of jealousy over his attention to a grief-stricken friend. It would be the height of selfishness. And Josie wasn't even trying to be like that.

After the funeral Ben rode in the limo with Meredith, and Josie followed them in his Mercedes, and she had held her tongue. From what Josie could see, Meredith would have no one, not a single soul, if Ben wasn't there to comfort her. No college friends or old business acquaintances, or even distant relatives had paid Meredith any visits. It was always Ben and Josie. Especially Ben. Ben had made all of the funeral arrangements. Ben had made sure Meredith ate dinner every evening and breakfast every morning. Ben had even hired an assistant to be there with Meredith, to wait on her hand and foot, but Meredith had insisted such an act of kindness wasn't necessary and fired the girl.

But it was completely necessary, Josie thought, as the funeral limo swung in front of Meredith's apartment complex and Josie drove ahead for a parking spot. It was necessary because Meredith needed the attention and wanted it solely from Ben, when Ben was already stretched too thin. But he was a good friend to Meredith in her hour of bereavement, and he never once refused her unrelenting need of his time. Josie had almost told Ben that he wasn't helping Meredith, that she needed to do things for herself in order to learn how to cope. But Josie again had held her tongue. Her relationship with Ben was still recovering from her outburst on his fiftieth birthday. When Meredith had phoned that Sunday morning and they had rushed to be by her side, the truth of where she stood in Ben's life had been placed on the proverbial back burner. And not to this day had that been resolved. Josie knew she had to be careful and watch her step. She had no good will to risk.

She ended up parking nearly six blocks away. By the time she walked back to the apartment building and made her way up to Meredith's floor, Ben and Meredith had been comfortably inside for nearly ten full minutes.

Meredith came through the flapping kitchen doors with a large bowl of tossed salad, three salad plates, and a bottle of vinaigrette. "I hope this is enough," she said as she set everything on the table. Ben was already seated, smoking a cigarette, and Josie joined him. When she saw what Meredith had prepared, she frowned.

"You don't have any food?" she asked her.

Meredith looked at Josie, and then she looked at Ben.

"This is fine, Mal," he said.

"What?" Josie asked. "I was just asking a question. I'm sorry but I'm hungry."

"Then why don't you go find a restaurant and eat," Meredith said with some degree of anger.

"I don't see why you have to get all upset, Meredith. I just asked a simple question. You ain't got to try and throw down on me because I asked a question."

"I just buried my brother," Meredith said, and she and Ben both glared at Josie. "I know that doesn't mean a whole heap to you, but it means everything to me."

"What does your brother's death got to do with this? I can ask—"

"Josie?" Ben said. Josie hesitated, and then looked at Ben. "Please," he said.

"What did I do?"

"Not now."

"But what did I do?"

"Ben," Meredith said in a low, measured voice, and he looked at her. "May I see you in the kitchen, please?"

Josie rolled her eyes and looked away. Asking herself to hold her tongue was like asking a baby not to cry, but she still didn't see where she had said anything wrong.

Ben put out his cigarette in the ashtray on the table, and then walked slowly into Meredith's kitchen. Meredith was leaning against the drainboard with her arms folded and her face seemingly flustered.

"She's got to go," she said as soon as Ben walked up to her.

"Come on, Mal."

"I mean it, Ben. I can't take her today. I'm two minutes back from my brother's funeral and she wants me to cook her a meal."

"That's not what she meant."

"I don't care. My nerves are shot. I just can't deal with her today. Send her home. Please."

Ben looked at Meredith, who didn't understand what she was

asking him to do, but he knew he could not say no to her. Not now, not when her disappointment was already overwhelming. "Okay," he said, and returned to the dining room.

Josie was still sitting at the big table, her small body leaning back and staring at Ben. He rubbed his mustache with his hand, which Josie knew meant that he had something heavy on his mind, then he walked around the table and stood beside her. She turned and looked up at him.

"It's best if you take my car and go on home," he said. Josie looked away, and then back up at him, her face betraying her hurt.

"Why? Because I asked her a question?"

"She's not herself right now, Josie."

"Neither are we, Ben. We haven't even had a chance to discuss our own problems."

"Don't worry about that. Just go on home."

Josie hesitated. "How are you going to get home?"

"I'll be all right," he said.

"I can come back and pick you up."

Ben stared at Josie. She had a heart of gold, he thought, even if nobody seemed to believe it. "I'll make it okay, Josie. You just go on."

Josie stood up from the table and allowed Ben to walk her to the door. When he opened the door, she turned toward him.

"Call me later," she said.

"I will," he said, and kissed her on the lips.

She looked around, at the too-neat apartment, and again at Ben, and then she left.

Meredith, as if she'd heard Josie's departure, came out of the kitchen and walked toward the living room.

"Help yourself to the salad, Ben," she said. "I'm going to change."

Ben nodded okay and Meredith disappeared into her bedroom. Ben felt lousy. Josie really did nothing wrong and did not deserve such treatment, but he also had to keep the occasion in perspective. Meredith was in pain, not Josie, and until Meredith was able to stand on her own again, he was going to support her.

They spent the remainder of the evening sitting in the living room listening to jazz. Meredith had changed all right. She wore a housecoat that appeared to be bare underneath to Ben, as the front flap constantly flipped open revealing her plump legs to the upper reaches of her thighs. Ben sat across from her, a cigarette in one hand, a glass of wine in the other, and every time Meredith crossed her legs, and then uncrossed them, he looked away. She was a gorgeous woman, he thought, who was going through hell. Any attention she could get, even negative attention, was going to be welcomed by her. He tried not to oblige her.

She sipped from her glass of wine. "The worst part about it," she said, "is the loneliness. I felt it the second I knew he was gone. He was all I had, you see. He was it. My world. The reason I got up every morning. And he was gone. My reason for living, for being, my world, was gone." She looked at Ben. "Can you imagine such loneliness?"

Ben hesitated. "Yes," he said.

Meredith seemed genuinely interested in this. "You can?"

Ben nodded. "Yes."

"What happened?"

"My wife died. We had been married for eighteen years."

"Eighteen years? My, eighteen glorious years," she said.

"No, they weren't glorious. I can't say that. She was ill. From the very beginning, before we even married."

"And you married her anyway?"

Ben hesitated, looking down at his glass of wine. "Yes."

Meredith smiled. "She was pregnant and you were a gentleman?"

Ben smiled, but very faintly. "No, she wasn't pregnant. I just happened to love her."

"But you knew she was ill?"

"Yes."

"What was wrong with her?"

Ben sighed. The memories would never fade. "She had numerous problems. She was bipolar; she was schizophrenic. She would hit the outer reaches of all of her disorders, sometimes in the same day."

"My Lord. It sounds horrible. Was she on any type of medication, Ben?"

"Not at first. I was in college when we first married. She was a waitress in a local cafe. She had a tenth-grade education but a sharp, impressive intellect."

"A beautiful mind."

"A beautiful mind. That's right. She was also nine years older than I."

Meredith smiled. "I would have never guessed that. Your wife was older than you?"

"She was. Older and wiser and very much what I needed. She calmed me down."

Meredith laughed. "Now I've heard it all. I assumed you were born cool, Ben. It seems so natural. I didn't know you actually had to work at it."

"I was impatient, and irascible, and I wanted what I wanted. Liz, that was her name, Elizabeth, taught me to settle down and to respect differing views and opinions and, yes, people."

"People like her? From the other side of the tracks?"

Ben nodded.

"I thought so. I could tell good breeding a mile away." Meredith said. "And you have that. Your parents were professional people, weren't they?"

Ben raised his glass to his mouth. "Yes," he said, and then sipped.

"They approved of your union with Liz?"

"They approved of everything I did. So they approved. Although my mother warned me."

"About Liz's mental problems?"

"Yes. She knew it was going to be hell. She pulled me aside and without mixing words told me that it would, that I would be Liz's nursemaid far more than her husband. She was right."

"And even with that warning from your dear mother, you married this uneducated waitress with all of these emotional problems, who also happened to be nine years older than you? You married her anyway?"

Ben nodded. "Yes," he said.

Meredith smiled greatly. Just the concept alone was unfathomable to her. "Why, Ben?"

"Because I loved her."

"And you thought love would conquer all?"

"I did then. I certainly don't anymore."

"I'm awfully glad to hear that. Because you're right. Love doesn't conquer a damn thing. Devotion does. Planning does. Making it up in your mind that this is the course to take and staying the course no matter what. That's what conquers all. That's what makes it sweet in the end."

Ben stared at Meredith, at the way the anger seemed to rise in her voice, at the look of almost wonderment in her eyes. Her pain ran deep, he thought. And it was entrenched.

"So," Meredith said, realizing that she was talking more about herself than anything Ben should need to hear, "whatever became of Liz Braddock? Was she institutionalized by the time she died?"

"No. I didn't allow that."

"You didn't allow it? You mean for eighteen years you . . . You're telling me that during the entire time of your marriage, all eighteen years, you kept your wife with you?"

"That's right. I had been warned. I entered that marriage, for better or worst, with my eyes wide open."

"Did she get better?"

"No. Progressively worse."

"And you wouldn't hospitalize her?"

"I couldn't. She was my wife. She wasn't playing a game. She was sick. She would not have been sick if it was up to her."

"How did she die?"

Ben paused. The worst memory of all. "Same way," he said to her.

Meredith, at first, didn't understand. And then she couldn't believe it. "Good gracious," she said. "*Suicide?*"

Ben didn't respond.

"Oh, God, Ben. It was suicide?"

The emotion of those old, painful days welled inside of him like a rushing wind. "Yes."

"But how? Why?"

"She couldn't take it anymore, Mal. She didn't want to be sick. She didn't want me to be her nursemaid. She used to be an independent woman. If anybody was going to nursemaid anybody it was going to be her nursing me. That's how she felt about it. But it didn't work out that way for her." Ben said this and then sipped his wine.

"And eighteen years later she ended it all?"

Ben nodded. He was called home. It was a cold, rainy, miserable night. He was meeting with fellow judges at the courthouse when the girl he had hired called him home. They were having dinner, she said. The girl was trying to talk about cheerful things, to keep the mood of the weather outside from penetrating in, but Liz kept talking about Ben. Where was he? Why wasn't he home with her? There's no court in session this time of night. He was with his woman. That was it. He was with his woman. The girl said she went on and on. About his woman. She had to fight off the females all her life, she said. They all wanted Ben. They felt he deserved better than an uneducated wait-ress like her. And she was old too? Liz knew there had to be another woman.

The girl stepped away for one minute. To walk into the living room and answer the ringing phone. One minute to tell the telemar-keter that no, they weren't interested in contributing to the police benevolence fund. One minute was all it took. Liz had stood up, walked into the kitchen, pulled out a butcher's knife, the one hidden on the top shelf in the far back of the cupboard. And it was over. In one minute. Eighteen years over. In one minute.

Ben leaned forward and sat his glass of wine on the table. He ran his hand through his wavy, short-cropped hair, and then he looked at Meredith.

"You'll get through this, Mal. You'll never get over it. But you'll get through it."

Meredith nodded, bravely, but the tears came anyway. Ben stood up quickly and hurried to her. "Oh, Ben," she said, reaching her arms up for him as he leaned down. He stood her up, and held her in his arms. Her sobbing was pronounced, and it was remarkable to Ben because he didn't think it was ever going to happen. She had been a tower of strength throughout her trying time, never shedding so much as a single tear. But now she was swimming in tears. "What am I going to do?" she kept asking. "What am I going to do?"

Ben looked at her. He pulled her face up to his and looked into her tear-filled eyes.

"Survive, Mal. That's what you're going to do. For your brother. For yourself. You are going to make it through. You understand me?"

"But it hurts so much. I didn't think it would hurt so much. The way they put him in the ground. That's my brother. Now he's in the ground? That doesn't make sense, Ben!"

And the sobbing returned, so forcefully that it seemed deafening. Ben's heart went out to Meredith, and his soul cried out too. His pain was once unimaginable too. He knew how she felt. That was why he lifted her entire body and carried her to her bedroom. Rest was what she needed. No more talk of how to get over it, how to get through it, or of what she was going to do if she couldn't. Rest for the body, the soul, and the mind was the only thing he remembered that seemed to work for him.

He pulled back her bedspread and then untied her housecoat. As he had suspected, she was naked, her voluptuous dark body staring back at him as if it were as ripe and as much in need of caressing as his always seemed to be. But he did not caress her. He removed the housecoat completely, and then laid her down in her bed. He moved to pull the covers up on her, but she stopped him. She grabbed a hold of his white shirt sleeve and pulled him to her. "Hold me, Ben," she implored, her big eyes filled with anguish and desire.

He held her. He leaned down and allowed her to pull him down to her, on top of her, and he held her as tightly as she held onto him. Her legs slowly separated and he could feel her bare breasts, her bare stomach, her womanhood below. All stuck against him, wanting him, needing him. But when she wrapped her arms around him, and her legs around his back, when their lips became a movement away from meeting, kissing, and when they were a short movement away from tossing all inhibition to the wind, he pulled away.

"We can't, Mal," he said.

"Ben, please," she pleaded, her pain already too much to bear. Ben sat on the edge of the bed and looked at his devastated friend.

"We can't," he said firmly. "Rest is what you need."

"I need you. Tonight I need you."

"Get you some rest. Can you do that for me?"

"Ben, please."

"Meredith!"

Meredith paused. And exhaled. "Okay," she said. "I'll try to get some rest. I'll try. But only if you'll stay here with me. If you won't leave me alone."

Ben sat there and stared down at Meredith, at her huge breasts twice the size of Josie's, at her body so full and toned and desirable. At her grief. And he nodded his okay.

India. Arie was singing "A Good Man" on the stereo, and Josie was lying on her living-room sofa staring at the African artwork that lined her walls. Her cordless phone was resting on her stomach, and a glass of sherry was in her hands. Without taking her eyes off of the wall of art, she picked up her phone, pressed redial, and listened once again for the machine to click on. "You've reached Benjamin Braddock. I'm unable to take your call. Please leave a message at the beep." And that was it. That was always it. Since her first dial and redial and the redial after that. He was scheduled to go on a three-day business trip to Oregon in the morning, and she couldn't even get him on the phone. She tried again and again. She hung up and kept staring at the wall, at one piece of art in particular. It was a beautiful painting of a village in Cameroon, and in the far corner of that painting sat an actual clock, the hands battery powered, and the clock itself seemingly so far removed from the artwork. The time was exact, because she had set it before her dial derby began. It was no longer 8:00 P.M., but 3:53 A.M.

CHAPTER 17

He watched her as she worked. She was working feverishly, from one assignment to the next, editing her own work and making sure that when she presented it there'd be no need for corrective action. He watched her. The way she struck her computer keys. The way her back was always straight, her braids always neat, her clothes always perfectly fit. For nearly an hour he stood at the plate-glass window of his small office and couldn't take his eyes off of Josie.

Finally, as nine in the evening turned into ten, Deuce walked out of his office and sat in the chair in front of Josie's desk.

"Working late," Deuce said, more as a statement than a question.

"Yep," Josie replied, squinting her eyes at the computer screen.

"Again?"

"Yep."

"I don't get it."

Josie glanced at Deuce, then began typing again. "Don't get what?" she said.

"This. You. Josie, you're the most beautiful lady this side of heaven and you're sitting up here every night as if this is all you've got to do."

"I'm just trying to get my work done, Deuce."

"You get your work done. This isn't about that and you know it. Your man should be out wining and dining you, showing you the world because you deserve to see it. What's up with that?"

"There's nothing up with that. Ben's out of town. Remember?"

"I thought you said he was coming back today."

"Right."

"Well is he?"

"Is he what?"

"Back in town?" Deuce asked.

Josie nodded. "Yes."

"He came back earlier today, didn't he?"

Josie hesitated. "Yes."

"And he hasn't even called you."

"And how do you know that?"

"Because I know him. At least I think I do. That dude is not right-eous, Josie, I'm sorry. Look at you. I could name fifty brothers off the top of my head who'd give their balls to be with you."

Josie laughed. "Bet you couldn't."

"And Braddock can't even pick up a telephone and tell you he's back in town? No way, man, I ain't trying to hear that. Something ain't right with that brother."

"Stop saying that. It's as if you take some pleasure in saying that. There's nothing wrong with Ben. When I press, he backs off, that's the nature of our relationship."

"That's stupid, Josie."

"If you knew how headstrong I can be sometimes, you wouldn't think so. I'm a lot to handle, bud. I admit it. My mouth speaks sometimes before I even think about what I'm saying."

"So he punishes you?"

"It ain't even like that."

"That's what it sounds like you're saying, Josie. The man is trying to stifle your creativity. He's trying to change who you are. He's trying to put a muzzle on you."

"What about you?" Josie asked, and looked at Deuce.

"What?"

"What are you trying to do?"

"I'm trying to be your friend. That's all."

"My friend?"

"Right."

"Then stop criticizing Ben. Okay? We've been through a lot lately, you just don't know. Meredith's brother died . . ."

"Who's Meredith?"

"Ben's assistant. Her brother just died and Ben's been trying to help her keep it together."

"Help her how? By neglecting you?"

Yes, Josie wanted to say. "No," she said instead.

"So this Meredith. Is she a looker?"

"What does that have to do with it?"

"Is she, Josie?"

"Yes, Deuce, she's a looker."

"She's talented?"

"She thinks so."

"Smart?"

"I guess so," Josie said.

"Older?"

"What does age—"

"Come on, J."

"Okay, yes, she's older."

"Boney or meaty?"

"Deuce!"

"Boney or meaty?"

"Meaty."

"Yeah, I thought so. I heard about Braddock. I heard he likes the classy types, the ones with some meat on their bones and sophistication in their stock. Women he doesn't have to teach. And he ain't never went for no younger females."

"You know all this?"

"Yes, I do," Deuce said.

"How?"

"I'm a journalist, Josie. I know how to check around. And L. L. Cool Ben's been around. Trust me on that."

"So what? I been around too."

Deuce laughed. "Yeah, right. Around nowhere," he said.

"You don't know."

"And all you did for him. I just don't get it. If it wasn't for you, those Florida women would have never been found out. You uncovered their scheme for him. You lost your job for him. You moved across the country for him. And he still doesn't have time for you? He's still too busy with Miss Meredith to bother with you? A looker like you? It ain't adding up."

"You can do all the adding you want, Deuce, and subtracting for all I care, but until you truly know Ben personally, you're wasting your time. Take those women in Florida. Even when they accused him of harassment, he wouldn't go public and say a bad word about any of them. Not one word. And I begged him to defend himself. But he wouldn't do it. They were misguided sisters, he said, and he wasn't aiding their fall. They didn't give a damn about his fall, but he cared about them. That's Ben. He's not like everybody else."

"Spare me, Josie."

"He's not. I don't care what you say. I know him. When I cut back on the emotionalism, he really responds to me."

"But that's not you he's responding to. You are emotional, Josie. Passion drives you. What you're telling me is that when you don't be yourself, he loves you. But when you're Josie, forget it. He doesn't want to have anything to do with you."

"He just wants me to slow down, Deuce. He likes that I stand up for what I believe in. Yeah, you're right, he does have some problems with me. He doesn't believe I think my beliefs through enough, that I don't count up the costs enough. But let's face it: it ain't like it's not true. I do jump to conclusions, and I am too emotional sometimes. I do take a stand without looking at alternative explanations first. But just because that's how I am doesn't mean I should want to be like that for the rest of my life. He thinks I can be better. And so do I."

"And I think you're just fine the way you are."

Josie smiled. "That's because you don't really know me. I drive him crazy sometimes, Deuce, you just don't know."

Deuce laughed. "Good. And keep on driving him too."

"If you want to know the truth, Deuce, I was glad he was out of town this week. It gave me a chance to think things through and do some reevaluating. And everything you're saying couldn't be farther from the truth. I'm the problem in this relationship. Not him."

"What about that anonymous phone call?"

Josie hesitated. "What about it?"

"Forgot about that?"

"I trust Ben. I'm not going to ruin my relationship because some stranger calls me on the telephone."

"But why would she call you, Josie, if nothing's up? Ebonically speaking, that don't make no sense. You have your doubts. You even told me you sometimes have your doubts about his fidelity, and this woman calls and confirms those suspicions. But now she's the liar? I thought you believed in truth, Josie. Not convenient truth. Not truth to soothe the soul. But truth."

"He didn't even deny it."

"What?"

"I asked him about it, but he wouldn't say anything. He wouldn't even deny it."

"Probably because it's true."

Josie shook her head. "Like I said, you don't know Ben. He doesn't play to pettiness. He gets accused, he's not about to try and prove his innocence to anybody. He just forgets you and moves on. Why he's still with me, after all the stuff I've accused him of, is the mystery of the ages."

"Ain't no mystery. He wants you to think it is, but it's not. You the man, Josie, that's why he's still with you."

Josie smiled. "You're okay, Deuce. You really are. If only you and Ben could get alone."

"Don't count on it. The brother loathes me and I can't stand him. He seems to have this vendetta against the so-called liberal press. He's never even given our paper an interview, which, by the way, my ace reporter could get, but won't."

"I'm staying away from that mine field."

Deuce chuckled. "I hear ya."

Josie looked at the clock. "Damn, it's late," she said, shutting down her computer. "I was going to stop by Denlex."

"He's still there?"

"I called his house thirty minutes ago and he wasn't there. So I guess so."

"He doesn't have a cell phone?"

"He does, but he rarely turns it on."

"You tried it?"

"Yep."

"Another confirmation," Deuce said.

"Of what?"

"Of a brother who doesn't want to be tracked down."

Josie laughed. "You are so wrong. You pull all these stunts with your ladies so you just assume every other man pulls them too." Josie stood up and put on her jacket. "It's guilt that's driving your suspicions, Deuce. Admit it, man."

"Okay, I'm done with it," Deuce said, standing too. "Braddock is a saint, we all know that."

"Whatever, Deuce."

"Come have a drink with me."

"I told you I wanted to go by Denlex."

"Just one drink."

"No. Why you ain't got no woman anyway? A good-looking brother like you. I'll tell you why, because you're too busy worrying about what I'm doing to be gettin' some for yourself." Deuce bent over, as if he had just been hit.

"Ooh," he said. "Low blow."

"You wish," Josie said. Deuce laughed out loud, proud of her quick comeback. But Josie still had Ben on her mind. She hurried out of the building.

The security guard escorted her up to the office of the vice president, talking all the while about how he wished he could find a woman sweet as she, and she smiled and felt good for a change. When she stepped off of the elevator and walked down the long corridor that led to Ben's suite, she could hear muffled voices—Ben's and a female's. It was so typical to her now, so in keeping with what she swore would not continue to make her do or say things that she almost always later regretted, that she decided to not let it bother her. He was a businessman with lots and lots of female friends, associates and acquaintances, and she just needed to chill and accept it. That was why she knocked on his office door before she entered. When she did enter and saw Ben and Meredith sitting at his conference table, working and talking, her smile could not have gotten bigger. Her strategy of learning to keep her cool was paying off already, she thought.

"Hi!" she said grandly, and her upbeat mood seemed to immediately rub off on him. He stood up from the table and hurried to her, smiling too.

"There's my girl!" he said, and lifted her in the air as he hugged her. Then he looked into her eyes. "Been behaving yourself while I was gone?" he asked her.

"No," she said, and he laughed.

"You'd better had," he said and touched her nose. Then he kissed her, long and hard. It was as if Meredith wasn't even in the room, the way he kissed her. He then let her down easy and walked back to the table. "You worked late tonight," he said to her, looking back as he walked.

"Yes," she said, following him.

"It's pretty late, Josie."

"It's pretty late, Ben."

He smiled. "Okay, point taken. You've got me on that one. Sit down," he offered, and she sat at the table. He sat down too.

"What's up, Mal?" she asked her rival.

Meredith smiled. "Oh, nothing much. How about yourself?"

"I'm good."

"Wonderful."

"I see you've been holding down the fort while Ben's been away."

"I try, dear, I try. I was home today, however, had no intentions whatsoever to come in at all. But Ben called and told me how much he missed me and how badly he wanted to see me so I braved the elements and came on in. It was a trap, I tell you, because ten hours later and I'm still here."

She said this and laughed. Josie could only manage a smile. Ben didn't call Josie when he hit town, but he called Meredith. If Josie hadn't turned over a new leaf, that alone would have fired her up. She'd be slinging accusations as if they were confetti. But she had turned over a new leaf. She wasn't about to let Meredith Chambers and her almost uncanny knack for pushing her buttons bother her.

"Don't listen to her, Josephine," Ben said. "She loves hard work. I could tell it the first time I met her. That's why I hired her."

"If she's been here for ten hours, how long have you been here?"

"I think my plane touched down around eleven."

"This morning?"

"Yes."

"You've been in town since eleven?"

"Yes, Josie."

"And you didn't even call me?" she said. It had slipped. Just like that. She couldn't do it. She just couldn't hold her peace.

"What is this, Josie? What are all these papers sprawled out all over this desk? Work, that's what. I haven't had a chance to hear myself think today, let alone call you."

"You called Meredith."

"To help me get some of this work done. Yes I did."

"But you tell her you missed her and you want to see her so badly.

Why would you have to tell her all that to get her to do her job? Am I missing something here?"

"It was a trap to get me in the office, I told you—"

"Am I talking to you?"

"That's enough, Josephine!"

"You don't tell me what's enough. I feel like a fool. How can you love me if you can't even take two minutes to pick up a phone and let me know you're still alive?"

"I had deadlines to meet, Josie, it's been hectic."

"Man, tell it to the birds," Josie said, standing up. "I don't even wanna hear that lame excuse. I gave you the benefit of the doubt. But you know what? You want this witch, then you can have her!"

"Witch?" Meredith asked, offended.

"Yeah, witch, bitch! Yeah, I said it. You've been using your grief to get Ben, don't try to act like you don't know what I'm talking about!"

"Good night, Josie," Ben said calmly, although shaken by her display.

"How would you feel if it were me, Ben? If I were spending all my time with Deuce? How would that make you feel?"

"Just leave, Josie, you're making the situation worse."

"I'm glad to get the hell out of here. And don't worry about the next time you don't wanna be bothered with me, because there won't be a next time!" Josie said this and hurried out of Ben's office. The tears were hot behind her eyelids as she walked away. It seemed so final to her now. So complete. There was no more drifting. No more life jackets and rescue boats trying to help them find their way. It was over. The end had come just when she thought she finally had a handle on the ever-changing tides. They were adrift. Oceans apart. Lost.

Deuce looked up from the front page article he had been reading. The woman that stood in front of his desk reminded him of an older, darker version of Beyonce Knowles. The same curves to her body, the same long hair, the same wide eyes and bright smile.

"May I help you?" he said.

"Your assistant said it was all right if I came on in. I'm Meredith Chambers," she said, and began removing her gloves. Deuce remembered that name, and stood up.

"I'm afraid Josie isn't here."

"I know she's not. That's why I am. May I?" Meredith motioned toward one of the small chairs in front of his messy desk. He nodded and she sat down. He walked around the side of his desk and sat down in the chair beside her. Josie had a right to think a chick like her would have the hots for Braddock, Deuce thought, watching her. She was fly. Had it going on in every department. Looks, attitude, style. If anybody could shake up the great judge, it was this chick, he thought.

"So you're Meredith," he said.

"Sounds as if you know me."

"I heard a little some'um some'um about you," he said.

"And I about you."

"What brings you to our woods, if not to see Josie? I know it isn't to give us an interview since no one from Denlex ever does. On orders from your boss, I might add."

He was ridiculous, Meredith thought, looking at Deuce, but he was good looking, and young. Exactly somebody who could easily be Josie's type. She decided then and there that her suspicion, based on little more than the way Josie said his name, was true. He had a thing for Josie.

"You know my boss?" she asked.

"I wouldn't call it knowing him. I know his lady."

"That's why I'm here. She mentioned your name a few days ago. I wanted to see if it was possible."

"If what was possible?"

"That she could be in love with you."

Deuce hesitated. "Now look lady. I don't know what she told you or what you may be implying, but—"

"Close the door, please," she said. Deuce looked at Meredith with one of those *check her out* expressions. But he got up and closed the door.

When he sat back down, Meredith crossed her legs. She was ready to get down to business. "We don't have a lot of time because I would rather not be seen by Josie. So I'm going to get to the point. You want Josie, and I want Ben." She said this and leaned back.

Deuce couldn't believe his ears. "Excuse me?"

"You want Josie. Or am I wrong?"

"Where would you get an idea like that?"

"Am I wrong?"

"Did Josie say something to you?"

"Yes, but not what you think. She merely said your name."

Deuce smiled. "Is this some kind of joke? Some kind of set up?"

"She evoked an emotion in Ben when she said your name. Benjamin doesn't show emotions that way. But he showed a spark twice, and both times were at the mention of your name."

"He hates me, and I ain't crazy about him, either. I'm the liberal media he despises. Remember?"

"You're the man who wants to take his lady away. Remember?"

Deuce paused. "And you're the lady who wants to take her man," he said.

"Now you get it. That is exactly right. I want Ben. I will tell it to you freely and deny it to the world if you tell it to anyone else. But I don't make miscalculations very often, Deuce. I'm a quick and usually accurate judge of character. You won't tell a soul. You want her too badly."

"And how badly do you want Braddock?"

"So bad that I can taste it. He is everything a man should be. I love him, and I want to spend the rest of my life with him. But there's a problem."

Deuce nodded. "Josie."

"Right," Meredith said. "And Ben's standing in your way."

"I'm still not gettin' this," Deuce said. "You've decided that I'm in love with Josie based on the fact that she said my name a couple of times?"

"Because Ben responded both times. That's the issue. Ben's response. He's as intuitive as I am. And he knows competition when he sees it. You're his competition, Deuce. You're young and handsome. He knows this."

"So he doesn't call her, stays away from her for weeks at a time, treats her like crap, but he's worried about me? I ain't buying what you selling, lady."

"I'm telling you what I know. He honestly believes that if Josie ever got the courage to leave him, you'll be waiting with arms wide open."

"Me and about seven hundred other guys."

"Case in point. She came by his office a few nights ago. She became livid because I was there."

"You were there the night Josie went by Denlex? The night Braddock came back from Portland?"

"Yes. Only he came back earlier that day. That morning in fact. And instead of phoning her, he phoned me. And she went ballistic. Of course she declared it was the end. But it never is with those two."

"Tell me about it."

"She asked him how he would feel if she spent so much time with you the way he has been with me. Although he was angry with her and would not back down, his entire countenance changed. Bingo, I thought, as I watched him. She hit a nerve. He was afraid that what she was saying could actually come true, that she could actually leave him for you. I could see it in his eyes."

"Okay, that was a few nights ago. Are they back together?"

"No."

"See, that's the rub for me. That's what I ain't understanding here, and trust me, lady, I'm a smart brother. According to you Braddock is afraid of losing her, but he does nothing to try and keep her. He calls you instead of her. He's been away a whole week and he doesn't even call her? That's not natural. No offense, but have you seen Josie lately? I mean she's it, she's . . . the total package."

"Have you seen Ben lately? He's perfect too. And I'm disinclined to use that word lightly."

"There's something between you and Braddock?"

"That's none of your business."

"Well, now, I don't know. He's calling you instead of his girlfriend, that sounds like more than a professional relationship to me."

"It's more than just a professional relationship, I'll say that. But it will never be what I need it to be until Josie Ross is out of the picture. You've got to get her out of the picture."

"Me?"

"Yes. She cares for you, and you love her. The two of you have far more in common, and you'll make a nice couple. You've just got to convince her that you're more worthy of her affections than Ben."

"If the way he treats her isn't enough to convince her, nothing I do or say ever will."

"That's where you're wrong. When I first met Ben I didn't think it was possible to penetrate that wall of his, either. I miscalculated Josie's influence in his life. But things have changed dramatically."

"Yeah, but you had the good fortune of a brother dying. I don't . . ."

"Don't you ever, and I mean, ever, mention my brother again. Do you understand me, Mr. Deuce?"

Her anger surprised Deuce. It seemed almost threatening. "Yeah, I understand. I didn't mean anything like that. I don't get glib about stuff like that, I really don't. I'm just saying that you had an event in your life that kind of pushed things along for you, that brought you and Braddock closer."

"That's why you've got to orchestrate your own event. You've got to make it happen. The time is perfect now. They're currently estranged and Ben seems content to keep it that way. He usually is. It's always Josie who comes running back to him with her little lame apologies and he takes her back. But if there is an intervening episode or a series of episodes, something that will help keep them apart, then your chances, not to mention mine, increase exponentially."

Deuce was in. He had to be. He wanted Josie just as bad as Meredith seemed to want Braddock.

"What intervening episode? You got something in mind?"

"I do. It's a simple plan, and it'll be very simple for you. But it should work."

Deuce looked at Meredith, at this classy lady scheming and conniving to win her man, and he was more than willing to participate. They deserved each other, he thought.

The protest was peaceful, as Deuce had expected it would be, and the few hundred demonstrators marched in lockstep outside city hall. "We want a voice, we want a voice!" they shouted, demanding that the mayor appoint more minorities to key government positions. Although Josie was all for that, she didn't see where she and Deuce both had to come along.

"To lend our support too," he said. "We're minorities after all."

Josie smiled. She liked Deuce's commitment to issues. Besides herself, he was the most passionate person she knew. They were now sitting in his little Datsun, because the rain had started to fall; Deuce was having a devil of a time getting his defrost to work.

"I need a new car myself, Deuce, so don't take this personally. But you need a new car."

Deuce laughed. "No thanks. Ol' Betsy's just fine. I'm not thinking about buying that plastic junk they're making nowadays."

"Spoken like a true twenty-eight-year-old."

"Got that right. And who says you need a new car? What's wrong with your Mustang?"

"It's old."

"That's all?"

"Basically, yeah. I'll just trade it in for a new one. I do it every so often, every three, four years."

"Well, if you got it going on like that," Deuce paused, "looks like you've traded in Braddock too."

Josie stared forward. "What makes you say that?"

"I'm your friend, J. Stop forgetting that. You may not tell me everything, but I do have two eyes. I can see a heartbroken sister when I want to."

Josie smiled. "What, you've broken so many hearts yourself that you know what it looks like?"

"Something like that. So what's the deal with the dude this time?"

"No deal."

"So it's on again?"

"I didn't say that, either."

Deuce shook his head. "This is crazy."

"What's crazy?"

"I hope you do change, Josie. He wants you to change so bad. I hope you change by leaving his ass for good this time. I mean, every time you get together with the dude it's something. That's not what love is about. Love is patient. And kind. And most of all, happy, Josie. But I haven't seen you truly happy since the day we met."

"It'll work itself out, Deuce."

"Yeah, you'll go running back to him like the good, little, whipped puppy you are, and he'll think about it, lecture you, then finally take you back. Until you say something else he doesn't like. That ain't even the kind of way you need to be living your life, dawg. But it's your life."

Josie smiled. "Got that right," she said.

Deuce put his hands up in surrender. It wasn't going to be as simple as Meredith thought, and he knew it.

"They're running for cover now," Josie said, and Deuce looked at the protestors. They all sought shelter either inside city hall or in their own vehicles as the rain intensified.

"There's nothing more here to report on, anyway," Deuce said, cranking up. "How's about lunch? You hungry?"

"Yeah. That sounds good. But only if you promise not to mention Ben."

"Oh, that'll be easy," Deuce said, driving away.

The crowd at Rhonda's was sparse, as it usually was after two, and Deuce selected a booth near the front of the restaurant. Deuce could see them as soon as he sat down, but Josie didn't even notice. Meredith glanced at him, as she and Ben sat in a back booth, deep into conversation about the new Akron plant. She waited for the right moment to come. But it didn't come, not after Deuce ordered drinks, not after he and Josie placed their food orders. Josie still had not noticed. Meredith knew at once that Deuce had to be proactive, and should have been from the moment they sat down, but Deuce didn't realize it until the drinks came and Josie still didn't see. He leaned toward her.

"I know I made a promise to you," he said. "But I may have to break it."

"What?"

"Ben's in the house."

Josie immediately began looking around, as her heart raced. And as soon as her eyes locked on to the back booth, Meredith, calm as could be, reached her hand to the side of Ben's mouth as if removing a crumb. Then she leaned over and whispered something in his ear. He laughed. From Ben's vantage point he could not see Josie. He was turned to Meredith and his back was turned to Josie, but she saw all she needed to see. She went to stand up.

"What are you doing, J?" Deuce asked her, pulling her back down.

"Let's just go."

"No. Why should we let that bastard run us off? Come on now. You can handle this. Forget him."

Josie sat down. It was easy for Deuce to say. Forgetting Ben, for her, was like forgetting you have cancer, or forgetting your name, or forgetting your heart. It may have been done before, but Josie had never seen it.

She looked at Meredith, at the way she touched his hand, his muscular arm, his shoulder, laughing and touching him as if she couldn't keep her hands to herself. Josie could have gotten angry, but she wasn't about to. He didn't want her anger. Look at him, he wasn't thinking about her. *Forgetting Ben may be impossible,* she thought. But she had to do something.

Ben turned around when the waiter arrived with their food orders, and he began eating and listening to Meredith. From his peripheral vision he saw an outline, a small, blurred outline that could have been—but he didn't even bother to look. As he ate and listened to Meredith, who was determined to keep his attention focused solely on her, he saw the outline again. He looked.

It was Josie. She was sitting at a table with Deuce and looking at a picture he was showing her. He stared at her, because he hadn't spent any appreciable time with her in over a month. The last time he saw her was almost a week ago, when she had flared up in his office. She had flown off the handle again that night, based on no real information, just raw emotion. But that was Josie. And when she looked away from Deuce's picture and at the booth in the back, she and Ben were finally face to face. When her eyes locked on to his, he dabbed his mouth with his napkin.

"Excuse me for a second, Mal," he said to Meredith, and then walked slowly over to Josie's table.

Josie was, by now, so nervous she could hardly contain herself. Was he coming to tell her something good, like he missed her, or something unbearable, like Meredith was now the one and that he thought she should be the first to know? Josie could never tell by looking at Ben. He knew how to control emotions. He knew how to walk toward her and not feel as if his heart was beating so loud that others around him could hear it.

"Hello," he said, looking exclusively at her. Deuce, surprised, glanced at Meredith. Meredith shook her head.

"Hey," Josie said and looked up at him. She swallowed hard.

"Late lunch?"

She tried to smile, but couldn't. "Yeah. We just came from a protest march over at city hall. Minority march."

"Oh yeah? How was the turnout?"

"Good," Deuce said.

"Not good," Josie said, glancing at Deuce. "A couple hundred people showed up but the organizers were expecting a whole lot more."

Ben nodded, and then stared at Josie. She looked different to him. He didn't know what it was. Had living on the edge of emotions taken her over, or was it just plain fatigue from too much emotion.

She wasn't taking care of herself properly and he could see it. He knew her. She didn't handle adversity well.

"You've been taking care of yourself, Josie?" he asked her.

"Yes," she said, but his stare forced her to tell the truth. "Sort of."

"What are you doing tonight?"

She hesitated. "Nothing," she replied, and Deuce shook his head.

"Eight o'clock, then?"

"Yeah. Okay," she said.

Ben nodded. "Okay," he said, stared at her again, and then he leaned down and kissed her on the lips. She closed her eyes, wanting more from him, but he pulled away. He smiled as she opened her eyes and he touched her lightly on the nose. Then he stood erect, glanced at Deuce, and left.

The biggest smile came on Josie's face.

Deuce shook his head. "You're sick, you know that?" he said.

"I know. But if it means I'll be with Ben tonight, I'll take that illness any day!" she said, and laughed. Meredith continued to try and push her buttons, but she didn't care about Meredith. Meredith had her time with Ben and that still didn't keep him from coming back to Josie. That was why Josie felt so high and happy. He came back to her. He came, not her. It was his turn now.

"That went well, don't you think?" Deuce said as Meredith opened the front door of her apartment and let him in. She then headed for the bar without breaking her stride.

"Stop being so sarcastic," she said. "It worked."

Deuce smiled. "It worked? They're hooking up tonight, but it worked?" Deuce sat down at the bar counter and shook his head. "That guy's got her in the palm of his hand. I couldn't believe how easily she caved."

"I told you work will be required to turn her around. She's the key. He'll move on, if she will."

"But she won't. That's what I'm trying to tell you, Meredith. You don't know how Josie talks about the dude. He's a saint in her eyes."

"He's a saint all right." Meredith said this with such force of bitterness that Deuce looked at her.

"You okay?"

"I'm fine," Meredith said as she sat a glass of wine in front of

Deuce. "I'm just realistic. Benjamin Braddock is the most ruthless, sadistic man I've ever met. That's a fact."

"Sadistic? Ruthless? What are you, out of love now?"

"Of course not. I'm just truthful about my love, and I want you to be the same. You have got to be more appealing to Josie. You've got to get her attention."

"I have her attention. She knows how I feel about her. She's no dummy. But it's Braddock, I tell you. Somebody's got to knock that halo off of his head."

"Yes," Meredith said. "You."

"And how? By more of those little sophomore schemes of yours? That shit don't work on somebody like Braddock. And Josie, man, I've never met anybody like her. I mean she's out there, you know what I'm saying? Far out. It takes nothing to make her thrilled to death and even less to make her miserable. She's very vulnerable. She's bound to be hurt."

"Better her than you," Meredith said and Deuce looked at her. She was so sure of everything. So certain. So smooth that Deuce knew something more was up with her. She called the man she loved sadistic? That didn't sound like a lovesick sister to him. There was something about her manner, Deuce thought as he sipped his wine and stared at his host, that didn't add up either. Was she one of those hard-up females who wanted Braddock no matter who she hurt in the process? Was she that much in love with that tight-ass? Or was there more to it than that? Deuce didn't know. All he knew was that a wealthy, conniving female like Meredith, a woman who could have pretty much anybody she wanted, had more on her agenda, far more, than just becoming Ben Braddock's lady.

CHAPTER 18

She looked out of her bedroom window just as Ben's Mercedes drove up and parked in her driveway. He was nearly twenty-minutes late but that was fine by her. She had just finished getting dressed herself. And it had been an ordeal. By the time she'd finally settled on what she would wear, a string-strap, black, sleek number, tight and low-cut the way Ben liked it, she had gone through nearly eleven different outfits. All were now thrown around on her bed, her floor, her dresser. The room looked like a salvage yard. She thought about tossing them under the bed or in the closet, in case they came back to her place tonight instead of going to his, but decided against it. Mainly because she didn't have any time to, but she had also expended so much effort in the selection process that now she was drained.

She was walking down the stairs, her high heels stepping loudly, as the doorbell rang. She walked across her living room and glanced in the mirror near her front door for one last look-over. She had done something revolutionary today: she'd allowed her beautician to remove her braids and cut her hair into one of those Halle Berry, low-cut, carefree, curly numbers. Everybody in the salon had thought she looked beautiful. She wasn't so sure.

She checked her lipstick, the diamond earrings Ben had given her for her birthday, and the diamond necklace she had given herself. Ever since she'd seen Ben at lunch she'd been preparing for this night. She hadn't even returned to work, except to pick up her car to drive to the salon, and now the moment had arrived. Everything, she thought, had to be perfect.

She opened the door. Her elation fizzled slightly as soon as she saw what Ben was wearing. He had on a dark blue suit, a white shirt, and a dark blue tie. His normal workwear, in other words. He probably hadn't even changed, but had left straight from work to pick her up. She'd spent all day getting ready. He'd just come on over. But it would take more than that to break Josie's spirit. She was swinging on clouds tonight. She was hopeful for the first time in a long time.

"Hi," she said gaily, ready for the evening to begin.

Ben took one more puff on his cigarette, then smashed the butt against the brick wall of Josie's townhouse.

"Hey," he replied, and then looked at her. Her hair stunned him. He had never seen her without braids. He stared at her, at her hair, and the way it brought out even more of the beauty of her face. He then stared at her dress, the way it was so low-cut and tight, the straps revealing her gorgeous brown arms and neck. He'd never seen her prettier.

"Wow," he said. "You look fantastic."

Josie, surprised by his reaction, smiled and moved slowly out of her door. Ben was Ben, she thought. Sometimes, like tonight, you could count on him to bowl you over. Other times you were on your own.

He took her to the Emerald, a ritzy restaurant on the banks of the Mississippi, and from the moment they were seated Ben became preoccupied. Local businessmen came up to their table like a faucet drip, one at a time, to shake Ben's hand and congratulate him without mentioning specifics, and to talk to him about some speculative ventures, to ask him about Denlex's "CEO situation." Ben smiled and laughed at their little jokes, and was generally cordial and respectful of each and every one. He seemed so relaxed in that world, Josie thought, as she sat back and watched him, that it seemed only natural that he would be the center of attention. But every time he seemed ready to pay some attention to her—and they both knew they needed to do some serious talking—another hand would come out and another anxious face would look down to congratulate Ben and then ask for an audience with him later in the week.

"What are they congratulating you about?" Josie finally asked him.

"Rumors that they're taking as fact," Ben said, and that was all he would say about it.

He was easily the most popular person in the room, and then his cell phone began ringing too. It was Denlex's PR man Sam Darrow, which only confirmed Josie's suspicion that something big was up. But since it was all business related and she would find out about it eventually, she didn't ask nor did she care to know what it was about. The restaurant had a room designated for phone calls, the majority of their clientele being business types, and Ben spent most of his time in that room. At one point Josie even told the waiter to take his plate of food in there. And she wasn't being funny, either. She actually didn't mind the interruptions. The night was still young, she thought, as she ate alone. It could only get better. It certainly couldn't get much worst.

After dinner they did not go, as Josie absolutely assumed they would, to some fashionable jazz club in the Twin Cities area or even in Uptown Saint Cloud, where the forty-plus crowd loved to gather and where the dress of choice was straight-up executive. He took her to a nightclub, a loud, youthful, thumpin' nightclub.

Josie tried to contain her own excitement as she walked into the club pleasantly surprised. The music, hip-hop and new-school R & B, was so in tune with what she loved that she wanted to start dancing immediately. But she held off and let Ben continue to take the lead. He was in her territory now. His lead, especially if it didn't go where she wanted it to go, wasn't going to last all night.

And the club itself, a kind of psychedelic, disco-style spot with big lights flashing, wasn't all that crowded yet, either, which was good. The dance floor gave you just enough room to get your groove on without forcing you to have to bump and grind strangers because of the lack of space. Ben found them a table against the wall, and as he pulled out Josie's chair, she whispered in his ear.

"This is great, Ben," she said, and he smiled.

"What would you like to drink?" he asked.

"Sherry if they've got it. Scotch if they don't," she said. Ben smiled and walked over to the bar.

Josie looked around at the wired crowd, and started moving with the beat. Two different brothers approached her for a dance before Ben returned with the drinks. She declined, but loved the attention. When Ben returned, she was practically dancing in her seat.

"Sorry about dinner," he finally said, after sitting down and sipping from his glass of scotch.

"Don't be. I know you had some business to take care of."

"But that's over now. My cell phone is off."

"Completely?" she asked.

Ben smiled. "Completely."

"Good," Josie said and started grooving again and looking at those assembled on the dance floor. "Where did you find this place?"

"You like it?"

"I love it. It's off the chain, boy!"

Ben smiled. "You can thank Whitney for this discovery. I told her to locate a place she thought you'd go for."

Josie smiled. "Good ol' Whitney. She'll do anything for you, you know that?"

"I know."

"Monster crush she has on you."

"I know."

"But what woman 'round there doesn't. Right?"

"You'll have to ask the women."

Josie smiled and turned her attention back to the dance floor. Ben liked her attitude tonight, the way she didn't seem driven by anything but having fun.

"I still can't get over this crib, Ben. It's tight. And here I was thinking we were going to do jazz tonight."

Ben shook his head. "I was tempted, I cannot lie. But no. You tolerate jazz for me. I'll tolerate this for you."

Josie smiled. "Rap, Ben. Hip-hop. Little R & B. Not *this*."

"What*ever*," Ben said the way Josie often said it, and Josie laughed.

"Wanna dance?" she asked him.

This was the part of the night he dreaded. Dancing to music he didn't care for, doing dances he didn't know. But he got up, took Josie's hand, and escorted her to the floor. Josie knew how to move so Ben planned to just follow her lead, but she moved way too fast for him. He unbuttoned his suit coat and tried to keep up, but he was laughing more than he was dancing. And when Josie placed her hands over her head and started shaking her body as if simulating some sex act, he knew he wasn't about to do that.

"Come on, Ben, you got it," Josie was yelling as she moved. "Just move to the beat, baby, that's all you've got to do!"

Ben moved to the beat all right, when the beat slowed down. He even started to feel more relaxed out on the floor. But as soon as the first brother moved into the picture and started dancing with Josie too, he gladly backed off. They could simulate whatever they wanted out there, he thought, as long as it didn't include him. He sat back down at his table, pulled out a cigarette, and smiled. "If they could see me now," he said jokingly to himself, and then he lighted his cigarette.

"I like the way you move out there," a voice said just in front of him, and he looked up. She was twenty-something with a long, narrow face and small, brown eyes. She stood at his table as if she'd been invited. He leaned back, took a slow drag on his cigarette, and stared at her, at her face first and then a quick look down at her body. And she had the body, he thought. Her outfit, a skin-tight, leather short set reminded him of that cat suit Serena Williams wore at a U.S. Open tournament once, and it didn't show an inch of anything out of place. He looked back up at her face, which he thought was pretty in an unremarkable sort of way.

"So you like the way I move?" he said to her.

"Yeah, I do. You reminded me of me when I first started clubbin'."

Ben laughed. "I see."

"May I?" She asked with more sophistication than her age would suggest, and Ben motioned that it was all right. She sat down, and then extended her hand. "I'm Rhea, by the way."

Ben removed his cigarette from his right hand to his left and then shook hers. "Nice to meet you, Rhea. I'm Ben."

"I take it this is your first time here?" she asked, when their hands released.

"It is."

"I thought so. I can always spot the first-timers."

"You're a regular?"

"Every week. I'd come every day if I could, but most nights I'm just too tired. It's my job. I'm a telemarketer. And I know, we're hated for interrupting y'all at dinner time when the last thing y'all wanna do is yap on the phone with us. Hell, I hate when I'm interrupted, myself. But it's a living."

Ben didn't say anything. He drank from his glass of scotch and looked around, at all the other interesting faces and bodies that were beginning to clog up the room.

"Some female dragged you out here, didn't she?" Rhea asked, and he looked at her.

"Not exactly."

"But you aren't here alone?"

"No."

"So where is the missus?"

Ben looked over to where he had left Josie dancing, but she was no longer there. He looked around, and around some more. Finally he spotted her near a wall dancing with a young brother who seemed to think it necessary to keep placing his hands on her hips.

"There she is. Near that wall back there. The lady in black."

Rhea looked. "Her? That's the female you were dancing with."

"Right."

"You came with her?"

"Yes. You sound surprised," Ben said.

"No. I mean, I am. But you? With her? Y'all ain't exactly what I'd call a match."

"You know about that, do you?"

"I know an odd couple when I see one. I mean, I don't even know the woman and can't tell you nothing much about her. But that female over there, that lady in black, she's wild, Ben. I can tell you that."

Ben looked at Josie, at the way she danced with total and almost reckless abandon, so excited that she seemed too high, way too excited for somebody with any kind of self control.

"So," she asked him, "what do you do for a living?"

"I work at Denlex."

"Office or plant?" Ben smiled.

"Office."

Rhea nodded. "Do you? I'll bet you're high up there too, aren't you?"

"I'm all right."

"I could tell. I could tell by the clothes. You can always tell by the clothes."

The last of the unrelenting series of songs, back to back to back, finally came to an end, and those on the dance floor began to disperse. Ben looked at Josie as her dance partner whispered in her ear. She smiled, shook her head, and then moved back toward her table.

"So, tell me, Ben," Rhea asked, noticing Josie's impending return too. "Do you freelance?"

"Freelance?"

"Do you see other people?"

Ben looked at Rhea, his eyes trailing down from her face to her body, and then he took a slow drag on his cigarette. He doused his cigarette and stood to his feet when Josie arrived back at the table.

"I'm through dealing, Ben," Josie said as she plopped down. "I'm dying."

Ben sat down too. "Why didn't you quit sooner, if it was killing you so?"

"Did you hear that music? How could I quit? It was intoxicating." Josie leaned back and seemed to notice Rhea for the first time. She folded her arms. "Hey."

"Hey."

"And you are?"

"Josie, this is Rhea," Ben said, introducing them. "She came over to keep me company while you were dying out on the dance floor."

"Nice to meet ya," Rhea said.

"Nice to meet you. And thanks for keeping him company. But I'm back now." Rhea glanced at Ben. Then she stood up. "See ya around, Ben," she said, and Ben nodded slightly. Rhea looked at Josie, who seemed so obnoxious to her, and then she walked away from the table, her tight leather suit capturing the attention of both Josie and Ben.

"What a hot ass," Josie said as she turned back toward Ben. "She was hitting on you, wasn't she?"

Ben pulled his glass of scotch to his mouth. "Wanna dance?"

Josie at first smiled, then she laughed. "I oughta say yeah just to scare your behind. And I would too. But you can forget that. I'm too tired to move, let alone dance."

Ben nodded. "Good," he said, and then laughed.

She snuggled against him as he drove fast along Highway 23. "Josie, you need to put on your seatbelt," he said to her, again.

"I told you I'm okay."

"No, you're not okay. Just put it on."

Josie rolled her eyes, slid back to the passenger side of the car, and buckled up. "Now, satisfied?" she said testily and looked out of the window. Ben glanced over at her. He had let her have her way tonight, drinking and dancing and having what appeared to be the time of her life. Now she was almost drunk. She worried him, sometimes frightened him, as he stared at the dark road ahead of them.

"Where are we going?" she asked.

"I thought we'd spend some time at the cabin," he said. "We need to talk, remember?" Josie smiled. Leaned back against the headrest.

"I love that cabin. It's so peaceful there. When you die, can I have it?" Josie said this and laughed.

Ben paused. "Yes," he said.

Josie turned her head toward Ben. "Really? You aren't going to leave it to your mother or your sister or your favorite charity?"

"I'm leaving it to you."

Josie paused. She didn't know if Ben was pulling her leg or serious. "Since when?"

"Since we left Florida and I got a chance to sit down with my attorney."

"You mean you actually have this written somewhere? That I get the cabin should something happen to you?"

"The cabin, the houses, the cars." Then Ben looked at her. "Everything."

Josie shook her head. "I was just kidding, Ben. You aren't gonna die. Why would you go and do all of that?"

"Preparation, honey."

"Preparation for what? You're fine. I was just playing around. Nothing's gonna happen to you."

"You never know, Josie."

"Oh, yes you do. You will not be dying no time soon, trust me on that. Tragedies like death don't befall people like you. You're too blessed. Things always work out for you."

"Right, until they don't."

Josie stared at Ben and the reality of their conversation made her nervous. He was right. *You never really know,* she thought. He could actually die on her. What was remarkable to her wasn't the fact of the matter, but the fact that she had never even thought about it. Not once. Ben could be here today and gone tomorrow, and she wouldn't be prepared for that by a long shot.

She opened her car window, hoping the fresh air would help sober her up. Ben had made arrangements for the inevitable. He had already seen to it that Josie would not have another financial concern for the rest of her life. A woman who wasn't even his wife, he had made provisions for her. That was why she felt an urgency in sobering up. If Ben were to die tonight, she couldn't handle it. He knew it, and that was why he was always backing away from her. Now she knew it too. She'd be a basket case, a self-destructive shell of a human being if something ever happened to Ben.

The fireplace had warmed the cabin by the time they got into bed. Josie didn't snuggle next to Ben, but lay with her back to him, still thinking as she stared at the fire across the room. Ben was surprised by her behavior, but he didn't press the issue. He knew she was still reeling from their conversation in the car. He was twenty years older than she. It was a pretty good bet that he would be leaving years before she would. And he had prepared the way for her. His attorney had advised against it. "You don't leave all of your earthly possessions to some girlfriend," he had said. And Ben had agreed. But he did it anyway.

"I want to apologize to you, Josie," he said.

"Apologize for what?"

"Everything. The neglect, the way I've been treating you lately. Everything."

"It's okay. You were helping out a friend. I can respect that, and I'm not exactly the understanding type." She said this and paused. A long, tense pause. Then she swallowed hard. "I think it's a good idea to tell you the truth."

Ben looked at her, at her bare back, her thin neck, part of her naked behind not hidden under the covers, and he swallowed hard too. "What's a good idea?" he asked.

"Space between us. A little time away."

Ben hesitated. "You okay?"

"Yes. I'm fine. I just think . . ." Tears began to appear in Josie's eyes. "I think you were right."

Ben did not respond. He could tell she was emotional. She was finally reaching a conclusion he had reached a long time ago: she had to slow down. She had to stop believing that the very reason for her existence was completely tied to him. Or it would be. When he was gone, when he was no longer on the scene for whatever reason, the foundation of her very existence would be shaken, to a point beyond devastation, maybe to a point beyond repair.

He reached over and placed his hand on her hip. She moved away from his touch.

"Good night, Ben," she said, through her tears. And he understood.

"Goodnight, love," he said.

CHAPTER 19

The rain came in a thunderous clap, and the huge Denlex building went dark as the lights flickered out and then came back on. It was eight at night and most of management was still in the building. But Ben was looking to get out.

He shoved some files into his briefcase, just in case he felt like looking them over at home, and began closing the lid. He was that close to a clean getaway. But Meredith, looking dashing in a loud lavender dress, came in.

"Well," he said, smiling, "looks like somebody's going to have a big night tonight."

"You like?" she said, and turned around like a model on a runway.

"I like."

She sat down in front of Ben's desk. "I hope Maurice likes."

"Maurice?"

"My date. I'm very hopeful." She looked up at Ben. He stood behind his desk in shirt sleeves, his briefcase closed and ready on his desk. She wanted to see if there would be even a flicker of jealousy.

"When did you meet this Maurice?"

"A few weeks ago. At a bookstore, can you believe it? He seems like a pretty decent guy."

Ben nodded. "You need to be careful, Mal. Everybody's pretty decent when you don't know them."

Meredith smiled. "You aren't worried about me. Are you?"

"You're my friend. Of course I worry about you. You're still very vulnerable right now, and susceptible to any smooth talker."

"You mean like you?"

Ben smiled. "Exactly," he said.

"No, Ben, I understand what you're saying. I do. But I can't spend another night alone. That's what it's come down to for me." Ben stared at his friend. She crossed her legs. "I turned forty yesterday," she said.

"Yesterday was your birthday? Mal, why didn't you tell me?"

"You have enough on your plate than to have to entertain me too. I'm sure Josie would agree with that."

Josie, Ben thought. He hadn't heard from Josie in nearly two weeks, since that night at his cabin. She'd concluded that they needed time away, and he hadn't argued with her. But he also hadn't banked on it taking this long.

"You should have told me, Mal," he said.

"You've done more than enough. Your kindness toward me has strained your relationship as it is. I couldn't bear to be responsible for any further problems." She was fishing. Deuce had told her that lately Josie seemed to be in the best spirits he'd seen her in months, as if she was resigned to something unpleasant, such as a breakup, or something wonderful, such as a certain togetherness. But neither she nor Ben was telling. Meredith had been trying daily to get the scoop.

"So," Meredith said, deciding to beat around the bush no longer, "how's Josie, anyway?"

"She's good."

"So it worked out, then?"

"What worked out?" he asked.

"At Rhonda's that time, two weeks ago, you were going to take her out or something, presumably to work things out. That's what I assumed."

"Oh, yeah. It worked out."

Meredith smiled. "You don't sound too certain of that."

"Do I? I mean, don't I?"

Meredith couldn't believe his lack of confidence. "Ben? You okay?"

He exhaled and placed his hands on his hips. "I'm okay, Mal, thanks."

"Is it Josie?"

Ben hesitated. He didn't discuss his problems with anyone, not ever, but tonight he was tempted.

"She's had an epiphany," he said.

Meredith smiled. "That sounds like Josie. And what great discovery has she made?"

"She loves me too much," Ben said.

"She what?"

"Knock, knock." Sam Darrow's voice was suddenly heard from outside the office. Meredith, still stunned by Ben's revelation, turned quickly. Sam walked on in. "Hello, Benjamin. Hello, Meredith."

Ben greeted him back. Meredith was still reeling. If what Ben said was true, and Josie was trying to wean herself off of him, her work just got a little easier. She knew she had to capitalize on the situation, and so did Deuce. But she also had to be careful. If she read too much into what Ben was telling her and Josie's so-called epiphany was more like a bump in the road than a life-altering event, then her actions could backfire. But just the thought that Josie was finally getting it raised the stakes. And Meredith was more than ready to move her planning into an elevated gear.

"You might wanna sit down, bud," Sam said to Ben.

Ben frowned. "What are you talking about, Sam?"

"Brace yourself."

"I'm braced. Now what is it?"

Sam smiled. "Word on the Street—as in Wall Street—is that Benjamin Braddock is among one of two finalists for CEO of Denlex."

Meredith smiled, then looked at Ben. Ben sat down. "One of two?" he asked.

"One of two, my friend. Congratulations," Sam said.

"You're certain of this?"

"Of course I am. Have I ever brought you wrong info before? You'll be getting a call before the night is done."

"Who's the other guy?"

"Fastower. Michael Herbert Fastower."

"Him."

"Yep, him."

"I thought you said there was a problem with Fastower?"

"There was, but nobody's saying what. Apparently it wasn't

worth revealing because I couldn't get anything after the initial buzz. He's still in the running."

"Who's Fastower, anyway?" Meredith asked.

"Big name. A one-time whiz kid at Haliburton. He's a heavy-hitter, no doubt about it. Smart. Harvard educated. Ambitious. Unlike Ben, he's been dreaming his whole life for this opportunity."

"He sounds like a shoo-in," Ben said.

"He would be. But the big boys don't like Fastower. And that's your saving grace, Ben." Sam looked at Ben. "Michael 'Fast-talker' is what they call him behind his back. He's a little too ambitious, too smart and smooth for them. You, on the other hand, are well known because you're already here, well liked because you know how to keep a low profile, and you have zero credibility issues. Word on the street is that you're the shoo-in," Sam said.

Ben leaned back, and then looked at Meredith. Meredith smiled greatly. "Wild," was the only word she could think to say.

"I told you I was gonna do it for you, boy!" Sam said with a sudden burst of energy, pumping his fist in the air.

"I am so happy for you, Ben," Meredith said.

"If it's true, it's incredible," Ben said.

"Yes, it is. It's wonderful," Meredith said.

"As soon as I got off of the phone with my contacts I came to you," Sam said. "I ran up ten flights."

"That's what I've never understood about the corporate world," Meredith said. "Why would Sam's contacts know before you, Ben, that you're one of two finalists?"

"That's just the nature of the business, Meredith," Sam said. "You notify your cronies so that Wall Street can begin to adjust before an official announcement, so it won't be a shock to their system. Then you let them get the word to the principals. That way it appears that your allegiance is with the bigger picture, with Wall Street, and not with just one or two men."

Ben smiled. "And it's also a cover should they change their minds and neither man will do. After all, they never said it themselves."

"They won't change their minds," Meredith said. "Not on you, anyway."

"Tell him, Meredith," Sam said. "Besides, their window of opportunity is too narrow. They've got to make a decision and an official announcement soon."

"What's going to be the strategy, then?" Meredith asked Sam. "I'm sure you have one."

Sam walked up to Ben's desk. "Okay," he said, his eyes focused exclusively on Ben. "You've got to keep a low profile. That's key. That's what distinguishes you from Fastower. Word is he's already planning a publicity blitz through the Midwest to drum up support, as if those old geezers on the board of directors are gonna listen to outsiders. But that's Fastower's style, and that's exactly what the board hates about him. But the good news is that he doesn't know it, so you keep a low profile, keep doing what you're doing, and you'll be fine. I guarantee it."

Ben looked at Sam, then past him at the numerous plaques on his wall, and to one particular plaque. "Man of the Year," it said, and it was from a small, local recreation center that he backed financially. It didn't make a ripple in the corporate world. No news media covered the ceremony. Not even Josie knew he had received it. But it was, to Ben, his greatest accomplishment. Because he didn't have to do anything but write a check every month, and that little gesture meant the world to them. If he was named CEO, he would have earned it through sweat and blood. The thrill of the chase could very well be more preferable than the capture. The capture would not be an end, but a beginning of more, more sweat, more blood. More. In the end it was not going to be an accomplishment at all. The more he would have to give, like former CEO Murdoch had found out, would still not be enough in the end.

"I'd better get going," Meredith said, standing. Ben stood up too as she walked around his desk, smiling as she came. "And I can't express how happy I am for you, Benjamin. Congratulations." She gave him a friendly hug. When they released, she kissed him on the mouth. Ben glanced at Sam as Meredith's lips parted from his. Sam could not believe his eyes.

"Oh, my goodness," Meredith said, as if stunned by her own behavior. "Did I do that? I did not mean to do that. I'm sorry, Ben. I am so sorry."

Ben removed his hand from around her waist and smiled too. "It's all right," he said. Although he knew that it wasn't.

"Hello?" Josie said into the phone. It was Scotty. "Hey, knuckle-head." She readjusted her laptop computer on her lap. She was in bed, in her nightgown, running search engines on the Internet.

"Hey, yourself."

"I haven't heard from you since my birthday, Scotty. What's up?"

"I was just thinking about you," Scotty said. "Can't I think about my best friend?"

"I give you permission."

"What you doing? No, no, let me guess. You're laying on that bed of yours pining away because Ben ain't there."

"I'm working, for your information. A source gave me some info that Oxidare may be involved in some illegal dumping that's making elementary kids sick. I'm just doing some background, although I'm not getting very far."

"And where's Ben?"

"I have no idea," she said.

"Wait a minute, now. Ben ain't there, and you don't care?"

"Scotty, I know you didn't call me to talk about no Ben. What's happened?"

"Nothing's happened."

"Liar."

"I'm in love, okay? Satisfied?"

"In love?" Josie asked.

"Yes, girl—as in happy."

"Who is it this time? A murderer, a thief, or a combination thereof?"

"Forget you."

"Who is he?"

Scotty paused. "Bruce."

"Again? The thief? I thought you said it was over, Scotty?"

"It was when I said it. But we worked out our differences."

"You need to quit, Scotty. You didn't used to be this hard-up."

"I'm not hard-up."

"Yes, you are. Why would you keep going back to that loser? A man who stole from you and tried to beat your ass? Please."

"He's changed, Josie, all right? Why do you keep running back to Ben?"

"Ben doesn't steal from me and he's never beat my ass."

"He's done something to that ass. That's why you keep running back to him. Well it's the same way with Bruce. I feel like he's the one."

"He's the one all right," she said. "The one in the next police line-up."

"I don't know why I even bother with you. I knew you wasn't gonna be happy for me."

"I'm not gonna lie to you, Scotty, and pretend it's all right what you're doing. It's not all right. Bruce ain't shit. He's a player. A user. He'll bleed you dry, then move on to his next victim. When he runs out of victims he starts over. You're just a part of the rotation, brother." There was silence over the phone. Josie leaned her head back. She had gone too far. "I'm sorry."

"Don't be. You're telling nothing but the truth as usual."

"You're a good-looking, smart, successful man, Scotty. You shouldn't have to take all that crap over and over again. Pretending that something is when it ain't." Josie could hear a car pull up in her driveway. She got up, cordless phone in hand, and walked toward the window. "And why? Just because you don't wanna be alone? Please. Peace of mind is worth it, take it from me."

It was Ben's Mercedes. The engine cut off, and then he slowly emerged. Josie's heart dropped.

"I'm not like you, Josie, I keep telling you that."

She began walking back toward the bed. "Listen, Scotty, I'll talk to you later."

"What? No you ain't giving me the brushoff."

"I'll call you back," she said.

"It's Ben, isn't it?"

"What is that your business?" Josie began shutting down her computer and removing it from her bed.

"And you're preaching to me? You doing the same thing. Ben shows up and suddenly your whole world revolves around him."

"It ain't even like that."

"Oh, yes, it is," he said.

Josie hesitated. Scotty was right. It was exactly like that. She sat back on her bed, her back against the headboard. "You know what? You're right. You are absolutely right. Now what were we talking about?"

Scotty laughed. "Don't even try it, Josie. Go on and hang up because I know that's what you're dying to do. I know you gots to be with your honey."

"What were we talking about, Scotty?"

"What you doing, girl?"

"I thought you called to talk to me," she said.

"I did."

"Then talk!"

"Okay, dang, don't take my head off. I was just trying to help your trifling butt."

"What were you talking about, Scotty?"

"Bruce, of course," he said.

Josie could hear the doorbell ring. He knew where she kept her spare key, so she didn't know why he was tripping. Sure enough, within seconds, she could hear him unlocking the front door and entering. Scotty continued talking, as she had requested, but she only half-listened. Ben was on her mind.

He walked slowly up her stairs. By the time he made it to the landing and appeared at her bedroom door, her heart was racing. He looked great, she thought, no look of worry about her absence in his life at all. Maybe content was the word, as he stood in her doorway, his hands in his pockets, his muscular body leaning against the door frame. Uncertainty, too, was what she saw when she looked at him. Contentment with uncertainty, as if he still wasn't sure if he should be there. She had stayed away from him for two weeks. Two long weeks, and he seemed the better for it. That was sobering to Josie, and that was why she was glad she decided to keep talking to Scotty.

"I still say you deserve better," she said into the phone.

"And I agree with you," Scotty replied. "And when better comes along I'll take it. But in the meantime—and just in case fairy tales really don't come true—I'll stick with Bruce."

"It's your life." Josie looked at Ben.

He moved, seemingly reluctantly, away from the door frame and across the room. He listened only slightly as Josie continued running her mouth on the phone, all but ignoring him. He glanced out the window at the empty street in Josie's quiet neighborhood. The rain was still pelting down, but less dramatically now. He still felt that sense of dread that began to overtake him when he got the call from the chairman.

He sat in the chair against the wall. Josie began laughing, as if her phone companion was just cracking her up. Ben sat back and watched her, watched her lift her head back and rub her shoulder, her V-neck nightgown revealing the cleavage of her large breasts. It had been months since he had touched her, not since the night of Deuce's get-together, and he'd been wanting her so bad lately he could feel it beneath the belt. He crossed his legs. He knew Josie. It was no accident that he hadn't heard from her in weeks. She had some serious thinking to do and he respected that. But enough was enough.

"Josie?" he said in the midst of another round of laughter from her. She looked at him, and then placed her hand over the phone's transmitter. "Why don't you tell your friend you'll call her back."

"It's not a her," Josie said, and then quickly regretted that she had said it. She removed her hand from the phone. "Listen, I have to talk to you later," she said into the phone.

"No, he ain't demanding that you hang up on me," Scotty said. "Put him on the line, girl. I can handle Ben."

"Okay. Talk to you later, bye." Josie hung up, then looked at Ben. "Yes?" she said.

"How you been doing?"

"Good. What about you?" she asked.

Ben nodded, with some hesitation. "Okay," he said. Their eyes finally locked onto each other. Josie wanted to jump from her bed and run to him. But she didn't. She'd finally worked up enough courage to function without the constancy of Ben in her every thought and action, and she wasn't about to throw it all away just because he showed up.

"Why haven't you called me?" he asked her.

"Why haven't you called *me*?"

"I didn't know it was a contest."

"I didn't, either."

Ben paused. "I'm one of two finalists, Josie."

"Two finalists? For what?" Ben didn't respond. "CEO?"

"Yes."

It was stunning news. She couldn't help but smile. "That's great. Congratulations."

"Thank you."

"You'll be running Denlex. That's really something. You deserve it, Ben, you deserve it so much."

"I appreciate that, Josie."

"Who's the other finalist?"

"Fastower. Michael Fastower. Well-credentialed, affable fellow from what I understand."

"But he won't beat you."

"He might."

"No way. What's he got that you don't have?"

Ben smiled. "Youth. He's six years younger. Sometimes that matters."

"That's crazy. You're older and wiser, and experienced in so many different things."

"If the selection committee is as positive as you are, I'll be a shoo-in."

Josie laughed. "Now you're talking right!"

Ben smiled and leaned his head back. Josie looked gorgeous to him, sitting there, so filled with life and vitality and such unbridled enthusiasm that it was almost contagious.

"I miss you," he finally said to her.

Josie didn't respond. She missed him too, more than he probably realized. But she had decided during her time away from him that she was no longer wearing her feelings on her sleeve.

Ben was disappointed by her lack of response, but he decided to keep plugging at it. "I'm used to getting four or five phone calls from you every day, and then suddenly nothing. Even Whitney was concerned."

Josie smiled. "She would be."

Ben smiled, and then his look turned decidedly serious. "Come here," he said to her.

He had said those two words to Josie many times before, when he wanted to hold her or kiss her or lecture her. Every time she had jumped at his command. But not this time.

"I don't see anything wrong with your two legs," she said.

Ben couldn't help but smile. "Good answer," he said. He stood and walked to the side of her bed. It was a change, seeing Josie like this, and he wasn't sure yet if he liked what he saw. He sat down on the edge of the bed. He smelled like a combination of cologne and tobacco. A combination she missed.

"Now," he said as he sat down, "is that better?"

"I guess," she said. She avoided eye contact. He was too close now. But he was the same old Ben, who never relented in his stare, who made her so nervous that she felt she had no choice but to stare back. And she did, looking at his mustache first, and then into his eyes. His soft, caring eyes. And as soon as she did it, as soon as her hazel eyes looked into his bright brown eyes, she wanted to cry.

His heart melted as tears appeared in her eyes. He leaned over to her and placed his hands on either side of her face. Then he kissed her, first on those eyes, and then on the mouth. Her body pushed back against the bed's headboard as he kissed her hard, and all of her resistance, all of her need to stay even-keeled, to let him know that she was no pushover any longer, flew away like a feather on a paper airplane as soon as she felt the warmth of his lips against hers. She placed her arms around his body and opened her mouth. He wrapped his tongue in hers and kissed her so desperately, so urgently, that she could feel the bones of her back pressed hard against the headboard. They kissed as if it had been years. When their lips finally parted, and their tongues finally relaxed, their breathing became so labored that they continued leaning against each other just to regain their composure.

"You miss me?" he asked her, his breathing even more erratic than hers, his sweet breath blowing cool air all over her warm face.

"Yes," she replied, and she could barely speak.

"How much, Josie?"

"I miss you so much. More than you will ever know." She said this lovingly, and sadly, because it was so true. He looked at her with such intensity, with such love and desire, that she grabbed hold of him again. And he kissed her again, even harder, even more passionately, even more desperately than before. He had never wanted her as much as he wanted her this very hour, and he had to have it in the worst way. That was why he forced himself to break away, to stop kissing the woman he could have kissed all night, because his need went deeper than a kiss. He stood up and removed his coat and tie.

Josie watched him, with thrill and apprehension, with a sense of uselessness and a sense of awe. She wished she were stronger; she wished she could say no the way she had that night at his cabin, when the realization that she was too needy, too damn dependent on this man, caused her to finally wake up. But she wasn't there yet. As she watched him, as she watched him remove his coat, slip off his tie, his shirt, his T-shirt, and then unbuckle his belt, she knew she was doing exactly as she planned *not* to do and was reentering a world she was trying to leave. But she couldn't leave. She craved him. He was her drug of choice. As he laid her down and lifted her gown off of her body, she knew she was like wiggling bait for the catch: hooked again.

He kissed her face and her neck and her breasts and her stomach, and then he did something he had never done before. He *tasted* her. It was so unexpected, and so exhilarating to her that she swerved her body, lifted herself up on elbows, and lay back down as his tongue massaged deep within her. She grabbed the sheet and squeezed it tightly as he lifted her thigh, her body jerking with excitement, too much excitement, and she finally jerked away from him and closed her legs. It was over, she thought. It had to be over. She didn't know if she could take anymore. But he stood up, staring at her, as if telling her telepathically that more was coming, to get ready for more, and then he removed his pants and boxer shorts.

He leaned down to her and turned her onto her stomach. When he lay on top of her and slowly slid in, his massive body gyrating hers in rhythmic, bed-shaking bounces that caused even him to yell out as she cried "Oh!" She cried out because it felt so good, and it felt so right. It felt as if she was never going to overcome this man, this big, wonderful, glorious man, that she loved too much.

Deuce Jefferson leaned back in his recliner and drank more beer. A rerun of an old *Sanford and Son* episode was on TV. Although Fred and Lamont may have been hilarious, Deuce wasn't feeling it. He was too busy thinking about Josie. He couldn't penetrate that wall for nothing in this world, and he gave it all he had. Since that day at Rhonda's, when Braddock had come to their table and told Josie he was taking her out that night, she hadn't been the same. She was too preoccupied with work, he thought, to be okay. But when he tried to make his move, he was rebuffed at every turn. She wouldn't have dinner with him or go for a drink with him or even have an innocent lunch with him. If she had broken up with Braddock, he thought, then it wasn't necessarily good news for him. Not the way she was acting. Now Meredith had just called and said she was on her way over. As if she could do or say anything that was going to change Josie's heart. Even when Josie wasn't with Ben, she still was with him, it seemed to Deuce. There was no interfering with that kind of love.

After watching yet another *Sanford and Son* episode and as *The Bob Newhart Show* was just beginning to run credits, Meredith finally arrived. Deuce fixed her a drink and they settled down in his living room. Meredith hadn't said anything substantial, just that routine pep speech of hers, where everything was going to work out and, whether he believed it or not, things were moving in their favor. Deuce was pretty well ready to tell her a thing or two about things moving, how they were moving more against them than in favor of them, when Meredith pulled out an 8-by-10-inch glossy photograph of a forty-something man with a short Afro, thick sideburns, and a smile as crooked as his teeth. Deuce picked it up from the table and observed it. The man did not seem familiar to him at all. He looked at Meredith. "Who is he?"

"What did you tell me was the biggest hurdle that had to be overcome before Josie would even give you the time of day?"

"Braddock."

"Not just Braddock, but his glow. Her almost inexplicable belief in his great decency."

"Right."

"What do you think is Josie's greatest asset?"

"That's an almost impossible question to answer. She has so many assets." Deuce smiled, and then sipped more beer.

"Name the number one."

Deuce paused. "Her passionate commitment to truth and justice and doing what's right. Her morality."

"And if she ever supposed that there was a character flaw in our friend, the judge, then that glow of his won't shine as brightly. Wouldn't you agree?"

"Josie is a different breed, Meredith."

"Nonsense. She's a woman. And not a very experienced one at that. She may believe that Ben is having an affair, and may even have some proof of it, but that in and of itself is not going to be enough. She'll internalize that. He sleeps around on her and treats her like crap, but he's still a good, decent man who holds everybody else in high regard. That's why women stay with unsavory men. They treat them horribly, but the women declare that they know the true side of their men. Then they don't blame the men at all, but their good looks and charm and the fact that the females won't leave them alone. I think that's Josie."

Deuce shook his head. "So we gonna tarnish Braddock's glow?"

"That's the idea."

"We're gonna tarnish the reputation of the man you love?"

Meredith hesitated. Deuce was sharper than she had thought. "If it will get Josie Ross out of the picture once and for all," she said, "yes."

Deuce smiled. "And you call Braddock ruthless?"

"I'm just looking out for my interest," she said.

Deuce looked at the photo before him. "And Sideburns here is supposed to assist in that?"

"Yes."

"So who the hell is he?"

"His name is Stuart Lindsey."

"Lindsey? Never heard of him." Then Deuce smiled, looked at the photo again. "Looks like a Shaft wannabe, if you ask me."

"Don't laugh, Deuce," Meredith warned. "He is not one to take lightly. This Shaft wannabe, as you call him, very well could be the man."

"The man? You sound like a bad movie, Meredith. What man?"

"The man who just might knock that halo off of Ben Braddock's head."

CHAPTER 20

"You didn't have to do this, Deuce," Josie said as her Mustang pulled out of the parking lot of the *Bullhorn Journal* and turned west on Saint Germain. Deuce buckled his seatbelt and smiled.

"I know I didn't have to do it. I wanted to. No woman should be going car shopping alone."

"And why not?"

"Salesmen's tongues wag when a female shows up on their car lots alone. Trust me."

Josie smiled. "Their tongues can wag all they want. It's my money."

"Agreed. But they're slick, Josie. They'll rip you off in the name of helping you out."

Josie's cell phone began ringing. "Oh, I know the game, Deuce. I hear what you're saying." She pulled her cell phone from her purse. "But you don't know me. Ain't nobody ripping me off, okay?"

Deuce laughed. "That's what they all say."

Josie flipped open her cell phone. "Hello?"

"Hey."

"Ben?"

"You sound surprised."

"I am, a little. What's up?"

"Nothing. Was just calling to see what was up with you."

"Oh. Yeah, now that is surprising," she said, and smiled. "Nothing's up. Just trying to survive in this harsh and cruel world."

"That sounds like something one of those *Bullhorn* commentators would say."

"How would you know that? Don't tell me Ben Braddock reads the *Bullhorn Journal?*"

"I read my girlfriend's stories all the time. The rest of it is pure happenstance."

Josie smiled. "You need to stop trippin'."

"Where are you? Sounds like you're on the go."

"I am. Where are you?"

"In my office."

"No meetings to attend?"

"Yes, but I started thinking about you."

Josie didn't respond. She didn't know what to say. He hadn't phoned her in the middle of the morning just because he was thinking about her in a long, long time. Now he was trying to act as if he phoned every day.

Her sudden silence disturbed Ben. He remembered a time when she couldn't stop calling him, sometimes four or five times a day. Now she never phoned. "Where are you off to?" he asked after it became clear she wasn't about to break the silence.

"I'm driving over to the Ford dealership."

"The Ford dealership? Why? Your car giving you problems?"

"No, not really. I just think it's about time I consider doing a trade-in before it does start giving me problems."

"That doesn't make sense, Josie."

"Why not? You do it all the time. You have three automobiles, remember? And all three are practically new."

"If I jump from a bridge, you're gonna jump too?"

Josie smiled. "I might."

"You'd better not."

"I'm just kidding, Ben, dang. I'm just going to look for another Mustang, that's all this is about."

"I thought you loved the one you have."

"I do, and I'll love a new one even better."

"What*ever*," Ben said the way Josie loved to say it, and Josie laughed.

"Going alone isn't a good idea," Ben said.

"What?"

"You shouldn't go to a car lot alone."

"Now here you go. I can take care of myself, okay? Besides, I'm not alone," Josie said, and looked at Deuce. "Deuce has been kind enough to go with me."

There was a pause. "Deuce?"

"Yeah. He's of the same opinion as you, that a woman is so feeble-minded that all a salesman has to do is smile and she's fresh bait."

"Why didn't you call me?"

"Call you? Since when have you had time to be bothered with me?" Josie did not mean it the way it sounded, and she could tell immediately that Ben was offended. But she wasn't exactly lying, either. "Your schedule is usually pretty tight, Ben," she said. "That's what I meant."

"Yeah, well, I don't want to keep you. Tell Deuce I said hello." Ben hung up the phone. Josie looked at her cell phone, shook her head, and then hung up too.

"How's boyfriend?" Deuce asked.

"Getting stranger by the day."

"Meaning?"

"Nothing. He said hello."

Deuce smiled. "To me?"

"Yep."

"That's a switch," Deuce said.

"I'm sayin'."

"He doesn't mind my tagging along with you?"

"Why should he mind?" Josie asked as she turned onto County Road 4 and downshifted gears. If he did mind—and to Josie that was a big if—it would be a beautiful development.

She came to check out a few Mustangs she'd spotted on the Internet, but instead spent over an hour checking out SUVs. She and Deuce were like kids in a candy store, admiring everything about every SUV they viewed, from the color to the seating to the rims on the tires. The salesman was pleased too, because he just knew he had a sure bet of a sale, especially when Josie agreed to test drive one of the Expedition models. But just as the salesman walked back toward the showroom to grab a tag, Josie saw Ben's Mercedes drive up and into the lot of the Mike Malcottt Ford Dealership. When he stepped out of his car, dropping his cigarette to the ground to button his suit coat, even Deuce was stunned.

"What's he doing here?" he asked as Ben began walking toward them. His guess was as good as Josie's, whose first instinct was to leave Deuce's side and run to Ben. But she decided to stay.

"Well, hello there," she said as he walked up. He smiled, which wasn't easy for a stern man like him, and as soon as he reached her side he became territorial. He placed his hand around her waist.

"Hello," he said. "Thought I'd come by and give you a little moral support."

"Ah, don't even trick that. You came by to make sure I didn't get ripped off."

"Since it ultimately would be my money that would be the source of the rip, I think I'm at least entitled to see the goods beforehand."

Josie smiled. The memories of last night, when he had made love to her in ways he had never before, still sent ripples through her body. She placed her arm around him and looked up into his eyes. "Whatever the reason," she said, "thanks for coming."

Ben smiled. His body was still rippling too, and to look into her eyes again made him want another round with her as quickly as he could get her alone. But he resisted the urge to even kiss her. He was in too deep as it was, he felt. He looked over at Deuce, whom he could sense was staring at him.

"What's up?" Deuce asked as soon as Ben looked his way.

"How are you?" Ben said.

"I thought Josie told you I was coming with her."

Ben continued to look at Deuce, as if he could not believe the nerve of the brother. "She did," he finally said. Josie, knowing when Ben's mood was turning combative, touched him on the stomach. He looked at her. "Made any decisions yet?" he asked her.

"No, not really. We were just joking around."

Ben frowned. "Joking around? I thought you were here to pur-chase an automobile?"

"I am."

"Then what are you joking about?"

"I didn't mean it that way, Ben. What I meant was that we were just . . ." She shook her head. "Never mind."

Ben looked at Deuce, whom he suspected had something to do with why Josie wouldn't be taking something as monumental as car shopping seriously. Before he could exchange words with Deuce, the salesman returned with the tag. His wholly confident walk slowed, however, when he saw Ben.

"An addition to our group, I see," he said as he walked up.

"This is Ben," Josie said to the salesman.

"Hello, Ben," the salesman said, shaking his hand. "The name's Ed. Welcome to Mike Malcott. You look like a man who would love an SUV."

"He's not car shopping, Ed," Josie quickly interjected. "He's just here with me."

"I see. You're a popular lady."

"Seems that way, doesn't it?" Josie said with a smile. Ben placed his hands in his pockets.

"Well, Miss Ross," Ed said, "ready for your test drive?"

"What are you test driving?" Ben asked her.

"This," she said smilingly, and Ben looked at the bright red, massive SUV that stood in front of them. Then he looked at Josie.

"An Expedition, Josie?"

"Just to see what it rides like."

"To see what it rides . . ." Ben exhaled. "This is not a game, Josephine."

"I didn't say it was a game, Ben. Dang. The man offered to let me give it a spin, and I said okay. That's what people do at car lots."

"I'm sayin'," Deuce said, and Ben glared at him.

"It was really my suggestion," Ed said.

"How much is it?" Ben asked.

Ed smiled. "You mean for the Expedition?" Ben didn't respond. "It's only fifty-two."

"Fifty-two?"

"Yes, but for your lady we can work something out. That price is just the start of the bidding. It's always negotiable."

Josie looked at Ed. "You told us it wasn't negotiable."

"Did I?"

"You did," Deuce said, and the salesman glanced at Ben. But Ben was staring at Josie.

"You're actually considering buying this fifty-two-thousand-dollar tank, Josephine?"

"She should have the best," Deuce said.

"Yeah," Josie said with a smile, not taking the situation nearly as seriously as Ben.

"Besides," Deuce added, "looks like your ride easily tops fifty-two thou', Doc. With maybe forty thou' on top of that. I mean, come on. And if it's good enough for you, hey. It's good enough for Josie."

Ben ignored Deuce. "Is this what you want, Josie? An SUV?"

Josie rolled her eyes. "Apparently not," she said. Then she looked at the salesman. "Let's go take a look at the Mustangs."

"If you want it, Josephine, I'll get it. But do you want it?"

Josie looked at the Expedition. It would be a ride to behold, that was for sure. But she couldn't afford it by a mile and the idea of Ben spending fifty-two thousand dollars on a vehicle for her, putting her even more in his debt than she already was, wasn't attractive to her anymore. "No, I don't want it," she said. "I'll stick with the 'Stangs."

"Are you sure?" Ben asked her.

"Are you crazy?" Deuce asked her.

"I'm sure," she said to Ben. "The jury's still out," she said to Deuce.

Deuce laughed and Ed, the main one disappointed, escorted them around the lot to a double line of brand-new Mustangs. Ben's cell phone began ringing and he began walking behind them as he answered it.

"He was bluffing, wasn't he?" Deuce asked Josie as they followed closely behind Ed.

"About what?"

"Buying you that Expedition, J., come on."

"He doesn't bluff, Deuce."

Deuce looked back at Ben, who was talking in a low voice on his cell phone, and then back at Josie. "Damn, girl. And you turned him down?"

"Hell, yeah, I turned him down. He already bought me a house, and he pays all my bills. But my car? My 'Stang? No, thank you. I ain't owing no Negro for that."

"You sound like the brother who drives around in a Rolls Royce and sleeps at the homeless shelter. His car means everything to him. Unnaturally so."

Josie laughed. "But he be looking good, though."

"I still think you should consider your boyfriend's offer," the salesman said to Josie. "A Mustang cannot compare to the ride you'll get in our front-line SUVs."

"I'm sure it can't. But I can't afford an Expedition, so that case is closed. Okay?"

The salesman understood attitude when he heard it. He, after all, worked in the public eye on a daily basis. But he didn't understand foolishness, and Josie, in his mind, took the prize.

Ben flipped shut his cell phone, and then moved toward the salesman. Josie could tell right away that something was up. "Ed?" Ben said.

"Yes, sir?"

"Is there a television set around here someplace?"

"A television? You mean equipped in one of the vehicles?"

"No, just a TV."

"Sure. Come with me."

"What's the matter, Ben?" Josie asked him.

"I don't know yet," he replied.

Ben began following the salesman toward the showroom. Josie hesitated, watching them as they walked away, and then she began following too. Deuce, there to tag along, tagged along.

There was only one TV, in the waiting area of the showroom, and the salesman, on instruction from Ben, flipped the channel from CNN to the local Channel 3. Deuce immediately recognized the man from the photo from the night before. Stuart Lindsey was being interviewed by a Minnesota business reporter. Lindsey, who was on satellite feed from Florida, was sitting behind a desk in what looked like one of those small, paneled-wall offices. His sideburns weren't as thick as those in his photograph, but he still looked like a Shaft wannabe to Deuce.

Ben's suit coat was now unbuttoned, and he had both hands on his hips. He stood in the middle of the small waiting room, a waiting room filled almost to capacity with customers, and Josie walked over and stood beside him. Deuce and Ed stood back.

"He overbilled clients," Lindsey said.

"Billing for work he didn't necessarily do?" the reporter asked.

"That's right."

"You know this for a fact, Mr. Lindsey?"

"Yes. I was his law partner. I absolutely know it for a fact. He would even get clients to lie if it would help win the lawsuit."

"You mean he would get them to withhold information . . . ?"

"I'm talking out-and-out lying. Ben Braddock was good at that. If he knew something wasn't true, if he knew those clients weren't injured, he would get them to claim they were, anyway. Whiplash and back injuries, that was his thing. And he made millions off of it."

"That's a strong accusation, Mr. Lindsey. You're accusing Benjamin Braddock of very questionable, very shady business practices."

"You don't know the half of it. That's why I'm telling my story now. When I read in the *Wall Street Journal* that he was one of two finalists for CEO of Denlex, I was beyond stunned. I sat back when the brother became a circuit court judge twenty years ago, and I didn't say a word then. I should have, but I was dealing with my own issues then. And I didn't have to say anything when he was nominated to sit on Florida's supreme court, because those beautiful and, I might add, truthful sisters said it all for me."

"You're talking about the women who accused Judge Braddock of sexual harassment?"

"That's right."

"You believe their accusations to be true even though evidence has surfaced that they may have had an agenda?"

"They might have had an agenda, but they were still telling the truth, in my opinion."

"Why are you coming forward now?"

"He's going to be running Denlex, that's why."

"It's not for certain yet, Mr. Lindsey."

"You obviously don't know Benny Braddock. He never loses. That's why I got in touch with y'all. When I found out he was up for CEO, I knew I had to speak up."

"But I still don't understand why, sir?"

"Denlex is a publicly traded company. That means the investment dollars of millions of average Americans could go up in smoke if a shady character like Braddock has any hand in it. It'll be Enron all over again. Only worse."

"These are some explosive allegations you're leveling against the senior vice president of Denlex," the reporter said. "Have you spoken to any federal regulators yet, or anybody in the justice department?"

"Look, I'm just telling what I know. People can take it or leave it. But Braddock as CEO of Denlex? That's going too far. The man is a racist against his own people. That's the level of man we're talking about."

"Why would you call Mr. Braddock a racist? Because of his well-documented, conservative, Republican views?"

"More than that. I remember when we were partners and he used to refer to poor blacks as savages. The middle- and upper-class blacks were cool with him. He didn't have a problem with them. But the poor, he hated. They were savages, he said. They were a drag on the race. That was his word. Drag. If it was left up to him he'd send them all back to Africa, that's what he told me. And more than once too. And you're telling me that's the kind of man the stockholders of Denlex want running their company? I don't think so."

The reporter then appeared on camera alone. "And that's the way it is. The former business partner of the man who just might become CEO of one of the most respected companies in Minnesota is speaking out. Loudly. His bottom line: Benjamin Braddock is not the man we thought he was. He is not the man for the job."

Josie looked at Ben as the reporter's piece ended. Josie could sense devastation, although it wasn't showing on his face. "You know him, Ben?"

"I thought I did."

"Who would put him up to these lies? The other finalist, Fastower?"

"I don't know."

"So what are we gonna do?"

"You're going to continue looking for an automobile," Ben said, still staring at the television set, still seemingly cool, but inwardly numb.

As soon as Ben arrived back at work and walked into his suite of offices, he could feel the stares. Everybody would look away when he looked toward them, and by the time he'd made it into his office, both Meredith and Sam Darrow had discovered his arrival and rushed in.

"How bad is it?" Ben asked them as he stood behind his desk. Meredith looked at Sam.

"We're bleeding," Sam said.

"Who's Stuart Lindsey, anyway?" Meredith asked, as if today was the first time she had ever heard of the man, as if she had no hand whatsoever in bringing his allegations to light.

"We shared a law practice over twenty years ago."

Sam looked at Ben. "Are those allegations true, Ben?"

Ben hesitated. "No."

"No to which allegation? Shady businessman or racist?"

Ben sighed and shook his head. He placed his hands on his hips. "Both," he said.

"Okay. Good. Like I said, we're bleeding. Those accusations, even if untrue, certainly don't help us, but there's still hope."

"What hope?" Meredith asked. "Ben was just wrongfully crucified in public, and I mean totally decimated, and you're talking about hope? Where's the hope, Sam? I say we kiss that CEO job goodbye."

"We aren't kissing anything goodbye," Sam said. "All Ben has to do is deny everything. They're lies and Lindsey's a snake trying to make a name for himself. That's all he has to say."

"Are you kidding me?" Meredith asked Sam. "You can't believe that yourself. The board of directors aren't going to just take Ben's word for it. The damage is already done."

"Not necessarily. If the bad press blows over, and if the board . . ."

"Come on, Sam."

"If the board is bold and the Street doesn't get antsy for an announcement, the chairman, who loves Ben by the way, may hold over a decision on CEO. We still may have a shot."

"I say Fastower is a lock," Meredith said, dismissing Sam's assessment. "And I wouldn't be surprised at all if he was the one who dredged up this Stuart Lindsey in the first place."

"That's why Ben has got to speak up," Sam said. He looked at Ben. "You've got to wipe your feet with this guy, Ben. You've got to totally discredit him and everything he said about you."

Ben sighed. "No," he said.

Sam looked at Meredith. Meredith was staring at Ben.

"What do you mean, 'no'?" she asked him.

"If the board wants to question me about the allegations, I'll answer their questions. But I'm not about to get into some verbal, tabloid fight with Stuart Lindsey. He's a good man who's had a lot of problems in his life. I'm not adding to them."

Sam couldn't believe it. First he looked at Meredith. Then he glared at Ben. "Let me see if I've got this straight. You don't want to add to *his* problems? Is that what you're telling me? The man who just accused you of being a liar, a thief—and, oh, yeah—a Ku Klux Klansman deserves your compassion? Is that what you're saying?"

"That's what I'm saying, Sam," Ben said so firmly that even Sam Darrow knew to back off.

The doorbell rang, and it was Deuce with a bottle of champagne. Josie was at first surprised, then glad to see him.

"I know," he said. "What in the world brings me to your door, right?"

"Right."

"I thought you could use some cheering up. It hasn't exactly been a banner day for you and Ben."

Josie smiled. What an understatement. "Come in, please."

Deuce, relieved that his uninvited visit was accepted, walked into Josie's townhouse quickly. He looked around at her home, at the black-and-white patterns throughout, as if her taste in design would reveal some secret side to her.

"Have a seat," she said, and he did, sitting on the sofa. She accepted his bottle of champagne and poured them both a drink.

"Now you sit down and relax," he said, patting the cushion beside his. She smiled, with drink in hand, and sat down too. "What were you up to, anyway?" he asked. "I hope I'm not interrupting anything."

"Nothing important. I was cleaning out my kitchen cabinets. That's something I always do when I'm upset."

"Okay."

"It's crazy, isn't it?"

"Only if they don't need cleaning out."

Josie laughed. "Sometimes I wonder."

"After you dropped me back at work this afternoon I got a little worried when you didn't come back to the office yourself."

"I know. I was just upset. Ben wouldn't talk about it and . . ."

"And what? And you began to wonder if those allegations were true?"

Josie hesitated. "No."

"Come on, Josie."

"Ben wouldn't do those things that man accused him of. I know he wouldn't."

"He's a conservative Republican, Josie. A black man. You told me yourself you used to call him an Oreo back in Jacksonville."

"That was before I got to know him, Deuce. He's no racist, okay?"

"But why would the man just lie like that?"

"I don't know, but that's exactly what's happened."

Deuce shook his head. "You're too smart for this, kiddo. I'm sorry. There are too many damn coincidences here. Women are calling you, talking about how they're sleeping with your man. He neglects you in favor of women like Meredith Chambers, who you can look at and tell is a tease. You notice all kinds of suspicious behavior from him, like staying out late at night and blaming it on work. And on top of all of that, woman after woman has already accused him of sexually harassing them."

"Those allegations were false, Deuce, I told you that."

"I hear what you're saying, but it adds to the pile, Josie. Now this new dude comes along with yet another tale of what kind of man Ben Braddock is. And you're still talking about how it's all lies? Come on, J. You're smarter than that. I mean, there finally comes a point when you have to check yourself and say, hey, wait a minute here. Ain't nobody that unlucky," he said. Josie leaned back and closed her eyes. She was emotionally drained.

Deuce looked at her. She was dressed in a maroon halter top and a pair of denim Daisy Dukes. Her breasts were large and her belly was flat. *Gorgeous,* he thought. And her face, her vulnerable, lovely face; he wanted to kiss her. And he would have, but the doorbell rang.

"Damn," Deuce said, and Josie looked at him.

"What's wrong with you?"

"I just really wanted to talk to you."

"You are talking to me," Josie said as she stood up and walked to her front door. She looked out of the peephole and could see that it was Ben. She exhaled, waited another second, and then opened the door.

"Hey," she said. "I didn't expect to see you tonight."

"I thought I'd swing by before I went home," he said as he walked in. He had a lit cigarette between his fingers and his tie was undone. He appeared disheveled to Josie. When he saw Deuce, of all people, sitting on her sofa, he stopped in his tracks. Then he looked at Josie.

"This is an early night for you, isn't it?" Josie said as she closed her front door.

Ben didn't say anything. He continued staring at her for an explanation, but she didn't see where she had to explain anything to him.

"Come on and have a seat," she said, walking toward the sofa. He watched her in her Daisy Dukes and halter top, looking like a prime piece of meat for an opportunist like Deuce Jefferson, and it all seemed to Ben to be the perfect ending to a hell of a day.

When Josie turned and noticed that Ben was still standing in the foyer, she smiled. "Come on, Ben, and sit down," she said, sitting down herself. "We won't bite you."

Deuce laughed. Ben took a slow drag on his cigarette, put it out in the big potted plant by the door, and then walked further into the home. He sat down in the armchair across from the sofa and crossed his legs.

"How's it going, Benny boy?" Deuce asked with a smile, and even Josie knew he had gone too far. Ben, however, was astute at not rising to the bait. He didn't bother to respond.

"You want a drink?" Josie asked him. "Deuce brought champagne."

"What is he celebrating?" Ben asked, and then he and Deuce glanced at each other.

"He's not celebrating anything," Josie said. "He just brought a bottle with him. Do you want any?"

"I have a bottle of scotch in the refrigerator. Get me that, with soda."

Josie shook her head. "You're a scotch man to your heart," she said as she got up and walked into the kitchen. Deuce purposely looked at her, at her body mainly, and when he turned back around, Ben was, as he had hoped, staring at him.

"So, Judge Braddock," he said, "you seem to be holding up quite well. Considering." Ben said nothing. "How does it feel to be called a racist?" Still no response from Ben. "Has to feel strange. I mean, a dude call me something as deplorable as that and I'm ready to have a case, you know what I'm saying? I'm ready to go to jail. But not you. You just stay at the car lot until Josie finds her the Mustang she wants, pay for it, and leave. Like you're some damn big shot, tossing money around like that. But, hey, it's your money. I'd let you do it too, if I was Josie. I, in fact, encourage her too. But that's between me and Josie. But tell me, brother, you gonna sue Mr. Lindsey or what?" Ben continued staring at Deuce without even thinking about responding to him. "Of course you won't sue. You can't sue if it's true, now can you? And he said he knew for a fact you sexually harassed those Florida women. Let's face it, Ben, all Josie really proved was that they had ulterior motives, but that didn't mean they were lying."

Ben exhaled. "Are you finished?" he asked him.

"I'm just getting started, partner."

Ben nodded. "Fine," he said. He stood up and began to head for the kitchen. But Deuce was out for blood. He was desperate, and tired of being upstaged by the likes of Braddock. As soon as Ben walked past him, he pounced.

"Her juice is sweet," he said.

Ben turned toward him, the frown on his face almost piercing. "What did you say?"

"You know what I'm talking about. Josie. She's got the sweetest juice I ever tasted, man."

The anger rose in Ben's heart so quickly that before he realized what he was doing he had grabbed Deuce by the catch of his collar, slung him up from the sofa, and punched him with a right so vicious that it stung Ben's hand. Deuce tried to fight back, swinging wildly, but Ben pushed him away from him as if he were a feather. Deuce fell against the sofa, but the momentum from Ben's violent push caused him to flip over it and crash-land on the floor. The sound of Deuce's crash landing was so loud that Josie came running out of the kitchen. When she saw Deuce on the floor, she stopped. Then she looked at Ben.

He exhaled. His anger, though now back under control, was still burning. He began walking toward her, his stomach churning like razor blades cutting against it.

"Get that bastard out of here now!" he ordered her, and then he walked away and up the stairs.

Deuce was still reeling from the punch. He couldn't believe a tight-ass bastard like Ben Braddock could handle him so decisively. He began to stand up, his face feeling like a sledge hammer had rammed it.

"Are you okay, Deuce?" Josie asked as she hurried to him and helped him to his feet. "What happened?"

Deuce was holding the side of his face with his hand. His anger now unhinged too. "What do you think happened? Mr. Perfect did this. Your angel of a boyfriend did this to me!" Then Deuce looked toward the stairs that Ben had already climbed. "I oughta go up those stairs and kick his ass!"

"That's enough, Deuce."

"Like hell it is. Who does that asshole think he is? He ain't gonna be handling me."

"What happened? Why would he hit you?"

"Why you think? Because he's crazy. I told you something was wrong with him!"

"Ben wouldn't just hit you like this, Deuce."

"Okay, he's still Mr. Perfect in your eyes. Believe in fairy tales, Josie, that's cool too."

"What did you say to him?"

"What did I what? What did *I* say to *him?* I can't believe you asked me that. Look at me, Josie. Look at my face! What words could make a civilized man do something like this?"

Josie didn't know what to think. She was already drained, already filled with too much relationship baggage as it was. Now this. She asked Deuce to leave. "Me? After what that asshole did you're gonna throw *me* out?"

"Just leave, Deuce, all right? It's tough enough."

Deuce looked at Josie, at the pain that pierced her entire body, and he nodded. "Okay, Josie, I'm out of here. He wins. That asshole wins again. But all I'm asking you to do, Josie, all I'm begging you to do, is to be smart. He ain't no saint. He ain't this great man you think he is. And the sooner you realize it the better off you'll be. We'll all be."

"Deuce, just, please just leave."

Deuce shook his head. She was so far gone in love with that jerk that it was pathetic to him. He knew he couldn't fight her feelings. Not now, when he himself felt humiliated. "Call me if you need me," he said to her, and she nodded. He looked one more time up those stairs, and it was taking every ounce of control he had not to lose all restraint and go up there and bring Braddock down. But Josie looked too pitiful already. He knew he wouldn't be hurting anybody but her in the end.

"I'll see you tomorrow," he said to her, and then he left.

Josie stood downstairs longer than she had intended, but she felt frozen in place. She knew Ben was upset by what Stuart Lindsey had to say, but he had no right to bring that attitude to her crib. That was how she felt. Angry now. He was fed up, she knew Ben was, but so was she. She stayed downstairs longer, to compose herself, then she headed upstairs.

Ben was lying on top of her bed, fully clothed, even his shiny Italian shoes still on his feet. One leg was propped up and one hand was hidden inside his suit coat as if he were posing for a gangster reel. But his face was devastated. It was that look on his face, of such horrific disappointment, that calmed Josie down.

"Come here, Josephine," he said, and she walked over to her bed. Then she lay on top of him. She rested her head on his chest as he massaged her back.

"What's going on, Ben?"

"I don't want you to have anything more to do with Deuce Jefferson."

Josie lifted her head and looked at him. "Why?"

"Because I said so."

"Not good enough. I work for Deuce. You're telling me to quit my job because you say so? No way."

Ben hesitated. "He's a liar."

"Okay," Josie said, sitting up on him, "let's get one thing straight. I don't want you decking guys because they're insinuating that they're hitting on me or whatever the hell it was. I can take care of myself. You understand me? I don't need to be under your or anybody else's protection. Got it?"

Ben looked at her. This was what he always wanted. A self-assured, independent Josephine. But now, in times like these, he didn't know if that was what he needed. "Got it," he said.

"Now tell me what's really bothering you."

Ben leaned his head back, staring up at the bedroom's ceiling. "I'm tired, Josie. I'm tired of problems and lies following me wherever I go. I thought Minnesota was going to be different. Our fresh start. But it's the same nonsense all over again."

"Who's Stuart Lindsey?"

"We were law partners together."

"He's lying?"

"Yes."

"Why?"

Ben hesitated. "I don't know."

"You do know, Ben. You have to know. Now what's the story?"

Ben exhaled.

"Josie."

"Josie nothing. I want to know what the hell's going on around here. I'm tired of this too. Now why would your former law partner tell all of these terrible lies on you?"

"I haven't seen or heard from Stu in over fifteen years, Josie. I have no idea what's going on with him now."

"But where would he get those allegations from? Something had to have gone on."

"It did. And he was right. When we were partners there was a lot of shady dealings. A lot of them. But he was the one committing the acts, not me. I dissolved our partnership as a result. And Stu never got it back together. Last I heard he was living somewhere in Miami and was on drugs."

"Damn. Your former law partner?"

"Yep."

"And you aren't going to tell anybody, are you?"

"Nope."

"But why, Ben? Your career is on the line."

"Stuart has always had difficulties in his life, Josie. I know you can't understand that, but it's true. I'm not adding to his troubles."

"He had no problem adding to ours."

"I don't live my life that way."

"What way?" Josie said.

"An eye for an eye."

"But *Ben*."

"No 'but Ben.' I'm not discussing that now, Josie. I can't."

Josie looked at him. He couldn't, he was right. She leaned down and allowed him to wrap her in his arms. He squeezed his eyes shut as he held her. The devastation of his good name raked over the coals again was too much for him to face. And the pain came not from a stranger, not from some enemy he should have suspected all along, but it came from Stu, a man he helped at every turn, a man he had once counted as among his closest friends. Shoot him, stab him, beat him up beyond all recognition. *Anything physical,* he thought, *would be preferable to this.*

Meredith arrived late to the small café on Division Street. Deuce waved her toward the back, where he was sitting, and after they had ordered drinks and lunch, Meredith leaned back.

"Don't be so impatient," she said to him.

"Impatient? Didn't you hear me? Even after Ben knocked the living crap out of me she still got rid of me. Not him. Me! How can you tell me to be patient? No matter what happens to Ben Braddock, nothing seems to be able to shake Josie's faith in him."

"You don't know what went on after you left."

"This morning at work she looked fine to me. So whatever went on was fine by her. And guess what? It don't include me. So much for your plan!"

"What did I tell you, Deuce? Ben Braddock is a mountain that has got to be chipped away. It will not topple all at once. But it'll fall, believe me."

"You are so sure of every damn thing when nothing's happening."

"Seeds of doubt are being planted, I told you that. But I agree, we will need to kick things into a higher gear. I will, as early as tonight, in fact."

"What's tonight?"

Meredith smiled. For every plan she had ten backup plans. "An opportunity for both of us," she said. Deuce, wary of Meredith but knowing that she was all he had, didn't even ask her to explain.

Ben was hanging up from a conference call with Akron just as Meredith was coming into his office. She was beautifully dressed, he thought, in that same yellow suit she had worn the first time he'd laid eyes on her, but she was visibly upset.

"Mal?" he asked as she walked in. She hurriedly sat on his office sofa.

"It's not right."

"What's not right? What's the matter?"

"Is it me, Ben?" she asked, and looked up at him. Tears were in her eyes.

Ben stood up and walked to her, his heart pounding with sympathy. He sat down beside her. "What are you talking about? Now settle down and tell me what's happened."

Meredith started rolling around a tissue that was in her hands. "You're going to think it's too silly."

"What, Mal?"

She looked at Ben. "It's Maurice."

Ben frowned. "Who's Maurice?"

"The guy I've been dating. Remember?"

"Oh, yeah. The guy you had the hot date with."

"Right."

"What about him?"

She cried harder and placed the tissue to her nose. "He's married," she said.

"Married?"

"Yes."

Ben exhaled. "I see. That's a damn shame, Mal."

"Is it me? I have such awful luck with men. It has to be me. But why, Ben? Do I give off certain clues?"

Ben smiled and pulled Meredith into his big, muscular arms. "Of course not," he said. "You're a wonderful woman, Mal."

Meredith cried in his arms. Then she looked up at him. "Is there another you out there somewhere? For the love of cloning, is there?"

Ben laughed. Meredith smiled. "You'll be okay, kid," he said.

"Promise?"

"Promise."

She leaned back on the sofa and crossed her legs. "I need help."

"You're okay."

"I'm serious, Benjamin. I need some cheering up because lately it's been tough." Then she looked at Ben. "Take me to Paris."

Ben smiled. "You don't think small, do you?" he said.

"I'm all I have."

"And you keep treating yourself too."

"Can you cheer me up?"

"Not in Paris, I can't."

"Okay," she said, standing up. "I guess I'll just go home and try not to think about him."

Ben stood up too. "That's a good idea."

"What about dinner tomorrow? Can you at least take me to dinner tomorrow?"

"No, I'm going to be in New York tomorrow. Remember?"

"New York?"

"Yes, Mal."

"Oh, yes! That's right. The big conference. Well, at least one of us
will have a little excitement." Ben didn't respond.

"You don't need an executive assistant with you, do you?" She
stared at him. Her preference was that he ask her, but she couldn't
risk it any longer. Even on her request he seemed reluctant. "I won't
get in your way, Ben," she added.

Ben smiled. It wasn't a question of her, but Josie was on his mind.
"I know you won't," he finally said. "And certainly you can come
too. Maybe we can check out some jazz together."

"The legendary Arthur Chambers perhaps."

"What do you know about Artie Chambers?" Ben asked.

"He's a first cousin of my ex-husband. And he still knows how to
blow that horn."

"All right. That would be great, Mal. I'll love to have you with
me."

Meredith smiled. She wanted to hug him, to keep the memory of
her on him, but she decided not to push her slowly evolving good
luck.

Josie was at Ben's home lying in his bed. She heard his car drive up
and she looked at the clock on the night stand. It was after one-thirty
in the morning. She shook her head. She knew he had a business trip
in the morning, a trip that would take him away from her for two
more days, and she wanted to give him a proper send-off. She had
been excited about it too, all through the night. But one-thirty was
far too late to be just getting home from work. She may have been
excited earlier, but now she was mad. By the time he had entered his
home and walked up the stairs to his bedroom, her fire was still
smoldering.

But he didn't know it, and smiled when he saw her lying there. He
had seen her car out front, a brand-new light green Mustang, and he
was pleasantly surprised. He was horny as hell, and she'd been on his
mind all day. Seeing her lying there, between his sheets, warmed him.

He walked over to her and bent down to kiss her forehead, but she turned over quickly. She was upset. And he knew, without asking, why.

"Josie."

"Good night, Ben," she said.

He exhaled. He could have sat on the edge of that bed and explained to her exactly why he ran so late tonight, but he didn't do it. She wouldn't believe him anyway. Her tolerance of his behavior had dwindled over the past month. She, as Meredith had recently told him, didn't take shit from him anymore. He still could have argued with her; he still could have pled his case. But he didn't. He decided to just let it be. He left her, showered quickly, and went to sleep in the guest room across the hall.

CHAPTER 21

She saw him coming but she did not move. She stared at him as he entered the old building and walked swiftly toward her desk. He had on his Oxford suit and tie, both a smoky gray, and he moved as if he was upbeat for a change. She had left his home before dawn this morning, while he was still asleep in the guest room, and just the fact that he would even sleep in the guest room had annoyed her. That was on top of her already being annoyed that he was still up to his old tricks, even after all of the crap they had to deal with, still coming home so late that he might as well not have come home at all. *I mean, really,* she thought.

"Good morning," he said as he arrived at her desk.

"Good morning," she said, her arms folded, her eyes staring at him.

"What time did you leave the house? I was asleep."

"I didn't pay attention to the time."

"But early?"

"Yes."

"Why didn't you wake me, sweety? You know I'm going to New York today."

"I didn't see you to wake you."

Ben hesitated. "I slept in the guest room," he said.

"How was I to know that?"

Ben could tell she had a decided curtness in her tone and manner.

But he remained upbeat. "Is there an office we can go into?" he said with a smile. "I want to kiss you good-bye."

"No offices are available that I know of," Josie said.

"Then walk me to my car."

"Can't. I've got too much work to do."

Ben stared at Josie. She was still upset with him, still angry because he had come home late or hadn't made apologies when he did come home, or that he had slept in the guest room, or all of the above. He was never quite sure what it was with Josie. He wasn't about to try and figure it out now. "Okay," he finally said, disappointed as hell. "I've got a plane to catch anyway, so I suppose I'll have to see you when I get back."

Josie didn't say anything, which disappointed him more. He stood there longer. He hated to leave town this way, but there was no reasoning with Josie when that attitude of hers was working. It was as if she was in the zone. Yet he looked at her once again to see if there was any way possible of breaking through that zone, that protective shell that now surrounded her like body armor, but there was none. And it hurt. He hated to leave this way, but he left.

Josie watched him leave, watched him slowly walk away from her without turning around, his once swift stride now a lumbering gait. As soon as he cleared the building's exit, as soon as his gray suit coat flapped by and out of sight, she walked up to the window and looked out. He walked across the street to his parked Mercedes and stood beside it, smoking a cigarette. He stared back at the building, as if he was trying to get up the nerve to go back in, but he didn't turn. He took a last puff, tossed his cigarette, and then got into his car and quickly drove away.

When Josie looked away from the window, from Ben, she saw Deuce. He stood at the threshold of his office door, his chiseled body leaning against it, his face both concerned and anxious as he stared unblinkingly at her.

Deuce watched Josie all day, from the time she returned from a story downtown to the time she was preparing to leave for the day. Earlier he had tried to woo her, asking her three different times to have dinner with him. She declined all three times, wanting nothing to do with anybody right now. But Deuce knew his window of opportunity was narrow. He couldn't shirk from drastic measures if they became necessary. That was Meredith's advice. Always have a backup plan, she'd warned him. And he did.

Josie, for her part, ignored Deuce's stares. She kept herself busy all day just to keep all the background noise off her mind, and it was working like a charm. Until her desk phone rang. When she picked up and there was a pause, she knew immediately who it was.

"What do you want?"

"And hello to you too."

"What do you want?" Josie said.

"Guess who's in New York with your man?"

Josie hesitated. "What?"

"You heard me," said that woman's voice. Josie didn't respond. *More drama,* she thought. Yet another scene from yet another drama she was being forced, once again, to participate in.

"You hear me, Josie? Ben is in New York, silly-ass. He's two-timing both of us now, the bastard. But I know the brother so I'm not exactly surprised. But I'll bet you are."

"I don't know what you're talking about."

"Ben is in New York, that's what I'm talking about. Don't you get it? He's in New York, but he's not alone. Chick called Meredith is with him. Meredith Chambers. She's one of his so-called executive assistants. I hear they've been a hot item for months now. Ben denies he even knows a Meredith of course. Like I'm that dumb. Like I don't check shit out. But that's Ben. That's the kind of man we're dealing with. But don't take my word for it. I'm just trying to help a sista out, but you don't have to take my word for it. Call his office. They'll tell you who went to that conference with him. Give his office a call."

She said this and hung up the phone. Josie paused before hanging up too. Her heart was pounding and her thoughts were running wild. Meredith was with Ben in New York? When he knew she wouldn't approve?

She immediately reached for the phone again to call Denlex, to find out for herself if it could possibly be true, but she decided against picking it up. She couldn't. What difference would knowing make? He was a full-grown man. If he wanted to be with another female, he was going to be with another female. Josie knew she couldn't make him act right. She couldn't make him be faithful to her. If he cared about her feelings at all he wouldn't have that witch Meredith Chambers within ten feet of him, anyway.

Josie also believed that she was beginning to learn Ben's ways, and she didn't like what she was learning. He was a player. Ladies Love Cool Ben, just like Deuce had said. And Cool Ben loved the ladies. Calling and getting all upset and crying her eyes out wasn't going to help a damn thing, especially not her. It was a painful realization, but she knew she couldn't keep going down like this. She couldn't keep allowing Ben, over and over, to treat her this way. But she could stop worrying about it. That was what she *could* do, and that was what she did when, instead of picking up that telephone and calling Denlex for some kind of sick confirmation, she turned back to her computer and got back to work.

The work of the conference had been exhausting but Ben still took the time to show Meredith the town. Although they journeyed to Greenwich Village in search of jazzman Arthur Chambers—and didn't find him, since he never would headline a club—they still didn't give up on the evening. They hung around, enjoying good jazz in a small club on Bleecker Street, where the conversations were muted because the real reason for the season was the music. And they listened to every note, listened like the jazz enthusiasts they claimed to be. Then they danced.

Ben and Meredith danced in the middle of the room. He in his Oxford suit and Vito Artioli Italian shoes, and she in her backless, Armani evening dress. They danced as if they were in love on the dance floor. The music was *It Just Happens That Way* by Mindi Abair, and it was played impressively, Ben thought, by the club's headliner band. Meredith knew how to move and so did Ben. When he dipped her, he smiled because she knew how to do it. She knew how to allow her hair to flow back and her neck to tilt just at an angle from his chest. When he lifted her back up, back into his arms, they were practically lip to lip. Ben stared at her lips, and then in her eyes. He stared at this goddess of a good-looking woman, and he could have kissed her. He could have pressed his lips into hers, and he knew she would have allowed it. But he didn't. He pulled her closer to him instead. Her back was bare, and the feel of that bare back made him grind against her on the dance floor.

She was pleased with his touch and the rhythm of his movements, because she knew she had done it. She had created a magical moment. He now desired her, and that was the perfect result. She had him, she felt for the first time, right where she needed him to be.

Josie was at home watching *My Big Fat Greek Wedding* on DVD when her doorbell rang. It was Deuce. At first she hesitated, because she had told him at work that she didn't want to be bothered. Then she opened the door.

"I couldn't help myself, Josie," he said with a smile. She looked at him, in his jeans and Sean John jersey, looking like the con artist she took him for. Although she wasn't feeling it tonight and couldn't smile, she did let him in.

"What are you watching?" he asked as Josie settled back on the sofa, her small feet tucked under her butt, her shorts and tank top making Deuce almost impatient with need.

"A movie," Josie said.

Deuce smiled. "I know it's a movie, J. What movie?"

"My Big Fat Greek Wedding."

"Your what?"

Josie almost smiled. *"My Big Fat Greek Wedding.* It's a comedy."

"A Greek comedy. Seems like a Greek tragedy the way you look."

Josie looked at Deuce. "What in the world are you talking about?"

"You, Josie. Look at you. You're nearly in tears watching a comedy. That should tell you something. Either that's a bad-ass movie, or something's wrong with you."

Josie exhaled. "Just sit down."

"No," Deuce said. "I don't wanna sit down. You might rub off on me. Misery loves company, you know."

"First of all," Josie said, getting an attitude, "I didn't ask your ass to come over here. I didn't ask for any company, okay? And second of all, you can always leave. Then I'll be certain not to rub off on you."

Deuce stared at Josie. Josie refused to look his way, but when his stare wouldn't quit, she did.

"What?" she asked angrily. He smiled.

"You're cute when you're mad."

Josie stared at Deuce, and then she exhaled. "Okay, you win. I apologize. All right? I'm just a little down in the dumps right now."

"And why are you?"

"Can you sit down for two minutes?" she said.

"I'd rather stand."

Josie smiled. "Ben's not here. He won't deck you. You don't have to be afraid."

Deuce smiled too. "You're wrong for that, J."

"I'm sorry. I couldn't resist."

"Answer my question. Why are you down in the dumps?" Deuce asked.

Josie's smile dissipated as she thought about the never-ending drama of her life. "I just am," she said.

"It's Ben, isn't it? He's the reason, isn't he?" Josie wouldn't respond. "You know what? This is crazy. I mean, look at you, J. You're the most beautiful, sweetest, kindest woman in the world to me. To every man. You don't have any business being down in no dumps, and alone on an electric night like this. I'd bet that bastard Braddock isn't alone, or down in the dumps."

Josie looked at Deuce. Everybody seemed to understand Ben. Everybody seemed to have such strong opinions about him. She wish she could be certain like that.

"I'm here for you, Josie. I'm your friend. I want you to feel that you can talk to me."

"What made Ben hit you the other night?"

"What?"

"Why did Ben hit you?"

Deuce hesitated. He knew what she was doing. He knew that she was grasping for straws, trying to find Ben's nobility again, trying to find a reason to love Ben again. "What did he tell you?" Deuce asked.

"Nothing, as usual."

"I told him that I thought Stuart Lindsey was telling the truth, and that your boy Ben is most definitely a shady businessman and probably a racist to boot, just like Lindsey said, and he became angry, not to mention violent, and, as you put it, decked me."

"Because of that?"

"Yes." Deuce said.

"You didn't mention me?"

"You? Why would I mention you?"

"Did you?"

"No, Josie. He just didn't like the fact that I agreed with Lindsey, that's all that was about." Josie nodded. And fought back the tears. "What's the matter?" he asked.

"Nothing."

"Josie."

"I said nothing, Deuce, all right?"

Deuce knew when to back off. He knew it well now. So he smiled. "Guess what?"

Josie looked at him. "What?"

Deuce pulled a small stack of CDs from his pocket. "I brought music."

"What?" she asked.

Deuce walked over to Josie's DVD. "Do you mind?" he asked.

Josie gave up. "Whatever, Deuce, okay?"

Deuce hated that she had such little enthusiasm, but he was determined to change that. He put on Mr. C's "Cha-Cha Slide" and then stood in the middle of the room and started smiling.

"Come on, Josie," he urged her, "let's turn this mother out!"

"You turn it out."

"Come on, Josie!"

"No, Deuce. I told you I wasn't feeling it. I'm not feeling it."

"You don't have to feel it. All you gots to do is dance."

"No, thanks. You dance."

"So it's like that?"

"Exactly," she said.

Deuce smiled and decided to do just that. He followed the instructions of the song and moved around the room hoping that he had the moves, but knowing that he didn't. Josie tried not to laugh, watching him, but when he whipped around so fast that his feet became entangled, causing him to fall to the floor, she laughed. She nearly fell over laughing.

"You need help, boy!" she yelled between laughs.

"Help me then," Deuce urged as he stood up from the floor. Josie shook her head. She wasn't up for this, she thought. But he was so cute standing there, a black man with no rhythm at all, and she felt she had to do it. She had to come to his rescue.

And they danced. Josie led the way, a teacher if ever there was one, although Deuce could hardly keep up.

"There ya go," she kept saying. "There ya go. Now you got it.

Now you got it. That's how it's done. Don't think about it, just move. Just move, Deuce. There ya go." Josie, before she knew it, was actually enjoying herself.

They danced and danced, through the new "Cha-Cha Slide" and the old "Electric Slide" and Ja Rule and Ludacris and, yes, even L. L. Cool J. And Josie didn't mind at all. She just danced. She lost herself in herself, and had a ball dancing and laughing as Deuce tried and tried but never quite got the rhythm.

Finally, when they were both already too tired, Deuce stumbled. Josie laughed. But he stumbled into her, causing her and him to tumble to the floor. Josie landed first and Deuce conveniently landed on top of her. She was still laughing, not just at the fall, but at the fact that Deuce had landed, of all places, right on top of her. She couldn't even imagine another man besides Ben on top of her. Now Deuce was right there. Looking good, smelling good, making her laugh. But when he stared at her, and his look was no longer playful and gay, but serious, she turned serious too. The feelings she began to feel, as Deuce lay there, forced her to realize the position he had really put her in.

"We'd better get up," she said weakly, but Deuce shook his head.

"Why, Josie? I'm free. And whether you know it or not, so are you. Don't you understand that? You don't owe Braddock a damn thing, not even respect. Because Josie, you may not want to admit this, but the man doesn't respect you. He does everything to push your buttons, haven't you figured that out yet? You're not his woman, you're his convenience. You're there when he needs you, but when somebody else is available, he forgets you. You. The best of the best, still not good enough for him. Well, forget him, Josie. Who the hell is he? Stop believing lies, J., that's not what you're about. That's not the Josie I love. That's the good little doll of a nervous-ass woman he wants you to be. But that ain't you. Stop being what you're not."

Tears began to roll from Josie's eyes as Deuce talked. She felt so empty and so alone and so used up that she didn't know what to believe. She looked at Deuce. He smiled.

"I love you, Josephine. You know I do. And I want to be your prince. I want to wait on you hand and foot. I want to look at you day and night, just stare at your beautiful eyes and your little button nose and your luscious, oh they are so luscious, lips. And I promise you this. I won't break your heart. I won't play you like love is some game and your heart doesn't matter. You know I won't. Me and you are the same kind of people, J. We're passionate and we believe in truth. And believe this, if you don't believe anything else I've said. You're good enough, Josie. Don't ever think that you aren't. You're more than enough woman for me."

Josie smiled through her tears and Deuce wiped her tears away. Then he stood up and helped her to her feet. They began dancing together in a slow drag, dancing to music that was not playing.

They arrived back at the Omni late, and Ben unlocked the door of Meredith's hotel room. He handed her the keycard, and she smiled and invited him in for a nightcap. He balked.

"If you don't come in," she warned, "all of your efforts at cheering me up will have failed miserably."

Ben smiled. "Oh, yeah?"

"Yes."

"You're a tough broad, Mal."

"Absolutely," she said.

Ben hesitated again, but then he entered her hotel room. While he walked around, taking a peek at the furniture and then the view, she hurried for the wet bar. By the time she returned to him with a glass of wine, he was sitting down on the sofa.

"Here you are," she said, and he stood to receive the drink. Just as he had stood up, Meredith leaned toward him and the glass bumped against her and spilled just slightly onto her expensive evening dress.

"Oh, no!" she said. "I am such a klutz."

"I'm sorry about that, Mal," Ben said.

"No, it's me."

"I probably should not have stood so quickly."

"Don't be ridiculous. It's me. I'm always having these crazy accidents. But here," Meredith said, handing Ben the remaining glass of wine, "you hold this before I do more damage. And will you please excuse me for just a moment?"

"Of course."

"You won't go anywhere?"

Ben smiled. "No, Mal," he said. "I'll be here."

Meredith smiled and moved slowly, as if in total control, toward the bedroom. When she arrived in the bedroom, she changed quickly, taking everything off and putting nothing on but a red, silk blouse that just barely covered her. She looked at herself in the mirror, put on her best got-it-together smile, and hurried back into the living area.

When she returned and walked over to the sofa where Ben sat flipping through a magazine, he stood up, and then looked down at the blouse that barely covered her, at her sizable, attractive thighs that were nearly completely uncovered.

"I hope you aren't offended but I didn't bring many clothes," she said as she sat down.

"We need to get that dress dry-cleaned," Ben replied, sitting down too, "if you expect to get that wine stain out."

"It'll be all right. I wasn't all that excited about that dress, anyway."

Ben smiled. "So you just toss it aside? An Armani?"

"That's right. I've had more than my share of good times in that dress, thank you. Like tonight." Ben looked at her. "It was wonderful, Ben. Thank you so much for taking me out. It did me a world of good." Ben nodded. Meredith crossed her legs, almost revealing way too much.

"I'm sorry we didn't get to see Arthur Chambers. That would have topped it all."

"I talked with the manager of the club," Ben said. "He said Art Chambers has become even more of a recluse. He doesn't know if he's even performing anymore."

"Now that's a shame, because I say older is better," Meredith said. Ben smiled. Meredith sighed, as if her depression was returning, and leaned her head back against the sofa. "I think of you as my best friend, Ben. As the only person in this world who seems to give a damn about me." Ben didn't know what to say. Meredith suddenly covered her face and began sobbing.

"Mal, what's wrong?" Ben asked, tossing the magazine on the table beside him.

"I'm sorry."

"What's wrong?"

"I just can't help it. I try, but it's so hard."

"Come here," Ben said. Meredith decided not just to move closer to Ben but to slide up onto his lap. Ben allowed it because of her state, and began to hold her. She looked up into his eyes.

"It just gets so lonely sometimes. I feel so lonely. So alone."

"You're not alone, honey. You have me and you have everybody at Denlex completely in your corner. Don't you forget that."

Meredith smiled through her tears. "I know you're with me," she said. "You're the only human being who's never hurt me. Can you believe that? You're it. And you'll never hurt me, will you, Ben?"

Ben hesitated. "No," he said.

"Kiss me, please." There was a pause, and she could tell he was torn. "I don't want anything from you, Ben, I promise you I don't. I just need to feel your lips against mine. I just need to know what it feels like to be kissed by somebody who cares about me."

Ben's compassion for Meredith overwhelmed him. Her life seemed so tragic, so void of what it means to be truly alive, and he knew he couldn't say no to her. He cared for her too much, just as she had said.

He pulled her body closer to him, hesitated again, but then he kissed her. She closed her eyes and leaned into the kiss. And she worked it. She worked it with her tongue and with her experience. She unbuttoned her blouse and removed it as she worked. He wanted to resist her, but it had been too long. And she was working it too hard. She even repositioned her body to face him, and saddled him, without breaking a stride. When he realized she was naked before him, he could not resist. His compassion had turned into passion and he started working it too. He kissed her chest and her breasts. Just as he was about to suck, just as he was about to cross the point of no return, he blurted it out. *"Oh, Josephine!"* he moaned, as he kissed Meredith. As soon as Josie's name slipped from his lips, his eyes opened and he stopped.

"Good Lord," he said.

"Ben, it's okay," Meredith said desperately, her entire body begging him to continue, her entire life-plan hinging on him to continue. But he couldn't. He had gone too far already. He leaned his head back.

"Good Lord," he said again, as if he could not believe it himself.

"Ben, please," she pleaded. "It's all right."

"It's not all right, Mal. Don't say it's all right."

"I told you I don't want any strings. I just want one night. That's all. Just one night, Ben. Please."

"No."

"Honey, it'll be good for us, for both of us. We're friends. We're close friends. We'll still be friends when it's over. I'm just so lonely. And I have no one. You're all I have, Ben. I just want to spend a night with you. With my friend. Just one night."

"I can't," Ben said, moving her from his lap. "Don't you understand that? I can't."

Meredith knew she couldn't let their friendship suffer too, a friendship that she knew was her only chance of ever getting through. So she gave up, for now. "Okay," she said.

Ben stood up. "I'll see you in the morning," he said as he walked slowly to the door.

"I'm sorry, Ben," Meredith said.

Ben turned and looked at her. She was putting her silk blouse back on and looking pitiful to him.

"Don't apologize, Mal," he said. "You did nothing wrong. You understand? It was me. I'm the one who apologizes. I'm the one who went too far."

"We're still friends?"

"Of course we are. Don't worry about that."

"Good night," she said, as if her pain was still too painful, and Ben understood.

He left her hotel room and walked swiftly to his. When he entered he began pacing, moving like a wounded animal from one side of the room to the other, his entire soul racked with an almost unbearable sense of guilt and burden. Everybody wanted him to be what they wanted him to be. Everybody needed him. Everybody wanted a part of him. And he gave. He gave part at a time, until nothing was left. Until what he wanted—what he needed—was blurred by their wants and needs.

And Josie. He stopped pacing when he thought about Josephine, his unlikely love. His sweet, caring, painfully impossible lady. She was one of many females in his life. One of many friends, associates, ex-girlfriends unable to let go. All of them thinking they'd discovered the prized man when they met him. But Josie was his woman. She was the one that wrenched at his heart. She was the one that drained him most of all.

He kept pacing. He didn't phone her. He couldn't bear to hear her continued demands for more of his time, more of his love, more of him. But he needed to hear her voice. He needed to hear her soft, caring voice. But he didn't phone her. He just walked.

* * *

The song now playing was old school: "If I Were Your Woman" by Gladys Knight, and Josie was glued against Deuce as they danced. She was in the valley, she felt, the valley of decision, but it was a calming place to be. Deuce had calmed her. He had made her laugh and he had calmed her down.

When the music stopped, and Deuce turned off the DVD player, that calming feeling began to disappear. Panic set in. He took her by the hand, his eyes staring deeply into her eyes, and walked her slowly toward the stairs. She moved not by her will, but by his. He wanted her so badly that *she* could feel it. And the feeling intoxicated her, as if it were not her, as if she didn't know what she wanted anymore and had allowed his want to become her need.

They walked to the stairs, about to take one step at a time, going up, going to a new place in Josie's life, to a new beginning she began to dread. Just when the fear was too heightened to bear, just when she held Deuce's hand tighter to support her weakening body, the phone rang. She nearly jumped out of her skin. Deuce was stunned by her reaction and grabbed hold of her, and she could not even mouth the words that she was okay.

She walked over to the phone just beyond the staircase. "Hello," she said like a whisper. There was a pause. And then the voice. The voice that still melted her heart. She sat down.

"Ben?" she asked.

"How are you?"

She couldn't speak. The tears welled up once again. She looked at Deuce. He sat down on the stair.

"Josie?" Ben said.

"Yes, I'm here."

"I didn't mean to phone you so late. I didn't plan to call you at all. But . . . But I miss you." Josie didn't know what to say. She wiped her tear, but others came. "I think we need to get some time away, honey," he said. "I've been thinking about that. We haven't really had enough time together. When I get back tomorrow evening I want you to be at the house, so we can plan a vacation. Just you and me. A couple of weeks at least."

Josie's heart should have soared. It was what she'd always wanted, time away with Ben. But her heart wasn't right. It was too deep in the depths of doubt and despair and confusion to soar at all. She couldn't even speak.

"Did you hear me, Josie?"

She exhaled. "Yes."

"And?"

"And what?"

"Josie, don't do this to me. I need you to hang in there, honey. I need you to understand."

"I understand."

"Will you be at the house tomorrow when I get back in town?"

She paused. "I'll see."

"Josie?"

"Yes?"

"Please," he said.

Josie almost looked at the phone. It didn't sound like Ben. Something had happened. "How's Meredith?" she asked.

There was a pause. A long, agonizing pause.

"She's there in New York with you. Isn't she?"

Another pause, and then he spoke. "Yes," he said.

"And I know, nothing's going on, right? She's your assistant and you needed her to be there with you. And you didn't bother to mention it to me because it's not my business, anyway. Is that the drill? Is that the line? I know it by heart now."

Yet another pause. Yet another slap in Josie's face. "I'll see you tomorrow, Josephine," Ben said, and then he hung up the telephone.

Josie looked at Deuce, who was staring at her, and then she hung up too.

The silence that suddenly engulfed the room was intense. They sat there, staring at each other, and then at the room itself. They were this close, this close to paradise. And Deuce was devastated.

"Good night, Deuce," Josie finally said, and Deuce wasn't surprised at all. *Braddock wins again,* he thought, as he stood to his feet.

"Good night," he replied. He was reluctant, disappointed, and heartbroken. But he left.

They had lunch the next day. *Josie's way of making amends,* Deuce decided, and to him she appeared almost unnaturally excited. After the emotions of last night, he couldn't understand why. She sipped from a club soda and smiled.

"Ben's coming back today," she said.

"Oh, yeah? The same Ben who's in New York with Meredith Chambers?"

Josie's fragile joy almost showed signs of bottoming out, but she held on. Not thinking about those little annoying details of her relationship helped.

"Yes," she said.

Deuce shook his head. "It doesn't take much to get you up, I see."

"What*ever,* Deuce. I just reached some conclusions last night."

"Conclusions? Such as?"

"Ben is worth it. He's worth holding on to. And I'm just trying to hold onto my man, that's all I'm trying to do. And, yeah, we've got some problems, damn right we do, just like all couples. But we'll work them out. If that makes me seem like a chump in your eyes . . ."

"It makes you a long-suffering woman in my eyes, Josie. It's L. L. Cool Ben I'm talking about."

"He's all right."

"Josie, he has Meredith Chambers in New York with him. Meredith Chambers! She ain't no Girl Scout, even you told me that. And she's gorgeous too?"

Josie hesitated, then looked at Deuce. "She's good-looking to you?"

He'd hit a chord. "Good looking? Josie, that lady's hot. She turned me on and she was all the way across the restaurant. You remember how seductive she was acting with Ben that day in that restaurant. Come on, that woman doesn't go to the Big Apple with an unmarried man and no fireworks pop off. Don't even try to tell me that."

"It takes two, Deuce. That's the conclusion I've reached. And Ben's not having it."

"You say."

"Damn right, I say. I know Ben. You think you do, but I know I do. And that's why I'm gonna be right at his house waiting for him when he comes home, and I'm gonna tell him how much I love him and I miss him and to hell with all this shit. You hear what I'm saying? I've decided I'm gonna trust Ben and to hell with the rest of it. And you're right. Ladies do love Cool Ben. You're absolutely right. But that don't mean Ben loves them."

She was over the cliff, Deuce thought. She was rationalizing, then compromising, then settling for what she could get. A woman like her, settling; he'd seen it all. "I'm happy for you, J., I am," Deuce said. "Don't mind me. I'm just jealous."

Josie smiled. "The truth at last."

"Don't rub it in."

"I won't. But I'm glad you admitted it. And, by the way, what did you tell Ben that forced him to knock you out the other night? And don't tell me that lie about Stuart Lindsey."

Deuce shook his head and smiled. "You are a cruel woman."

"Tell me."

"I told him your juice was sweet."

Josie smiled. "That's all?"

"I'm not talking about fruit juice, Josie."

"Duh? I know that. But that's all you told him?"

"Yeah."

"And he decked you just for that?"

"Yes."

Josie laughed. "See there! I told you he loved me!" She began to stand up. "I've got a ton of stuff to do so I'm gonna take the afternoon off."

"Are you requesting to take the afternoon off or are you demanding to take it off?"

Josie stood at the table and smiled. "I'm asking you if I may take this afternoon off."

Deuce smiled. "What's in it for me?" he asked.

"Deuce!"

"Okay, damn. Yes. You can take it off. But I expect to see you bright and early tomorrow morning."

"Deal. Thanks, Deuce. And see ya."

She left. Deuce leaned back. He couldn't believe how bad his luck was turning. It was hopeless and he knew it. But he looked at Josie as she walked away, at the joy she felt over her man coming back home, and that was why he had to have her. He wanted somebody to feel that way about him, but not just anybody. Josie, she was the one. He knew in his soul that she was the one for him. And just as she felt Ben was worth the fight, he felt that Josie was worth it too.

He pulled out his cell phone and dialed. Then he waited. "Rain," he finally said into the phone. "It's me. Yeah. It went terrible, how do you think? But, listen, it ain't over yet. I need you to do one more favor for me. Just one more, Rain. No, no phone calls. This is different. But you've got to do it now."

Josie went to the mall to find just the right see-through gown with some ridiculous animal on the front, which always seemed to make Ben smile. Then she went grocery shopping. By the time she made it to Ben's house she was exhausted, but she wanted to do it right for a change. She wanted to cook for him and serve him up an evening he wouldn't soon forget. That was what she wanted to do. When she walked up to his front door and saw the small envelope that rested against it, everything changed.

To Ben, from Dawn, the envelope said, which guaranteed that Josie would open it. Not right away, however. She unloaded her groceries and her negligee, put them inside the house, sat down on his sofa, and then opened the envelope. Nude photos of a beautiful, exotic-looking, dark-skinned female were inside, and a note: *Hope you like them, Benny. They're just like the last ones. Call me later and we can do it again! Love, Dawn.* Josie looked at the photos again, and at the note again, and then she shoved both back into the envelope.

Ben pulled into his driveway later that evening and was relieved to see Josie's Mustang at his house. Their relationship needed some serious work, he knew better than anyone. *But not tonight,* he thought. He needed her tonight. Not talk. Not plans. Her.

He walked slowly across his sidewalk, his movement not what you'd expect from a man as needy as he. But that was why he moved slowly, to keep some control, to at least project an image of somebody who wasn't as hard-up as he truly was.

He walked up his steps, unlocked his door, and entered his home. The first thing he noticed were groceries sitting in bags in his foyer. The next thing he noticed was Josie. She was coming toward him, and not very lovingly either, with what he could only detect was a stack of photos in her hand.

"Who's Dawn?" she asked him.

Not again, he thought. "What?"

"Who's Dawn?"

"I don't know any Dawn."

"Like hell you don't."

"Don't you talk to me that way, Josie."

"Does this refresh your memory?" She held up one of the nude photos. "Do these refresh your got damn memory?" She threw all of the photos violently at Ben. He tried to catch them, but the force of the throw caused all of them to tumble down. Josie's anger was palpable as she walked past him, staring at him, and then she left his home.

Later that same evening, Josie was at her own home clearing out her kitchen cabinets. She was on her knees on top of her drainboard when her phone began ringing. She kept reaching for dishes on the top shelves and placing them on the drainboard, the feelings inside of her causing her not to think, but just to go through the motions. Her answering machine clicked on. But when the beep sounded and a message was to be left, she stopped and listened. There was a long pause of silence, and then a click off. Josie paused too, but then she continued pulling down dishes from her cabinet.

Ben was sitting by the fireplace in his bedroom, wearing that colorful smoking jacket Josie had given him for his birthday, a glass of wine and a cigarette in his hand, as he placed his telephone back on the hook.

CHAPTER 22

Months came and went and the winter settled in. Josie didn't think it was possible, but life actually went on. Life without Ben wasn't happy, or even hopeful, but it wasn't a roller-coaster ride, either. She went to work; she went home. She didn't consider herself bitter, although Deuce and any other man interested in her would beg to differ, but she felt like her old self again. Happiness wasn't what she was about, independence was.

She had disengaged. That was how Deuce saw it. A kind of willful, deliberate, stop-the-world-I'm-getting-off disconnect. He tried to ignite her passion again, with jokes and small talk and shouts of crusades yet to be trumpeted, but Josie wasn't interested.

She continued to go to work every day, and then go home. But she wasn't having anything else. She felt used. Just when she was ready to fall deep into that blind trust that love required, just when she was ready to say to hell with facts, bring on the fiction, just when she was ready to settle for less, she was stunned. She was stunned by life itself, and how cruel it could be. She was stunned by love itself, and the brutality of the hurt.

Yet that hurt, that same brutal hurt, took on a form all its own one night in the dead of winter, when her doorbell rang.

It was nine at night and she was already in bed. She tried to watch television, but found herself flipping through channels as if she hated everything she saw. Her doorbell rang, and then she heard loud banging almost simultaneously. She got out of bed, put on her robe, and hurried downstairs. But she didn't get there fast enough. Her front door was rammed once, and then again, and then it broke loose and flew open. Policemen in SWAT-team riot gear came charging in. She immediately stood frozen on her stairs.

"Get down, now!" the officers yelled, and Josie quickly raised her hands and crouched down. They rushed her on the stairs, while other officers began searching through her home.

"What is this about?" she kept asking, but she received no response, just orders to be still and quiet or she would be sorry. And they handcuffed her.

"Are you Josephine Ross?" the lead officer asked as he stood her to her feet.

"Yes. What's happening?"

"We received numerous phone calls of drug activity at this address. We have a search warrant."

"Drug activity? *Here?*"

"We have a search warrant. It'll be better if you were to tell us everything you know."

"What are you talking about? There's no drugs in my home. Are you out of your mind?"

"Settle down, lady."

"Settle down my ass! This is a terrible mistake you're making!"

"We're following up on credible information, so I suggest you cooperate. If you're clean, fine. This will all be over rather quickly. But if you're not . . ."

"Sarge!" an officer yelled from Josie's patio outside. The sergeant, who was questioning Josie, immediately left her side and hurried outside. Another officer sat Josie on the stairs and insisted that she remain silent. And she sat, until the sergeant returned. Josie was then officially placed under arrest.

Ben grabbed his briefcase, turned off his office light, and was within ten feet of the elevator when Meredith came out of her office.

"Hey, boss," she said. "I didn't know you were still here."

"Had to reroute some backloads," Ben said as he moved up to the elevator and pressed the button.

"I thought I could get out of here by five for a change," Meredith said, walking up to the elevator behind him, "but I was wrong as usual."

"It's been a hectic week."

"It has. And you know what? I'm going to just treat myself to the biggest drink a bartender will be willing to make for me." Ben smiled. "Wanna join me?"

"I'd better pass, Mal. I'm going to try and get some work done at home."

"All work and no play makes Ben a dull boy."

"I understand that. But I've got too much to do."

"It's your life." The elevator door opened and they both stepped inside. "But I still wish you'd reconsider. It'll be fun."

Ben looked at Meredith as they rode down. She wore a green, leather coat and what they used to call go-go boots. When she turned toward him he could see a white cardigan sweater underneath, her large breasts in that sweater appearing larger than usual. He had come so close with her, he thought, remembering vividly that night in New York. His actions still embarrassed him every time he was around Meredith. That was why he declined her offer once again. Going anywhere with her, especially given the level of horniness he was feeling these days, would be dangerous.

"Benny, it's just a drink."

"I know," he said, "but I'd better pass."

Meredith shook her head. "I'm only asking you to go for a drink with me, Ben," she said, again, as the doors of the elevator opened on the ground floor. "But I understand. You've got a lot to do. Still, it's a standing invitation."

"I appreciate that," he replied, as he watched her work those hips as she slowly walked away.

At home he didn't bother to eat. He went upstairs instead and lay on his bed. His intentions were to rest for a few minutes, and then get to work. But his plan went awry as he fell asleep within minutes of closing his eyes. When the phone began ringing, he had been asleep for nearly an hour.

"Hello?" he said, still groggy.

"Ben?" said the voice on the other end. It was Josie. Ben hesitated. He hadn't heard from her in months, not since the night he'd returned from New York. "Ben?"

"I'm here, Josie. What is it?" The sound of sniffling could be heard through the phone. When he realized she was crying, he exhaled. *What now,* he thought. "What's wrong?" he asked her.

"They came to my house."

"Who came to your house?"

"The police. They came to my house and said I was under arrest."

Ben frowned. "Josephine, what are you talking about?"

"They arrested me."

Ben hesitated, as if he couldn't believe his ears. "They *what?*"

"I'm in jail, Ben."

Ben sat up on the side of his bed so quickly that he became dizzy. "Good Lord, Josie. What's happened?"

"They said I had heroin hidden on my patio. They said I had drugs at my home, that I was selling drugs, Ben."

Ben ran his hand through his hair. He knew the law. He knew the court system. He knew the seriousness of what she was telling him.

"I want you to listen to me, Josie."

"Can you get me out of here?"

"Yes, honey. Yes, I will. But I need you to listen to me."

"They said they received all these phone calls about me, about how I had all of this drug activity at my home and how people were in and out like I was some big-time drug dealer, Ben."

"Josie."

"But they're lying. That's not even true. Nobody be in and out of my house, I mean, nobody, and I've never done drugs in my life."

"Listen to me, Josie."

"I told them they're making a mistake. I told them . . ."

"Josephine?"

There was a pause as she seemed to understand how emotional she was becoming. "Yes?" she said.

"You are not to tell them anything else, you hear me? Not a word. You have no statements to make. You sign no documents. You agree to no interrogations. I don't care how innocent you are. Do you understand me?"

"But I didn't do what they're claiming I did. I didn't do anything wrong."

"They don't care about that, honey. They don't care. You just do what I said."

Josie paused, and then exhaled. "Okay," she said.

"I'm on my way. This will work out, honey, I promise you. You just . . ." Tears began to well up in Ben's eyes at just the thought of Josie in jail—in *jail*—caused him to want to fall to his knees. But he quickly composed himself, for her. "You just hang in there, Josie. You just keep your mouth shut and wait on me. All right?"

"Okay."

"Okay," Ben said.

There was a pause. "Ben?"

"Yes, sweety?"

"Hurry."

His heart dropped through his shoes. How much more did they have to take? "I will, honey," he said. "I will."

Ben was sitting on a bench at the station, his back against the wall, when Josie was finally released. He sat quietly in the same expensive suit he had been sleeping in, his body anxious and exhausted and almost too horrified to move. But he knew he had to be strong for Josie. She had never been arrested before in her life. Not for anything. Now she had a felony hanging over her head. The woman he had thought was all but out of his life for good, the woman who had tossed nude photos in his face, was back in his life in spades. Either they were destined to be together, or doomed to be together. Either way, Ben decided, as he looked up and saw her walking out of the electronic security door, they were going to be together.

He stood up. Josie wore a pair of jeans, a jersey, and a pair of tennis shoes, an outfit he knew she threw on when the cops allowed her only a minute or two to dress. Her braids were frazzled, some even coming loose, and her eyes were wide and appeared terrified. *They'd better know whose woman they're dealing with,* Ben thought angrily of the cops as he watched Josie come toward him. He inspected every inch of her body for bruises, cuts, visible marks of any kind of brutality.

When she arrived at his side she just stood there, her face refusing to look up at Ben's, her entire body seemingly cast down by the burden of her own weight. Then she just fell against him, her head leaning into him so hard that he almost stumbled back. He held her. He wanted to pick her up and carry her away from there. But he didn't. She was trying to be strong and he was going to let her. He walked her out instead.

He sat her down and buckled her into the passenger seat of his Mercedes, but by the time he had walked around to the driver's side and stepped in, she had unbuckled her seatbelt and slid across the seat to sit next to him. He usually didn't allow it, but he didn't say a word this time. He buckled them both into his one seatbelt, and she leaned against him. She wasn't crying about the ordeal she was enduring. She wasn't complaining about the injustice of it all. She was just clinging, clinging to Ben as if he were her security blanket. She was floating in a new ocean now, and she wasn't even trying to pretend to know its depths. She needed him. He knew it. And she knew it more.

He took her home, although he didn't think it was a good idea. But she wanted to go home. He pulled into the driveway of Josie's townhouse, and she got out of his car before him and hurried around to the side of her home. Ben quickly got out and followed her, looking around, unsure of what, exactly, was going on in this world of theirs.

Josie saw where the cops had been digging, the light of her patio illuminating the entire area. She had a few plants she was trying to grow against the side of her wall, and the flower bed had been upturned, the few plants thrown out, and that was where they supposedly found the goods—over thirty grams of heroin. Thirty grams? Heroin? Josie shook her head. Then she looked at Ben, who looked so worried to her that she felt a need to reassure him.

"I don't do drugs, Ben."

Ben nodded. "I know."

"And for them to think I would take thirty grams of heroin and bury it in my backyard, not even in my backyard but right on my patio, is ridiculous. I'm being set up. How can they not see this?"

Ben paused. Nothing was simple anymore, he thought. "Let's go inside," he said.

Josie stared at him, and then she looked at her plants lying helplessly above the earth. She could have planted them again, to give them a fighting chance, but she had no fight left in her. She went inside her home.

Ben ran her bath while also making phone calls. After she had bathed, dried off, and put on her negligee, he was still making phone calls. He was lying on her bed, still fully clothed, his eyes closed by exhaustion as he talked on the phone. Josie sat on the edge of the bed till he finally hung up.

"Well?" she asked. "They're going to drop the charges?"

Ben shook his head. "No."

"No? But I didn't do anything."

"I told you I know that, Josie."

"Then you need to call somebody."

"I called somebody."

"Then call somebody else."

"I called everybody, Josie. Everybody. I called everybody."

"But why can't they do anything?"

"Because it's drugs, Josie. Because heroin was found at your home, Josie."

She stared at Ben, as if the reality was just beginning to sink in. "What are you saying? I could go to prison? You're saying I could go to prison?"

"I'm saying we are going to have to let the process play itself out. We're going to have to get you an attorney."

"You're an attorney."

"I'll oversee your defense, but we'll need somebody on board."

"But why?"

"For the trial, Josie, you know why. For the preliminary hearing where we'll try to get these charges tossed."

Josie once again stared at Ben, and it was a steely, hard, frightful stare. "How long could I get?" she asked him.

"It depends on a lot of factors, Josie."

"How long? Give me the maximum."

"Hopefully at the preliminary hearing . . ."

"Ben, please. Give me the maximum."

Ben paused. "If the charges end up being possession with intent, that is, if a jury decides that you not only had a stash of heroin for your own purposes, but you had it with the intent to distribute, then . . . Then we're talking about ten to twenty years."

If Josie was a balloon, she would have deflated. Life itself seemed to seep out of her. Ben reached out to touch her, to comfort her, but she moved away and stood up. She then walked toward her bedroom door.

"Thank you for everything, Ben," she said. "But I'll see you to-morrow."

"Josie, don't do this."

"Good night, Ben."

Ben looked up at the ceiling. It was tough enough. Yet Josie was ready to shut him out once again, and make it tougher. He got off of her bed and walked to her. She stood there defiantly, her leg shaking, her arms folded, as if Ben's inability to correct this monumental wrong made everything that was happening to her his fault. When he moved to kiss her on her lips, to kiss the woman he hadn't kissed in months, she turned her face away. He couldn't be her hero, so he was her enemy now. It was *his* fault. *His* burden. Another nail in *his* coffin.

Meredith was startled when she opened the door of her apartment to leave for work and saw Deuce standing there. He had a newspaper in his hand and a look of chilling horror on his face.

"I can't talk right now, Deuce," she said as she tried to move forward, but he pushed her back into her apartment and slammed the door.

"Are you out of your fucking mind, Meredith?"

"Now you hold on here."

He threw the newspaper toward her. She caught it. "Did you see the headline? BENJAMIN BRADDOCK'S GIRLFRIEND ARRESTED ON DRUG TRAFFICKING CHARGES. Drug trafficking charges? And guess what drug it was?"

Meredith, reading the headline herself, smiled. "Heroin."

"Yes! And don't try to act like you know nothing about it because I know better!"

"Sit down, Deuce."

"What could you possibly be thinking? Drug trafficking, Meredith? How could you do this to Josie?"

"I will tell you everything as soon as you sit down. Now sit down and calm down."

Deuce looked at Meredith, at the way she seemed to revel in his outrage, but he had to know what in the world she could have been thinking. He sat down.

"Okay," Meredith said, setting her briefcase on the table and sitting down too. "Ben and Josie have been apart for months now. Yet Josie will have nothing to do with you, and Ben's having nothing to do with me. I asked myself why. That's when it came to me."

"What came to you?"

"We miscalculated, Deuce. It wasn't Josie. It was Ben. It wasn't Josie."

Deuce hesitated, trying to figure out what Meredith had just said. Then he shook his head. "I don't know what the hell you're talking about, lady. What wasn't Josie?"

"We thought Josie was the one so in love with Ben that we had to change the image of Ben in Josie's eyes. We had to knock that halo off of his head, remember? Well, we did that. Those nude photos did it. They've been separated for months now. It worked. But it didn't work too, because Josie wasn't the problem. Ben was. He was the one who couldn't get over Josie. He was the one who had this puritanical image of Josie that couldn't be shaken. Yeah, we did part of our job. He's nothing in her eyes. But she's still diamonds in his, until now."

"Let me see if I'm following you. You ruined Josie's life—you put her in danger of many years in prison—so you could screw Ben Braddock?"

"Yes. No, no! Of course not."

"But she could go to prison, Meredith!"

"Oh, come on. Even if she's convicted she won't do any time. She'll get probation, perhaps, but no jail time. She's never been in trouble a day in her life. It'll be perfect for us, don't you understand that? Ben Braddock is ambitious if he's anything. He will not sacrifice his career or his good name for anybody. I suspect he'll hang in there with her initially. He'll have no choice. She'll be depending on him. But then his ambition and the fact that he views himself as this great moral man will take over. He won't be associated with somebody involved in drugs, I assure you. Not for long, he won't."

"That sounds great, Meredith. For you. But excuse me if I don't see how this is such a perfect plan for me."

"That's because you're not thinking outside the box, Deuce."

"Don't give me that corporate-jargon crap. I guess I need to change my paradigm too."

"She's dirty now. Don't you get it, Deuce? You didn't stand a chance with her because she didn't feel you were on her level. Oh yeah, she talked the street talk and tried to walk it too, but why would she be with a man like Ben? A man with background and breeding if nothing else? Because that's how she sees herself. She shuns high society, but she courts it as well. And you, my friend, didn't make the grade. She didn't see you as being on her level. Now she's on your level. She's a little dirty now. She's been arrested. She's been to jail. And even if she gets off scot-free, what man of background and breeding is going to want her? Let's, as she would say, get real. You, Deuce, represent the best of the rest for her. By my action alone your chances have increased a hundredfold, my friend. So before you start accusing me of ruining everything, you'd better live and learn. I know what I'm doing. I always know what I'm doing."

Deuce leaned back. He was in bed with the devil. He knew it. He also knew that the devil was speaking the truth. Josie never viewed him as her equal, he could tell that from the first day they talked. He was a little too down-home for her. Her childhood might have been rough, but his was too rough. He was too rough. Josie was too clean.

Now she suddenly wasn't clean anymore. She had a little of life's slush on her too. He knew Meredith was right. He also knew he had to have Josie. He had tried to get her legitimately. He had tried to woo her with his charm and personality, but it hadn't worked. Meredith, in one bold stroke, changed the entire dynamic. Now Deuce did stand a chance. He decided, right then and there, to take that chance. He had to have Josie. That's all he knew. And nobody else was offering up any other way to get her.

Ben spent his morning at home, calling lawyers and private investigators, and talking with the chief of police about the details of just what kind of case they had. By the time he was showered and dressed and pulling into the driveway of Josie's townhouse, it was late afternoon. And Josie was still in bed.

She didn't even move. She just lay there, staring up at Ben, seeming to listen passively as he told her that he had just hired one of the best criminal defense attorneys in the country for her, and that he was flying in today, and that a battery of private investigators were also on the case. Josie listened, but she didn't appear at all fazed. Ben tried to smile, to help lift her spirits, but she just lay there, staring at him, as if unable to be moved.

Ben didn't go into work at all that day. He thought he would—he needed to—but he couldn't. Josie was like a zombie going through the motions of life. He told her she needed to get out of that bed; she got out of bed. Then she just stood there. She showered because he said she should; she ate because he cooked her a meal; she sat out on the patio with him because he asked her to.

Ben was devastated. He smoked his cigarette and sipped wine and stared at Josie as they sat together. She sat on the patio like some sick old lady in a nursing home. Given up and left to die. In one night, one terrible night, something had happened to Josie that Ben never thought possible. She had lost her passion. She had lost her will to fight, a will that he had admired so deeply. He crossed his legs and doused his cigarette. "Josie, don't do this," he finally said to her. She looked at him.

"You've got to fight back, honey. You can't go soft on me now. If you don't fight back, this thing can do you in. You hear me, Josie? Josie? Now come on, honey. You aren't behaving like the woman I love."

Josie stared at Ben, and all she could think about were the nude photos she found at his home, the phone calls from his other woman, and the trip to New York he took with Meredith. She wasn't thinking about him. She didn't want to hear a word he had to say. Had Dawn been behaving like the woman he loved when she had posed naked for him? Was Meredith? Were any of his women?

She left the patio and went back to bed.

CHAPTER 23

Scotty Culpepper arrived at the Saint Cloud Regional Airport early that next day. Ben was there to meet him and the two friends shook hands vigorously, and then hugged. Scotty was Josie's best friend. Because of his love for Josie and his closeness to her, he had become a man Ben trusted. Ben also knew, however, that Scotty was a man of great emotional range, not unlike Josie herself, and he had been devastated over the phone when Ben told him the news. But he had to pull himself together and suck it up before he made it to Josie's house, Ben felt, or he would only make a bad situation unbearable. That was why Ben met him at the airport.

"Where's Josie now?" Scotty asked when they stopped embracing. "She drove you drunk yet?"

Ben smiled and took the luggage from Scotty's hand. He had forgotten how good looking a man Scotty was, with those big, whimsical eyes and that thick, long, black hair he wore in an Indian plait. Although it was wintertime and Minnesota didn't play when it came to harsh weather, Scotty wore a yellow, open-front shirt with a pair of white, cotton pants. He also had the audacity to have a pair of sunglasses hanging from the top bridge of his shirt. *Sunglasses in winter,* Ben thought as soon as he saw them. But that was Scotty.

"She's home," Ben said. "She didn't feel up to coming to the airport. And no, Scotty, she hasn't driven me to drink yet."

"She's all right then?"

Ben paused, then shook his head. "No."

"No?"

"She's in bad shape. She's not even fighting back."

"Josie? *My* Josie? I have to see that to believe it. I expected her to already be on the job clearing her name, getting on everybody's last nerve. I expected her to have at least written a letter or two to the President of the United States by now."

"I know," Ben said as they began walking.

"She's that bad for real?"

"For real," Ben said. He couldn't believe it, either. "But she'll be all right, especially since you're here."

"But where did the drugs come from? I don't understand what's happening."

Ben placed his hand on Scotty's upper back. "Remember what we talked about on the phone last night, Scott? Remember how I told you I needed you to be strong for Josie?"

"I know. I will be. But . . ."

"No *buts*. We don't know anything yet. Nothing. We will know it all soon. But you're going to have to wait it out just like the rest of us. I know it's hard."

"Hard? Child, please. It's torture."

"You're right. It is. But if it's tortuous for us, Scotty, imagine how Josie feels."

Scotty looked at Ben, at this good man who didn't seem to mind that he was walking through a public airport with a gay man close to him, and Scotty felt grateful, not for himself, but for Josie. He was grateful that Josie, that his Josie, had Ben.

Nothing. Not happiness, not concern, not even contempt. Josie showed no emotion whatsoever when Scotty walked into her home. Scotty was stunned. He'd never seen Josie quite so subdued. He looked at Ben.

"Scotty's here, Josie," Ben said, but Josie lay in bed without uttering a word. She looked at Scotty, stared at him, but she didn't say a word.

"I know you ain't trying to act like you don't know me," Scotty said with that quirky smile of his Josie always loved.

But Josie just lay there, looking at him, seemingly recognizing him, but not connecting with him at all. Ben walked over to the side of the bed and sat down.

"You aren't going to speak to Scotty, honey?"

Josie looked at Scotty. "Hey," she said.

"Hey? That's all you got to say? At your thirtieth birthday party you nearly broke my neck with affection. Now all you can say is hey?"

"I'm tired, Scotty."

"You think I'm not tired? I've been on a plane all morning. And I know Ben's tired. We're all tired. What makes you so special?"

Josie almost smiled. "You don't understand."

"You got that right. I don't understand. I don't understand why your big behind is lying in some bed this time of day. I don't understand why you don't get out of this bed, put on you some clothes, and handle your business, Josie. This ain't you. Some welfare queen, yeah, I can see it. But you? The slash-and-burn queen? No. You need to quit trying to front, girl, quit trying to act like you don't know what's going on, and get with the program. If not for yourself, at least do it for me. And Ben."

Josie looked at Scotty. "Ben? Do it for Ben? Child, please."

"Child, please what? Did I say something offensive?"

"Ask Ben," Josie said, and both she and Scotty looked at Ben. Ben stood up. He knew Josie well enough to know when it was time to exit.

"I'd better get back to the office," he said.

"Yeah, the office," Josie said derisively. "Go on back to the office."

Scotty couldn't believe Josie's insolence. "What's wrong with you, woman? Why you dissin' Ben like that?"

"Why he be dissin' me?"

"The man works hard, Josie."

"Scotty, it's okay," Ben said, and he tried to smile. Then he extended his hand. "Take care of her," he said. Scotty gladly shook Ben's hand.

"I will, man," he said. "Come by later on."

"We'll see," Ben said. He looked back at Josie one more time, and then he walked out of her bedroom.

"Don't start," Josie quickly said.

"You need to quit, Josie."

"Just don't worry about it, okay? You don't know what's going on."

"I don't?"

"No."

"Then enlighten me." Scotty folded his arms.

Josie turned over in her bed. "I'm not even sweatin' it, you hear me? I'm not even thinking about dealing with that stupid stuff right now."

"From what I can see, you apparently aren't dealing with anything right now. And this is definitely not the time, Josie, to be sensible."

Josie turned back over and looked at Scotty. "What?"

Even Scotty had to smile. "That didn't sound right, did it?"

Josie smiled. *Finally,* Scotty thought, a *smile.*

"No, it didn't," she said. "But nothing you say does. So hey."

"All right, Miss Thang," he said. "Keep on with yo' bad self. But payback is a bitch."

"Like you?"

"Uh huh," Scotty said, and then they both laughed.

They met in Ben's office, Lewis Hirsch, the lawyer, Campbell Gates, the lead P.I., Scotty, Meredith, and Ben. They sat around the conference table more silent than verbal. It had been nearly three weeks since Josie's arrest, three whole weeks, and the news wasn't good.

Everybody looked at Ben. He leaned back and began rubbing his mustache, seemingly buried in thought. Scotty was worried too, because he'd never seen Ben so worried, though he didn't fully understand what all of the legal doublespeak he was hearing truly meant.

"Maybe with more time," Campbell Gates said, "something will turn up. But Ben, I've known you too long to jerk you around. Your girlfriend's case doesn't look so good. Even if what she's saying is true . . ."

"It's true," Scotty said quickly and glanced at Ben, as if he expected Ben to defend her too. But Ben was someplace else, his mind completely engulfed in a train of thought well beyond the current place and time.

"Somebody may very well have planted the heroin," Gates said, rephrasing himself. "But trying to determine who did the planting is like trying to determine who dropped that needle in a haystack. Drugs don't carry serial numbers, Ben, neither can you extrapolate prints from processed powder. That's the problem."

"What about enemies?" Meredith asked, and everybody looked at her. "Somebody had to hate her bitterly to leave twenty-thousand dollars worth of drugs buried in her backyard. Did you look into that part of the equation?

"We did," Gates said. "But there, again, it's an almost impossible thing to decipher. I mean, she's a journalist. Of course she has enemies, plenty of enemies. But the kind that would do as you say, would be willing to leave twenty-grand of heroin around to snare her? That's where it gets tough."

"Did you talk to Josie about it?" Meredith asked him.

"We asked her to name names, but she could only think of the Florida women who leveled those sexual harassment charges against Ben, and the mayor of Saint Cloud. Well, you see, that's what you call running into a dead end."

"But you still have to check it out," Meredith said, and Gates nodded his agreement.

"And we did check it out," he said. "There was just no connection there. Not to any of these people and drugs. We even went back and reviewed every case Miss Ross has worked since her days as a reporter in Alabama and Florida and here in Minnesota, but nothing stands out, and I mean nothing. Almost all of her reporting has been political or social-consciousness stuff. She did very little criminal work."

"You're assuming it has to be a criminal," Scotty said, "or some drug kingpin or something. But it don't have to swing like that. And you know what I was thinking? I was thinking that maybe this is more about Ben than Josie. It could be that woman who's been making those anonymous phone calls to Josie, somebody like that. Somebody who wants Ben so bad that she'll stop at nothing to get him."

"You may be right. But what can we do? Investigate an anonymous woman?"

Meredith leaned back, and then she shook her head.

"So what you're saying is that you have nowhere else to look? You've exhausted all your avenues already?"

Gates nodded. "We follow leads, Miss Chambers. There are none in this case to follow."

"But are you looking at the bigger picture?" Meredith asked. "I think Scotty may be on to something. Maybe this entire matter has nothing to do with Josie. Maybe it's Ben they want. Maybe somebody's trying to get to Ben through Josie."

"Again, we've looked at all of that too. I have a battery of guys on this case, Miss Chambers, it ain't just me. And they worked overtime on this, for Ben."

"Stuart Lindsey came out of the blue," Meredith said. "Have you looked into his background?"

"Yeah," Scotty added. "What's his problem?"

"He works in a legal-aid office in Florida. He has numerous financial problems and, yes, he does have a drug problem. He's been an addict for years, but his drug of choice is crack, not heroin. Not ever. Stuart Lindsey, drugs, and financial problems have gone hand in hand for nearly twenty years. That's nothing new. And it's no secret either. Now, yes, there is some concern that he may have been paid to discredit Ben. Sure, he may have. But we believe it's more likely that somebody associated with Michael Fastower, Ben's competitor for CEO, is the source of the payments, rather than some drug source."

"But if Fastower paid Lindsey to discredit Ben, he could have hired somebody to plant those drugs as a way of discrediting Ben too," Scotty said.

"That's true. That's about the most viable possibility. But if that is the answer, then we're doomed. You will never trace that connection, I guarantee it. Fastower's nobody's fool. You will never tie his hands to this, not even to the person he may have paid to do this. And we have our doubts about his involvement to begin with. Fastower doesn't play the game that way. Never has. He'll scandalize your name, and be sleazy about it too, but he won't commit felonies of the kind in question here. Planting drugs is not his thing. We followed that road, but it was a dead end too."

Ben looked at Gates. "What's your bottom line, Camp?" he asked.

Gates looked at Lewis Hirsch. "The bottom line, Ben," Lewis said, "is that the drugs weren't planted."

Scotty nearly jumped up. "What y'all trying to say?" he asked.

"The evidence says it, " Hirsh replied. Then he looked at Ben. "She told us an untruth."

Ben's expression went unchanged. Scotty couldn't believe it. "You trying to say Josie lied to you? That's what you're trying to say? Ain't no way, man. Josie has never, and I mean ever, told a lie. She doesn't tell lies."

"She was arrested before."

Ben looked at Hirsh. He paused, as if to make certain he'd heard his old friend correctly. "Arrested?" Ben asked.

"I'm afraid so."

"For what?"

"It was during a pro-choice rally when she was in college," Hirsch said. "Some of the protestors were also smoking joints. Those were the protestors who were arrested. It doesn't sound like a big deal, I know, but it's a big deal. Josie told me that she had never been arrested before and she told me that she had never done drugs of any kind before. Both were lies. I think she thought that her arrest had been expunged. And it was, but we were able to find out the facts. Ben, if we're able to get this info, you better believe the prosecution team already has it."

Scotty looked at Ben. He didn't know what to say.

"Smoking a joint in college," Meredith said, "doesn't mean you'll end up with thirty grams of smack outside your patio door."

"Right," Scotty said. "That's what I'm talking about. You're putting two and two together and getting nine, and we're sitting up here letting you do it. That episode was so nothing that Josie probably forgot all about it."

"Or she wanted to conceal it." Lewis looked at Ben. "Josie's smart, Ben. She knows how important information is. Now I don't believe she was trafficking in drugs. I don't believe that for a second. We may be able to get the intent charges dropped. But the possession will have to stand. People just don't leave twenty-thousand dollars worth of drugs lying around to frame somebody. They could have accomplished the same result with a lot less dope."

"And, yes," Gates said, "we looked into the money angle too. When Miss Ross left Florida to come to Minnesota, she sold her condo down there. Sold it and netted, after expenses and mortgage pay-out, nearly forty-thousand dollars out of the deal."

"I had her bank that money," Ben said.

"I know, and she did. For a hot minute. Then every dime was eventually withdrawn, including twenty-two-thousand dollars at one time."

"Twenty-two-thousand dollars?" Scotty asked, stunned.

"Yes. And what she did with that money is anybody's guess. The trail ends at the point of withdrawal."

All eyes turned to Ben. He stood up.

"Where are you going?" Scotty asked, standing too.

"I have a lunch date with Josephine," Ben replied as he began walking out of the office.

"Can I come?" Scotty yelled after him.

"Yes," Ben replied.

"You come too, Meredith," Scotty said, inviting Meredith along. "You ask good questions, girl."

Meredith rose immediately. It was all turning out better than she could have ever hoped or planned. Not only was Ben questioning Josie's sainthood because of the manufactured chain of events, but Josie herself had created reasons to question it. She'd lied. Saint Josie had lied. Meredith gladly followed Ben and Scotty to confront the lady in question. She followed them not believing her good luck.

They went to The Pier for lunch, a small restaurant on the river. Ben fully expected Josie to question why Meredith had to come along, but she didn't question it at all. She took a seat in the booth next to Ben and stared out at the water that surrounded them, as if the reason for the get-together had nothing whatsoever to do with her.

The conversation, at first, was strictly on the nostalgia tip, as Scotty spent most of the time remembering the good old days when Josie was the mouth of the south and every big shot in town hated the sight of her. Including Ben, at first, he said.

"Ben?" Meredith asked with a smile.

"Oh, yes. He had to. Josie would write these horrible articles about him. Just horrible. One of them was titled, "Justice in White, Black, and Oreo."

Meredith laughed. "Are you serious?"

"Am I lying, Ben?"

"You're dead on, Scotty."

"And after she wrote the articles she would get mad at Ben for not calling her and congratulating her. I said, 'J., people don't normally call and congratulate their executioner.' But she insisted that Ben was so different, that nothing affected Ben."

"How did the meeting go?" Josie asked, interrupting the comradery that she felt was focused too much on her.

"Terrible," Scotty said, his honesty preventing him from ever being diplomatic. Then he looked at Ben.

Ben exhaled. "Before we have lunch, honey," he said, "I need to ask you a few questions."

"Okay."

"Scotty," Meredith said, "why don't we go see what's cooking at the buffet."

"You go, girl," Scotty said, "I need to hear this." Meredith looked at Ben.

"It's all right, Mal," Ben said. Then he looked at Josie. "You were arrested before." He said this not as a question, but as a matter of fact, and Josie immediately began shaking her head.

"No, I wasn't."

"In college, Josie. Your record was expunged."

There was a pause. "How could you find out about that?"

"You told me you were never arrested and you told me you never did drugs, honey."

"I didn't."

"You were arrested for possession of marijuana, Josephine."

"But it wasn't true. I was there. Yeah, I was there. But I was there to attend a rally. Some people in my area were smoking joints, but I wasn't one of them. Those cops grabbed all of us and stuffed us in paddy wagons. They didn't care. I wasn't smoking anything."

Scotty shook his head. "Josie, Josie, Josie."

"It's the truth, Scotty."

"I didn't say it wasn't."

"You know what? I don't care what y'all think."

"You what?" Scotty asked. "You'd better care, Missy. Your ass the one on the grill, girl. Not ours."

Ben, knowing Josie's limits better than anyone, hugged her. She tried to fight his embrace, but her emotions were beginning to run too high. She leaned into him.

"And since the cat's been spotted in the bag," Scotty said, "let's pull that sucker on out. What about the money, Josie?"

Josie frowned. "What money?"

"The money you got for your condo, Josie."

Josie looked at Scotty, and then she looked at Ben. "What about it?"

"I told you to bank that money," Ben said. "To put it in an IRA."

"I did bank it. I didn't put it in no IRA, but I banked it."

"Josie, why you doing this?" Scotty asked with a disappointed, concerned look on his face. "This me, and Ben. Why you lying to us?"

"I'm not lying, Scotty," Josie said, showing more fire than she'd shown in weeks. "I did put that money in the bank. And it's my damn money anyway. What my money got to do with any of y'all?"

"In the rule of law," Ben said, "the prosecutor has a burden of proof to carry. They therefore usually need to show motive and means. Motive for the crime, and the means to commit or carry out the crime."

"What does that have to do with me?"

"That condo money shows means, Josie," Scotty said. "It shows a way for you to pay for all them drugs!"

"Pay for what drugs?"

"Don't play dumb, girl," Scotty said. "Your attorney, Lewis Hirsch, had his people check into it. All that money you say you put in the bank has been withdrawn, including a one-time withdrawal of twenty-two thousand dollars."

Josie paused. "It's not what you think," she said almost half-heartedly.

"Then tell us what it is," Scotty said.

Josie looked at Ben. "I gave it to my mama," she said. And then she looked at Scotty. "Okay? It's always been her dream to have breast implants and I gave her the money to get it done. I also bought her a car with the rest of the money, and I paid for my sister Martha to take some cosmetology courses. And by then the money was pretty well gone. So I'm sorry to disappoint y'all, but I had nothing left to buy drugs."

Scotty smiled, and then he laughed. "You took the money for your retirement, for a little nest egg for you when you got old, and bought your mama some bigger tits?" He laughed. "Now that sounds like you. Any other story I wouldn't have believed for a million dollars. But bigger tits? Now that's Josie!" Josie almost smiled. Scotty caught her. "She almost smiled, Ben! Look at that. She almost smiled!"

Ben looked at Josie, who looked up at him. "I swear to you, Ben, that's where the money went."

"Okay," Ben said dryly, in his trademark flat affect.

*   *   *

Later that evening, Josie was sitting in bed. She was trying to take her mind off of everything by doing a crossword puzzle and watching the six o'clock news. Scotty was in the bathroom adjacent to the bedroom putting on his facial cream for the night, and Josie was already in her nightgown too. It had been one of those scary days for her, where it had seemed as if her past was trying to lay claim on her present and destroy her. That was what it had felt like. Simple things, like an arrest that never should have happened and giving money to her family, had been viewed as some sinister plot to prove that she was indeed a drug kingpin. She wanted to smile every time she thought of how absurd the idea really was, but it was no laughing matter. Those prosecutors were serious. They weren't laughing at all.

She looked up at the television set just as a picture of Fastower appeared on the screen.

"And now in business news tonight," the anchorman began. "Corporate-giant Michael Fastower has now been tapped to become the president and CEO of Denlex, beating out the company's current vice president for the top post."

Josie sat erect. "No!" she yelled.

"No what?" Scotty yelled back from the bathroom.

The anchorman continued: "Benjamin Braddock, as you may recall, was at one time considered the leading candidate for the post until a string of bad publicity, including allegations by his former law partner of improper business practices and the arrest of his girlfriend on drug trafficking charges, greatly reduced his chances. Fastower . . ." Josie leaned her head back.

"How could they do that?" she yelled, and Scotty, his face white with cream, came into the bedroom.

"Girl, what's your problem? What are you talking about?"

"Fastower won."

Scotty, who had no idea what Josie was talking about, decided to revert to form. "Yo' mama," he said.

"Ben was up for CEO of Denlex."

"I heard."

"But they gave it to Michael Fastower."

Scotty looked at the television set. "Really?"

"Because of me, Scotty. He lost out because of me. Damn! Damn! Damn!"

"Just settle down, Josie."

"Those assholes! How can they do that to Ben? He wasn't the one arrested. I was. And I wasn't even considered his girlfriend anymore at the time."

"Now that's news to me," Scotty said.

"Me and Ben had been separated for I don't know how many months when I got arrested. I didn't think we were ever getting back together."

Scotty walked up to the bed and sat on it. "Thanks for not telling me."

"I just couldn't talk about it, Scotty. It was too painful to talk about."

"What happened?"

Josie hesitated.

"Come on, girl."

"Some woman left her nude photographs at his house. She also left a note suggesting he call so they can do it again."

"That's a bold bitch," Scotty said.

"I'm sayin'."

"What did Ben say?"

Josie paused. "Nothing."

"Josie, you didn't. You didn't even confront him?"

"I had all the proof I needed, Scotty."

"So you didn't even ask the man if it was true?"

She paused. "I asked, in a way."

"In what way?"

"I threw the pictures of the bitch at him and left."

Scotty shook his head. "You will never change. You will never give a man the benefit of the doubt. He's got to be perfect or he can't be with Josie. That's why I think you chose to be with Ben in the first place. He was as close to perfect as you was ever gonna see. And the things that man has sacrificed for you."

Josie looked at Scotty. "What are you talking about? What sacrifice?"

"Josie, think about it. Ben knew that he was in line to be CEO. He probably wanted it badder than anything he ever wanted. I mean, what man in his business wouldn't want the top job? He knew what was at stake for him when he went downtown to bail you out of jail. He could have laid low. He could have sent lawyers down there to take care of that and stayed out of the way. But that didn't even cross his mind and you knew it. He'll do anything for you, Josie. Anything! Like the time he flew you to Florida for your birthday? What man we know would do something like that? And what did you do for his birthday? You bought him an ugly-ass jacket he hated and cussed him out. And as soon as somebody comes to you talking about how terrible Ben is, from some woman who probably wants him herself, you treat the man like dirt and kick him to the curb."

"I let him come back."

"This time, yes. Because you need him now. You're clinging to him now like you're a bitch going overboard and he's the last hand grabbing your ass. And what does he do? He only hires one of the most expensive lawyers in the country to represent you and a team of some of the most expensive P.I.s. But that don't even faze you. Because that's Josie."

Josie didn't know what to think. Ben did a lot for her, she'd be the first to admit it. But it was all that other stuff, all that mess and drama, that had racked her nerves too much.

"You know what I've learned, Josie?" Scotty asked, and Josie looked at him. "I've learned that sometimes things aren't what they seem. I know you believe in facts and truth and all that. I know you're Miss Crusader from way back. But Ben deserves the benefit of the doubt, Josie. He's earned it. You need to treat the man better."

"Me?"

"Yes, you. Like tonight. You hear the news about that CEO thing and it hasn't even occurred to you yet that he may be off somewhere hurting inside. All you can think about is how you might have lost the job for him. It's all about you. But nobody thinks about Ben. He's so strong. He can handle it. That ain't nothing to him. But I've been around him these last few weeks and I'm telling you the man is in pain. He's so worried about your crazy butt that he can hardly function. And you don't even bother to give him a call."

"I used to call him every day, Scotty, remember? Four or five times every day. And he wouldn't even take my calls."

"Because, once again, you were overdoing it. You're an extremist to your heart. You go all out in one direction or the other. Never a middle ground with Josie."

Josie exhaled. "I know."

"Am I right?"

"You're right," Josie said.

"You just need to check yourself, girl, that's all."

Josie leaned her head back just as the doorbell rang. Scotty went to the window and looked out. He saw Ben's Mercedes parked on the drive.

"It's just Ben, child," he said.

Josie's entire face lit up. "For real, Scotty?"

Scotty looked at her. "Yeah. What's so surprising about that?"

Josie jumped from the bed, ran down the stairs, and flew open her front door. As soon as she saw Ben, who was taking a last puff on a cigarette, she jumped into his arms. She wrapped her legs around him and held him tightly. He entered the house and closed the door behind him, and then fell back against that door. He had been craving her for so long, craving this very moment. And now that it was here, he was desperate.

"I love you so much, Ben," she said the way she used to say it, and his heart raced with excitement.

"I love you too, Josie," he said. "I love you too."

She kissed him. She pressed into him as if she couldn't breathe without his breath in her. He placed his tongue in her mouth and held the back of her head. They kissed, undaunted, for nearly a minute. Then he began carrying her, kissing her still as he walked, up the stairs and into her bedroom. They stopped kissing only when Scotty came out of the bathroom.

"Scotty?" Ben said. And then he smiled and set Josie on the bed.

"Hello, Ben. You appear to be in good spirits this evening."

"I guess I am. How are you?"

"Good. And you?"

"Scotty?" Josie asked.

Scotty rolled his eyes. "I'm talking to Ben."

"Scotty?" Josie said, again.

"Yes, Josie?"

"Get lost," she said. Both Scotty and Ben smiled.

"I will, but only for Ben," Scotty said, and then walked briskly out of the room.

He closed the door behind him and walked downstairs, smiling as he went. *Josie's off again,* he thought, *to yet another extreme.* Now she was going to smother the man to death. All because Scotty told her that she didn't treat Ben right. Now she had to prove him wrong.

She was going to treat that man and treat that man until the last thing he needed was treatment. Scotty shook his head. *That's Josie,* he thought.

He sat on the sofa and phoned Bruce in Florida. He filed his nails as he talked. He was amazed, absolutely stunned, to catch Bruce at home.

"You ain't doing the town yet?" he asked him.

"Not yet."

"I'm flabbergasted."

"Don't be. I'm not as untrustworthy as you think I am."

"Is that right? Well excuse me for misjudging you."

"You're excused."

"So now that the bullshit's out of the way. Why haven't you hit the road yet? I'm sure the boys are waiting on you."

"I figure I'll wait on your ass," Bruce said.

Scotty smiled. "Really?"

"Yeah. Why not?"

"You make me wanna come home tonight."

"Can you?"

Scotty sighed. "Unfortunately, no. I'm still not ready to leave Josie yet. Although she's beginning to come around."

"It's about time."

"I know."

"And I'm glad she is. For your sake," Bruce said, "because I can't stand her, know what I'm saying? She never liked me and I never liked her."

"I know it, Bruce. But what can you do?"

"Daniel called."

"That queen knows I'm still in Minnesota. What did he want?"

"He said he was just calling to say hey to me, thank you very much. He also said your precious art gallery was doing just fine without you."

Scotty laughed. "Yep. That's Danny boy."

What sounded at first like a little bed-shaking, lovemaking activity upstairs, a minor noise Scotty chose to ignore, became a furious round of bounces, as if the bed was lifting up and plopping down, over and over, and then faster and faster. "Damn!" Scotty said, and looked up at the ceiling.

"What is it?" Bruce asked.

"Some serious banging going on up in this mother."

"Ben and Josie?"

"Who else?" Scotty said. Josie started screaming as the banging sounds intensified, and Scotty couldn't hold in the laughter.

"Man, what's so funny?" Bruce asked.

"Josie, child. She got the do-me holler going like a song, Bruce. You oughta hear her. 'Ah! Ah! Ah!' And it's so high-pitched it sounds operatic. Ben bangs, she hollers. A bang, a holler. Like a damn song!"

Bruce laughed. "You shouldn't be listening to that, man."

"And how do you suggest I not listen? I'm down here minding my own business. They bringing it to me. They're the ones trying to break through the ceiling, not me."

"I thought she was crazy, but give me a break. How can she think about screwing at a time like this?" Bruce said.

"I'm glad she can think about it. She need to think about it. She hasn't been thinking at all, and that's been her problem. This is exactly what that heifer needs."

"She needs an attitude adjustment, that's what she needs."

"Don't even try that, B. She has good cause not to care for your behind and you know it. You did, after all, steal from me. You did, after all, try to beat my ass. Remember all of that? So don't act like she's just being devilish."

"Devilish?"

"As Michael Jackson might say."

"Michael Jackson? Man, please. Let me get off this phone."

"Get off the phone? Why? I offended you?"

"No, man, I'm trying to wash some clothes. I'll call you back later."

"Sure, Bruce."

"Scotty, come on. I'm telling you the truth. I gotta go."

"I have cordless phones all over that house, boy. You can talk and wash at the same time, if you wanted to."

"Well maybe I don't want to. How's that?"

"More like it."

"I'm sure. Bye, Scotty."

"Asshole," Scotty said, and hung up the phone.

But he still had to endure nearly five more minutes of bed-rocking, roof-stomping ain't-that-much-lovemaking-in-this-world lovemaking till it finally slowed to an almost rhythmic rock, and then, to Scotty's great relief, stopped. And total silence ensued.

Upstairs, where the noise had originated, Ben lay still for a few moments longer, and then slid off of Josie and onto his bare back. The sweat was all over his chiseled body and his breathing was so intensely heavy that even Josie got concerned. She turned sideways and looked at him.

"You okay?" she asked.

He smiled. "I'm fine," he said, and pulled her against him.

"You got that right," she said with a smile as she lay her head onto his chest and pressed her fingers into the ridges of his abs. "That was incredible, Ben."

Ben smiled and began stroking her hair. "Think so?"

"I know so. I thought I was gonna pass out about ten different times. I mean damn."

Ben laughed. "We almost got a little carried away."

"It was another dimension, I'm telling you." Then she paused. "You think Scotty heard us?"

"I have no idea."

"I doubt it. The door was closed. But if he did, I'll never hear the end of it. Dang, I hope he didn't."

Ben smiled. And then he stopped stroking Josie's hair and looked at her. "What brought this on?" he asked.

"What brought what on?"

"Josie, you could barely speak to me without getting upset. Now you open your front door and literally jump into my arms? Why?"

"Because I love you."

"You loved me when you couldn't stand me." She laughed. "So what changed your mind about me?" Ben asked.

Josie hesitated. "Two reasons," she said.

"Number one?"

"I saw the news. Denlex selected Fastower."

Ben nodded. "That's right."

"It's unfair, Ben. The only reason they gave it to him was because of me. What I do shouldn't have anything to do with you."

"Well, it does, Josie. You have everything to do with me. That's just the way it is. And I didn't lose out to Mike Fastower because of you. He was the best man for the job."

"No, he wasn't."

"At this time in my life, yes, he was. Besides, I'm not particularly interested in taking on any more responsibility. Not now. You're enough." Ben said this with a smile. But Josie didn't return his affectionate gesture.

"The second reason for my change of heart," she said as she lay her head back onto Ben's sweaty chest, "is because of Scotty."

"Scotty?"

"He talked to me. He said you were so worried about me you couldn't hardly function."

Ben began stroking Josie's hair again. "Oh, yeah?"

"That's what he said." She looked up at Ben. "Was it a lie?"

Ben looked at Josie, and smiled. "What do you think?"

"Ben, I don't know. That's why I'm asking you. You've got to start telling me how you feel. You've got to stop holding everything in like you do. I can't read your mind. If you're in pain, say so. If you're worried about me, tell me that. We'll both feel better if you open up some." There was a long pause. Josie waited for a response, but Ben didn't say a word. She exhaled and lay her head back against his chest.

"Bear with me, Josie," he finally said. Josie hesitated.

"I think I'm over you," she said.

As soon as she said those words, Ben's hand began stroking her hair slower, with much less vigor, as if he was suddenly caught in an absent-minded, slow-motion time warp.

"What's that?" he asked.

She looked up at him. "I think I'm over you."

His heart dropped and his entire body felt limp as he looked into Josie's sexy, beautiful, but now confident eyes. "Are you?" he asked.

"I think so. The obsession. The desperation. The insecurities. I think I'm moving beyond that now. You told me a long time ago to make friends, you remember that?"

Ben hesitated. "Yes," he said.

"You said they aren't going to be perfect, so don't expect them to be. And Scotty sort of said the same thing tonight. He said I expect perfection from people, especially from you. But not anymore. You aren't perfect. That's what I never fully understood. And I don't expect you to be."

"In other words," Ben said, trying to smile but too mortified to pull it off, "I'm not your hero anymore."

Josie looked at Ben and Ben stared into Josie's eyes. For her, it was an exhilarating feeling. An awakening. For him it was terrifying. "That's right," she said. "I don't think I need one now."

Ben tried to smile again, and then he pulled her closer to him. He was concerned with the implications, deeply concerned, but he understood them. It was a painful but necessary rite of passage for Josie. She had seen enough. Now even the mirages stung. And she had to protect her heart. Not with insecurity or desperation, the way she had tried to do it all along. Now she was protecting her heart with strength, and courage, and peaceful contentment. The same way he did years ago, after too many heartbreaks and too much disappointment also forced him to tone it down.

Nearly two hours later, Josie came downstairs. Scotty was practically asleep lying on the sofa and that fact wasn't lost on Josie. "I know you ain't got your funky feet on my couch," she said with a smile.

Scotty looked at her. She had on a robe and bedroom shoes, and was all aglow. He smiled. "And I know the last thing on your mind is this couch," he said.

Josie sat down on the sofa, quickly placing Scotty's head in her lap. "You heard everything, didn't you?" she said, touching his long hair.

"What?"

"Don't *what* me. I'll bet you heard it all."

"I don't know what you're talking about."

"Okay. Play dumb. But I'll tell you what, you should have been there, sweetheart," Josie said.

"I was there, sweetheart. I thought that bed was coming through the roof."

Josie laughed. "I knew you heard us!"

"Where's Ben?"

"He's coming down."

"He can hang a long-behind time for an old man. I mean, damn. You think he's taking Viagra?"

Josie slapped Scotty upside his head. "No, he ain't taking no Viagra. Are you?"

"If I needed to I would. But I estimate well, I'm about thirty, forty years from that need just now."

"Yeah, right," Josie said as Ben, fully clothed in his suit and tie, came walking downstairs. Scotty sat up to get a good look at him. Although Scotty was smiling, Ben looked like his regular, serious self.

"Hey, stud, how was your nap?" Scotty asked, and Josie playfully hit him.

"My what?"

"Your nap. Josie said you was up there all those hours getting some much-needed rest." Josie was smiling too.

"Did she?" Ben said, still serious, still unable to take the joke for what it was.

"She did. You must have been tired, all I can say."

Josie broke into laughter. Ben glared at her as he stepped into the living room. "Come walk me to my car, Josie," he told her, and she began getting up. "I'll see you later, Scott."

"Take care, man. And make sure you get you some more rest."

Josie laughed again. Ben glanced at Scotty, and then headed out the door.

"What's his problem?" Ben asked Josie as she followed him outside.

"He's just trying to be funny."

They walked slowly to Ben's car. Ben pulled out a cigarette and lit up as they walked. Once he made it to his car's door, he turned and looked at Josie. "I'm sure my neighbors appreciate this scene," she said, looking down at her robe. Ben looked at it too, unable to forget the round of lovemaking they had just endured.

"Is Scotty joking around," Ben asked, "because he heard us?"

Josie nodded. "Yep. We were pretty loud from what he claims."

Ben smiled. "Oh, well. That's what you get for having a house guest."

Josie laughed. "You're the one who called him."

"And you're glad I did. Aren't you?"

"Yes. Yes, I am. Thank you."

Ben nodded as he took another puff on his cigarette. He was staring so hard at Josie's body that she became uncomfortable and folded her arms.

"You'd better get out of this weather," he said. Then he reached out and hugged her. She fell into his warm embrace. "I love you, Josephine," he said as he held her.

She closed her eyes. And paused.

"I know," she finally said.

Ben's heart dropped as he held her tighter. He had never felt more alone and more needy in his life. When they stopped embracing, Josie looked at him, at his mustache and then into his bright brown eyes, and she smiled.

"Drive carefully," she said. Without waiting to hear his response, she began walking back toward her house.

"I'll call you later," he yelled after her.

"Good night, Ben," she yelled back, without turning around.

Ben watched her as she moved toward her front door, looking more graceful and sophisticated now, and he suddenly had an urge to run to her, and hold her again, but he resisted. His loneliness wasn't her problem. He wasn't going to make it her problem. He, instead, got into is car, cranked it up, and drove home.

CHAPTER 24

"We're going to whose house?" Scotty asked again as Josie's Mustang turned onto Foley Street.

"Whitney's house. Ben's secretary."

"I still don't understand, Josie. What does she know?"

"She has some information for me."

"And she couldn't just give it to you at the office? It's closer," Scotty said.

"She's off today for one thing. And she doesn't have any business with it, for another thing."

"She doesn't have any business with it?"

"If Ben finds out she has it she'll be fired," Josie said.

"Ben wouldn't fire her for helping you out."

"Yeah, right. You don't know him like that. If she breaks the rules, she gots to go. Period. That's how he operates."

"Well, if she does get fired it'll be all your fault."

"Exactly."

"Then why you puttin' this lady's job on the line?"

"Because I need the information, Scotty, dang. I'm in trouble, in case you forgot. And those high-rent folks Ben hired ain't worth a damn. They're turning everything around and trying to blame me. So I've got to get on my own case because, like you said, this is my ass on the grill."

"Oh, Lord," Scotty said. "She's back. One bang from Ben and she's slashing and burning all over the place."

Josie laughed. "Got that right."

"Although I still don't see how this secretary can help your case."

"I'm just following a hunch, that's all. It might pan out, it might not. But I've got to clear my name. And whatever it takes, I'm clearing it."

Scotty shook his head. "Remember when you were catatonic?"

"I remember."

"Remember when you were so zombie-like you could barely say my name?"

"Yes, Scotty, I remember."

Scotty hesitated. "I liked you better then," he said.

Josie reached over and slapped him upside his head.

"Ouch, woman!" he yelled. And then they both laughed.

Whitney came back to her dining-room table with a small folder in her hand. Josie anxiously reached for it, but Whitney drew it back.

"It's my job, Josie, if Mr. Braddock finds out."

"He won't."

"He'll view this as a breach of confidence and he'll fire me, you know he will."

"He won't find out, Whit."

"Don't worry, honey," Scotty said, as he took a seat at the table. "Josie's a mess, but she ain't no snitch."

Josie looked at Scotty. "What a backhanded compliment," she said, and Scotty laughed.

Josie looked at Whitney. "But he's right, Whit. Ben won't find out."

Whitney exhaled. "Okay," she said, and sat down at the table too. She opened the folder and handed Josie a list. Scotty leaned toward Josie and looked too.

"Okay, what am I looking at exactly?" Josie asked.

"That's a list of all of Mr. Braddock's appointments since the day you told me to start searching, since the day you received that anonymous phone call."

"What's so special about that day?" Scotty asked.

"That was the beginning of our problems," Josie said. "I mean, we had our share before then. But everything started snowballing after that."

"Do you recognize any of the names, Josie?" Whitney asked her.

Josie kept looking over the list. "No," she said. "And I mean not one of them."

"They're mostly big names in the business world. That's why that list is confidential. A lot of those visits involved talks about mergers and acquisitions and other matters that Denlex doesn't like to keep in the public eye."

"Damn," Scotty said.

"What, Scotty?" Josie asked.

"Almost all of those names are females."

Josie nodded. "Yeah, I noticed that too. But that figures."

"Why so many females?" Scotty asked Whitney. "I thought the world of business wasn't very kind to females."

"But apparently Mr. Braddock is because they come and come often. He gets a lot of visits from the ladies." Whitney said this and glanced at Josie.

"I still don't know what we're looking for, Josie," Scotty said.

"I believe it's a female."

"The person who planted the drugs?"

"Yeah. I believe a female is behind all of this. It's somebody who's in love with Ben, and they're trying to get me out of the way."

"But that private detective Ben hired said that theory didn't hunt."

"Didn't hunt?"

"You know what I mean. He said the street value on that heroin was too much money for a jealous lover to go that far. He totally dismissed that theory."

"I believe he's totally wrong. What else could it be? Think about it, Scotty. First, I start getting these anonymous phone calls from a female claiming to be Ben's lover. Then every time I turn around I'm suspicious of Ben about something, and it always concerns some female. Then those nude photos show up at his house. It's the same theme. A female is always at the root of our problems."

"And you believe somebody on this page can be the one?" Scotty asked.

"Yeah, I do."

"But who?" he said.

Josie shook her head. "That's the problem. I don't recognize any of these names." She then looked at Whitney. "What about you, girl?" she asked her. "Anybody on this page stands out to you?"

"Not really," she said. "I mean, they were all friendly with Mr. Braddock but they were all business people too. So, no, I can't see it. Besides," she said, as she handed the paper back to Josie, "the one that stands out in my mind ain't on that paper."

"Who?" Josie asked her.

"Miss Chambers."

"Miss Chambers?" Scotty said. "*Meredith?* That sweet lady?"

Josie pointed at Scotty and shook her head at Whitney. "Sweet my ass," she said. "But that's a man for you. Too busy thinking downstairs to have much left up." Whitney laughed. "But you think Meredith wins the prize, huh?" Josie asked Whitney.

"Oh, yeah. Easily. You should see her around that office, girl. If Mr. Braddock works late, she works late. If Mr. Braddock eats in the cafeteria, she eats in the cafeteria. If Mr. Braddock farts, she farts."

"But Meredith?" Scotty said, still surprised.

"Yes, Scotty, sweet old Meredith. She's had designs on Ben since the first day she showed up at his job."

"Then why didn't you suspect her?" Scotty asked Josie.

"Suspect her?" she said.

"Yes, Josie."

"Because."

"Yeah," Whitney said to Josie. "I know what you mean, girl."

"Well I don't," Scotty said. "So please enlighten me. Because why?"

"I can't picture Meredith planting drugs or hiring somebody to plant drugs. I can't see her going that far. I agree with Whitney, she'd be number one on my list too, but not for those reasons. She's irritating and nauseating and she gets on your last damn nerve over and over again. But she's mainly just a flirt."

"Now I'm lost," Scotty said. "I am truly lost, because I thought that was the point. You said some female was behind the whole shebang. You said this female wanted Ben so badly that she'd do whatever she had to do. Then you describe Meredith Chambers as exactly that kind of woman. Nobody on that list fits the profile, if Whitney's remembering correctly. And Meredith is good because she surely had me fooled. So why aren't we investigating her?"

Josie looked at Whitney, and then she looked at Scotty. He had a point, she thought.

* * *

Johnson Marketing was a large ad agency in the heart of Minneapolis. Josie and Scotty waited nearly twenty minutes in the narrow hall outside the human resources department before anybody would even see them. And then it was a low-level, blond-haired staffer named Ann who escorted them into a small office.

"I'm sorry about the delay," she said, closing the door, "but we're in the middle of hiring an entire department and we're beyond swamped. Please sit down." They sat down in front of the small desk that Ann sat behind. Then Ann smiled and crossed her legs. "Now, what can I do for you?"

"I'm Miss Ross. And this is Mr. Culpepper. We're here to compile a little information on one of your former employees—for background, that sort of thing."

"And you're with?"

Scotty looked at Josie. They had not even discussed that part of the plan. But Josie didn't skip a beat. "We're reporters," she said. "With a new business periodical out of Saint Cloud. We're doing a series of articles on successful area businesswomen. And one of the women we're interested in profiling is Meredith Chambers."

Ann smiled. Josie was relieved. "Oh, yes. Meredith."

Josie began pulling a notepad and pen from her hobo bag. "She did work for Johnson Marketing? Correct?"

"That's correct. She was with us for nearly fifteen years. She was an assistant to our former president. A very able assistant, I might add."

"She was a well-regarded employee then?"

"Absolutely. An excellent employee. I wouldn't have a bad word to say about her. If that's what this is about."

Josie glanced at Scotty. Scotty was staring at Ann. "You wouldn't say anything bad about her," Scotty said, "but what about any of the other employees?"

"No. Nobody. Meredith Chambers was an exceptional worker."

"You knew that she worked here," Josie said, "and that she was an exceptional worker while she did. But did you personally have any dealings with her?"

"Yes. She was somebody's advice I always sought. She's a good person. Of course it's against company policy for me to get into any real details with you about any of our employees, but I'll say this: Meredith Chambers is worthy of any accolades your paper wishes to give her. And if your paper is looking for unpleasant information on Meredith, if that's what this is really about, then I can stop you now. Because you're wasting your time."

"Why did she leave?" Josie asked.

Ann hesitated. "Off the record?"

Josie nearly jumped from her chair. "Absolutely," she said eagerly.

"Mr. Garner, he was our former president. Paul Garner. He was the victim of what we call around here a bloodless coup and was ousted as president. Meredith thought it was unfair, which it was, and she quit in protest. We all talked about quitting too, around the water coolers, you know, but Meredith was the only one with the courage to do so."

Josie leaned back. Then she closed her notepad. Meredith Chambers was nothing short of a saint in this woman's eyes, a modern-day Joan of Arc. Even Scotty understood it too, as he rose to his feet and began thanking the staffer for her time.

"Yes, thank you," Josie said, rising too. "We won't waste your time any longer."

"I wish I could tell you more, but there's really nothing more to tell. She served us very well." Ann then stood up. "Have you seen her?" she asked them.

"Yes," Josie said, placing her notepad in her hobo bag.

"How is she?"

"She's good. She's with Denlex now."

"That's right. Their human resources department did inquire about her. When she left here she told us she was going to retire. Forty years in the corporate world was quite enough, she said at the time. I guess she changed her mind."

"Looks that way," Josie said as she placed the strap of her hobo bag across her shoulder and turned to leave. She suddenly turned back and looked at Scotty.

"What?" Scotty asked, but she didn't respond. She couldn't. She looked at Ann instead.

"Did you say forty years?" she asked her.

"Yes. She said working in the corporate world for that long was enough."

"But that's impossible."

"What's impossible?"

"Meredith Chambers could not have possibly been working any-where no forty years," Josie said.

"Excuse me?" Ann said.

"She's only forty herself."

"So what, J.," Scotty said. "She lied about her age. Big deal."

"Listen, Ann," Josie said anxiously, as if she knew she was on to something. "I just want to make sure we're talking about the same Meredith Chambers. Could you describe her for me?"

"Well, yes," she said. "She was kind of a tall lady, perhaps Mr. Culpepper's height, but maybe a little shorter. She was about seventy years old, had long, black hair, a nice face—"

"Whoa," Scotty said, astounded. "Back up a minute here. Back the hell up. Seventy? Did you say *seventy?*"

"She was around sixty-five, seventy, somewhere up there, yeah."

Scotty shook his head. He couldn't believe it. Josie smiled. "Tell me something, Ann," she said. "Was this nice, elderly Miss Chambers active at all in the African American community?"

Ann hesitated. "I don't understand."

"You mean, she ain't black, either?" Scotty asked the confused staffer.

"Why would you think she was black?" Ann asked.

"No reason," Josie said, leaving quickly, satisfied that she had just uncovered the beginning of some serious cover-up. "Thanks again for your time. Come on, Scotty."

"A seventy-year-old white woman," Scotty said, shaking his head, as Josie hurried him out the door.

Scotty drove Josie's Mustang like a madman, from Minneapolis back to Saint Cloud, and he didn't break speed until they were pulling into the parking lot of the *Bullhorn Journal*. Deuce's Datsun wasn't around, which was a relief to Josie, as she didn't have time for him. She and Scotty hurried into the building and settled at her computer.

"How are we gonna look up information on Meredith if we don't even know the witch's real name?" Scotty asked this as Josie pulled up the Internet. She immediately logged onto the Denlex Web site and began searching for anything at all that she could find on Meredith. She and Scotty didn't know her real name. But neither did Denlex.

But her search turned up blanks. The only mention of Meredith at all was in an article on Ben, where she was simply noted as his executive assistant. Josie leaned back and exhaled.

"Damn," she said. "I thought they'd have at least some write-up on her, where she'd blurt out something personal, something that can give us a clue to who the hell she is."

"She ain't Meredith Chambers, that's for sure," Scotty said, leaning back too. "It's a lost cause, Josie. That woman probably has so many different names that she don't even know who she is anymore."

"She had a brother," Josie said, as if suddenly realizing it herself. Then she looked at Scotty. "She had a brother."

"Had?"

"He died. Strangely enough, he committed suicide. But what was his name?"

"Probably something made up too. But he killed himself? Damn. A black man?" Scotty said.

"Hines. That's it. Hines Lowe." Josie then began pecking feverishly on her computer keys. She conducted an Internet search of his name. When one article turned up, she and Scotty both leaned close to the computer screen.

Drug dealer gets twenty years. That was the article's title. They read on, about how one-time successful musician Hines Lowe was sentenced to serve twenty years in prison for his reputed drug trafficking on the north side of the city. To Josie's shock, the city wasn't Saint Cloud, or anywhere else in Minnesota, but Jacksonville. In Florida. The sentencing judge wasn't some obscure nobody they'd never heard of, either, but Ben.

"Ben," Josie said, stunned.

"Ain't that a bitch," Scotty said. "Ben was the judge who sentenced Meredith's brother to twenty years in prison."

"That's the connection, Scotty. I was wrong. She wasn't some jealous lover. She wasn't some female in love with Ben. She was trying to destroy Ben."

"But why would she plant drugs at your house if she was trying to destroy Ben?"

"Because she knew."

"She knew what? She knew what, Josie?"

But Josie didn't respond. She was too busy staring at the computer screen, too busy musing over the prospect of finally getting some answers.

"So that's the connection," she said. "Ben had thrown her drug-dealing brother in jail, and the heifer wanted revenge."

"I still don't see how she would get revenge on Ben by planting drugs on you, at your house. And heroin of all things. Unless . . ." Scotty hesitated. The implication of what suddenly occurred to him was almost exhilarating. "What kind of drugs was Mr. Hines convicted of selling, J.?"

Josie, understanding clearly what Scotty meant, quickly began strolling further down the article, and then bingo. There it was. She looked at Scotty, and smiled.

"Heroin," she said. And they both jumped up.

"Okay," Scotty said excitedly. "Let's calm our behinds down and think for a moment. We've got the information. But what do we do with it? Go to the police?"

"So they can botch it up? Hell nall," Josie said. "We're going to Ben. He'll know what to do."

Scotty agreed. They made a copy of the Hines Lowe article and then hurried for the *Journal*'s doors. But as soon as they were going out, Deuce Jefferson was coming in.

"Josie, hey," he said excitedly. "What's up, dawg? I thought you were still on leave."

"I am. I just needed to get something."

"So how you been? How you been holding up?"

"Good, Deuce. Thanks for asking." Scotty cleared his throat. "Oh, I'm sorry. This is Scotty, Deuce. He's a friend of mine from Jacksonville."

"Hey, Doc, what's up?" Deuce said as he extended his hand. Scotty gladly shook it.

"Wish we could stay longer," Josie said, "but we've got to run."

"Oh, pity, Josie," Scotty said. "And Deuce here seems so nice." Scotty saw Deuce as an opportunity to finally meet somebody interesting, somebody, as he saw it, with prospects. Deuce saw it as an opportunity too, but not because of Scotty.

"You're staying at Josie's place, Scotty, or—"

"Yes, I'm at Josie's."

"Maybe I can come by sometime. I need to talk to Josie about a story anyway."

"Which story?" Josie asked.

"Oxidare's illegal dumping."

"Oh, yeah. It's ready to run," Josie said.

"After you fact check it, it will be. When do you think I can come over?"

"Tonight," Scotty said.

"Not tonight," Josie said. "We have some business to take care of. Especially since it's practically night already. But tomorrow would be good. Come for dinner. I've got a feeling we may be celebrating."

Ben, however, didn't seem to be in a celebratory mood at all. He was in his living room on the sofa, with Josie sitting on one side and Scotty on the other. They were so excited about the news that Ben had to tell them both to settle down.

"But Ben," Josie said, "we've found the connection! Hines Lowe was a drug dealer you sentenced to twenty years in prison. The drug he sold was heroin. Heroin was planted at my house. Case closed."

"Nothing's closed, Josie. You've connected Hines to me with a case I only vaguely remember. It's an interesting connection, but that's it."

"That's it? What's that suppose to mean?"

Ben knocked the ash off of his cigarette, and then leaned back and crossed his legs. Josie found it remarkable that he would still be dressed so formally, in a suit and tie, when he was long since home for the night. "All you've established is that Hines Lowe may have had a reason to be upset with me, and that Meredith has been deceptive. But that's all you've established."

Scotty shook his head. "But that's motive and means, Ben. Hines Lowe had the motive and Meredith had the means. Especially after her brother killed himself. She was ready to get you good then. And that's why she took that stash of drugs he used to sell and planted them on Josie."

"Her brother sold heroin seventeen years ago, Scotty," Ben said. "And he spent sixteen of those years in prison. I doubt seriously if he still had a stash for Meredith to plant."

"What are you saying?" Josie asked. "Are you still defending her?"

"Of course not. The motive evidence is compelling. But tying Meredith to all of this isn't. Not yet."

"But why not, Ben?"

"Because it won't hold up in court, Josie. We can't just go into court and say that Meredith planted those drugs because she had a vendetta against me. Her brother, they will say, had the vendetta. Her brother, they will say, had the means. But her brother's dead."

"But it may get the jury to think more than one way," Scotty said, and Ben agreed.

"Yes, it may," he said. "But it may not."

Josie leaned back and closed her eyes. Ben was right. Some of those jury verdicts she'd covered over the years had her cockeyed, they were so crazy. She couldn't leave her fate in the hands of a jury. She could get twenty years if she did. Ben was right. She needed more.

"Well," Scotty said, standing up, a feeling of drain overtaking him, "come on, J. We'll just have to keep on searching."

"I know," Josie said. Then she looked at Ben. "Good night, Ben." She kissed him lightly on the lips. His heart raced when she kissed him and he placed his hand around her waist. "I know Meredith is your friend," she said, "and I know how loyal you are to your friends. But that woman's behind all our troubles, Ben. And I'm going to prove it."

Ben pulled her against him. "I know you will," he said and smiled, seeming as calm as she was excited. He still was so certain of everything that Josie wished she had his confidence too.

But when she moved to stand up, to leave with Scotty, he wouldn't release his hand from her waist. She looked at him. His bright brown eyes seemed pained now, as if the prospect of her leaving him alone tonight was too much for him to take. In some ways his look, and his reaction, astounded her. He didn't normally have any problems when she left his side. But in other ways, especially lately, she wasn't surprised at all. She looked at Scotty. Scotty already understood.

"I'll see you tomorrow, child," he said, walking toward the foyer. "Good night, Ben."

"Don't wreck my car!" she yelled after him.

"I'll think about it!" he yelled back as he promptly left the house.

For a full hour after Scotty's departure, Josie told Ben everything that happened in the course of her day. Without mentioning her contact with Whitney, she went through a litany of events, including the trip to Minneapolis and how stunned she and Scotty had been when they found out that the real Meredith Chambers was a seventy-year-old white woman. She laughed as she talked, and her passion was animated, but to Ben, as he sat back quietly and listened, it wasn't the same. There was a hesitation in Josie now, he thought, a sense of restraint, as if she'd been stung too many times and was determined to be more cautious now.

Even in how she related to him, he could see the difference. She didn't cling to him the way she used to. The way she was about to leave without asking if she could stay, something she had always done, was stunning to him. She said she was over him, that she didn't need him to be her hero anymore. Watching her all night, beaming with confidence and that harnessed, careful excitement, made him believe her. But it also made him feel more alone with Josie than he would have felt in a dark, empty room.

That was why he took her upstairs. He had to have her in the worst way. Every time he looked at her, every time she laughed, every time her beautiful, heavenly eyes looked into his, his heart sank deeper into an abyss he knew was of his own making. His life was measured out he thought. His life was orderly and straightforward and disdainful of any change in plans. But Josie had put the fire under his feet. Having her had kept him on his toes. As he walked her up the stairs of his home, as he undressed her in his bedroom and then held her in his arms, kissing her, he could feel the same fire she gave him begin to unnerve him. Nothing was orderly anymore. Nothing was straightforward anymore. Because he loved Josie, and loving Josie was no game. It was work, hard, challenging, unpredictable, messy work. The kind of job he used to wonder if he was willing to take on. But now, as he held her, as he burned with the desire to never let her go, he couldn't even imagine any other way.

Josie couldn't imagine it either, as he kissed her, as his head wedged itself between her legs and he kissed her all over. And when he entered her, when he turned her on her stomach, pulled her up to him, and entered her from the back, that same exhilaration she'd felt the night before—when he had made love to her so intensely she had nearly passed out—overtook her again. He pumped against her and squeezed her breasts and stood her on her knees as he moved in deeper. There was a time, she remembered, when she had to practically beg for this. Now she didn't even have to ask. It was all so beautiful, so intoxicating, and so different to her in every imaginable way that she couldn't help but smile. She couldn't help but enjoy the moment, enjoy, without any reservations, what was once the rarest of occasions in her life.

CHAPTER 25

"Caldwell Electronics, may I help you?"

"Fred Caldwell, please."

"May I ask who's calling?"

"Josie Ross."

"One moment, Miss Ross."

Josie leaned back against her headrest. From the parking lot she could see Scotty inside McDonalds, receiving their order. After he picked her up from Ben's, smiling like he just knew what they had been up to all night, the last thing she wanted was Micky D's for lunch. But Scotty was all of a sudden so hungry and it was on the way, and since she hadn't had anything to eat either, she had stopped. The Big 'n' Tasty was on sale for ninety-nine cents so she'd ordered it, but she wasn't even thinking about food. Meredith was on her mind.

"Josie and the pussycats," Fred's upbeat voice could be heard on her cell phone. "How are you, doll?"

"I'm doing all right, Fred. What about yourself?"

"Any day that I'm above ground is a good day to me."

"I hear that."

"How's that hotshot husband of yours?"

"He's fine. And he's not my husband, Fred."

"Not yet. But any day now. Right?"

"We'll see."

"Give him time, Josie. He'll come around. He'll be eligible for Medicare when he does, but he'll come around."

Josie smiled. "You're crazy, you know that?"

"I know it."

"How's Angela?"

"She's Angela. She never changes. That's why I love her. But she's fine. She's taking up Tae Bo now."

"For real?"

"Can you imagine? As if that woman didn't have enough moves in her arsenal. I mean, she's perfected the art of spending my money. Now Tae Bo. What's next?"

Scotty walked out of McDonald's with a bag of food and got in Josie's car. "Who are you talking to?" he asked as soon as he sat down.

"Fred," she said.

"Oh, Freddy. Tell him I said hello."

"But I let her do her thing," Fred said into the phone. "You know how persuasive she can be."

"I know. She can get anything she wants out of Ben."

"Oh, Benjamin's an old softy when it comes to Angela. They love each other to death."

Josie exhaled. "Yeah, I know."

"Tell him I said hello, Josie," Scotty said as he bit into a burger he had pulled from the bag.

"Scotty says hello, Fred."

"That's right. Scott's down there. Angela told me he was going to offer you moral support."

"He's offering me something, but I haven't decided if it's a good thing yet." Josie smiled as she pulled her burger from the bag.

"Benjamin told me about that nonsense, Josie. How are you holding up?"

Josie paused. "I'm okay. I'm better I think."

"Good. Lewis Hirsh is on your case. He's one of the best attorneys around. You'll be fine."

"I hope so, but that's why I'm calling you, Fred. I know you work with private investigators a lot."

"Not a lot, but I work with them."

"Think they could check somebody out for me?"

"Related to your case?"

"Yep."

"Sure they can. Let me get a pen here. Just a moment."

Josie unwrapped her burger, and then looked at Scotty. "This isn't a Big 'n' Tasty, Scotty. This is fish."

"That's mine," Scotty said, taking it back, and then handing Josie another sandwich to unwrap.

"You bought two sandwiches, Scotty?"

"Damn right I did. I'm hungry. You got a problem with that?"

"Okay, Josie," Fred said. "Sorry about that. I've got a million pens on my desk and none of them work. Now shoot. What's our subject's name?"

"Meredith Chambers. At least that's the name she's using."

"Whoa," Fred said. "That's a popular lady."

"Excuse me?"

"My people already vetted her. Months ago."

Josie stopped unwrapping her sandwich. Scotty sipped from his super-sized orange soda and looked at her.

"What is it, J.?" he asked her.

"You mean somebody already asked you to check her out?" she asked Fred.

"Yes."

"But who?"

"Benjamin."

"Ben? Wait a minute. Ben asked you to check out Meredith Chambers?"

"He did. You sound surprised."

"I'm beyond surprised. When did he ask you? After I got arrested?"

"Oh, no. It was a good while back before you got arrested."

"Are you sure?"

"I'm positive. He had just gotten in from New York when he called. It was late at night. I remember it well."

"What did he say?"

"He said the same thing you're saying. He needed me to have this woman checked out. And I did."

Josie could barely believe what she was hearing. "What did you find out?"

"You'll have to get with Benjamin on that, honey. I discuss my reports with no one but the person from whom the request came."

"Understood," Josie said. "And thanks, Fred," she added.

*   *   *

Ben was seated behind his desk, his feet propped up and reading glasses on as he perused a stack of acquisition projections, when his desk intercom buzzed. "Mr. Braddock?"

Ben became immediately upset that his instructions not to be disturbed were not being followed. He reluctantly pressed the button. "Yes, Whitney?" he said.

"This is Helen, sir. At the front desk. And I apologize for disturbing you."

"Where's Whitney?"

"She's off, sir. This is her day off."

"Yesterday was her day off."

"Yes, sir. And today."

Ben exhaled. "What is it, Helen?"

"I didn't mean to bother you, but a Miss Josie Ross is here to see you, sir. I tried to explain to her that you weren't seeing visitors without appointments but she . . ."

"Send her back," Ben said.

"Sir?"

"Send her back."

"Oh. Yes, sir."

"And Helen?"

"Sir?"

"Wherever Miss Ross comes to this office she's to be let in without exception."

"Yes, sir," Helen said. "I did not know, sir."

"Okay," Ben said and buzzed off.

He continued reading through his projection papers while he awaited Josie's arrival. It was only one in the afternoon but it had already been a hectic day. He had three different meetings, all intense, including one with his new boss Michael Fastower, and he had a working lunch with Lewis Hirsch. If they couldn't show cause for a dismissal at the prelim, Hirsch wanted Josie to plead out to simple possession, get sentenced to a few hours of community service, pay a fine, and call it a day. Ben knew it had to be an option on the table, and he knew he eventually would have to present that option to Josie. *But not now,* he thought. She was just coming out of her shell, just getting her passion back and will to fight. He wasn't about to squash that spirit just yet.

She didn't look too uplifting, however, when she walked into his office. Scotty was following behind her, but she was moving way too fast for him.

"Why didn't you tell me?" she asked as soon as she walked up to his desk.

Ben leaned back and looked at her over his reading glasses. She was in a pair of black jeans and a plain-green T-shirt with one of those thin, army jackets covering her. Just seeing her made his heart flutter.

"Why didn't I tell you what?" he asked her.

"You had Meredith investigated months before I got arrested?"

Ben hesitated. "Who told you that?"

"You was on to that bitch months before this shit hit the fan?"

"Josie, calm down."

"Why didn't you do something, Ben? This would have never happened if you would've done something!"

Ben removed his reading glasses and threw them on his desk. "Sit down."

"No, thank you."

"Sit down!" Ben said angrily. Josie hesitated, and she wanted to go there too, but she sat down. Ben looked at Scotty. "You, too, Scott," he added.

Scotty took a seat in the chair beside Josie's. Ben sat his papers on his lap and squeezed the bridge of his nose with his fingers. Then he looked at Josie. She appeared to him to be more sad than angry now.

"You spoke with Fred?"

"Yes."

"When?"

"Today. Not long ago. What difference does it make? Why didn't you do something about Meredith?"

"You don't even know what that report contains. Do you, Josie?" Josie hesitated. "No."

"Yet you're in here upset that I didn't do something about something you don't know anything about."

Josie closed her eyes and then leaned back. "Okay, you're right. I was just so shocked. You had me thinking Meredith was this great friend of yours."

"I thought she was."

"But you don't anymore?"

Ben paused. "No," he said.

"But why? What happened?"

New York happened, Ben thought. Meredith's wild attempt at seducing him. It was one attempt too many, he'd felt, and he felt it when he looked into her eyes. He'd seen his share of lusting women before, more than his share, those who wanted to tear off his clothes as badly as he wanted to unclothe them. But that wasn't what he saw in Meredith's eyes.

"There's no magic reason, Josie," he said. "I just decided to do some investigating."

"Fred said you called him the night you returned from that business trip in New York, the night I found those nude photographs at your house. Did those photos have something to do with it?"

"Yes."

Josie hesitated. "So you now agree she's behind what's happening to me?"

Ben nodded. "I never said I didn't agree with that, Josie."

"But last night you acted like we didn't have enough evidence to tie her to anything."

"We don't. Not quite."

"What did that report say?" Scotty asked him.

"The same information you guys uncovered."

"What's her real name, Ben?"

"Alisha Lowe."

Scotty laughed. "Alisha?" he said.

"Yes. Fred's people did mention, however, that Meredith may be into prostitution."

"Prostitution?" Josie asked, stunned. "That woman was a street-corner ho?"

"Not street corner. High flyer all the way. But Fred's people wouldn't go that far. This was only what her neighbors suspected because of all the men in and out of her apartment at all times of night. They didn't have any proof of this."

"I believe it, though," Scotty said. "I can see the hooker in her."

"Yeah, right," Josie said.

"It's true. I'm psychic like that. Take that sweety pie Deuce."

Just the mention of that name caused a reaction from Ben. He looked at Scotty and began rocking slowly in his swivel chair. "What about him?" he asked.

"He's got the hots for Josie, that's what."

"Scotty!" Josie said, astounded that he would even mention that, and then she looked at Ben.

"I saw it sister," Scotty said, not backing off. "The way his gorgeous behind kept looking at you. Child, please. That boy got it so bad even Stevie Wonder could see that. Now you're pretty. I hate to admit it but you've got it going on, so it ain't like it's a surprise. But I must say that brother kind of took the cake."

Ben's heart dropped. "What do you mean?" he asked him.

"Nothing, Ben," Josie said. "He doesn't mean a damn thing because he's just running off at the mouth the way he always does."

"What do you mean, Scotty?"

"I mean the brother got it deep down, to the ground, bad. Maybe worse than you."

Ben seemed stunned by Scotty's comment about him. Were his feelings that obvious now? Was he that far gone? He glanced at Josie.

"He'll do anything to get Josie," Scotty said, "that's all I'm trying to say. The brother's whipped. But Josie wasn't thinking about him."

"Thank you!" Josie said, as if Scotty's last comment exonerated her.

"Although she did invite him to dinner tonight."

"Scotty!" Josie said.

"Dinner?"

"Yep." Scotty said.

Ben looked at Josie. She quickly shook her head. "He just want to go over some stories I was working on, Ben, that's all. It's work. Don't listen to Scotty."

"Anyway," Scotty said, "getting back to this Meredith mess. Or should I say Alisha mess? What I don't understand, and I thought about this a lot last night. Some people might have been doing other things, but I was thinking."

"Forget you!" Josie said.

"But what I don't understand," Scotty continued, "is why would Meredith want to get you, Ben?"

"Duh," Josie said. "He sentenced her brother to prison, Scotty."

"For selling drugs."

"That's right."

"That's what I don't get. He was a lowdown drug dealer. He was her brother, but he was a drug dealer. Meredith is a smart lady. How could she want revenge on somebody who didn't do anything but sentence a guilty man to prison?"

"Because that man was her brother, Scotty," Josie said, as if it were obvious. "Because she probably didn't think he was guilty. She probably thought he was innocent."

Ben's chair-rocking suddenly stopped. "Or she knew he was," he said.

"What?" Scotty asked.

"I'll be damn," Ben said. "That's it."

"What's it?" Josie asked.

But Ben was thinking beyond Josie and Scotty. His eyes even trailed away from them. He felt suddenly enlightened. He felt as if he had figured out another piece of the puzzle, and, like all the other pieces, it was sitting right in front of him. And that was the key. That was the connection he knew was out there somewhere. But he had to do this right.

"Is Deuce still coming over to your place tonight for dinner?" he asked Josie.

"What's going on, Ben?"

"Is he?"

"Yes. But what's going on?"

"Okay."

"Okay? Okay what?"

"He's telling us to get lost, Josie," Scotty said and stood up.

"I'll talk to you later," Ben said. Josie, frustrated beyond words, shook her head. If she ever even tried to understand how Ben's brain worked, she decided, she'd go crazy. Little problems he jumped all over. Big problems didn't even faze him. *Forget him,* she thought, as she and Scotty left his office. He was, as far as she was concerned, no help at all.

Deuce Jefferson leaned back on Josie's sofa and smiled. "Coming from you it's a compliment," he said.

"I mean it," Josie said, sitting beside him. "It was one of the best articles I've seen. The research was flawless."

Deuce laughed. "A woman by the name of Josie Ross deserves all of the research credit, thank you. You came through for us, babe."

"What about Oxidare? What's been their reaction?"

"Oh, they're hot. We've sunk tabloid journalism to its lowest lows, according to their press release. Like yeah, and you're killing babies."

"I hear that."

Scotty entered into the living room with drinks.

"Here you are, Deuce," he said gladly as he handed him a ginger ale. "Ginger ale for the gentleman, and sherry for the lush."

"I oughta throw it on you," Josie said playfully as she took the glass of sherry from Scotty's hand. He sat down in the chair across from Deuce.

"So, Deuce, tell me," he said, crossing his leg, "are you into new things?"

"That's enough, Scotty," Josie said.

"I'm just kidding, dang. You know I'm just kidding, don't you, Deuce?"

"I hope so."

"I am. I got me somebody, thank you."

"Yeah, a thief."

The doorbell rang. "But at least he's *my* thief," Scotty said.

"Just get the door."

"You get the door."

"I have company, Scotty." He sucked his tongue, but he went to answer the door.

"Expecting somebody?" Deuce asked.

"Nope. But it could be Ben."

Deuce hesitated. "Ben? You called me over here when you knew Ben was coming?"

"I said it might be him. But what's the big deal? That fight y'all had is ancient history now."

"It was hardly a fight."

"Well whatever it was, it's over now."

"Ben," Scotty said jovially as he opened the door. Then he frowned. "Hello, Meredith," he said.

Deuce nearly jumped out of his skin when he heard Meredith's name.

"What's wrong?" Josie asked him.

"Nothing. It's just feels weird, that's all."

"Ben is not going to hurt you, Deuce, all right?"

"I know he's not."

"So don't sweat it. Especially since he brought Meredith along. My ass was on the grill. Now it's Meredith's time."

Deuce looked at Josie, then he looked at Meredith as she walked further into the home. She had seen Deuce's car out front so she wasn't surprised to see him. But she was definitely curious.

"Hello, Josie," she said as she walked in. "How are you holding up, dear?"

Josie ignored her. It was enough, she thought, that the witch had to be in her house. She wasn't about to make nice about it too.

"Have a seat, Mal," Ben instructed Meredith. She paused, but then sat down in a chair.

"I didn't expect to find Mr. Jefferson here," Meredith said as she sat down.

"You know Deuce?" Josie asked, surprised.

"I wouldn't call it knowledge. I've seen him at Rhonda's a time or two. Once, I think, with you."

"Mal?" Ben said.

"Yes?"

"I know about your brother."

Meredith paused. Deuce looked at her. "Pardon me?" she said.

"I know about Hines Lowe."

Meredith smiled. "What are you talking about, Ben?"

"I sentenced him to twenty years in prison."

"What?" Deuce asked, astounded.

"Oh, yeah, Deuce," Josie said. "That witch over there is out to get Ben. That's what this is all about. And her name ain't even Meredith. It's Alisha."

"Alisha?"

"*That's* what I said," Scotty said with a smile.

"He was arrested for drug dealing," Ben said. "For trafficking in heroin."

"The same brand of drug," Josie said, "that just so happened to have been placed in my backyard."

"And I thought you was on our side," Scotty said to Meredith. "I thought you was some sweet, little, nice spinster lady just trying to help Josie out. I thought you was her friend."

"My friend?" Josie said. "Please. She's the last human being on earth I'd consider a friend. She's behind everything. I know she is now. Those anonymous phone calls, Stuart Lindsey, those nude photographs of that so-called 'Dawn' lady. Everything!" Josie began to get emotional. Ben walked over to her and sat down beside her.

"I'm okay," she said.

"Sure?"

"Yes."

"All right," Ben said. Then he pulled out a cigarette and lit it.

"This is all very interesting," Meredith said, rising, "but . . ."

"Sit down, Mal," Ben said.

Meredith looked at him and glanced at Deuce, and then she sat back down.

"Hines was arrested for drug trafficking," Ben said, "but he was innocent."

Both Scotty and Josie looked at Ben. "Innocent?" Josie said.

"Yes. Wasn't he, Mal? He was no heroin dealer. Not that meek and lowly musician. Not the man who just wanted to be left alone. He wasn't trafficking drugs." Then Ben paused, his eyes staring unblinkingly at Meredith. "You were."

Josie was so stunned that she grabbed hold of Ben's arm. Scotty's jaw dropped open. "What?" he asked Ben, but Ben was staring at Meredith.

"You were always the brains of the family," Ben said to her. "You were always the one with the plans. But Hines was a good man. He couldn't allow his baby sister to go to prison. He wouldn't allow it. So he went instead, for sixteen years. That's a heavy burden to bear, Meredith. And what's remarkable is that you're still dealing drugs. Even after what your brother went through. You're still at it. All those midnight trips of yours and late-night visitors. Your neighbors think it's prostitution you're dealing in. But it's been drugs all along. That's why it was easy for you to plant that stash at Josie's house, and then call in false reports. You're shady from way back."

Tears began to well up in Meredith's hard, cold eyes. "You sent him to prison," she said. "This is all your fault. You sent an innocent man to rot in prison!"

"No, Meredith," Ben said, "you did that. Because you knew he was innocent. Because you remained silent while he served all those years in prison just to keep you free. But the truth imprisoned you, didn't it, Mal? And revenge, misguided revenge, became the only way you knew to get your release."

Meredith just sat there, staring at Ben as if she were staring through him.

"I needed a hook," Ben said. "A connection. Something that would tie it all together, that would make sense of it all. And I found it. Mutual interest. Meredith and Deuce."

"Deuce?" Josie said and looked at Deuce.

Deuce immediately shook his head. "I don't know what he's talking about. Me and Meredith? You crazy."

"Mutual interest made a partnership lucrative for you both," Ben said.

"What the hell are you talking about? What mutual interest?" Deuce said.

Ben paused. "Meredith wanted Ben Braddock. You wanted Josie Ross."

Deuce laughed. "What?"

"You're in love with my woman, Deuce. Which is usually fine with me. People can't help how they feel, but you became obsessed with her. And that's what I didn't understand, until today. You were obsessed with Josie, and I was in your way."

"What is this? Some kind of joke? What? You're upset that they didn't pick you to head Denlex? Is that what this is about? They screwed you so you're gonna try and put the screws in me?" Deuce said.

"Meredith wanted to get to me," Ben said, ignoring Deuce, "but Josie was in the way. That was where it all came together. I'm sure Meredith approached you and I'm sure she didn't give you all the details, that's not her style. But whatever she told you, you fell for it."

Deuce shook his head, although even Josie could see that his confidence was dwindling as fast as ice on a hot tin roof. "What does any of this have to do with me?" he asked.

"Meredith," Ben said, "didn't want my friendship or, as she probably told you, my love. She wanted my head on a platter. I became convinced of it, but I got stumped there. *Why,* I kept asking myself, would she keep trying to seduce me if she hated me, if all she wanted was revenge? It didn't make sense. But, oh, yes it did. The revenge was in the seduction." Ben said this and looked at Meredith. "That has to be the answer," Ben continued. "You wanted to have sex with me to snare me somehow, to trap me into impregnating you, maybe, but I doubt that. You hate me. The last thing you would want to have was my baby. No. It had to be a sex crime. You wanted to get my sperm inside of your body so that you could have your proof, have my DNA, when you cried rape. That's what you were going to do. Weren't you, Mal? You were going to cry rape. And then I, too, would know what it felt like to have my back against the wall as an innocent man wrongfully accused. Just like your brother."

Meredith didn't respond. She couldn't. Deuce, however, was dumbstruck. He knew there was something more to Meredith's story than her undying love for Braddock. He knew there had to be more. But he never dreamed it would be *this*.

"I still don't see what any of this has to do with me," he said, but with a lot less zest.

"Josie got in the way," Ben said. "She kept getting in the way of Meredith's scheme. And that's when you became a natural ally to Meredith. She needed you desperately if her plan was going to work. Because she knew, just as everybody else knew, how obsessed you were with Josie. Even Stevie Wonder could have seen that." Ben said this and glanced at Scotty. Scotty smiled.

"And you worked with Meredith. You schemed with Meredith. You became part and parcel to everything Meredith needed you to become," Ben said.

"Man, get out of here," Deuce said, getting angry. "This shit whacked! Why would she plant drugs on Josie? You tell me that! How would planting drugs on Josie help her cause?"

"Because she knew."

"She knew what?"

"She was the first human being to discover something rather odd about me, that hurting Josie was absolutely the most effective way to hurt me."

Josie looked at Ben. Her mind felt so confused she didn't know what to say or think or even believe. She thought this was about Meredith. She thought this little gotcha session was all about Meredith. But Deuce too? She looked at him. "Deuce," she asked him. "Is it true?"

Deuce turned toward her and placed her hands in his. He could take her rejection. He could even take her scorn. But he couldn't bear her hate. "Josie, listen to me," he said desperately. But she didn't want to hear it.

"Is it true?" she asked.

"Josie."

"Please just tell me if it's true, Deuce. You were working with Meredith? You were trying to destroy me too?"

"You know I wasn't. I'm Deuce. Remember? I'm your friend. But Josie, sometimes the game is rigged. Sometimes breaks don't come to dudes like me. We have to make our own breaks."

"I could have gone to prison for years, Deuce. Don't you realize that?"

"No. I didn't have anything to do with that, Josie. I swear to you I didn't. I didn't know she was gonna plant drugs at your . . ."

Everybody looked at Deuce. Then they looked at Meredith. But she wasn't crushed, or even concerned. She was as defiant as ever.

"Am I supposed to be scared now?" she said to the faces that stared at her. "Am I supposed to break down in tears now and confess my evil ways? It'll be a cold day in hell if you're expecting anything like that from me."

"Damn," Scotty said. "The nerve you got. Your little scheme backfired and you're mad at us?"

"Nothing backfired," Meredith quickly corrected him. "I know what I'm doing." Then she looked at Ben. "So you put a few things together, did you? Whoopie for you. Well that doesn't change a thing. I would have gladly told you the truth. Yes, I planted those drugs at your silly little girlfriend's house. I knew how it would devastate you. And it did. I took pleasure in seeing your torture. I took pleasure in seeing you looking like death warmed over every time you came to the office. It was wonderful. You needed to feel something. Now you can see how I felt when you totally disregarded the evidence and convicted my brother anyway. And you did it so cruelly. You did it in such a way to ensure that every appeal would fail. You're good. I'll give you that. You're real good. But I'm better. Because nobody, and I mean nobody, can trace those drugs to me. It'll just be my word against yours. And who's going to believe your word after all the controversy you've been connected to? From those women in Florida accusing you of sexual harassment to Stuart Lindsey accusing you of everything else, who in hell is going to believe you? You're just a distraught boyfriend who'll do whatever it takes to help his woman. You have no proof of anything. Just a lot of words. That's why you'd better not rest. Not for a moment. Because, yes, you may have figured this scheme out. But I'll still get you. One day, some way, I'll still get you. You will finally pay for what you did to my family. Yeah, I planted that heroin at Josie's house. And I don't even care about that. Because you're going down, Benjamin Braddock. That's all I care about. You're going down!"

There was a long pause. The room seemed to deflate with the pain and the devastation of love and hate and unrelenting revenge, with too many swirling emotions. And the silence was deafening.

Until Ben reached into his inside coat pocket, and pulled out a small recorder. He rewound it briefly, and then pressed play.

"You will finally pay for what you did to my family," Meredith said, her voice heard loudly and clearly over the recorder. "Yeah, I planted that heroin at Josie's house. And I don't even care about that. Because you're going down, Benjamin Braddock. That's all I care about. You're going down!"

At first everybody was stunned, especially Meredith, who never thought Ben had it in him. He trusted people, was her calculation. He would never suspect his friend, was her miscalculation.

The room remained numb with silence, until Scotty started laughing. "Oh, man, oh, man," he said. "You know how to put on a show, girl. Complete with confessions and venom and all kinds of hatred and despair. It was so good Ben had to tape it. And looks like you're right, Meredith. Somebody *is* going down. But it ain't gonna be Ben!"

Josie looked at Scotty and she wanted to share his joy. She tried to smile, to understand as he did that the worst was over now, but she looked at Deuce. And she couldn't pull it off.

CHAPTER 26

He came out of his office as she placed the last of her personal effects into the small cardboard box. She saw him as he walked toward her, but she did not look his way. He moved slowly, as if the hesitation in his steps would make her understand. But she didn't, and she never would. He had played a game with her very life, a Russian roulette, and she was never going to understand that. He was betting on human nature. He was betting on Ben breaking her heart so that he would be there to pick up the pieces. But Josie knew better. She knew love was nothing like that. If Deuce had loved her, as he now so mightily claimed, then he wouldn't have wanted her to fall to pieces in the first place.

Although Josie was exonerated of all charges and Meredith was poised to do some serious time in prison, she didn't feel vindicated. She felt betrayed. That was why she didn't even look at Deuce when he walked up to her. She placed her loaded box into her arms and began moving swiftly from behind her desk. Her goal was to get away without having to say a word to him, not one word. But he caught her by the arm.

"You don't have to quit, Josie," he said. "You don't have to do this."

Josie looked at him, and he had those same sad, caring eyes that once drew her to him, that same devil-may-care wild Afro that she thought meant he was a rebel too, that same look of compassion that she just knew made him one of the good guys. But there was more to him than that, and she could see it now. She looked at him as if she could look through him. This man she once thought the world of had committed, in her mind, an unspeakable horror. He had taken her trust and her friendship and baited them on his hook for his own purpose, for his own selfish lust that had nothing to do with her. She wasn't a person to him anymore, but a conquest, a challenge, a prize ready to fulfill the emptiness in his soul.

She looked at him as he held on to her arm, and his eyes, his once caring eyes, made her want to cry. His smile made her want to slap it off his face. His black skin made hers crawl. And she snatched away from him.

"I was only trying to help you, Josie," he said, his voice trembling for understanding, his hand suspended in midair as if he still had a hold on her. "You've got to believe me. Ben Braddock didn't mean right by you. He had you so messed up emotionally that half the time you didn't know if you were coming or going. It was always something with that dude. He wanted to change you, Josie. How could anybody want to change a beautiful soul like you? He wanted to take your spirit away until you were just like him. And I couldn't have that. I'm not proud of how I went about it. I'm not proud of how easily I let that crazy-ass Meredith dupe me into believing in her scheme. But I did it for love, Josie. My love for you. I thought my love would be all you would need."

"You didn't care what I needed, Deuce. Stop kidding yourself. What you did you did for you, for your needs. You left me twisting in the wind, dying in pain, because of what you wanted and what you thought you had to have. At least Meredith was doing her dirt for the love of her brother. And she wasn't trying to kid herself, either. But you are lower than the low, Deuce. Because it was all about you. And you still don't understand that."

Josie looked at him one more time. She gave him a hard, cold, angry, sad look. And then she began to walk away.

"Josie, wait," Deuce said, in one last-ditch effort to stop her, but she kept on walking. "I never took you for a quitter," he added, when all hope seemed gone. And it worked. She stopped, and looked at him.

"I once took you for my friend," she said. "I guess we were both wrong."

Deuce's look of confidence melted like snow before Josie's very eyes. He may have wanted to apologize, or he may have wanted to explain the reasons one more time. But she didn't care either way. She was done.

She kept walking toward the exit. The newsroom was bustling with activity and she was just another distraction in that room. But she didn't mind that either. She thought she had found a home at the *Journal*. She thought she had finally found a place of refuge where the only thing that mattered was your compassion for the voiceless and your concern for God's blessed earth. But it was no different there. The *Bullhorn Journal* talked a good talk, and drew her in with the promise in their walk, but in the end, when it mattered to her, it was bull.

As she passed the discard bin, the huge trash can where reporters placed all unwanted documents and other sensitive materials in need of shredding, she stopped. She looked at the cardboard box in her arms, a box filled with her personal effects, the same box she carried away from the *Herald,* and the *Gazette* before that, and was now carrying away from the *Journal*. She tossed it. She threw it all away. Something had to change, she decided. This carrying out a box filled with another broken piece of her life, as if it were a reminder of just how fragile her very existence could be, was getting old. She was tired of it. And she left it where it landed.

Ben and Scotty were standing next to Ben's Mercedes when Josie came out of the *Bullhorn Journal*. Ben was wearing shades and was casually dressed in jeans and a polo shirt. Scotty wore a warm-up suit. It was a nice, sunshiny day. One of the few in Josie's recent memory. And they were all upbeat.

Especially Josie, who put on her sunglasses and ran across the street as if she were as free as a bird and wanted the world to know. She jumped into Ben's arms, and Ben's shades nearly flew from his face as he was forced to twirl her around.

Scotty shook his head. "Just kill the man, Josie. Just give him a coronary right here, right now."

"What if I give you one, how about that?"

"I'm sure you'll try."

Josie's feet touched back down, and she smiled and looked at Scotty. "You always got to have something to say, don't you?"

"Always, girl," Scotty said.

"Josie?" Ben asked.

"One day I'm gonna have something to say to you," Josie said jokingly to Scotty, and then she looked at Ben. "Yes, dear?" she said to him.

"I have an idea."

"Oh. Okay, I'm listening."

"It occurred to me that since we're taking Scotty to the airport, anyway, since we're going to be right there, I thought we could all take a trip."

Josie hesitated. She didn't get it. "Because we're going to be at the airport, we should get on the plane? Is that what you're saying, Ben?"

Ben couldn't believe it himself. "Yes," he said. "We should take a trip."

"Where to?"

Ben paused. "Las Vegas," he said.

Josie smiled. "Vegas?"

"Yes."

"For what?"

"A vacation, for one. We both need it. And while we're there, who knows?"

Josie slid her glasses down on the bridge of her nose and looked at Ben. "Who knows what?"

Ben seemed nervous as he hesitated before speaking. Josie smiled. She'd never seen him quite so uncertain. "People have been known to get married in Las Vegas," he said.

At first Josie couldn't believe he'd said it. She stared at him as if there was some punch line following. But there wasn't. "People have been known to get married there?" she said.

"Yes, they have. And I thought that maybe, perhaps, if we're there, since we'll be there, we could . . . We could . . ." He paused, and looked at Josie.

"We could what?"

Ben released a heavy, slow exhale. "We could consider getting married ourselves. To each other, I mean."

Scotty laughed. "Now that's a good idea. Being your wife may be the only job she can keep."

Ben and Josie didn't even look Scotty's way. They were staring at each other.

"What about it?" Ben asked her.

"What about what?"

He paused again. His look was so pained that Josie almost smiled. "Will you marry me?" he asked her.

She looked around, at the old warehouse of a newspaper building and the dead-end street that encompassed them. But it was, to her, the perfect setting. She looked at her man, at her middle-aged man who now seemed as desperate as she once was.

"Sounds tempting, Ben," she said. "Awfully tempting. But I'm not sure if you're ready yet."

Ben stared at her with astonishment on his face. Not ready? *Him?* Scotty was laughing already, and Josie was too. Then, as if suddenly realizing the joke, Ben joined in as well. Even the truth was funny sometimes. Because, in truth, he didn't know if he was ready, either.

TERESA McCLAIN-WATSON holds a bachelor's degree from Florida State University and a master's degree in history from Florida A&M. She is the author of three additional novels, *Plenty Good Room, Surviving Mr. Right,* and *Loose Lips.* She currently resides in Florida.